Sept

Remember

September Remember

BY

ELIOT TAINTOR

PROSPECTA PRESS

WESTPORT – 2015

Prospecta Press
P.O. Box 3131
Westport, CT 06880
www.prospectapress.com

Cover and book design by Barbara Aronica-Buck

Paperback ISBN 978-1-63226-025-3
eBook ISBN 978-1-63226-026-0

To Bill
And to all other members of A.A.

CONTENTS

FOREWORD

I remember the dashboard in the boy's truck when he came to pick me up. There was maybe a rubber crocodile mascot on that dashboard. Or there was something funny and cute dangling from the rearview mirror, maybe that rubber crocodile; I was so drunk. Maybe it was a lobster.

The boy didn't drink and he told me that the reason he was so boringly sober was because he was an alcoholic and he was going to Alcoholics Anonymous (A.A.). A few weeks later, I asked him to take me to my first A.A. meeting. It was exactly like what you see in movies—men and women in a basement of a church, talking about being drunk or about not being drunk. One guy wore paint-splattered coveralls; one woman in a power suit looked like a famous blonde actress. Outside, after the meeting, the night was fully resigned into winter; it was February, frost. I felt delicate like an infant and like an infant I also felt hysterical.

An alcoholic on awakening is much like a newborn baby—fragile and without any defense against a very sober world. *September Remember* begins with a terrifying—and darkly funny blackout—the sort of a blackout that pulls you right into the mind of a drunk on the loose. Reading it, I was reminded of my AA friend picking me up in his truck, the uncertainty of that boozy hazy evening. The blackout is not the story of *September Remember*, but it's that darkness that will suck you into this story.

When published, *September Remember* was a best seller, and the first known novel that put A.A. into literary consciousness. It's been out of print now for over 60 years.

The book is full of language and prejudices that are reflective of its time. That was the time of America between the two world wars: more than twenty years before Martin Luther King's "I Have a Dream" speech, years before women made it out of the kitchen into the living room, and years before new immigrants were only recognizable by the derogatory terms used to describe them. In that way, *September Remember* can be treated as a historical document that mentions Alcoholics Anonymous, but it is much more than that: its mythology is essentially A.A.'s, a story of rebirth and redemption.

In the beginning, a non-drinking alcoholic is completely unprepared to face the very sober world and all the responsibilities it takes to live in it. Not only that—there are people who have been hurt by alcoholics in blackouts, often the people who are most dear to those same alcoholics. For an alcoholic, remorse is like a heavy mattress, and nothing can get you out from underneath its constant weight unless it's booze, which you drink to forget whatever it is that is making you feel the guilt. But, occasionally, guilt and remorse is what wakes you up. For Avery "Rick" Rickham, the hero of *September Remember*, the guilt and remorse were what woke him up after a bender inspired by his violent quarrel with his only daughter. An old friend takes him to his first A.A. meeting and it's all men and women in a church basement just like it is in the movies, just like it was for me decades after the book came out.

A.A.'s program has barely changed since its inception in 1934. It's hard to know how many people it has kept sober for the past 80 years—its strict confidentiality prevents the keeping of records—but it's safe to guess the number is in the millions. For a modern member of A.A., it is an illuminating experience to read this book and realize that the language of recovery hasn't changed either and that the principles are the same: alcoholics helping other alcoholics to achieve sobriety. Rick being taken to his first meeting by a friend in A.A., newly sober Rick being teased by some of the old-timers, Rick trying to help someone else get sober, Rick being tempted by booze, or dealing with a friend's relapse—all of that is par for the course for the modern member of A.A., too. As are more difficult situations, such as infidelity or those really tragic ones such as suicide, or death—both topics that the book deals with, both of which are familiar to *this* alcoholic. (There was another A.A. boy—not the first boy—who once serenaded me terribly, embarrassingly, at a summer barbecue. He died of vodka in the fall.)

Although not exclusive to alcoholics, grim experiences tend to congregate around addicts. It's a strange kind of specialness. I remember on joining AA, someone said to me: "prepare to have your heart broken," when I mentioned the friendships I was making in the program. I have had it broken a few times since then—mostly because people, even sober, relapse, just as I did, and almost killed myself in the process. When I came to A.A. for the second time, I was desperate, like all the alkies in *September Remember*. One such character, Bill Griffith (a fictional Bill Wilson, the founder of A.A.), says, "I am willing to do anything. Anything. If there is a God, will He show Himself?" Griffith has a sense of light and ecstasy, as he says, followed by great peace, which then brings him to sobriety.

Today, A.A. is only one of the options on the addiction treatment menu. For me it was the only way I knew. The rigorousness of the program, the simplistic adages like "Easy Does It" are what helped me to simplify everything in the beginning of my sobriety—twice. Twice, in A.A., I was a newborn baby, except I already had a life and it was a big confusing mess when I came to from my many blackouts. With the help of A.A., the mess became a little smaller and easier to understand. I have never found God and I have never stuck with the traditional A.A., the way it is described in the book, but I credit my life to it—with its many bumps and all its messiness.

There's a saying in A.A., "The program is not a way of life but the way to life." I've used A.A. as a springboard to my own sobriety and till this day I use most of its principles in helping me maintain that sobriety. In *September Remember* the reader will have a unique opportunity to see how the earliest member of Alcoholics Anonymous used the program to come to and maintain theirs. It's a view well worth the time to experience.

— Jowita Bydlowska,
author of *Drunk Mom*

INTRODUCTION

September Remember, originally published in 1945, has been obscured by time and is known to only a few as the first Alcoholics Anonymous novel. It was written by Gregory Mason and Ruth Fitch Mason under the pseudonym Elliot Taintor. For a time it was a best seller, but it has been out of print for almost seventy years now. As with many best selling novels of the past, in terms of content and style, it now can feel somewhat dated. Nevertheless, the book still holds more than passing interest to contemporary readers.

I came across this novel in the course of researching the writers Thomas Boyd and Margaret Woodward Smith, the parents of Betty Grace Nash, who was the co-owner of the Ridgefield (Connecticut) Press, where I had my first teenage job. In the late 1920s, Thomas Boyd had an affair with the poet Ruth Fitch Bartlett, and left his wife for her. Ruth left her first husband, Walter Bartlett, for Boyd, and the couple subsequently married and moved to South Woodstock, Vermont,

Thomas Boyd became an active communist in the early 1930s, influenced by what he saw during the stock market crash and subsequent Depression, as well as by what he experienced personally—as a writer unhappily working with publishers, whom he believed exploited writers. In 1934, Boyd ran a spectacularly unsuccessful campaign for governor, garnering just 177 votes statewide.

After Boyd passed away in 1935 at just 37, likely from the effects of being gassed during World War I, Ruth Fitch Boyd became a literary agent. In1937, she married anthropologist and writer Gregory Mason. They collaborated on two novels, *Danbury Curve* and *September Remember.*

After some further research, I learned that *September Remember* is considered the first novel ever to include Alcoholics Anonymous as part of its storyline. And it was evidently one of the best-selling novels of 1945. When I decided to reprint this book, I expected I would need to contact the heirs of the authors for permission. Researching the novel's status at the Library of Congress, I discovered that its copyright expired in 1972 and had never been renewed. Unbeknownst to all, *September Remember* had fallen into the public domain and had become freely available for reprinting, but as so often happens with out-of-print books, its status was clouded and unclear until now.

During the intervening seventy years, many of the attributes of addiction and recovery described in the book have remained unchanged, giving the novel a certain timelessness and ongoing appeal. Both because of and regardless of its time and place, *September Remember* tells a fascinating story.

September Remember

I

TIME AND TIME AND TIME AND TIME

The windshield wiper jerked two precisely uniform arcs against the rain that came out of the darkness like water out of a great hose, directed at the car by a gigantic, prehensile thumb. Clockwise. Counter-clockwise. The narrow rubber arms always seemed to hurry, but always moved with infuriating regularity. Clockwise. Counter-clockwise. Avery Rickham found himself wishing that the damn contrivance would over-reach itself, go past the neat curve with a fine spurt of energy, or fall short in comprehensible human fatigue. In this petty struggled between Man and Nature, his sympathies were all with the erratic violence of the storm. He was seized by an irrational hatred for the cunning mind that had set this absurd gadget to cope with the wild sweep of wind and rain.

He was a man given to sudden irrational hatreds. Glorying in them. Ashamed of them. Dominated by them. A big man, hunched into the front seat of the small roadster, his knees jutting above the dashboard, his heavy shoulders braced but sagging against the leather seat. He had a dark, defiant face. Irregular features. Arresting in their odd emphatic angularity. Strong dark hair. Desolate dark grey eyes.

Clockwise. Counter-clockwise. Rick had only to reach out his hand and turn a plastic button and the busy arms would stop in their tracks with a protesting squish. But he could not reach out his hand. He could not summon even that meager amount of physical or mental energy. His last dime's worth of tenacity had been spent in getting into this car with Joe. He felt like a man sliding into a foxhole, hiding from the enemy—only the enemy was himself.

Joe had pulled him out of jail early this morning for "Drunken and Disorderly Conduct." Christ, had they booked him for "Assault and Battery" too? He couldn't remember. And he couldn't forget.

Fear gripped him. Fear worse than anything he had known in his long years in the bush. Worse even than the time when he had come back from his first mule trek to locate a fresh stand of *sapota* trees and the half-drunk native chicle foreman had started bragging. He had begun by boasting that he was not afraid of snakes, he was not afraid of crocodiles, he was not afraid of *tigres*. The next minute Rick could foresee that he would reach a resounding and dangerous climax and yell that he was not afraid of *gringos!* This would not be so good. It would not be good at all. Especially as the man had an old Colt .44 and Rick was unarmed. There had seemed hardly room between the living green walls for Rick to turn his mule, but he had twisted quickly in his saddle and looked the native in the eye.

"Are you never afraid of *yourself, hombre?*"

It had worked. With a cry of terror the man had somehow kicked his mule past Rick and pounded ahead along the narrow trail. When Rick finally overtook him he was sitting quietly on his mule, a chastened *mestizo*.

Poor devil. Rick understood the native's terror now. He had hated the world in those days but he had not hated nor feared himself. It was hell not knowing what you had done. Or what order you had done what in. You could sleep off most of the physical agony of a hangover. His head was still pounding but his stomach had quieted to a sort of groggy queasiness. Only the mental nausea had not diminished. He could not remember. And he could not forget. Isolated incidents kept swimming at him like the shadows of sharks on the floor of the ocean, but something came first . . . something pleasant . . . not part of this green seaweed and shark-fin nightmare . . . and yet part of it.

Gail! Gail had put her arm through his and lifted one eyebrow in a way that made her look disturbingly like her mother. She had wanted him to go with her to a cocktail party, "Not every gal," she teased, "has a father who pops out of a jungle and . . ."

"You make me feel like Tarzan!" Rick had laughed, but the moment had been enormously important to him.

In one desperate week after his wife's death in childbirth he had put all their money in trust for this daughter who had survived; arranged for

Adelaide's sister, Emily, to look after her; resigned from his position as consulting engineer in a New York firm and found a field job with a chicle company in Campeche. For nearly eighteen years he had knocked about the world on roving assignments with one of the big oil companies between jobs with the chewing gum firm. For nearly eighteen years he had tried to forget Gail's existence, except for the month he had spent at home when she was five and found he could not stand New York nor the engaging child who was too close a replica of Adelaide. After that he had fulfilled his paternal instincts by sending her occasional odd presents—a few ancient Mayan pottery whistles one of his archaeological pals had dug up and given him in exchange for a tip on the location of a burial mound, serapes woven by Indians and dyed with crude brilliant colors, jadeite beads from the tomb of a high priest who had made difficult astronomical calculations in Yucatan before the Saxon barbarians had learned to multiply and divide. Strange gifts for a little girl in a brownstone house in the East Sixties. Gifts that Gail had proudly displayed to him recently, arranged in a special cabinet in her room, while he stood beside her and cursed himself in his heart for a selfish fool. At that, it had not been any belated sense of responsibility for her but a worse than usual bout of malaria and a better than usual offer from the Home Office that had brought him back to New York.

"You will go with me?" Gail had insisted and Rick had known that she was asking for more than a chance to show him off to her new friends. She was seeking his approval of those friends. The moment was important to her too.

Emily had made it quite clear that she considered the Mantons impossible people. "Paul is good looking," she had admitted reluctantly, "but his mother is in some fashion business and they belong to what I believe is known as Café Society."

Rick had brushed Emily's remarks aside—she was obviously old-fashioned and narrow in her social judgments—and found a sweet new brand of happiness in Gail's appeal to him. It was a fine proud feeling.

And she had been lovely, coming gaily down the stairs to meet him in a short black dress with a white fur jacket slung over her shoulder and a silly white flower on a scrap of black veiling tilted over one eye. The costume had definitely not been chosen by her Aunt. Rick had felt both annoyed and touched by Gail's attempt to appear smart and alluring and her achievement of incongruous innocence. If she had been any other woman in the world he would have looked her over as a cute little trick and missed the innocence completely. Hell, he couldn't have other men looking at his daughter like that. In baffled concern he had vowed to protect her, to warn her somehow, but all he managed to say was, "Isn't it sort of hot for that fur thing?"

Gail had laughed the way women laugh when men act as if clothes had anything to do with the weather. "Of course it is," she agreed as they stepped into the slanting September sunlight, "but I wanted Daphne Manton to see it."

The Manton apartment on the East River had been as full of phony notables as a gossip column. "That's Daphne Manton," Gail had waved excitedly at a slim woman with blued hair curled in a crisp high pompadour, "Doesn't she look French? Paul and I call her *Madame de Maintenon* and she always wears that special shade of blue to match her hair. Even her fur coat is that color. It's famous as the 'Manton Blue'."

Mrs. Manton had put a possessive arm around Gail and turned to Rick. "Isn't your daughter a darling, Mr. Rickham, and so photographic! I've been trying to get her to model some of my ridiculous hats—but of course her Aunt disapproves. Really you know the Powers' Model List reads like the Social Register these days."

Rick had taken a martini from a silver tray, downed it at one gulp and reached for another glass. He had dismissed Emily's opinion of these people as old-fashioned. Now he had found himself defending her attitude with quick anger behind his words, "I'm afraid I quite agree with Gail's Aunt. In my day nice girls never allowed their photographs to appear in the papers and certainly not as advertisements."

"Oh Daddy, how quaint!" Gail had laughed and he had not liked the sound. There was a false high note in it.

"But don't you see," Mrs. Manton had persisted, her curly blue head tilted to one side as she studied Gail with shrewd appraising eyes, "it's her air of innocence that is so engaging."

Rick had felt fury pounding in his veins. Damn this woman for seeing and putting a commercial value on the very quality in Gail he had just discovered and determined to protect. He had reached for another cocktail. "Apparently I have been too long in the bush to understand your civilization!" He had handed Mrs. Manton her world with emphatic irony. "The Indians in Central America defend their daughters."

"What a thrilling life you must have had, Mr. Rickham!" Daphne Manton had side-stepped the impact of his anger and left him feeling like a sententious grey-beard. "Indians fascinate me. I feel the way D. H. Lawrence's women do about primitive men. But I suppose Indians today are quite dull and dirty, and civilized men are merely dull. You must tell me about them sometime. Gail has been talking of nothing but her father for days."

A boy with smooth dark hair had come toward them and greeted Gail with a casual, "Hi, darling."

Gail's face had lighted with a warm happy smile and she had given her father's arm a quick, confident squeeze. "Daddy, this is Paul."

Rick had stiffened. He had been absurdly angry at Daphne Manton. The woman was a fool, but he admitted that except for her influence on Gail he might have found her an attractive and amusing fool. This was different. This was like two continents facing each other across a narrow channel, armed and ready to fight. This boy was handsome—too handsome. His mouth was petulant and there was no openness in his face. No stability.

Clockwise. Counter-clockwise.

"Lansing Patterson . . . Lansing Peterson . . . what the hell was that guy's name at Harvard?" Rick spoke out loud.

Joe's laugh filled the small car, silenced the pelting rain and the sucking sound of the windshield wiper. "You mean the fellow who was always chasing chorus girls? Gosh, I haven't thought of him in years . . . last time I heard he was trying to beat Tommy Manville's record. What in the world put him into your head?" Joe turned from his intent concentration on the slippery black road and looked at Rick curiously for an instant, but Rick didn't answer.

He was back at the Manton cocktail party watching Gail cross the crowded room with Paul . . . Paul who was like someone Rick had known . . . Paul who was not necessarily a playboy just because he reminded Rick of Lansing Somebody-or-other at Harvard. Rick had gulped another drink and told himself he wasn't being fair but his instinctive, violent dislike and distrust of Paul Manton could not be silenced—and weren't instincts sound, protective mechanisms, coordinated memories, warnings of experience, and wouldn't man do well to heed them as animals do?

Daphne Manton had taken Rick's arm authoritatively and herded him about the room like a small sheep dog driving a large ram. Titles crackled around him like dried grass. Slightly seedy titles. A Georgian Prince, a Polish Countess, an ex-ambassador, recalled because he had disagreed with the President's foreign policy before Pearl Harbor, the divorced wife of an English Earl, who had been in Hollywood and was beautiful in a tired, scornful way, a thin Frenchman with an old name and a new aptitude for getting along on the shady side of American business, two Russian Princesses, a man who knew Washington-behind-the-scenes, two more Russian Princesses. Mrs. Manton gave Rick rapid by-lines as she introduced her guests.

Rick had grabbed another martini. Didn't the woman know that Russian Princesses come a dime-a-dozen! Hadn't she ever heard of the Soviet Union! Didn't she realize that anyone could jam an apartment with this type of riff-raff simply by providing free drinks! Hell, if Daphne Manton liked this crowd, thought these people cosmopolitan, that was her affair. But it wasn't Gail's. How could Adelaide's daughter be impressed by this spurious bunch, this cheap notoriety? The more upset he had become about Gail the more he drank and the more he drank the more upset he became about Gail. He had watched her, laughing with Paul and a group of younger people, a cocktail glass in her hand, her voice too shrill, her manner too provocative.

God damn it. She looked as cheap as the rest of them. He ought to grab her by the nape of her neck and drag her out of this place. Instead, he had reached for another martini. The liquor was catching up on him. In Belize and Playa Carmen he had been able to pour it down, get roaring drunk, if he liked, and sober up and carry on with his work. But there had been an increasing and alarming number of times the past two or three years when he had needed several stiff shots in the morning. The "hair of the dog" idea was bad stuff. He'd been half-cockeyed or sunk with the jitters through three or four successive working days. And since his return to New York even a few drinks seemed to hit him. Hit him hard. And fast. He—Avery Rickham—who not so long ago had been known as the best "holder" in the *cantinas* of Central America. And his hangovers had changed. You could stand a "head," but how could you cope with the choking mental depressions which had engulfed him recently. He'd better watch out. He'd had plenty now, but you couldn't take a party like this without drinking. One of the Russian Princesses had been telling him about the rubies her mother had lost in the Revolution. He didn't believe a word of it. She'd probably been born in the Bronx . . . in the Zoo. That was funny. Damn funny. He had laughed and the Princess had batted long eyelashes at him in startled inquiry.

"Where's Manton?" he had asked suddenly, catching another martini from the butler's tray. He'd like to meet Manton. What sort of a guy would stand for a party like this going on in his place? He had asked Emily about Paul's father but she had been vague, having heard only that Mr. Manton had made a pile on Wall Street.

The short fat man who knew Washington-behind-the-scenes had laughed. "Oh, you wouldn't catch P.J. at one of his wife's shindigs. He's off fishing. Always off fishing . . . or shooting. Belongs to clubs in Florida, clubs in Maryland, clubs in Canada."

Smart guy, Manton, Rick had thought. *He* didn't have to stick this party either. He could grab Gail and get the hell out. He had pushed his way toward her. She was perched on the arm of a "Manton Blue" couch, with Paul sprawled on a cerise cushion at her feet, his head just touching her knee.

"We're leaving," Rick had said, *"now."* He had realized his tone was wrong from the look that came over Gail's face.

"Not *me*," she had said and leaned closer to Paul.

Her face had been a perfect target. Before Rick knew what he was doing he had slapped it. Quickly, as a cat slaps.

The noisy room had become abruptly silent. The ambassador was gone. The divorced countess was gone. The Russian Princesses were gone.

Gail was gone. Rick had been dimly aware of Gail rushing from the room, her hand to her cheek, of Paul hurrying after her, of Gail in a small voice saying goodbye to Mrs. Manton. With magnificent fatherly aplomb he had paid no attention. He had finished another martini without haste. Daphne Manton and the man who knew Washington-behind-the-scenes were standing in front of the mantel looking at him. Suddenly he had remembered that Gail had said this fat fellow was taking Mrs. Manton out for dinner. Rick had gotten to his feet nonchalantly, found his hat and coat, made his farewells with careful politeness.

In the street the cool night breeze from the East River had cleared his head for a moment. He must find Gail. He had asked the doorman if he had seen a girl in a black dress with a white fur jacket. The doorman had called a cab for her and had added that "the little lady seemed in a big hurry." God, he thinks I'm an old fool chasing after a kid. Rick had considered socking the doorman in the nose, but it hadn't seemed worth the effort. What he needed was a drink.

Had he gone to the Monks Club first, or to those three or four bars in the middle fifties? He hadn't been in the Monks Club since the night before he sailed for Central America. He had left it plastered then. He had entered it in worse shape last night, but not too drunk to sign a check for his back dues. "Pay your dues in toto is a gentleman's moto," he had shouted. The words had seemed to rhyme. To be hilariously funny. He had pulled his check book out this morning and studied the stubs. There were two made out to the club. He must have cashed the second to buy drinks at the bar for the late revelers. *Late* revelers. That was it. He must have gone to those bars in the middle fifties first.

He rolled his head from side to side on the leather upholstery of the car as if the physical act might shake loose his memory. It seemed to function only intermittently. Had he lost it when he left the Mantons'? The devilish part of these alcoholic blackouts was that he always suspected the worst. Magnified his evil deeds. He couldn't remember making any effort to find Gail. Had he even thought of her after talking to that doorman?

Was it because he had made no effort to find her that he had drawn a blank? Or vice versa?

There had been a big dark prostitute somewhere around 48th Street and 7th Avenue. They had argued about her price and she had finally agreed to meet him outside a hotel on 8th Avenue. And then stood him up.

There had been Jimmy Smith at the Monks Club. He could remember welcoming Jimmy vociferously, although he had never particularly liked the fellow. Jimmy had seemed only pleasantly squiffed just the way he used to be in the old days. Carrying a load, but not getting emphatic about it. Rick had been emphatic all right. He had bet a guy when the war would end and the guy had quibbled about the terms. Rick had started to fight him. Good old Jimmy had stopped the fight by offering to buy them both another drink.

There had been the sailor on 42nd Street. He could remember places but not time. Time and Time and Time and Time.

"You looking for the same thing I am, Buddy?" the sailor had asked. Pete. That was the sailor's name. A good, humorous name. A good, humorous sailor.

Rick had had an inspiration. They would go to a hotel and inquire if their wives had returned. They might get away with something. No harm in trying anyway. They figured that Rick, being in civilian clothes, had better do the talking.

A small, dapper clerk in a shiny blue suit had leaned over a desk at the end of a narrow entrance hall. To his right was an old-fashioned elevator, occupied by a yawning colored boy, and a steep stairway covered with a dusty red carpet.

"Has my wife come in yet?" Rick had begun. "The tall red-headed one," he had added, seeing that the clerk was about to ask the name.

"No sir, she's not in yet," the clerk had replied without a flicker of curiosity.

And there they were. They had tried again, plus a cigar wrapped in a dollar bill, but no soap. Rick wasn't sure how many hotels they had gone into, each dingier and more disreputable than the last. It had seemed like a bright idea. But it hadn't worked out.

There had been two girls talking to a man on a street corner. The man had done a quick fade-out when Pete had barged up to them and grinned, "Our wives, Buddy." The blonde with the red sandals had grabbed Pete.

"Dora always goes for the Navy," the other girl had said, slipping her arm through Rick's. He had brushed it away angrily. Now it came to him suddenly that the gesture must have reminded him of Gail's when she had asked him to go with her to the Mantons' cocktail party. The girl had given him a resentful look and then laughed uneasily. Hell, she'd get more dough out of this big guy than Dora would out of her sailor. Dora was a softie, always cutting rates for men in the Armed Forces and calling it patriotism.

"How much?" Rick had asked.

"Ten bucks." The girl had added a fiver to make up for him shoving her away.

The sailor and the blonde were turning into a mouldy-looking hotel, with a pretentious lobby that had obviously seen better days.

"Dora and me—I'm Lucille—got our own private rooms here." H. Peculiar Henry! She sounded as if she were actually bragging about it! Rick had followed her down a dark hallway, smelling strongly of insecticide. There was nothing here to remind him of a long, clean white corridor in a New York Hospital down which he had run headlong, scattering interns and nurses in his flight from the closed door of a delivery room eighteen years ago. Nothing except that damn disinfectant. Smells and music were like elephants. Twin white elephants that never let you forget. He had laughed harshly and Lucille had given him a startled, apprehensive glance.

The girl had pulled her dress over her head and tossed it on a chair before Rick finished pushing the old-fashioned bolt on the door. Her body was slim with hard, compact, little curves. But she looked cold. "Even an American whore can be hot." The phrase had slipped into his mind. He had sat on the edge of a low sagging bed, trying to undo the knot in his tie, trying to remember who the hell had said that.

It was old Bill Baker of Bakersville, on Baker's River, in Baker County, Virginia. Bill had been on the prowl for a school teacher with a voluptuous figure and an unfortunately prudish attitude. Betty—somebody—in Puerto Barrios. The local tarts, sitting around the Boca Dorada saloon in their flimsy pink, blue, cerise dresses, had made no headway with Bill Baker. Every time the half-breed guide, who acted as a pimp on the side, approached Bill hoping to start a deal with, "This whore in blue dress say she like speak you private," Bill would fix his drunken stare on the plank ceiling and chant, "I wanta get my mits on Betty's tits," baffling the pimp and his stable of part Indian, part Spanish, mostly negroid wenches.

"*El Senor* like buy rounda drinks, *sí?*"

"Sure thing." Bill would pull out his wallet and order the best imported Mexican *Cuahtemoc* for the whole crowd. He was generous but he was adamant. Presently the pimp would try again.

"Excuse, Meester Baker, this whore in yellow dress say she like speak you private."

Neither the question nor the answer had ever varied. Bill's ludicrous refrain would boom out again. But *el Americano del Norte* made them all laugh, and he bought plenty of beer.

Beer. That was an idea. Rick had rung for the bellboy and ordered half a dozen bottles at the exorbitant prices of twenty-five cents per. Lucille had brought two tumblers from the washstand, concealed behind a faded green baize screen. She had sipped hers, made a face and given it up. Looking impersonally at her slim legs and flat stomach, she had observed that girls who went in for booze got fat and flabby in no time. "Beer," she had added solemnly, "don't do a girl no good."

"No good for you, no good for me," Aleece had said of cognac. Was that the difference between a French whore and an American? This kid didn't give a damn how stinko he was. He had been a kid himself in Paris just after the Armistice. *"Tu ne peut pas m'aimer parce que j'ai trente quatre années et j'ai habité avec un Australien."* Wonderful logicians, the French.

Aleece had been his third. The first had been a brown-haired, intellectual girl he had picked up after a Harvard-Yale game, near the Touraine in Boston. She had worn a tweed suit and sturdy oxfords and he had actually taken her for some guy's date when he first spoke to her. Dolly Seymour had been his second. He had been stationed in Winchester and been given two days' leave in London before embarking for France. She was a little like Dora, he thought. She had made a vow not to take anyone but a man in uniform till the war was over.

The first three. Silly business counting them. Adolescent. "Americans are sexually adolescent," a Russian General had proclaimed in a high class bordello off the Nevskiy Prospekt, run by a *Madame* Miroir.

"The mirror is man's worst invention," Rick had said out loud.

Lucille had looked at him as if he had suddenly lost his mind. "What's the big idea?" she had asked nervously. This guy had acted queer from the start. She had sidled off the bed and pulled her dress from the back of the chair.

"Mirrors make you think about yourself all the time," Rick had explained patiently. "Ever hear about Narcissus looking at his own image in a brook and falling in love with himself? Mirrors cause a man to love himself. Or hate himself." Rick was wound up now. He had lifted the last bottle of beer, not bothering to pour it into a glass. "Mirrors are the reasons for complexes, neuroses, psychoses, drunkenness and suicides."

Lucille had grabbed her shiny black purse containing Rick's ten bucks from the chipped bureau, unbolted the door and slid out.

He ought to get the hell out too. But he had thrown himself back on the bed and roared with laughter. H. Peculiar Henry, but she was funny with her scared rabbit eyes. In the next room a radio had blared out suddenly.

"Come to me, I've waited so long for you,
Come, I'll sing a wonderful song to you,
Come, come, because I love you so."

A Friendship sloop in a little land-locked harbor in Maine. A slim colt of a girl. He had never touched her. Everyone in the town thought that he had. All the fishermen and the postmaster and the storekeeper were sure that he had. But he never had.

It was her forehead that had bowled him over. The direct, clean line of it, straight up at the sides like a Greek temple with the perfect arch at the top. "And seen strange lands from under the arched white sails of ships." Her forehead had the arrogant curve of a billowing mainsail, coming into port at dawn. A skinny girl, asleep in the cockpit. And the wind over salt water. And the scent of spruce and pine off the hot damp land.

The old tune had jogged his memory and his nose had taken it up. The twin white elephants were busy.

> "Stay just as you are,
> Don't ever change,
> You're divine, dear."

A tall, honey-haired girl with a figure like the Winged Victory. The widow of a Division Manager in the United Fruit Company, she had hated the tropics, but from a perverse inertia had stayed on after her husband's death. Rick had alternately loved and fought her for two years, drunk and sober. He mostly drunk, she mostly sober, but neurotic. Neurotic as hell. Which mattered most—the Winged Victory or the little girl in Maine, who hadn't even warmed him when she sat in his lap? Christ, he has maudlin. And he didn't honestly know the answer . . . *"C'est curieux, la vie."*

"C'est curieux, la vie." Before the Australian, Aleece had had *"un grand amour avec un Anglais,"* who had written her a letter which she kept at the bottom of her jewelry box. "It is only you I love and I am marrying a nice English girl tomorrow. *C'est curieux, la vie.*"

A saxophone had broken in from the radio in the next room. How flat a sax is after a cello. As flat as Lucille after Aleece. Now a violin began to show off. That was cheap. Like organs in movie houses and chimes except in churches. To use decent, beautiful things for shoddy purposes . . . for advertising cathartics. Cheap announcers, cheap tenors, cheap little musicians . . . cheap whores. Lucille had a decent body but a cheap, soap-opera mind. God, how she had looked at him when he started talking about mirrors. He laughed again at her frightened, stupid, brown eyes . . . millions of voters had eyes like Lucille's . . . eyes with no mind behind them . . . timid eyes, begging for security, welcoming paternalism in any form—fascism, communism, Fourth Term.

A cartoon in the old *Masses* showing a couple of prostitutes soliciting two men, and the caption, "Of What Truth Are These Things The Lies?"

What the hell was wrong with a society where lies and cheapness flourished? What had happened to America since Oliver Wendell

Holmes, Jr., said that a man's greatest satisfaction came from doing a good piece of work and leaving it *unadvertised*? Mirrors and cities. Self-admiration. Advertising. Mass production and mass dependency. Blackout curtains at the windows of ratty hotels and monstrous office buildings and Park Avenue apartments only a "Realtor" could call homes. Scared city dwellers listening behind blackout shades for the sound of a plane in the night. Great silver bombers swooping out of the sky like fate . . . like an instrument of evolution. London . . . Berlin . . . New York . . . gone like the cities of the Mayas he had seen with the jungle growing over them till from his plane they were just bumps against the sky. The Tower of Babel was a great story—Christ, what a story. Only no one had ever paid any heed to it . . . like War. He'd made the world safe for Democracy along with the rest of his generation . . . and look at it now. "We did it before and we'll do it again." Time and Time and Time and Time. Add a bombing plane to the Tower of Babel and you'd have something. Bombing planes swooping, circling . . . his mind had been circling something all night and veering away from it. Something important.

A knock at the door. God, he had forgotten to bolt it when Lucille went out. Was she coming back with another customer? It might have been five minutes . . . or five hours since she left. His watch was in his vest pocket. He reached for it now. Hell, Lucille wouldn't knock. It might be the police . . . places like this were probably raided once in a while, just for the effect in our highly moral, hypocritical, whore-and-mirror civilization. There ought to be a fire escape off the one narrow window . . . if he could make it. He pulled on his shoes as noiselessly as possible . . . if he didn't move they might think the room was empty and go on. But the knock was repeated and a voice whispered, "Hi, Buddy. You still there?" Thank God, it was Pete.

"Come on in, Sailor," Rick had called. Pete was a good guy. He was glad to see Pete.

They had gone to a couple of bars and Pete had kept tilting his cap further and further over his left eye. It had reminded Rick of something . . . something his mind refused to remember. They were drinking beer with Rye chasers. "Not Rye with beer chasers," Pete would insist solemnly as if the distinction made a vast difference. He had a trick, when he wanted to make a point, of whistling out of the corner of his mouth and, at the same time, bringing his arm back and with the descending whistle swooping his right hand and pointed forefinger downward, like a dive bomber. It was humorously emphatic. He did it to describe the little yellow bastards swarming over an American cruiser off Guadalcanal, zooming out of the sky like Jap beetles.

Rick had said the Army doctors thought he was too damn old to get into this fight. Anyhow, he still had a splinter of shrapnel in his leg from the last one. He pulled up his trouser and showed Pete. Funny, how you wanted to do the same damn thing over again. He'd give his shirt to get out to those islands and shoot hell out of the Japs. Pete said it sure was hell all right, only most of the time his ship had been on the receiving end. He had a burn on his shoulder as big as a fish where they'd grafted skin from his own ass. Lousy stunt to pull on a guy. But the docs would let him go back pretty soon now. And things would be different. You could bet your sweet life they would.

Rick had moved an empty beer bottle, a glass, and a mustard jar around the sloppy counter. Pushing them carefully into position. The bottle was a German machine gun nest. The mustard jar was their artillery position. The glass was his squad moving forward under fire from both sides. He was back in Chateau Thierry fighting *"les sales Boches."*

"Let's go, Sailor." Suddenly Rick had shoved the beer bottle and mustard jar together so that they struck the glass. It fell on the floor and smashed. They could hear the bartender grumbling as they lurched into the street.

The dim-out gave Broadway a malevolent air, but it wasn't as late as Rick had expected. A night club with a striped canopy and a doorman in the costume of the Russian Imperial Guard was just closing. Why had he wanted to punch a doorman in the nose? Where had there been three Russian Princesses batting mascaraed eyelashes at him and chattering about the rubies they had lost in the Bronx Zoo? He had looked around him bewilderedly. People in evening dress were complaining about the scarcity of taxis. Rick had heard Pete's sharp whistle, seen his arm zoom gaily. Then Pete had clutched the post of the canopy and been sick in the gutter. A woman had shrieked in dismay. A young man in an opera cape and a high silk hat had said in a loud disgusted tone, "No wonder we're losing in the Pacific if that's what our sailors are like."

Rick's fist had shot out. The young man had crumpled to the sidewalk. Women had screamed. Men had milled around . . . not turning on him . . . this wasn't any free-for-all. The doorman had shrilled his whistle. Taxis had honked. People had scurried into them. Pete had swayed, turned, yelled, "Scram, Buddy, scram!"

Rick had stood there looking at his fist with a puzzled, triumphant smile. He remembered now. He had done what he had been aiming to do . . . he had smacked the whole cheap, phony Café Society in the face. Hard. Intending to hurt. Not as a cat slaps. God, that was it. That was what he had done.

Two policemen had come shouldering through the crowd, asking brief questions. Someone had picked up the young man, dusted off his opera cape and hustled him into a taxi. Someone had pointed at Rick. One of the cops had him by the arm.

"You hit a guy, Buddy?"

"I hit my daughter!" Rick had stared at the policeman in baffled misery.

"The bird is nuts," the cop had remarked to his companion, and tightened his hold on Rick's arm. "You better come along quietly, Buddy."

Rick had been quiet. He was sobering fast now. He was quiet in the police car. He was quiet when they got to the police station, where a sleepy Sergeant had taken his name and address. "Drunk and Disorderly. Assault and Battery," the Sergeant wrote in the blotter as the cop who had brought Rick in stated the charge. It seemed reasonable enough to Rick . . . but irrelevant. Of what truth are these things the lies?

He had hit Gail. He had to see her. But he couldn't call her from a police station at four a.m.

Would they let him call anyone? "Joseph Augustine Kelly," he had said, "at the Harvard Club." He had had lunch with Joe. He had ordered a couple of old-fashioneds and Joe hadn't touched his. Funny damn thing for Joe Kelly to be on the wagon. Only Joe had insisted he wasn't on the wagon . . . he just wasn't drinking today. He had made quite a point of it. Rick couldn't see what difference it made what you called refusing a drink. But Joe was an advertising man, maybe he thought labels mattered. Maybe they did. He had been on the wagon himself for fifty-nine days once . . . that was the longest he'd ever been able to stay off liquor, though he had aimed at a year several times. God damn booze anyhow. He was through. He'd never have another drink as long as he lived. Never. We did it before and we'll do it again. Time and Time and Time and Time.

The Sergeant had said, "We'll let you call him in the morning. Better sober up first." But he hadn't refused. Perhaps the Harvard Club had had an effect. Lucky as hell Joe had mentioned that he was staying in town for a meeting last night. Luckier still that Joe was Irish and a Catholic. Joe had known how to pull wires. Rick still couldn't get all the details straight. The guy he had socked evidently didn't crave publicity either. He was the son of a well-known lawyer and had been out on a party without his wife. The story had been killed in the newspapers. Had they taken Avery Rickham's name off the blotter? He had heard the phrases—Drunk and Disorderly—Assault and Battery. He had seen Joe paying his fine. For what? Disturbing the Peace. Boy, was that a laugh. Disturbing the Peace . . . in September, 1943.

II

REPRIEVE

Clockwise. Counter-clockwise. Rick turned his head slowly to look at Joe. Joe's hands on the wheel were relaxed and steady, his wrists flexed, letting the car have its head through the skiddy darkness. The way you let a mule pick his own path over the side of a mountain, your rein loose but your hand ready for a quick firm pull. Funny, how smart men always seemed to treat cars and boats and planes like animals, humoring 'em a bit, coaxing 'em along. Joe was smart all right. He'd been smart this morning at the police station.

"You're a hell of a good friend, Joe." Rick managed to get the words out. And felt like a fool. You can't thank a guy for the sort of thing Joe had done for him. He slumped back watching the endless black road, his past pulling at him, a long wet black ribbon, heavier, blacker than the ebony asphalt . . . as if the asphalt had melted into a dark, pervasive liquid, oozing into every crevice of his existence, tarring everything it touched. Which was everything. It engulfed not only the present but the past.

He had never been happy. He knew that now. Never in all his life. His mind scurried around like a faithful dog, bringing sticks for his approval. "You were happy playing first base at Exeter," his mind would bark hopefully. "And that summer after the war . . . a Friendship sloop in a little land-locked harbor and a slim colt of a girl with a forehead like a Greek temple. How about that? Skating with Adelaide at Lake Placid . . . the sharp snow-cleared air and the bonfires around the lake at night and the music . . . and Adelaide in a short black velvet skirt and white fur jacket and small round muff . . . professionals toe-dancing in the spotlight, but the crowd watching Adelaide and Rick waltz, because they were young and in love and Adelaide was beautiful." No not even that.

He rejected them all. They didn't seem real now. They didn't have anything to do with him.

The Winged Victory had asked him once how he kept going when the black monster of a hangover clutched him. It was just before they broke up in a furious argument, he blaming her hypochondria, she pointing to his drinking as the cause of their intolerable relationship.

"You hang on like a beaten prize fighter, hoping for the gong," Rick had said. "Your mind tells you the damn depression will end sometime. It has ended before. You don't believe your mind. You hear it only dimly, as a punch-drunk fighter hears advice yelled from his corner."

Dimly. You hear only dimly. Had Joe actually said just now, "Sure, I'm a friend of yours, Rick. But that isn't the point." A funny thing for Joe to say. There was a quizzical smile at the corner of Joe's wide mouth. The smile stretched to a grin as Joe turned for a quick look at Rick's startled face.

"I thought that might get you," Joe laughed, "You haven't heard a damn thing I've been saying. But it's true. Friendship is beside the point."

"You mean . . ." Rick puzzled over the statement, "that you'd have done what you did this morning for any drunken bum?"

"Well, I might not have pulled quite so many wires for any other guy," Joe admitted, "but I'd have gone to bat just the same. Every A.A. would. It's part of our program."

"I don't get it, Red," Rick said. Not that it mattered. He had seen a picture of five men on a rubber raft in the middle of the Pacific—one of them just a kid with a thin, haunted face who looked as if he might jump overboard before a rescuing ship turned up. He felt like that now. Too damn exhausted and hopeless to care about the meeting they were heading for in White Plains.

Joe had dragged Rick into a drug store near Times Square when they walked out of the jail; had filled him up with coffee and tomato juice and suddenly started talking about a bunch of ex-drunks who called themselves "Alcoholics Anonymous." Joe was one of them and proud of it. His voice had boomed out in the small booth, making Rick's head pound harder than ever—if that were possible.

"It's the God-damnedest organization, Rick . . . it's like seeing

Lazarus rise from the grave . . . 'dead drunk' isn't any figure of speech, it's a fact. We say 'sober fact,' and 'dead drunk,' and boy we're right . . . you *are* dead when you're drunk . . . dead to the world. There isn't just one Lazarus in A.A., there are a thousand Lazaruses, not one miracle—a thousand miracles . . . you see them with your own eyes every time you go to a meeting . . . swine being turned back into men. . . ." He had tugged at his wild red forelock. "I'm not exaggerating, Rick. I haven't been so happy since I pitched that no-hit game against Yale."

Rick had held his head in his left hand and lifted the shaking cup to his mouth, taking small careful sips of coffee. When Joe said, "You go over to my room at the Harvard Club and sleep it off. I'll pick you up late this afternoon and take you to a meeting in White Plains," Rick had agreed. His resistance had been so low that if Joe had suggested jumping off Brooklyn Bridge he would have agreed to that too.

Clockwise. Counter-clockwise.

Joe pulled the car over to the side of the road and stopped so abruptly that a Packard skidded around them with an indignant blast of its horn. Clockwise. Counter-clockwise. The busy arms jerked to rest.

"Helping other drunks helps us, see?" Joe said, "Reminds us of the messes we used to get into ourselves. Keeps us on the beam." He got a cigar out of his breast pocket, struggled with the cellophane wrapping, bit off the end, struck a match and finally spoke while the flame died and darkness came back over his strong humorous face with its high beak of a nose.

"Look, Rick. You're serious about laying off the stuff, right?"

"Right."

"And I gather you've tried to stop plenty of times on your own?"

"I've tried," Rick said. God, how he had tried. For the last five years. Cutting it down . . . cutting it out . . . drinking nothing but beer—until a case of beer caught up on him—never drinking alone . . . never drinking in the bush . . . never drinking except in the bush . . . never drinking before dinner . . . never drinking except before dinner . . . never drinking with women . . . never drinking without women . . . going on the wagon . . . and falling off the wagon. . . . Time and Time and Time and Time. "I stuck it once for fifty-nine days." That was his record. Before and since, the twenty-first day always threw him. It was a damn queer jinx. "I've been aiming at a year, but I've never made it."

"The wagon isn't any good. Not for a real alky, it isn't."

Joe was making the same point he'd insisted on at lunch when he had refused an old-fashioned. "What the hell difference does it make what you call not taking a drink?" Rick protested feebly.

"One whale of a difference. When you're on the wagon part of your mind is always looking forward to the bender you'll go on at the end of your stretch. The A.A.'s go at it another way. We're only dry for twenty-four hours. That's all. Any dope can lay off liquor for one day. Different psychology, see?"

It probably made sense. Rick heard himself asking how the hell anyone could tell whether he was a "real alky" or not, but he felt as if someone else were saying the words. His despair had changed suddenly to a conviction of unreality, which was even more frightening. Usually the sensation that he was not there at all, the need to pinch himself to establish his identity, was a separate mood. Tonight it had hit him in the middle of the familiar depression. He turned down the window and let the dark damp air blow across his face.

Joe was saying, "You have to answer that yourself, Rick. Put it this way: do I control liquor? Or does liquor control me? Can I walk into a bar and take one drink and walk out? Or does one drink make me feel there's not enough booze in the whole world to satisfy me? And how about a shot in the arm in the morning? That's a pretty sure test. If you need the hair of the dog, you're an alcoholic."

"I guess I am." Rick spoke slowly, almost indifferently. After last night, after other nights and days of fear and misery, he was ready to admit that he couldn't control his drinking. It seemed pretty obvious, but he couldn't see how it helped.

Joe, however, sounded pleased. "Good for you, Rick. That's the first step and you'll be surprised to find what a tough one it is for most A.A.s. It was for me. I kept kidding myself that I was just a hard drinker, telling myself I could handle it. I didn't tumble to the truth until I realized that alcohol is a poison to some people. Yup, just the way sugar is to a diabetic . . . or pollen to an asthmatic. The point is nobody blames a diabetic.

Nobody scolds him, or preaches at him. If he wants to stay healthy he damn well avoids sugar. Right? Okay, so Joe Kelly avoids liquor."

"How?" Joe was trying to help, but he seemed to be talking all around the point. Rick turned the window up and shivered, his body shaking as if in an attack of malaria.

Joe gave him a sharp, anxious look and pressed his foot on the starter. Clockwise. Counter-clockwise. The windshield wiper leapt into its routine. "What you need is coffee. Good hot coffee and plenty of it. Ought to be a dump along pretty soon."

It was a dump all right. A lonely-looking Greek was reading the funnies behind a deserted counter. "Hi, Aristotle." Joe called all Greeks Aristotle and they all responded with bewildered grins. Rick stretched his legs in a narrow booth and moved a tall sugar-shaker and a napkin holder across a spotted table top . . . an empty beer bottle, a glass, and a mustard jar . . . a bartender grumbling as they lurched into the street. He wondered what had happened to Pete . . . and Dora . . . the patriotic whore. Joe put two thick white cups of coffee on the table and went back for a couple of slices of coconut pie. Rick gulped the coffee. It wasn't bad. Strong and bitter but not bad. He could feel the heat rushing through him, thawing him out as if he had been half frozen in a snow bank. He straightened his shoulders and pulled out a pack of cigarettes.

"More mocha, Aristotle," Joe shouted and pulled at his wild red hair. "That's better, Rick. Couldn't have you falling asleep at your first meeting."

"I guess I'm not much of a prospect, Saint Augustine. I couldn't seem to keep my mind on your lecture."

"Guess I'm not much of a lecturer," Joe laughed. "I'm so full of this A.A. stuff that I don't know where to begin—or where to stop. But don't say you're a bum prospect—yet. Wait till you see some of the other guys who've made the grade." He laughed again and his voice boomed on in the small stuffy room. His voice that was like Saint Patrick's charming the snakes out of Ireland. It wasn't Irish really, and it wasn't a brogue at all, but an intonation of vastness. A vast melancholy and a vast humor. "It's that voice of yours, Red, not your wit that got you on the *Lampoon*." Rick had kidded Joe their sophomore year at Harvard. Now he felt Joe's voice seeping through his mind the way the coffee had rushed through his body. Warming it. Waking it to life. Joe was talking about the town drunks who'd done fifty stretches in the County Jail; about the rich bastards who'd been in and out of fancy institutions; about the men who'd been lawyers and engineers and ended up behind the eight ball, sleeping in Bowery flop-houses, spending their days on the "Beach," panhandling nickels to buy "smoke."

The rain had stopped and the lights of White Plains were clear in a suddenly opening sky. As if by the same miracle the blackness of Rick's depression had lifted . . . the outer world matching the inner . . . what the devil was that called? Rick puzzled over man's pathetic attempt to fit the prodigal indifference of Nature to his own small moods . . . Pathetic . . . Pathetic fallacy. Joe maneuvered past a crowded bus and pointed out the County Center where the A.A. meetings were held. The parking lot was jammed with cars.

"All these belong to ex-drunks?" Rick asked.

Joe laughed. "Mostly Bingo addicts. Me, I'd rather be an alky. More interesting."

They climbed a wide flight of stairs to the second floor and looked down from a balcony onto a room where hundreds of people sat hunched over little squares of cardboard. The announcer would call a number in a bored, emphatic voice and hundreds of eyes would shift anxiously from left to right; hundreds of hands reach tentatively toward a pile of lozenges. There was none of the reckless gaiety of roulette; none of the compelling excitement of the whirling wheel, the click of the ball, and the clipped fatality of the croupier's, *"Messieurs, Mesdames, faites vos jeux. Les jeux sont faits."* Rick turned away from the stupid mediocrity of this timid game of chance and followed Joe up the stairs. His hands were cold and clammy. He wiped them furtively on his trousers, not wanting to shake hands with anyone, not wanting to meet these screwy strangers after all.

Fifty or sixty men and women filled a small smoky room with loud voices and laughter. Cheerful crowd anyhow, Rick thought. He'd been afraid they'd be a dreary-looking bunch of self-righteous reformers. Then his mind side-tracked illogically. Hell, they didn't look like drunks. Too damn normal. They could never have known his crazy despair . . . never have done the fool things he had done . . . Gail. . . . He must telephone Gail. She ought to be home now.

"Hi there, Joe." A stocky man, with round brown eyes and a flute player's curved upper lip, detached himself from a group near the door.

"Kidd Whistler—Avery Rickham. It's Rick's first meeting," Joe said.

"That so? When were you drunk last, Mr. Rickham?" Whistler had the aggressively strong grip of short men.

"Last night." Rick was surprised that he felt no impulse to add, "None of your damn business."

Whistler balanced on his toes like a cheerleader getting set to jump up and down in front of the grand stand, "Good for you, Rickham. Got to be honest about it. I could have told anyhow from your hand. Clammy. Sure sign of the jitters, eh, Red?"

Joe gave a quick look at Rick to see how he was taking it. He wasn't blowing up for a wonder. You couldn't miss Kidd's exuberant good will. "Kidd has done a swell job on a lot of pretty hopeless drunks from here to Georgia. Sat up all night with a guy who had a loaded gun and was planning to use it on himself. I'll give you his phone number in case you ever get that way, Rick."

Phone. He had to call Gail. Now. "Is there a telephone booth in the building?" Rick asked.

"Downstairs. On your left. Want me to show you?"

"No, thanks. It may take quite a while." Rick hurried off, missing Kidd Whistler's wink at Joe.

A distant hopeless whirr buzzed in his ear like a late November fly against a window pane. He jangled the hook impatiently. "The line is busy. We will call you back in twenty minutes." "Hell, no," Rick shouted into the mouthpiece and banged up the receiver. He had been annoyed when he had tried to reach Gail earlier in the day by the mechanical indifference of dial phones, nostalgic for a human voice saying, "Number, please." Now, the cheerful assumption that he had nothing else to do but hang around for twenty minutes—and why always twenty? Why not fifteen? Or twenty-five—sent him pounding furiously up the stairs.

People had started to settle down on rows of folding chairs, but Joe and Kidd Whistler were still standing near the door.

"You owe me a buck, Kidd," Joe shouted, slapping Rick on the back. "Good boy. Kidd bet me a dollar you'd never show up . . . or turn up stinko in a coupla hours."

Whistler pulled out his wallet, and his flute player's mouth rippled into a wide grin. "Glad to pay up on that bet," he turned to Rick, "I figured your call was a phony . . . no pun intended . . . had the same stunt pulled on me once. Drove to hell and gone to pick up a drunk whose wife wanted him to go to an A.A. meeting. Never works out right when a wife or mother tries to shove a guy into A.A. You got to want this thing yourself, brother, and don't forget it. Well, this fellow seemed okay in the car. A bit over-hung, but okay. When we got up here, first thing he asked, just like you did, is there a phone in the building . . . and vanished. Boy, when he came back you could smell his breath clear across the room, but he acted real nice and quiet till he started to snore. In the middle of Hank Frost's speech—I think it was Hank's—he rolls off his chair and into the aisle."

"What the joke, boys?" A tall, slender woman joined them. Rick had noticed her when he first came in—a lovely pointed face like a Medieval saint—and wondered how any husband with a wife like that could be a drunk. Joe introduced her as Sylvia Landon and added that he and Rick had been friends, drunk and sober—but mostly drunk, since college.

"Joe's a real friend," Sylvia Landon smiled at Rick and slipped her arm through Joe's, "the kind of a friend who's always there when you need him most."

"He was around when I needed him this morning," Rick agreed, "yanked me out of jail."

"I don't see any prison pallor," Sylvia smiled, "your stay must have been brief. I did a ninety-day stretch two years ago for heaving a rock through a stuffed shirt's window."

Rick looked incredulously at the lovely pointed face with its luminous spiritual quality, but he could find nothing baffled and angry in the serene blue eyes, nothing belligerent. "Sounds like a pious idea," he ventured.

"The judge didn't think so." Bitterness edged Sylvia's low voice. "Joe knows what a mess I made of things. He got my sentence reduced."

"Good old Joseph Saint Augustine Fix-it Kelly," Rick reverted to the phrase which had always gotten Joe's goat at Harvard.

"Hey, cut that out." Joe sounded the way he had at college. He looked at his watch. "Time to get going, Kidd. Keep an eye on Rick, will you Sylvia? No phony phone calls, boy."

The two men ambled down the aisle together. Kidd Whistler rapped on a large oak table and went up on his toes in a cheerleader's gesture. "Well, folks, this is the regular Wednesday evening meeting of the White Plains Group of Alcoholics Anonymous. I guess you all know me, but for the benefit of any new members I better say that I am an alcoholic—and how. Sorry I can't tell you my sad story tonight because we've got a good friend here from the Greenwich group and in just a minute I'm going to turn the meeting over to him. First, I've got a couple of announcements to make." He picked a bunch of papers off the desk. "Here's a letter from New York about the Annual Dinner. It's going to be a bang-up affair with swell speakers. If you missed it last year, don't miss this one. I've got a stack of tickets right here, so be sure to come up after the meeting and get yours. Now here's a . . ."

Rick squirmed in his chair. It was small and the back stuck into his spine. What the hell had he gotten into anyway—a God-damned Rotary Club?

With quick perception Sylvia Landon leaned toward him and whispered, "Kidd's a bit too much of an organizer, but he's a salesman. When he gets through selling shoes he sells A.A. He's started groups all over the country and he keeps in touch with them, puts pep in the old ones. He really does a lot of good." She seemed to be persuading herself as well as Rick and he relaxed gratefully, stretched his long legs into the aisle, and decided to stick it out.

Joe was standing next to the oak table now. His reddish hair on end, his red-brown eyes alert as a setter's, his voice booming out with its rich intonation of vastness—a vast melancholy and a vast humor. You could feel the crowd respond. Liking Joe. Liking what he was saying.

The crowd in the Roosevelt bar—New Orleans, not forty-fifth

street—had liked Joe too. The way he had flourished his wallet, pulling out a wad of fifty-dollar bills, handing Rick a bundle. "A little expense money, pal," he had shouted and the crowd had felt good about it. People never seemed to envy Joe his luck, never complained that he got all the breaks. He had a way of making them forget the "quiet desperation" of their own lives, of swooping them up and into his wild, adventurous world. A tired-looking jobber from Kansas City had attached himself to Joe like an elderly Saint Bernard to a frisky young setter. He had insisted on treating them to *Ramos* fizzes till they finally broke away and settled down in Joe's room where a huge fan zoomed like an aeroplane over their heads.

"Here's the story, Rick." Joe had flung his panama in the general direction of the bed.

"Shoot." Rick had made himself comfortable by throwing his legs over the arm of a dust-covered chair. "Your cable didn't give me much of an idea what was up." It had come at a fortunate moment though. Rick was about due for a vacation and at loose ends as to where to go, since avoiding New York had become almost a mania, so Joe's "On big Hollywood assignment. Chicle Camp story. Fat salary for you technical advisor. Meet Roosevelt New Orleans. Cable how soon you can make it," had seemed like a good gamble.

"You know my firm handles one of the big chicle accounts. . . ."

"I ought to." Rick's eyes had darkened with the memory of the week after Adelaide's death when he had rushed into Joe's office demanding a field job somewhere—anywhere—so long as it was far enough away from New York.

"Right," Joe had hurried on, "but you didn't know—only a few pulp editors know—that Joe Kelly has been trying to crash the fiction market. I figured the pulps would be an easy way to start." He gave Rick a sheepish grin. "Well, I'd just sold a chicle yarn when I happened to hear that Paradise Pix was planning a big picture on some American enterprise in the Tropics—coffee—fruit—sugar or. . . . Boy, why not chicle?" Joe's grin widened into confidence. "I grabbed my manuscript, hopped me a plane to the Coast, and did the Movie Magnates ever fall for it, especially the ants in the bush."

"Ants in whose what?"

"Don't get funny now. You're my technical expert, not my gag man. The ants are the big scene. Wait till I come to that. It's terrific." Joe reached for his briefcase, pulled out a luridly covered magazine. "You can read it later, I'll just hit the high spots now. The heroine, a beautiful Maya Princess, is writing her senior thesis at College on chicle, the sacred confection of her ancestors. The *sapota* tree was the only wood used in the great Maya temples, or haven't you run into any archaeologists? Anyhow, this gal wants to see how gum is produced and the company invites her to visit a modern chicle camp. It's a swell layout, everything as clean and fancy as a dairy at the World's Fair, situated on a narrow peninsula jutting into a big silvery lake. Romantic. Only there's a drought which is holding back the flow of sap in the middle of the rainy season. . . ."

"Oh yeah," Rick protested.

"Don't be so damn literal. The drought is important. You'll see why in a minute. Now for the hero. He's a handsome young timber cruiser who's in trouble with the boss. He falls for the Princess. And how! The villain is a Maya Indian who worships the beautiful Princess and is even crazier about the beautiful *sapota* trees. He's a religious fanatic, see? He can't stand the idea of the sacred sap being wrapped up in neat little packages of gum and chewed by alien people in strange cities. So he starts a forest fire on the other side of the lake with the wind blowing toward the camp. He knows the woods are full of army ants, the big man-eaters. They can't swim and their only way to escape from the flames is to make for the peninsula. But he isn't leaving anything to chance. Ants love honey as much as bears. In the night he spills a trail of wild honey right down to the edge of the camp.

"Now the villain is close to the drainage ditch just outside the camp. His work is nearly done. Soon the ants will smell the gringos and go for them. Then he will rescue the Princess in a *cayuca*. But his foot catches in a root. He falls. Furiously he slashes at the root with his *machete* and cuts his heel. The ants smell his blood, they're on him, his screams wake the camp. A tethered mule neighs in agony as the ants reach *him*.

"'Ants!' yells the *chiclero* on watch. The Princess wakes from her hammock to a scene of wild confusion. Enter our hero. He shouts to the men, points to the chicle. Silvery, snow-clean chicle bubbling in great pots. They swing the kettles and spill the boiling chicle into the drainage ditch. As the ants hit the chicle they curl up like paper in a plumber's torch. The Princess is saved."

"Very realistic!" Rick laughed, "Screen credit to Joseph Augustine Kelly."

"Nope." Joe tugged at his red cowlick. "My name isn't big enough. Paradise dragged in a real writer, Jay Karnes."

"Tough luck," Rick could feel Joe's resentment like a blast from the zooming overhead fan. The fun was knocked out of things for him, too. "Is this guy Karnes working with us?"

"Hell, no. He's got too much pride and money. Last week he had to get an armored car to move his bonds from one New York bank to another." Joe laughed. "We've got a free hand—practically. And the chicle people are all for it, so long as we give an honest picture of the business. That's where you come in. Paradise plans to do the shooting in Central America. They'll want 'takes' of natives climbing trees. . . ."

"Chicleros zig-zagging *sapotas."*

"That's the stuff," Joe approved. "Now you sound like a technical expert. We might have one of the poor bastards fall and show how the company takes care of him and his family. Sorta corny, but I'll want you to work out a lot of real 'shots' to give the public the story of chicle. I've got three months leave on full salary, plus our pay checks and expense account from Paradise. Boy, are we all set."

"Where do we start?" Rick asked. His trip to New Orleans struck him as pretty screwy if Joe was planning on going right back to British Honduras.

"Right here, in a whore house in New Orleans!" Joe howled. "Paradise is paying Jay Karnes plenty to sign the story and the *bordello* is *his* idea. It's his only idea so far."

It had been hot that week in New Orleans, hotter than British Honduras. And they never did find the whore house Jay Karnes had suggested—liquor and women and gambling all in one spot. But they had a whale of a time looking. There had been bagnios with women and liquor, joints with liquor and gambling. They had done a thorough job of investigation and had wired Hollywood every night to report their progress. Then Joe had hit on the idea of using Lee Christmas in the story. Rick couldn't see what Lee Christmas had to do with the Epic of Chewing Gum. Joe had said, "You just don't recognize Hollywood genius when you see it, Rick. Hell, he's perfect. He was a filibuster, wasn't he? And he met these spig revolutionists in the Red Light District of New Orleans, didn't he? After running a train through a red signal because he was color blind and thought it was green. And Bonilla declared he was the engineer they were looking for because there weren't going to be any stop lights in their revolution. Jay Karnes wanted the story to begin in a brothel in New Orleans, didn't he? And Paradise hired us to do a chicle picture, didn't they? Okay, you have to pull the two things together somehow. Lee Christmas would do the trick. He'd fought in Central America, hadn't he?"

Rick had said he thought Joe had hired him as a chicle expert, but he guessed he was turning into a technical adviser on rum and whore houses. It had been one hell of a bender from New Orleans to Honduras, into the bush and out. Then Rick had gone back to his job and Joe had headed for Hollywood. Nothing had ever come of the picture, so far as Rick knew, but something had happened to the crazy, red-headed Irishman.

The flimsy chair creaked as Rick straightened to look at Joe now.

"Yes, sir," Joe was saying, putting one leg over the edge of the speaker's table and pushing aside a stack of A.A. pamphlets. "I come by my boozing ways honestly. Nothing illegitimate about it. My old man was a Saturday night drunk. He'd come out of the mill with his pockets bulging and stop with the gang for a coupla beers. . . ." There was a quick burst of laughter and Joe looked around with a grin. "Sounds familiar, doesn't it? He ran true to form all right, rolling home at five a.m., boiled as an owl, shouting fit to wake the dead—and the neighbors. My mother would get him to bed, warn us kids to stay away from him, and go off to early mass. . . ."

Rick could hardly believe his ears. In all the years he had known him, Joe had never mentioned his family. Rick had met Joe at baseball practice freshman year and asked him around. Some of the snobs in

Rick's crowd had tried to high-hat the skinny red-headed "Irish."

"Prep?" Joe would laugh. "Sure and I attended the Loyola Parochial School and Lowell High." But there would be a "want to make something of it, pal?" gleam in his red-brown eyes. By the end of sophomore year Joe Kelly in his old brown sweater, with his famous left-handed curve, and his odd squibs in the *Lampoon*, had become one of the Big Shots in the class. It could happen even at Harvard. A few die-hards had continued to mutter that there must be something damn fishy about Kelly's family, others accepted the romantic legend, which had somehow got around, that he was an orphan, but for the most part, Joe was invited everywhere and not expected to reciprocate with weekend invitations. Only Rick had worried secretly, afraid that Joe was ashamed of his family. Now, here was Joe talking openly about them at his cockeyed meeting.

"Sure, I inherited the taste for liquor and the inability to handle it, but I went my old man one better. I didn't just get drunk Saturday nights. Neither did he when he came up a bit in the world. You know how the Irish are at politics—a kind of natural talent like putting a hook on a ball." Joe swung his left arm as if he were winding up for a pitch. "My father's cronies set him up in a cigar store when I was twelve where he could sorta keep an eye on the ward heelers. It meant that we kids had to keep an eye on him and the store. It meant that he had a fine chance to close up early and slip around the corner to a saloon, but I never saw him reach for a bottle in the morning. He left that improvement to his oldest son. You'd think, wouldn't you, that Joe Kelly would've been the last guy in the world to become a drunk. I saw what a mess it made of my mother's life, what tough going it was for us kids. It stands to reason that I—well, there isn't any reason in an alcoholic's mind. I didn't touch the stuff in college—partly because my sister and I pricked our fingers and made a solemn pact, signed in our blood, at the ages of nine and seven, never to touch a drop, mostly because I was in training and broke all the time anyhow. But in France it was different. You'll hear a lot of guys say they started drinking in the last war, blaming it on trench nerves. It wasn't like that with me. The Latin way of drinking appealed to me— wine and cognac. I kidded myself that it was different from my old man's beer with Rye chasers—the poor man's potion—but it was poison just the same. It took me years to find out that one drink is dynamite for me. One drink is too much—and it is never enough. That's what we alcoholics are up against. We can't be moderate drinkers. Ever. Maybe if Bill Griffith had started A.A. twenty years earlier, my old man wouldn't have been run over by a beer truck. Maybe. He was a stubborn cuss. I get to thinking about him sometimes and the Flexible Flyer he gave me for Christmas when I was eight and the ball games we'd go to and then I know how lucky we A.A.s are. It's a funny thing to call a bunch of rummies lucky, but I mean it. We've found a way to live without liquor. Sounds sorta negative, like a guy who's learned to walk without a leg." Joe looked around with his wide, confident grin. "Okay. I'll make it stronger. We've found a way to live. Period."

Rick heard the applause; heard Joe introducing the next speaker, a large Italian who worked as a chef in a Stamford hotel and who kept marching across the platform with an imaginary book in his hand, saying, "I reada the book, see? Paja seven-one where they tell about the twelva step. I say to myself, 'Tony Trombetta, thatsa right. You are powerless over the alcohol,' and I taka the number one step. So Then I taka the number two step. For me that is easy. I knowa God since I been small as a young olive tree. God will helpa me out. For Tony the number two is small step lika this. For some is biga step lika this. . . ."

Rick wasn't paying much attention. He was thinking about Joe. And his family. It explained a lot of things—why Joe used to vanish out of their lives every summer vacation, with never a post card from a ranch in Arizona or a camp in Maine—why he got such a kick out of handing out those fifty-dollar bills in the Roosevelt bar.

The man across the aisle was getting to his feet. He had a thin, scholarly face and a careful look. Not timid but careful. He put his feet down precisely as he walked to the front of the hall, removed his spectacles and wiped them carefully.

"My name is Duncan MacKenzie and I am an alcoholic." He made the statement without emotion, as if he were about to testify in a court room. "I have been thinking over what Joe Kelly said about his father— or to be exact. . . ."

Rick was sure MacKenzie would always be exact. He didn't need to make a point of it. There was an exact crease to the trousers of his grey pin-stripe, an exact part to his thinning grey hair. MacKenzie would be the morose kind of drunk, the kind you saw sitting alone at the end of a bar. Not kidding with anyone. Not getting any fun out of it. Hell, what fun had he gotten himself the last five-six years?

"I've been thinking about my own father," MacKenzie continued. "He was a distinguished lawyer and a distinguished drinker. I always wanted to be like him. I got kicked out of my first prep school for my unsuccessful experiments with alcohol, but I worked like the devil at college and law school, where my father had made a brilliant record. When he took me into his firm I imagine most of our friends thought I drank too much because I had an inferiority complex. They were quite right. I did have one. Not so much because I lacked my father's brains, as because I did not have his head for liquor." He gave a wry smile. "You see my ambition had transferred itself, I knew I could never be as good a lawyer as my father, but I kept on trying to be as good a drinker. I was a failure at that too."

He took off his spectacles, wiped them with a neatly folded white handkerchief and put them back in his breast pocket. "I have sometimes been called a typical Scot, which usually means in the popular mind a dour, reserved, solitary person. I was not, however, a solitary drinker. I wanted to be the center of a crowd. A few drinks made me feel as popular and witty as my father—at first. I seemed to have a great many friends when I was drinking. I seemed to be a regular fellow. I even became a member of the 11:40 Club.

"This remarkable organization had half a dozen members in the town of South Orange where my wife and I were then living. We were all alcoholics—although, of course, none of us admitted that self-evident fact. We thought we were getting by. We were pleased with ourselves. We made sounds of somewhat contemptuous pity when we heard about friends who got tickets for drunken driving—or were carted off to sanitariums. *We* could handle liquor. *We* got to our jobs every day. On the 11:40. We took a curious kind of pride in passing by the saloon near the ferry on the Jersey side. And usually we made a point of skipping the first one on the New York side. Conscious of having demonstrated enormous self-control, we would stop at the second or third saloon on Chambers Street for our eye-openers. At this stage of the game I had not started the drink-before-breakfast habit, but I should have guessed by the reek of cloves and peppermint that some of my boon companions had.

"Eventually we would reach our offices. Whether we arrived at two or at four o'clock depended not on our business appointments, but on which side of Chambers Street we happened to be—one had a lot more saloons than the other. When I finally got to my office I would be a fiend for work—most of it unnecessary. I would rush through the motions of looking up briefs, looking up minute points of law, dictating long unimportant letters. I was absolutely no good.

"Often several members of our Club would meet after, quote, work, end quote, and have a few pick-ups on the way to the ferry. Or we might even stay around New York and make an evening of it. But it was a point of pride with all of us to telephone our wives, and to get home at some hour of the night and catch the 11:40 the next day.

"This program continued for a surprising number of years. Thanks to my secretary who would say in a convincing voice, 'Mr. MacKenzie will be in conference all day tomorrow. I am sorry the only time he could see you is between four and five.' It is amazing how many good-for-nothing drunks are protected by the loyalty of secretaries and wives. Maybe, the answer is that the men who don't get this extraordinary loyalty end up in asylums, or morgues—so you never hear of them. You can guess what happened in my case. After a while I couldn't wait till I got off the ferry for my first drink; after a while my secretary couldn't even make appointments between four and five. Finally, a long stretch of D.T.s disqualified me for membership in the 11:40 Club. Then a lot of doctors in a lot of expensive sanitariums tried a lot of 'cures' on me. . . ."

Rick wondered why there was a sudden burst of laughter at this. The crowd certainly had a grim sense of humor, but MacKenzie gave a dry chuckle.

"Evidently some of the rest of you have been 'cured' too. I didn't stay 'cured.' As a last resort I came to High Pines. Someone had told my wife about Dr. Wales. Gradually he got me to a point where I could recognize my own infantilism and he advised me to go to an A.A. meeting in Greenwich. You could say that A.A. did the trick, but I don't think that would be quite honest. I owe a lot to A.A. *and* to psychiatry. It was the combination that worked with me. I know some of you feel that A.A. is the one and only answer to this problem of alcoholism. As I see it that is a childish and dangerous form of group egotism. Dangerous because your justifiable pride in the A.A. program may turn into a stupid resentment of psychiatry. And you know what the book says about the dangers of resentments to an alcoholic. . . ." He stopped speaking abruptly, as if he felt that he had lost touch with his audience, and walked down the aisle, his precise eyebrows pulled into a frown.

Joe pulled at his red forelock, his voice jerking people back to attention. "I'm glad Mac said that. I think he's right. I wonder how many of you know that the Greenwich Chapter started out by meeting at High Pines. One of the finest women in the New York group was there and some of the New York members used to come out regularly every Friday night to see her. Hank Frost would join them from Cos Cob. I'm sorry he isn't here tonight because he still doesn't hold with foolin' around with psychiatry. I'd like to hear him and Mac argue the subject. There's nothing I like better than a good argument. Maybe that is a hangover from my drinking days. I was the greatest argufier in ten States. But Hank had to work late tonight at his boatyard, so I've asked Sylvia Landon from the New York group to tell us about women alcoholics."

Rick pulled his long legs out of the aisle and shoved back his chair for Sylvia to pass. She moved with an easy grace, looking in her deep blue linen dress like a Medieval saint returning unhurriedly to her place in a stained glass window.

"I am an alcoholic." She made the statement in a quiet voice as if she were announcing her faith before a flaming pyre. "It was very hard for me to say those four words at first, so now I say them to myself every morning when I wake up. And now they give me courage. I think it is harder for a woman to admit that she is a drunkard—or is that just an alibi of my sex? Society seems to be rather indulgent toward a man who drinks too much, but promptly and thoroughly disgusted by a lady in her cups. It isn't a pretty picture, I grant you, but Society makes it very easy for a woman to become an alcoholic. We women have too much leisure—oh, not now, during the war—now, there is never time to do all the work we want to do." Rick noticed the tensing of her jaw and the way her hand tightened on the corner of the oak table. "But usually even women who call themselves busy have time on their hands. Leisure is a lovely word, but a dangerous one for a potential alcoholic. Look at Duncan MacKenzie. He at least got the 11:40—some strong habit kept him that much on the beam. Then look at your average woman. Average— there's a word I could never face.

"My family brought me up to believe that I was something special. That I had a beautiful, special destiny waiting for me. Not that I had to make any great effort to achieve it. Just that they made me feel I was prettier and cleverer than the 'average' girl. It was easy to agree with them. When I married the most eligible young man in our small upstate New York town everything seemed to be working out according to my stars. Remember that line—'The fault, dear Brutus, lies not in our stars but in ourselves that we are underlings.' I not only wouldn't admit that, I couldn't. It was a wonderful discovery that liquor could make my dream world seem real. The crowd we played around with did a good job of Saturday night drinking at the Country Club. It was fun for them. For me it became fantasy. I could pretend that I wasn't just a young married woman at a small town dance. I could be a *femme fatale* in the International Set. A few drinks took me from the Riviera to one of those fabulous English country house weekends. But it wasn't enough to feel like a Far-away Princess only on Saturday nights. There was the whole dull week to live through—shopping—going to lunch with the girls I grew up with—playing bridge in the evenings. Pretty soon I found I could keep the Saturday night dream world going all the time. It was a lovely discovery. At first I used to get up for breakfast with my husband and talk conscientiously to the maid about meals, but it really hardly seemed worth-while. It was easier to stay in bed in the morning; pleasanter to start drinking as soon as I woke up. I told my friends I was writing a novel. I couldn't waste my time going to luncheons. That was a fine idea too. It made me sound special. Feel special. I bought a typewriter. I bought reams of white paper and yellow pads and carbon and soft pencils and boxes of paper clips and folders and envelopes. But there wasn't any place where I could keep the, any place where I could work—drink—undisturbed. I needed a studio. I got one. A wonderful room over the garage with a fireplace and a big table and a big couch. I'd go out there in the morning—if I could get up in the morning. I kept a bottle in the drawer of the desk. At first I used to rush back to the house at five, take a shower, slip into a dinner dress, and have a shaker of cocktails ready when my husband got home from his office. If he smelled liquor he would think I had just been sampling the martinis. Then, one day he found me passed out on the couch in the studio with an empty gin bottle beside me and the cover still on my typewriter.

"You see what I mean about women and leisure. A man would have had to get up and go to a job. I had all day with nothing to do. I didn't blame my husband for divorcing me after the passing out on the couch in the studio became a regular scene. The funny thing is that I was really relieved in a way. I told myself I didn't want to live in that dull little town all my life. It was the town's fault. I didn't want to write a novel anyhow. I wanted to go to New York. I wanted to be an archaeologist. My mother sympathized with me. She was sure my husband had never understood me. I was sensitive. Special. She blamed him for my drinking. I had never touched anything stronger than sherry at home. Her daughter could not have acted like that without cause. I must have been terribly unhappy. Of course, I agreed.

"I wasn't going to drink in New York. Everything would be different in New York. It was for a while. I found an apartment near the University. I enrolled for graduate classes. I met new people. I was excited and happy for a while. Then I failed an exam in physical anthropology—you can imagine what happened. A few drinks made me feel sure that my professor had been unfair. She was a brilliant woman with a thin ugly face. Obviously, she was jealous of me. A few more drinks put me back in my glamorous dream world, a few months put me in an alcoholic ward. Jane Post visited the ward. She talked to me. She left me a copy of the A.A. pamphlet. When my mother rushed to my rescue, telling everyone I had had a nervous breakdown from overwork, Jane talked to her. My mother got me out of Bloomingdale. She took me to a hotel. I stood at a long window looking down into a narrow court-yard lined with neat rows of garbage cans—I wanted to jump. . . ."

Rick clutched at the arms of his chair—and there were no arms. He could feel the abysmal compulsion of a street below him. Once in a hotel room in Havana he had crawled out of bed before dawn and shoved a great carved chest in front of a balcony window. His knees had been shaking from rum and malaria but he had managed to add a flimsy wicker chair and a solid table to his barricade. It had been a slow fumbling process in which his frantic instinct of self-preservation had not once been impeded by a doubt. Only when he woke late in the day had he surveyed the barricade with a mingled horror and a detached curiosity. Why the hell should a man who felt the impulse to jump go to all that ridiculous trouble to save himself? Yet he had repeated the same crazy performance the next night and the next.

The palms of Rick's hands were wet with fear—fear for himself, fear for the slender woman in the blue linen dress. She had stretched out her hands in a spontaneous gesture of gratitude, "A.A. has held me back from that window. A.A. is teaching me how to live with myself—I don't mean that I am cured of alcoholism—none of us are—but A.A. has given us a reprieve." There was applause and Sylvia hesitated, "I never told anyone about wanting to jump out of that window," she added, "I didn't know I was going to tell it to you tonight, but that is another thing A.A. does for us—it helps us to be honest with ourselves . . . to tell the truth about ourselves. . . ."

That was it! Rick sat up suddenly. He felt as if a Venetian blind had been pulled up in front of his eyes. He had been looking at the world through slats, seeing only streaks of light, narrow glimpses of people. These A.A.s let you see them through a clear pane of glass. They were real. More real than anyone he had ever known. He knew them better than the Winged Victory, better than the slim colt of a girl with a forehead like a Greek Temple, better even than Adelaide. He knew Joe as he had never known him in Harvard or New Orleans. He was among friends. He was not alone any more.

III

SALT WIND AND SUN

Rick woke to sunlight slanting through yellow organdy curtains and the sharp salty tang of mud-flats. He was used to waking in strange beds, in strange hotels, in strange lands—hammocks swung between the tall columns of *ramon* trees—the narrow berths of coastal steamers—mosquito netting draped over wide brass beds in European hotels from Lima to Hong Kong. This moment of orientation no longer filled him with uneasy fear as it does the infrequent traveler. He enjoyed watching his sleepy mind turn and sniff like a cat to discover its whereabouts. But this place was strange . . . because it was familiar. Familiar as his boyhood. That was it. Falmouth. He stretched, happy for an instant, and then remembered.

This was Joe's house in Riverside, Connecticut. Joe had brought him back after the A.A. meeting in White Plains. H. Peculiar Henry, this must be Thursday! Time and Time and Time and Time. The Mantons' cocktail party had been Tuesday afternoon. And he had not seen Gail since . . . since. . . . Remorse hit him. Harder than it had in the dark foxhole of Joe's car. A different kind of remorse. He had been down for the count then, groggy with self-contempt, self-pity. Now he was thinking of Gail. The poor damn kid with a drunk for a father. He'd fix things up with her somehow. Start being a decent parent . . . a slender woman in a blue dress with the face of a Medieval saint . . . a careful man in a precise grey pin-stripe . . . a fat Italian acting out "I taka the first step so" . . . and Joe. Joe pulling at his wild red forelock, his voice booming out with its rich intonation of vastness—a vast melancholy and a vast humor. If they could do it he could.

He stretched again, testing his muscles tentatively. The twitching nerves of the jitters had almost gone. Swinging long legs out of the canopied maple bed he pulled on his clothes. Joe must be up. He could catch an early train to town with Joe and see Gail before he went to his office.

The cheerful aroma of coffee and bacon led him to a small dining room where Joe was chatting with a large colored girl in a candy-striped pink dress. American breakfasts were tops, Rick thought. Other nations could beat us at other meals . . . Italy for lunch—spaghetti with meat sauce and great garlic-rubbed bowls of green salad . . . England for tea—hot buttered scones and Devonshire cream and strawberry jam. You had to grant the brussels-sprouters a knowing way at the tea table . . . France for dinner, obviously . . . but breakfast in America. Especially in New England.

"What train are you taking?" Rick asked, spooning into a dish of fresh applesauce.

"The 8:13. But look, Rick, why don't you stay out here for a few days? When I called your office yesterday I said you were sick—you were sick, you know—and that you'd be back to work Monday. Stick around and we'll fill you up with fresh air and as much A.A. talk as you can stomach. There's a meeting in Greenwich tomorrow night."

It was decent of Joe but—"I've got to see Gail," he said, watching Joe pour coffee into a large white cup decorated with gold scrolls of hearts and flowers which entwined the word, "Father," in flourishing letters. Where the hell had Joe picked it up? Probably somebody's idea of a joke. H. Peculiar Henry, being a father was no joke.

The coffee was good, strong and black. "Any Italian in it?" Rick asked.

Joe nodded, "We mix 'em. Why not ask Gail out for the weekend? Emerald is off on Thursdays, but Gail could come tomorrow or Saturday."

It might make things easier at that, Rick thought. He could see Joe's dock through the bay window and a rowboat halfway out of water, tilted on its side in the mud. If he could sit on that dock with Gail and watch the gulls, or row her around the harbor, he might be able to talk to her. How could a man apologize to his own child, explain that he had not really hit her but a whole phony society, without telling her all sorts of things about himself? The things that made him tick . . . sailing with his father in the old catboat at Falmouth . . . skating with Adelaide at Lake Placid. He would have to face even that. Talk to Gail about her mother—about their marriage—if he could ever hope to show her what was wrong with Paul. But how could he manage it in the brownstone house where he and Adelaide had lived with such gay security and such unforeseen brevity?

"Call her up now," Joe urged. "The phone's in the hall under the stairs."

But Gail was not at home. Emily said she had gone off to the Poconos for a week. "With the Mantons?" Rick asked in furious certainty of the answer. "I couldn't stop her, Avery." Emily was the only person who still called him by his first name.

Grandfather Avery used to say, "Avery is a good name, boy. Don't you ever let anyone make you think that Cabot Rickham would have been a speck better!" Grandfather Avery had been a tall, authoritative man with a crinkly white beard and high leather boots. He would stalk along the Charles and people would turn and point him out as "quite a character." He had run away from home at seventeen and sailed around the Horn and come back to Boston with tall tales of San Francisco in '49 and only enough gold for pretty Abigail Bronson's wedding ring. Later he had amassed a respectable fortune in a respectable manner, but he regarded this as merely the normal and quite dull procedure of a gentleman and preferred to recall his youthful adventures to a youthful audience of one. Avery would sit entranced in a book-lined study on Beacon Street listening to his grandfather's stories—men had been dropping like flies on the streets of 'Frisco from scurvy and an old miner had told Grandfather Avery to eat a raw potato every day. He had carried one in his pocket and he would pull out the very gold knife he had pared it with and show it to his small grandson. Avery had always been disappointed because he had never pulled out the potato too.

Gail was older than Grandfather Avery had been when he sailed around the Horn. And Gail was a child. A lovely, willful, un-self-reliant child. What had happened to America? It was becoming a country of adolescents. He had known men who were still college boys in their thirties—and proud of it.

Rick's mind switched back to Emily's voice on the telephone. "Gail seemed terribly upset when she got home from the Mantons' party. She wouldn't tell me what the trouble was and she usually does, but I couldn't get a word out of her. She just rushed up to her room and started throwing things into a suitcase and dashed out of the house."

Fury pounded in Rick's temples. Fury at Gail. Fury at himself. He had failed her again. If he had gone directly home from the Mantons' instead of barging around the town getting plastered he might have prevented this. Emily had sounded worried and Emily was not the worrying kind. H. Peculiar Henry, was Emily afraid that Gail might elope with that impossible Manton boy?

Rick stormed into the dining room and shouted incoherent phrases at Joe. He was going down to the Poconos. Now. He was going to drag Gail away . . . by the hair of her head if necessary . . . from those cheap, ridiculous Mantons. Joe was lucky. Joe didn't have a daughter who fell for a Lansing Somebody-or-other with a fashion-female mother. He'd be damned if he'd let Gail marry Paul Manton. She came of good sturdy stock. . . . He was pacing the length of the dining room from the bay window to the pine corner-cupboard and back again.

Joe watched him with a quizzical look. "Easy does it, Rick," he advised. "That's alcoholic talk."

"The hell it is." Rick flung himself into his chair and gulped the last swallow of cold coffee. "I'm not planning to get drunk if that's what you mean."

"You may not be *planning* to go on another bender, but any alky who gets in a rage like that is sure heading for one. Don't kid yourself Rick."

"That's what *you* think, Saint Augustine." Rick's voice was angry. He was angry at Gail, at himself and at Joe. Joe ought to know him better than that. He wasn't a weak sister who couldn't stay off liquor for even one day.

Joe pulled out his watch, folded up the *Tribune* and pushed back his chair. "I take it you're going to town with me and then down to the Poconos. And a fine scene that will be. And whatever do you imagine

your girl will be after doing, the high-spirited colleen that she is?" Joe
had a way of putting on a mock Irish accent when he was most in earnest.
"I suppose she'll be falling into the arms of her loving father. The devil
she will! She'll be off with this lad of hers, or I miss my guess. An' who'll
be to blame for that, I'm asking you?" He opened the kitchen door and
called to Emerald in his normal voice that Mr. Frost would be bringing
in a bunch of fish and he'd fry himself a mess of them for supper. She
could set the table for one. Mr. Rickham was leaving.

Rick heard Emerald's rich Negro laughter. "That Mr. Frost, he sure
is the fish-catchin'est man I ever see. He knows the ways of all them
smelts, flounders, blackfish, snappers and porgies," she rolled the names
off with the relish of a Charleston fishmonger.

Rick followed Joe to the front steps. A tall, round-shouldered man,
with great curved eyebrows which gave him the look of a friendly barn
owl, was shambling up the walk between rows of late zinnias.

"I fixed it up for Hank Frost to take you fishing today," Joe
explained. "He said he'd go A.W.O.L. from his boatyard. But I guess he
won't care. Hank is always glad of an excuse to go fishing. Hi, Hank,"
he boomed. "Looks as if you'd lost your customer."

"The hell he has." Rick surprised himself by his sudden change of
mind, the unexpected enthusiasm in his own voice. He hadn't been fishing since he had gone after barracuda and amberjack off Chinchorro
Bank. He lifted his head to the salty tang of the incoming tide.

Hank looked Rick over, then followed Rick's eyes to the dock.
"Nothin' like a day on the water for what ails you. Nothin' like it anyhow.
Tide's 'bout right for stripers. We'd better get going. Hey, Red," he
shouted above the whir of the car Joe was backing out of the garage.
"Better tell this friend of yours where he can find some fishin' duds."

"Emerald'll fix him up," Joe called back, turning the car out of the
narrow driveway.

Rick pulled on an old pair of dungarees and tugged at a T-shirt to
get it under his belt. It must have flapped like a tent on Joe. No luck
with Joe's sneakers. No luck at all. He went down the stairs, envisioning
drearily what the mud would do to his tax oxfords, and found Hank on
the back porch.

"Dug these up in the garage," Hank pointed at a large pair of rubber boots, an over-size wind-breaker and a Block Island cap. "Happened to remember that Tony had parked 'em here last time he went out with me. Tony's a big guy too—for a wop."

Carrying four oars, two anchors, a tackle box, bait pail, clam rake, two thermos bottles, and a paper bag of sandwiches Emerald had handed them, they made their way to the dock.

"Seems like quite a load," Rick commented. He had always prided himself on traveling light in the bush.

"We ain't takin' nothin' extry," Hank said defensively. "Better to have too much stuff here, than somethin' ashore when we need it. I was aimin' to try three kinds of fishin' . . . that is, if you got the stomick for it. How's the stomick actin' today, brother? Mine uster turn over somethin' awful."

"Okay." Rick grinned, remembering the applesauce, oatmeal, fish cakes, bacon and coffee he had stowed away at breakfast—the first real meal he had had in more than thirty-six hours. "The prisoner ate a hearty meal."

Hank laughed at the old joke. He had shoved the boat off, arranged their junk with practiced neatness, and now directed Rick to let go the painter and hop in.

Hank was in the after-seat, so Rick crawled carefully forward. It struck him as an odd arrangement, but it might mean that Hank was planning to have Rick do the rowing while he trolled. Hank patted the side of the boat affectionately, as a man will stroke the flank of a prize-winning horse. "Nice job, eh? Built her myself down to our boatyard . . . fifteen-eighteen years ago." The skiff was round-bottomed with fine slim lines. "Paint her grey so's the city fellers 'round here can't foller me too easy just when I've picked me a good spot." He grinned and pulled on the long ash oars.

Rick located the other pair and slid them into the oarlocks, noting approvingly the rims of leather to keep them in place if you had to drop them in a hurry when a fish struck. Hank evidently classified him as a city fellow with a hangover who couldn't pull his own weight. He'd show him that he hadn't spent eighteen years in the bush for nothing. "How about our weights?" he asked, resentment showing in his tone. "Wouldn't the boat balance better if we changed places?"

"How much you weigh?"

"One-ninety, I guess."

"'Bout what I figgered. I'm one-eighty-four, myself." Rick was surprised. Hank was a skinny-looking guy. "Had it doped out that when we start trollin' we'd take turns on the oars. That way you can fish right over my oar, like my old woman does, an' I can lay my rod at my feet, so's I can net your fish easy and bait both hooks. If we strike bottom out in them bass rocks I can free both hooks."

It sounded reasonable enough, but Rick didn't like being put in the position of an old woman. He gave an angry tug on his right oar and caught a crab. Hank guffawed.

"Don't you go takin' no offense now at me comparin' you to my old woman. That ain't no insult, Mister. Wait till you see her land a twelve-pounder."

Rick laughed and pulled more evenly on his oars. The boat had an easy run, light but steady. As they skimmed under the dark span of the railroad bridge, a train rumbled overhead and Hank shook his fist. "Blasted idjits!" he shouted above the roar. "Hustlin' themselves into New York City when they coulda stayed in God's country."

"Right," Rick agreed, though he had always regarded this section of Connecticut as too suburban. Not exactly the Great Open Spaces. "You can have my share of New York."

"Don't want it." Hank spat in a southeasterly direction. "New Haven's my idea of a town. Been Frosts going up there to Yale college since way back. To my way of thinkin' civilization ends when you enter East Port Chester and don't rightly start up again till you hit the real south after jumpin' the states of New York, New Jersey and Pennsylvania. Them states is amorphous. Sourlands. Why I won't even go visitin' an A.A. meetin' in Jersey. If a man ain't got the brains and commonsense to get outa Jersey he might as well stay drunk. . . ." Hank cocked an owl eye at Rick, "I get real riled up thinkin' about this country. American history's kind of a hobby of mine you might say. Got a lot of old volumes belonged to my Grandfather—set of the *Federalist* and all Spark's biographies. Couldn't rightly say which I like best—readin' them old histories, ketchin' me a bigger bass than the old woman, or gittin' a nice wing shot at a broad-bill. See that little hump of trees?" Hank pointed back toward the stone abutment next to the Power Plant, "That's Park Island. Good spot for blacks. Broadbills don't mostly come in this close."

"You mean you shoot black ducks over there, right under the Powerhouse?"

"The ducks is there, brother," Hank chortled as if letting Rick in on a private joke, "but these here foreigners, like Joe, don't take no notice on 'em. Go traipsin' up to their clubs in Milford or down to Maryland, leavin' me sittin' pretty with plenty of broads, blacks, mallards, and an occasional whistler, not countin' the mergansers which is too fishy for anyone exceptin' a wop. Ducks is smart. No foolin'. They head into the Powerhouse marsh figgerin' as how no hunter'll go so close. No one does but me. I know all the guards at the plant. When they hear shots from the direction of Park Island they can count on its bein' me. Usually is. Sometimes they investigates so as no saboteur will take advantage of this situation. Mostly, if it's me, I put up a recognition signal. If it's not, the guards tell the guy to beat it. Which makes it pretty soft for me."

South of Park Island was a half mile sweep of marsh, pocked with mudholes. They would be lovely small lagoons at high tide, Rick noted, wishing he could stop rowing to wipe the sweat from his eyes. His T-shirt was soaked and a regular river was running down his spine. Hell, the least exertion seemed to make him drip like a man in a Turkish bath. He had always blamed it on malaria. Nights when he'd have to get up three times—or more—to change his pajamas. Quinine would do that. But so would booze. Maybe he'd been doing a bit of alcoholic dodging all the time. Not being willing to admit that liquor had anything to do with it. His arms felt like bits of spaghetti, but he bit his lower lip and pulled on. Hank seemed able to keep up a regular easy dip of his oars and a regular easy flow of talk. It was all Rick could do to listen. "That's one of my blinds," Hank nodded toward some brownish bushes above the rocks. "Be usin' it real soon now. October's the sportin'est month we got round Cos Cob harbor—fishin' kinda merges into huntin' in October. Feller can pull a blackfish up with one hand and shoot a black duck with t'other," he chortled, shipped his oars and stretched like a lean black bear in the sun. Pulling out a pack of *Wings*, he offered one to Rick. Rick's hand shook as he held the cigarette toward a kitchen match.

"Easy does it, brother—that's one of our A.A. slogans. Never had to apply it particular to myself. Never was much of a one to rush things." Hank cocked a kindly but inquisitive eye at Rick. "Reckon you're the nervous kind?"

Rick nodded. The A.A.s seemed to go in for leading questions—like Kidd Whistler last night. He took a long drag on his cigarette and decided to try the direct attack himself. Giving Hank a friendly grin, he asked, "If you aren't the nervous type, what was your trouble?"

Hank blinked. "Fair enough, brother. We kinda get the habit o' pouncin' on new members. All with the good intention of givin' 'em a hand. There's been a heap o' fine and fancy explanations o' my case, but I dunno as I rightly hold much with any of 'em. Joe now—he's got it figgered that I had some inferior complex on account of the Frost family uster build the solidest small craft to slide down the ways south of Friendship in the State of Maine. Mebbe so. I was always hangin' round the Yard when I was a kid, admirin' the prints of early clippers and such and studyin' on the plans of old whalers. Got so I hated my Pa for turnin' out toy boats for Yacht Clubs—Snipes and Lightnin's and Frost-bites. Mebbe that's why I took to runnin' round with the railroad gang down to the station, drinkin' varnish and loafin' on the streets of Greenwich— my mother uster call it Grennich like the foreigners do—mebbe I was just ornery and wanted to raise hell. Ever hear o' Gresham's Law? I read how it applies to money but it fits me like an old shoe. Sorta figgered it was smart to talk like the town bums and ain't been able to stop ever since. Bad language sure drives out good grammer mighty easy. I'd learned better but I couldn't speak like an educated person now if I tried. Like I was tellin' you, Frosts always went up to Yale College—but not me, not Henry Cotton Frost, the Third—own damn fault if you ask me. Own damn fault that I lost the Yard, too. After my Pa died I got so sore at the whole stinkin' business that I'd go a-breezin' up to Commodores o' Yacht Clubs who knew how to ride a fine Wall Street storm, and me half seas over, and bawl 'em out for the baby's bathtub craft they was orderin'." He let out a loud laugh at the memory. "Bunch of landlubbers a-comin' into the Frost Boat Yard not knowin' the difference between a yawl and a ketch. Great Uncle o' mine up to Saybrook come down an' called a directors' meetin' and threw me out on my ear."

"Tough," Rick commented inadequately.

"Yes and no," Hank pondered, "War done the Yard a good turn. We're makin' P.T. boats now for the Coast Guard. They're nice honest craft too. I figger my ancestors wouldn't be ashamed of the Yard any more. And I'm a hell of a sight happier doin' the job I'm doin' there than I ever was fussin' with accounts and profits and losses on them jimcrack lapdogs my Pa called boats."

Hank tossed the stub of his cigarette overboard and started rowing. "How about tryin' for stripers first? Then at low water we'll get clams. Fish for blacks on the first two hours of the flood, which is the best time for 'em on the rocks where we're headin'. Then we'll have the last o' the flood to hit the weaks, which is stickin' round late this year."

"You're a regular fishing clock," Rick laughed.

"Have to be to get 'em. Some of these foreigners goes for weaks in the up-stream channel at low water and for blacks on the ebb and wonders why they don't get nothin' except bergalls," Hank snorted derisively.

Rick was catching on to the fact that Hank used the term 'foreigners' to apply, not to 'wops' or 'polacks,' but to commuters. It took Rick back to his childhood and to his father's rage at the 'summer people' who were 'spoiling' Falmouth when he was a boy. Although the Rickhams had been actually only summer people themselves, they had inherited their house from a great aunt and so had some claim to roots, which Mr. Rickham had assiduously cultivated and vociferously defended even to the extreme and unpopular extent of refusing to contribute to a new golf club.

Hank gestured with a flip of his right oar toward a long wooded point about three miles eastward, black in the seaward shine. "That's Tod's Point. Best beach this side of Stratford. And one time we put it over on the foreigners. Had quite a fight with the property owners along Lucas Point to get the Town Meetin' to rent it as a public beach. Can't nobody use it much now account of gas rationing. Still and all it's right for a town on the water to have its own beach." Hank took two heavy rods of lancewood from the bottom of the boat. The hooks were rigged to a gut leader, which connected to the line by a brass swivel, so that the spoon and hook could turn freely. He pointed out the spot where he had tied a piece of red yarn on each line to mark seventy feet, so he'd know when he had it let out. Rick watched him tie a large kitchen match about a foot above both leaders. This was a new one.

"What's the idea?"

"Ketches the seaweed and keeps it from coverin' the bait." Hank looked pleased with himself and directed Rick to fish on the outside because a hooked bass is apt to rush inshore to break the line over the rocks. Hank put a long sandworm on one hook, so that the whole shank of the hook was covered and the tail left dangling. He reached for the other rod but Rick grabbed it first.

"Hey, I'm not your old woman. I guess I can bait my own line."

"You sure keep your finger right on the trigger, brother. Yes sir, I bet when you was liquored up good you got into plenty o' fights." Hank winked one owl eye amiably. "No need to take offense. There's particular tricks to every kinda fishin'. I was just aimin' to show you some of the way I been pickin' up for the last forty years. Reckon you could show me some yourself. What you ketch down South America?"

"Barracuda and amberjack." Rick could feel the throb of the motor launch, the pull in his arm sockets against the tug of the great fish, the smell of salt spray, see the sudden arc when the barracuda curved across the sky, but before he had a chance to get going on a modest description Hank pointed a nicotine-stained finger toward a couple of boats that were putting out from shore near the Riverside Yacht Club. Rick had noticed a varnished skiff shoving off from the seawall in front of a red brick house and a graceful woman in blue slacks and a yellow and red plaid shirt picking red and yellow zinnias in a garden that sloped to the water's edge. The foremost of the boats Hank indicated was a white, round-bottomed job with lines similar to Hank's craft. Trailing it was a broad red skiff.

"Bert 'pears to figger it's a good day for stripers too."

"What?"

"Bert Sammis. Guy in the white boat. Knows his fish all right. Ain't

exactly Neptune but the fellers in the red boat acts like he is. Always
hangin' 'round to see which way Bert's headin'. I've seen Bert hide hisself
in a crick bed to throw 'em off . . . damn nuisance how they trail ya.
Them guys'd pull into two inches o' slime if Bert did."

Now the varnished skiff was squishing through the water only
twenty feet away. "Hi, Hank," the bow oarsman yelled, a ruddy-faced
fortyish man in a peaked red hunting cap.

"Hi, Jim. Nice day."

"Sure is. You aimin' for stripers?"

"Yep. Ought to be bitin' real good."

"You think Mead's Point worth tryin'?"

"Should be. Tide's right."

"Looks like Bert's headin' for Greenwich Cove."

"Could be. Bert'll git 'em if they's there and they had ought to be
there."

"Thanks, Hank. We'll keep out of your way."

"Hell, it's a free ocean. Riparian rights stops at high water mark,
brother. Luck, Jim."

"Luck, Hank."

The varnished boat pulled ahead and further toward the middle of
the harbor. Hank watched it quizzically. "Guess I got Jim puzzled. He
don't know whether to follow Bert or me. Feller with him's a funny guy.
One of these here commuters, but mostly he commutes from Old Greenwich to Cos Cob. Gets on the train in the mornin' and hops right off
agin at the second station. Keeps his fishin' togs and junk down to Jim's
place. Scared his wife'll ketch on as how he ain't goin' to New York."
Hank chortled. The varnished skiff was taking a wavering course, first
heading toward Goose Island ahead of Hank and Rick, then edging over
toward Bert's boat and its dogged red follower.

"Nice boat he's got though—for a flat bottom. Round one like this
is better for trollin', but that skiff is good for duckin'. I'm buildin' me a
Barnegat sneak box now over to the Yard. When I get me any spare time.
Only good idee ever come outa Jersey."

Three other boats were waiting off Goose Island. One beside the
faithful red followed Bert; Jim and two others swung in behind Hank.

"'Pears to be my day," Hank grinned, obviously pleased.

Rick's shirt was drying in the warm September sun. He could feel the tension going out of his arms and strength seeping in, as he reeled out his line. A small green heron stood aloof on one brown rock, while a flock of neat black and white terns crowded gregariously on another. Suddenly Rick's rod was nearly wrenched from his hands. The reel shrieked like a startled kingfisher.

"It's a big one," yelled Hank. "Play him careful. Don't give him no slack whatever you do. And remember, easy does it."

After stopping the slight headway on the boat with one back push of the oars, Hank dropped them and began reeling in his own line. He kept his rod tip at extreme distance from the boat and at right angles to it, knowing well that bass love to dive into rocks and to snarl one line over another. This was obviously a patriarch of basses—from the way Rick's stout pole was bending—and he seemed to know all the tricks.

Quick as were the two men, and alert, the bass was quicker, more alert. He rushed toward the boat so fast that Rick's fastest reeling could not take up all the sickening slack, then he cut over toward shore, leaped out of water right over Hank's singing line, dove back, and toward the very bottom. The glimpse they had showed him enormous.

"Twenty pounder!" Hank gloated. "Hold him, boy."

But now the big fish was coming at the boat again, on Rick's side. Though there was a slight pressure on that zigging green cord it was not fish, it was the weight of Hank's line and bait and swivel added to the slack in Rick's. A black-streaked silver form shot under the boat, leaped out of water again five feet from a brown boulder awash in a tangle of weed on the inshore side. The fish went down in the weed. Rick reeled on. In came the end of his line, limp and empty. Empty not only of fish but of Hank's line, too, and of its own swivel and leader and spoon. The bass had cleverly yanked it over a sharp edge of rock six feet above the end of the metal leader.

"Sufferin' Portygee!" was all Hank said, then with infinite sadness slowly reeled in his own line.

Rick said nothing. But his eyes were dancing. This was fishing! Fishing worthy of Chinchorro Bank or Ambergris Cay or Key West or

Avalon. And this was the mouth of Cos Cob harbor, where commuters complained they caught only bergalls.

Hank pointed to his tackle box, rusty, salt-caked from the wear of twenty seasons. Rick rigged on a new spoon and swivel and leader, put on a huge sandworm, then added a smaller one—hoping against hope to lure that big fish out again.

Hank grinned. "We'll never see *him* again." He spat a brown stream on his own intact bait, which swirled out astern as he leaned on the oars.

After two more turns around Goose Island Hank headed for the reef making eastward from Murderers' Island, a half mile offshore. "Uster git my best 'uns here," he muttered.

Rick had let his line out ten feet beyond the red thread which once had marked seventy feet, but now marked only perhaps sixty—what with the piece the big bass had taken. He was idly watching the pearl-backed gulls on Diving Rock when his hook caught on something very solid.

"Hold it, Hank, I've caught the bottom." Hank stopped the boat with one quick backward bite of the oars, then gently urged it sternward.

"Reel in slowly, don't put no pressure on it or you may cut the line again on a rock, leastways bend the hook."

Suddenly Rick's reel sang again, thirty feet of line went directly away from him fast.

"Bottom's movin' eh?"

Then the line went slack, and Rick's heart went sick. To lose two big ones in fifteen minutes, that would be too much!

"Reel him, reel him, don't give him no slack to spit out that hook."

Sweat cascaded off Rick, rolled down his wrists, covering his hands. His wet thumb slipped off the reel ratchet—giving the fish more slack. He was cursing himself audibly, furiously. Why must he show himself such a duffer to Hank, he who had fished all the Seven Seas, muffing everything like a dub.

"Slow but sure, haste makes waste, easy does it. You ain't lost him, he's still there. See that!" The line tightened again, went off southward in the general direction of Oyster Bay across the Sound. "If it's bottom it's an earthquake.

"Take it easy, this'll be a long fight, but we'll get this one." Hank was grim, tense, but he had finished reeling in his line and he was reaching for the landing net.

The gesture gave Rick new confidence, he forgot his shakes, forgot the sweat which was blinding him, and bent over the reel. The fish was sulking now, coming in gradually, with only an occasional sideways rush of three or four feet.

Rick had the click off the reel now to save wear. The taut, wet line came in steadily, silently. A dark shape was rising into view, black, heavy-shouldered. Not built like a striper, Rick thought, but he pushed his mind back on his job.

"Don't let him bump the boat now, easy now, don't reel no more, hold him right there, I can get 'im."

Hank's sinewy blue-denimed arm snaked the net at the end of the long handle under the dark fish. He lifted hard, there was a splash, and Rick's heart sank again. But Hank had slid his other hand down the net handle, leaning way over the boat side as he did so. Rick instinctively leaned the other way to prevent a capsize, and in doing so he brought the fish in nearer. The gunwale dipped to within an inch of the water, then held as if it rested on a rock. This boat was truly "built right."

A quick lift by Hank and the fish lay writhing and flapping in the net coils on the bottom of the boat. Hank was on it like a cat on a mouse.

"Great Mother Mackerel," he exclaimed, "it's a blackfish! An' a grandaddy. We won't take no more chances on this 'un." He opened his clasp knife; with a crunching sound the fish's backbone was severed.

Hank opened his tackle box and got out his scales. He put the scale hook under the tough upper lip of the fish. Rick noticed the lower lip was even bigger and tougher, like some enormous hard negroid human lip. Teeth showed, blunt crunching teeth, as big as a man's incisors but blunter—to crush clam shells with.

"Eight pound and a quarter, second biggest I ever see! Boy, you sure seem to 'tract all the big 'uns. An' you break the rules—first time I've heard o' blackfish caught by trollin'."

They paddled idly to a shining strip of sand beach on the north side of Murderers' Island and got out of the boat to stretch their legs and "take the weight off'n our tails," as Hank put it.

A few minutes later Hank became abstracted in watching a swirling patch of water between two small rocks a few yards from the northern end of the beach.

"Don't move, look!" he whispered, "them two rocks where the water's swishin'. Ain't no tide current there, somethin's movin'." Distinctly they saw the head of a large fish poke out of water, rub angrily against the farther rock. It fell back, then lifted and rubbed the rock again. This time they could see most of the back with the long dorsal fin, a silver back, with longitudinal black stripes.

"A striper," whispered Rick, "spawning maybe."

"No Siree, t'ain't spawnin'. That's your bass, Mister, an' it's tryin' ter rub your hook outa its mouth against that rock. In all my fishin' days I never seen the like o' that!"

Again the head rose, rubbed angrily at the rock. Rick was moved with quick compassion, as he'd been when he'd seen a wounded duck try to escape the jaws of a swimming retriever.

"If on'y we had a shotgun now." Very cautiously Hank picked up a large stone, rose to throw it. A silver streak shot for deep water.

They trolled for bass while the sun rose higher and hotter. Rick peeled to his shorts, smeared himself with sunburn lotion he had found in Joe's bathroom despite Hank's contemptuous advice that "too much sun is bad for the human body."

At noon they beached the boat with a sharp *grck grck* on the shelving beach of Sand Island. Hank opened a paper bag of lunch which Emerald had provided; he flourished a thick rye bread and cheese sandwich southwestward toward the narrowing head of the Sound. "If you look sharp down thataway you can spot the Empire State buildin' . . . that is if you care to see it. Most folks seem to think it's somethin' remarkable."

Rick followed Hank's scornful glance and saw faint lavender shadows seeming to rise from the horizon waters like a mirage. "Hell's delight, I'd just as soon forget New York."

Hank grinned approvingly.

Rick unscrewed the top of a thermos jug and poured hot coffee into red plastic cups. "Think of all the dives in the shadow of that building.

Think of all the poor dopes sitting in smoke-filled rooms drinking. Beer leavings in glasses, the sour smell of whiskey spilled on sawdust, and wet chewed cigar butts. And here we've been all morning out in a boat in the clean sun and wind—*not* drinking."

On a near point of land Rick could see an apple tree. How glad apple trees are, he thought, lifting their gnarled limbs like tough old men basking in the soft September sun, still vigorous, still loving life.

Off the eastward marsh grass a great blue heron dropped angrily between two white gulls which had been poaching on his fishing grounds. Easily capable of eluding the heron with their greater speed, the gulls seemed to decide good-naturedly that there was enough fishing for all, for they flew up-harbor a quarter of a mile, chuckling to each other as they went.

A clump of trees on Tod's Point was filled with the elliptical forms of sleeping night herons. A pair of fish crows flew in and out of the branches scolding, but they could not ruffle the solid languor of the great hunched herons.

"You got quite a manner o' speakin', brother," Hank chuckled, "Yes, sir, here we been sittin' in the clean sun and wind—not drinkin'!"

IV

TEN OF DIAMONDS

"Hey, Joe, the ten of diamonds was good in dummy." Kibitzer Crunden pointed the stub of a cigar over Joe's shoulder. He was a large amiable guy, who always managed to grab the seat behind the regular bridge players and followed the game with vociferous attention.

"Sorry, partner." Joe reached in his pocket for change. They had passed the lagoon in Bruce Park, where Hank said you could catch blue crabs, and were nearing the ugly bulk of the Power Plant. No time for another hand.

"Joe's got flounders on the brain. Or is it ducks, Joe?" His partner kidded good-naturedly.

Joe let it ride. He'd had Rick on his mind all day, but he couldn't tell these fellows about Rick—or about himself for that matter. They'd look at him with embarrassed, evasive eyes. Kibitzer Crunden would shake his bald head and puff out his fat cheeks, and go home and pour himself a double shot and say to his wife, "Always thought that Joe Kelly was a queer duck." Damn funny thing how you could play cards with the same bunch of men morning and evening for years and not know what made them tick. He could state their names, occupations and bridge habits. Tom was a corporation lawyer, with grey hair, a distinguished nose, and an aversion to raising an opening bid unless he had at least four trumps, headed by an honor, and a couple of aces on the side. Dick was a smooth young-looking broker with a perpetual tan toning into his light-brown hair and carefully informal tweeds. Dick had a weakness for Blackwood's four no trump even before you settled on a suit. Harry was a mild, middle-aged banker, with a modest, almost apologetic mustache, and a tendency to take unnecessary finesses. It didn't add up to much. Oh, he knew where they all lived, their approximate incomes, their wives' first names, the age and sex of their children. It still didn't add up to enough. Not enough to make you feel you could tell any one of them what was going on inside you. Didn't they care? Didn't they have any curiosity? Or were they afraid? Were they deliberately—perhaps desperately—sticking to the safe surfaces of life because they were afraid? As if trouble were contagious, as if by admitting the existence of insecurity they might jeopardize their own safety. So that when someone they "knew" went off the deep end, got arrested for drunken driving, landed in a divorce court, or jumped out of a window, they averted their eyes and hugged tighter to their little rubber boats.

Joe watched Harry putting the cards neatly into their case, leaving a quarter on the window ledge for the brakeman. Tom was reaching for an important-looking pigskin briefcase on the rack over their heads. Dick was adjusting the brim of his brown felt hat. He looked at Joe's battered green object with a lifted eyebrow. "How about taking up a collection and buying Irish a new fedora?"

"You boys don't understand." Joe studied his hat with seriocomic pride. "This hat is just about perfect. No old newspaper man would be seen dead in a bandbox item like Dick's. There's a regular technique for getting 'em in proper shape like aging Roquefort cheese. If you're in a hurry you can do a pretty fair job by buying a package of dust, covering thoroughly and letting stand one week, then, being careful not to shake off any dust, you put the hat out on the back porch in the rain. If you are unlucky enough to run into a stretch of bright weather I have discovered that by holding the hat under a shower for half an hour you can achieve quite a realistic effect. Of course, a few grease spots help if artistically applied, especially around the band, and it is wise to ravel the ends of the ribbon a bit. Nothing really equals kicking around the bottom of a car, preferably a model T, for three or four months, but, as I say, gentlemen, this hat is practically perfect, considering the fact that I have only worked on it for two years."

"Joe's a sketch, all right," Kibitzer Crunden commented, as if he were forgiving him for the ten of diamonds.

Sunlight still glanced off the pond across from the Riverside station where the kids skated in winter, but the community garden patches that ringed it looked ragged now, with only a few sprawling tomato vines and sturdy green rows of broccoli. Joe climbed the steep wooden steps, crossed the bridge and went down another long flight to get his car. They were nice guys all right, but they didn't seem real. Not the way Hank and Sylvia and Kidd Whistler and all the other A.A.s did, even the ones you only saw once or twice at meetings and never said two words to again. You knew what made them tick. They were the kind of friends you made in college or in the last war, like Rick and Jim Bradway. The kind you never expected to make again. That was it. It was like going through Belleau Wood together. You were fighting the same damn enemy. You had the same hopes and fears, defeats and victories. If Rick could get it—the sense of companionship, of not going it alone. The all-in-the-same-boat feeling. Not each one in a separate rubber boat like the guys on the train. Hiding something. Hiding themselves. The way the A.A.s would get up and talk at meetings, really let their hair down, made other contacts seem thin and superficial. Other people shadowy.

Monica hadn't understood that. Lots of wives didn't seem to understand. Hell, you couldn't blame them for not trusting a man who had sworn off over and over again and then reached for a bottle. Monica had reason enough for not believing in him. He'd heard other men say that their wives resented the time they spent going to meetings and on A.A. calls. Monica had said they were losing all their friends because he was in White Plains or New York every night and he had said, "What friends has a drunk?" But Monica hadn't liked it. She hadn't liked his telephoning at the last minute when they had a dinner date with the Crundens that he had to stay in town to help Sylvia Landon out of a jam. Funny, because it was Monica who had saved the *Saturday Evening Post* article on A.A. and given it to him in the first place. Stop thinking about Monica. Think about Rick and Hank.

Joe turned his car down the steep grade of Buxton Lane. He hoped they had had luck today. Hoped Hank's slow, easy humor had calmed Rick down. Rick had been in an ugly mood. Hell, he had probably hopped a train by now and was raising Cain with Gail.

Rick was on the side porch, his long legs stretched out in a rickety deck chair, as Joe came up the steps. He flourished the latest copy of *Life* angrily. "Of all the God damn stinking sheets," he shouted, "typical of your whole moronic civilization. Here, look at this, Joe. *Life* goes to a party. So what? If they want to run a picture magazine, okay. The dopes who go to the movies every night and think with their eyes can have it. But why the lengthy captions? Why the smart, wise-guy, pretentious, long-winded comments? That's what gripes me." He threw the magazine down in disgust.

Joe laughed, but he was worried. Rick apparently was still in an alcoholic mood. He picked up the derided copy, smoothed out the slick heavy paper and pointed to another spread. "You're prejudiced, Rick. They run some damn good stuff. And they're a swell advertising medium."

"Advertising!" Rick snorted.

"Okay. Okay," Joe grinned, "I'm not going to let you get started on that now." They had sat up all one night with a bottle of rum in a native hut in Santa Cruz de Bravo, arguing about advertising. Rick had stated grandiloquently that advertising was robbing the American people of initiative, was producing canned mentalities and moreover was destroying the souls of a lot of honest ex-newspaper men. "Meaning me?" Joe had asked. "Meaning you, Saint Augustine." Rick had shaken his head mournfully. "You were a good guy at Harvard, a good guy on the old *Sun*, and look at you now. If advertising doesn't finish the job, Paradise Pix will."

"What we need," Joe said now, "is a drink."

Rick looked at him, startled. Probably he meant some damned soft slop. But Joe led the way to the kitchen and started a kettle of water, measuring out coffee and telling Rick where to find the cups.

"Sound idea," Rick approved. "They serve coffee before meals in a lot of places. Silly the way Americans think coffee has to follow a meal."

"You talk like one of the left-bank boys after the last war," Joe said, "but you did a good job cleaning these babies. That's a sizable blackfish, all right."

"Eight and a quarter pounds." Rick's voice boomed with pride. Fishermen, radio commentators, and actors have no false modesty, Joe thought, but a fisherman's boasting always seemed naïve and somehow engaging. "Hank says it's the second biggest he ever saw in these waters," Rick went on. His long face had color on the high cheekbones. It had been yellow as a winter apple yesterday.

Leave two men alone in any kitchen with no female interference and the resultant meal will usually have the taste and tang of food cooked over a camp fire. To add to the illusion Joe suggested that they take their plates and the coffee pot out on the side porch. Crickets filled the early darkness with their autumnal chirping and a light breeze stirred the maple leaves.

"Stick around and we'll take you duck shooting as soon as the season opens," Joe said. "Look, Rick, I've been thinking about you all day. Why don't you move out here with me for a while? I've got plenty of room now to put you up and it's a hell of a lot easier to cut out liquor in the country than it is in New York.

It was decent of Joe. Damned decent. But it wasn't the answer for him. This country seemed tame after the bush. The fishing had surprised him but you couldn't get away from the fact that the place was only an hour from New York. The town of perpetual cocktail parties. The town where people seemed to think that the only possible form of hospitality was to offer you a drink. "How about stopping in for a highball tomorrow?" or "Drop in for a martini before dinner." Every old friend he had run into had wanted to celebrate their reunion with a drink. Every new man he had met in business had immediately suggested hoisting one.

"I can't manage it here, Joe," Rick said. Flee alcohol, that was it. He could go to the mountains of Colombia, where he knew a tribe of Indians who drank only ritualistically, at planting and harvesting. He could catch a boat next week. The fall fiesta would be over by the time he got there and he would see no liquor until spring. That would give him six months start anyhow. "I've got to have a different set-up. Different scenery. Different associates."

"New associates. Right," Joe said, "That's what A.A. does for you. I've got more honest-to-God friends in A.A. than I've had in all the years since college. But why new scenery? It's been tried plenty and it never works out. I heard of one fellow who went to an island in the South Seas and a storm washed a keg of rum ashore. Another guy shoved off to the Arctic to escape booze and a bunch of explorers came along and taught him to eat the alcohol jelly from his stove. He killed himself. Kind of extreme cases, maybe, but they prove my point. You can't run away from liquor—or yourself."

"The hell you can't. I'm going."

"You tried it once, Rick, and look what happened."

"What do you mean?" Rick was angry now. There was a point beyond which even Joe's friendly concern seemed a damned intrusion.

"You know what I mean, Rick." It was a difficult business to say what he had to say, but Joe didn't hesitate. "You ran away after Adelaide died. You left your kid. Shifted your responsibility to your wife's sister. That was adolescent behavior. No matter how you look at it."

"I saw that Gail was comfortably fixed," Rick said defensively. He was holding on to his temper, but he didn't like this. He didn't like it a little bit.

"Comfortably fixed! Hell. Does a child need a parent? Death took her mother. Self-pity got her father. I'm giving it to you straight, Rick, because it's my guess that is why you started drinking. You feel guilty about it, yourself. Only you don't want to face it. You were yellow in nineteen twenty-five. Are you going to be yellow again? Walk out again just when Gail needs you? Just when she has found a father? Can't you think about her for a change? Except to get angry and threaten to bust up her life the way you did this morning."

Rick got up with a jerk that sent his chair clattering. He strode to the far end of the porch and back, pushing chairs and tables aside as if he were hacking his way through the bush with a *machete*.

"God damn it, Joe, you don't know what you're talking about. You don't know what I did to Gail when I was drunk Tuesday."

"Whatever you did," Joe said slowly, "it couldn't equal what I did."

Jim Bradway had gone back to Joe's apartment with him for a nightcap after one of those business sessions with an out-of-town client which involved going the rounds of all the fancier night clubs. It was the fourth straight night Joe had been out "drinking on account," as the agency called it, and the liquor and late hours had piled up on him. They had turned in through the dark garden on East Fifty-third Street and climbed the stairs to Joe's apartment. Joe could see the living room as it had looked when he switched on the lights. He had never wanted to see it again. It was a pleasant room. A man's room with large leather chairs, clipper ship prints and, between the high French windows opening on the small garden, shelves and racks reaching to the ceiling. They were filled with trophies—silver cups Joe had won for public speaking at the Loyola High School and for track at Harvard, a German helmet, and his collection of guns. Jim and he had both been pretty tight when he had started showing them off—a pair of pearl-handled dueling pistols he had picked up in Virginia, an old Tower musket, a Civil War sword, a Spanish fowling piece with a butt inlaid with silver, a German 8 mm. Mauser from the last war, and his first rifle, a twenty-two Stevens single shot, the executioner of many a squirrel.

"You didn't shoot Gail," Joe said now, stretching his right hand out and aiming his forefinger at Rick like a pistol. "You didn't point a Colt .45 at a guy you loved like a brother." Jim had been the kind of a friend Rick was. Not the kind you play bridge with on a train. The kind you'd been through hell with. They had been in the same outfit overseas, but Jim had taken a job in Chicago and hadn't moved to New York till after Rick left, so Rick had never met him. They would have liked each other, Joe thought. They were both big men, uncomfortable in cities. "You didn't think you were back in Belleau Wood. You didn't forget that a gun was loaded. You didn't pull a trigger and see your pal fall . . . look up at you . . . with . . . with a calm surprise in his eyes . . . no . . . ." Joe's voice was almost a whisper now, "no reproach in those eyes . . . just surprise. You didn't yell at him to get up and quit horsing around. You didn't see his eyes go . . . queer. You didn't turn cold sober and take his pulse and find him dead."

Rick took another turn on the porch. Emily had sent him a clipping about the "accidental shooting," as the papers called it. It had happened a year or so after the crazy Hollywood chicle job and by the time the mail caught up with him, Rick had thought it too late to write Joe. Anyhow, what the hell could you say in a letter? What the hell could he say now for that matter? He put his hand awkwardly on Joe's shoulder.

"You make me feel like a heel, Joe. Human reactions are pretty low when you come right down to it. I'm sorry as hell for you but it makes my own troubles seem damn small potatoes—the whole business of Gail pretty easy to cope with after what you've been up against."

Joe shook himself like a dog coming out of deep water. "That was more or less the idea," he grinned. "I figured it might make you feel better, so I took the plunge. And believe me it was a plunge. I've never been able to talk about it to anyone till this minute—except Monica. And that was different. That was plain, continuous hell for both of us."

"Where's Monica now?" Rick asked. He had heard that Joe had married Jim Bradway's widow. It had sounded like a screwy idea but natural, in a way, he supposed. Tragedy could bring two people together as well as propinquity. The nearness of sorrow was a closer thing than any geographical accident. It had been that way with him and the Winged Victory. They were both unhappy people. The sadness behind her triumphant beauty was what had first attracted and then annoyed him. Joe didn't answer for a long minute. Come to think of it he hadn't mentioned Monica the other day at lunch and she obviously wasn't around now. Rick kicked himself for asking.

"She took Jimmy out to California. He'd had pneumonia and the doctor thought the change would do him good." Joe paused. "That's the story for publication. She went before Christmas last year and God knows whether she's ever coming back. Hell, I'm not blaming Monica for getting out after two years of my coming home drunk night after night till she was scared I'd kill her son in one of my crazy fits of remorse. He's a good kid—only he looks exactly like his father—the same trick of pulling his mouth down at the left corner, the same quick way of using his hands. It used to drive me bats."

Like Gail and Adelaide, Rick thought. You couldn't stand seeing likenesses and special gestures repeated. If Joe had a son would he pull at his cowlick the way Joe was doing now?

Joe took a snap-shot out of his wallet and tossed it over to Rick. By the brief light of a match Rick peered at the group—a slim dark-haired woman with an alert narrow face, a sturdy small boy intent on holding the head of an Irish setter toward the camera. Behind them were tall fluted columns and a large brick house.

"Where was it taken?" Rick asked inadequately, not knowing how you could comment on a wife and stepson who had walked out on a guy.

"Jim Bradway's house back of Greenwich. That's where we lived, God bless us. It was about the size of the Country Club and about the only thing Jim left. He'd been getting a big salary, but they hadn't saved a nickel. You know how it goes. I thought the least I could do was to help Monica stay in the place if she wanted to. And she did. So I paid the taxes and the upkeep for a couple of years. Then after we got married I tried to persuade her to sell the house but she was crazy about it and Jimmy had grown up there. She thought he'd miss it. I don't know. He seemed to like me a lot. Hung around me all the time. I could have taken him fishing here. He could have had a dinghy at the Yacht Club."

Falmouth and the husky little catboat Rick's father had taught him to sail. Long sun-splashed days squinting at the peak of a sail on an old gaff rig, nosing her closer to the wind, or spilling the wind in a puff, then letting her out on a reach. Long hours sitting on the rickety dock at low tide, his short legs dangling, his stubby fingers struggling with knots, achieving neat half-hitches, bowlines and squares, being properly scornful of grannies, splicing with awkward determination, and his father a patient oracle with a pipe and an occasional coveted nod of approval. Grandfather Avery had been a romantic, adventurous figure but Rick thought now of his taciturn, circumspect father with sudden understand-ing—and envy. He and Joe were missing something all right. Most likely you could never have that special companionship with a girl, but Joe might have done things with that sturdy kid of Monica's. No wonder young Jimmy had followed Joe around. Monica must be a fool. It was a damn shame. Joe the gregarious, Joe the life of the party, Joe the joker with the quick insight and sympathy was a lonely guy. Lonely as Rick, the angry tilter at windmills.

"Look, Joe, if that invitation still holds I'd like to park out here with you for a while."

Joe's face lit up. Even in the dimness Rick could feel rather than see the change in his expression, could hear the warmth come back into his voice. "Well, now I've an even better idea. . . ." Joe developed his plan with growing enthusiasm. There was an apartment over the boathouse-garage some former owner must have put in for a chauffeur; he could fix it up and camp out there weekends. He'd like to spend a couple of nights in town anyhow. Then Rick and Emily and Gail could take over the house for a few months. That is, if Rick thought it would work out. If he could persuade Emily and Gail to try it. They could pay Emerald's wages and let him eat with them when he came out.

"Hell, we'll rent it." Rick seized on the idea with eagerness, seeing a boyish Gail in faded dungarees sitting on the rickety dock splicing rope with slim red-tipped fingers.

V

THE SPIRAL GALAXY IN ANDROMEDA

Fog was a damp grey screen at the west window where Rick stood listening to the muffled sound of Joe's car going up the hill in a cautious second gear. Across the dull pewter-colored harbor the Power Plant huddled like a dim frightened monster. Fog had been soft and white on the high hills of Santa Marta. Softer, whiter than rabbit's fur thrown off twigs into Rick's face. Mules and men had panted through the still softness along an invisible trail carved in the rock with nothing under it but space and fog. He had been terrified and happy with the exhilaration that comes from danger and the snow-like enchantment of the fog. But this greyness was like trying to breathe with your head in a pillow of dirty goosefeathers. A smothering melancholy. This was a day to crawl into a hole and pull the hole after you. To shut yourself in a small closed room . . . with a bottle.

Wednesday without a drink. Thursday without a drink. All the Wednesdays, Thursdays, Mondays, Tuesdays, Saturdays, Sundays for the rest of his life without a drink if he followed the A.A. program. If he *could* follow it. It was harder than the wagon had ever been. At least on the wagon you could look forward to the bender you could go on when you had finished your stretch. Joe had had exactly the opposite idea. Joe's voice came back to him from the foxhole darkness of the small car. "We're only dry for twenty-four hours. That's all. Any dope can lay off liquor for one day." Think about today. That was it. Okay, Friday without a drink, he added to himself, pacing Joe's narrow living room with clenched fists.

The red and yellow jacket of *Alcoholics Anonymous* caught his eye. Joe had left the book conspicuously on the maple desk. Rick reached for it now as he had grabbed at tufts of grass on that trail above Santa Marta.

He had been amused and annoyed at the way the A.A.s had talked about THE BOOK at the meeting the other night—as if it were the Bible—as if it had all the answers. The cover was torn, the margins showed emphatic pencil marks, and whole paragraphs were heavily underlined. He whiffled the pages rapidly. He had the impatient, curious type of mind which can never start a book methodically at the beginning. Isolated sentences leapt at him—"If we were to live, we had to be free of anger"—"Resentment is the number one offender."

He had been proud of his own rages. Cultivated them. Like a crazy gardener pulling up tulips and fertilizing dandelions. How often he had shouted, "Righteous indignation is dead. What America needs is more righteous indignation. Our ancestors had the guts to denounce evil in anger. Where are our Cotton Mathers? Our Patrick Henrys? Our Jonathan Edwardses?" He would look furiously around the bars from Guatemala to Rio and people would laugh with the ready indulgence men have for a drunk and say, "Hear! Hear! Right you are, big boy!" A sick feeling of shame came over him now. Had his ravings ever made any real sense? Had he ever followed his loud alcoholic words with sober action? Wasn't most of his invective motivated by a personal grouch? A bitter frustration because he, Avery Rickham, had been cheated by life. Didn't it all go back to Adelaide's death, the idea that Fate was against him? He had been honest the other night when he answered Joe's question, "Do you control liquor? Or does liquor control you?"

He leafed back to a spot where Joe had turned down the corner of a page. Unconsciously, he smoothed it out and was struck by the incongruity of his gesture. For a man who began reading a book in the middle, blatantly disregarding the author's considered arrangement of ideas, to be careful of the physical condition of a volume seemed pretty ridiculous. He would start on the first page and read every damn word. But this was the gist of it, evidently. Here were the Twelve Steps the big Italian had acted out. He noticed that Joe had bracketed several points with a marginal note that the Twelve Steps could be reduced to five. Rick grinned. There was an advertising man for you—valuing brevity at so many dollars per half inch of space. Punch home your selling points in easy-to-remember slogans. Like fixing up the Ten Commandments.

Probably some smart guy had gone after Moses. Here he was feeling like Hank that THE BOOK was a veritable Bible. So damn good that you shouldn't monkey with it.

He got up and rummaged around Joe's desk for a pencil. Advertising men could be counted on to have soft pencils and big yellow pads anyhow. Step number eight said to make a list of the persons you had injured. Okay, he'd try it. And he'd shoot the works and make amends as number nine directed—where and when he could.

His list had to start with Gail. There was no getting away from that. He supposed most men put their wives' names first. That was one thing he would never have done. If Adelaide had lived he would never have turned into an alcoholic. There he went again. Excuses. Self-pity. Last night Joe had accused him of running away—of being yellow. He had been pretty sore at Joe. But it was true. And Joe still didn't know what had happened at the Manton party. It wouldn't be easy to win Gail back. A wife would have more tolerance than a daughter. Emily had said that Gail idolized him. That would only make it tougher. It was always easier to forgive the people about whom you felt indifferent. Thank God, Joe and Hank had saved him from rushing after Gail in anger yesterday and making a bad matter worse. He had never been a patient person. He'd damn well have to learn patience now—the patience of a man sitting on a rickety dock watching a small boy practicing bowlines, figure eights, and sheepshanks, the patience of the boy himself. There had been a time when he had not been beset by vehemence.

Rick stared at the yellow pad and wrote W.V.—Winifred Vickers, his Winged Victory. Was there anything he could do about her now? Had he ever been sober when he saw her? Had he ever really given a damn what she felt or thought? That day at the races . . . she had worn a white silk dress and a hat with white feathers like a gull in flight. The tropic wind had blown the pleats of her skirt close to her long rounded legs, had fluttered the wide sleeves like wings, giving her the quality of sculpture—of arrested motion. She had been gay and beautiful, sitting in the box under the flapping awning, greeting friends, sipping a long pale green drink of lime and rum—but they had gone back to her house quarreling. Why? He couldn't remember. There had always been an inhuman quality in their relationship. Passion without affection. Hell on wheels. And he had blamed her and her neurotic headaches, which he had told her with repeated cruel directness were nothing but nerves. He had walked out of her life without a word. Would it do any good to write her now? Any good to her? That was the point.

Bill Driscomb—names came at him without his own volition. To hell with Driscomb. He was the head of the New York sales department. What did he know about the guys who did the real work in the bush? What did he care? He sat on his fat ass and drew a fat salary—bigger than Rick's—more in one day than the natives who climbed the *sapota* trees made in a year. Sure, he had a resentment against Driscomb. What right guy wouldn't? Sure, he'd told Wharton when they had a couple of drinks together one night at Wharton's club, that Driscomb was an incompetent fool. Did the drinks have anything to do with it? Wouldn't he say the same thing again sober? He scrawled a large irritated question mark after the name.

All morning the steady hum of the vacuum cleaner had been in his ears. Now it had stopped with an expiring whine and the stillness reminded Rick of the ominous silence when the engines of a great ship suddenly cease in a fog. He almost expected to hear the strident wail of a fog horn, see the grey hulk of another liner looming perilously near. Instead, there was a sound like a shutter banging in the wind. Only there was no wind. He threw the front door open and dampness slid past him into the hall "on little cat feet." The thumping was more distinct, repeated with the intermittence of thunder. The regularity of machine-gun fire. That was it. Some Coast Guard outfit—or harbor patrol—must be practicing. If only he could get into the Navy. Go steaming into those little islands in the Pacific with a bunch of sailors like Pete. Fight the damn Japs. Instead of fighting himself.

He slammed the door and turned back to Joe's living room. Under the old brass student's lamp with its green glass shade was the book with a torn red and yellow cover. That was his fight. He knew damn well the Navy wouldn't take him at his age, with a piece of shrapnel in his leg and alcohol in his blood. It was escape that was getting him again. The romantic appeal of Guadalcanal and Attu, like the magic of the *Sierra*

Nevada de Santa Marta, and all the inconceivably green fields of adventure. His enemy was liquor. His enemy was himself. His war was not on some far-flung battle line, but here. But now. In this small pleasant room in Riverside, Connecticut, shut in by fog. An island in time and space.

From the kitchen came the low, rich sound of Emerald's singing:

"Got to go down in that Valley,
Got to go there by myself,
Ain't nobody here can go with me,
Got to go there all alone."

Mournful words. Mournful tune. But Emerald's voice had an oddly comforting quality.

There was no sunset. The greyness deepened, blue washed in. Water and sky matched with a darker line of shore between. Lights went on in the Power Plant, turned it from a huddled monster to a protective fortress. The cat's eyes of Joe's car gleamed in the blue darkness. Rick had things to talk to Joe about—questions that had been shouting for utterance all day, filling the silent house with a Socratic argument between THE BOOK and himself. The basis of A.A. was religious. That was okay. Rick wasn't irreligious—exactly. He believed there was some Order in the Universe, some Supreme Spirit. He was willing enough to accept the A.A. phrase, "A Power greater than ourselves." A lot of people must have trouble with the word "God," or they wouldn't need this circumlocution. Funny how ruthless was the "tyranny of words," as Stuart Chase called it. But that wasn't what bothered him. It was the idea of prayer. The gist of THE BOOK was that you couldn't stay "dry" by yourself. You had to ask help from God, "as we understand Him," but how could he, Avery Rickham, expect this great remote Spirit of the Universe to pay any attention to him?

He put the question to Joe when they sat for dinner before a driftwood fire. Will Beebe had sent him a New Year's card showing a picture of the constellation of Andromeda with the lines, "The Spiral Galaxy in Andromeda is as large as Our Own Milky Way. It is one of 100 Million Galaxies. It is 680,000 Light Years Away. It has 100 Billion Suns. WHO

ARE WE TO WORRY?" He quoted it to Joe now. "That's the way I feel. Who am I to worry? And by the same token who is God to worry? He's got bigger plans on a vaster scale. He must be too damn busy to bother His head about a bunch of drunks. Do you guys actually imagine He'd snatch a bottle out of my hand?"

"The good old *reductio ad absurdum*," Joe laughed, "It used to be your favorite method of argument at college, didn't it? Of course, this business isn't as simple as that. But honestly, Rick, if you pray to God to help you, you won't reach out your hand for that bottle."

Rick watched Joe cut the end of one of his thick Tampa cigars. "It's easier for you, Joe. You're a Catholic. You're got the habit of prayer. I haven't prayed since I was a kid. Not since I lost the idea of a benevolent bearded Gentleman, sitting up in the clouds and looking remarkably like my Grandfather Avery—even to the riding boots. Think of the Galaxy in Andromeda. Think how infinitesimal this earth is and then think of . . ."

"The fallen sparrow?" Joe grinned.

"Damn it, you Jesuits always have some glib answer. Do you seriously think God gives a hoot more than you or I do for a dead sparrow in the dust of the road? With a war going on? With men dying every day?"

"Didn't *you* care as a kid? Didn't you ever wrap a bird carefully up in a shoe box and dig a hole in the back yard and put some blackeyed susans on it and feel kind of sad inside? Maybe we were closer to the spirit of God as kids."

"You sound like Wordsworth, 'Heaven lies about us in our infancy, trailing clouds of glory,' or something. Isn't Wordsworth sort of old hat to be falling back on now?" There was a familiar ring to their dialogue. Their positions hadn't changed much since college except that Rick's attitude was different. Then he had debated with Joe for the hell of it, now he desperately wanted to be convinced against his reason. He found himself envying Joe the faith he had once ridiculed.

Joe went over to the book shelves which ran across the whole north side of the room from floor to ceiling. He switched on a standing lamp, looked along an upper shelf and reached for a small volume. "Is this any better than Wordsworth?" he asked, tossing the book at Rick.

"M . . . yes." Rick flicked the pages rapidly. "I'd forgotten about James. Damn unlucky that we got to Harvard too late to have him."

"I've heard that one before," Joe laughed. "You were always grousing about the great good days being gone, my lad. Bill Griffith never mooned around Cambridge talking with guys who knew James, but he based the A.A. philosophy on the *Varieties*—or didn't you notice?"

"M . . . yes," Rick nodded absently.

"Remember the line about religion being a 'plurality of saving powers, a more of the same quality as oneself, that one can in a crisis make contact with and be saved'? I'm not sure whether it's here or in something I read about James, anyhow it's the answer to your problem of God reaching out and snatching a bottle from your hand, isn't it?"

"Good point, Saint Augustine. But you and William James together could never make me believe in miracles."

"The A.A.s will." Joe spoke with assurance. "You'll see miracles to equal the loaves and the fishes at every meeting you go to—if you've eyes to see. Isn't it a miracle when a man who's been a down-and-outer, a drunken good-for-nothing bum sleeping in flop houses and drinking 'smoke' on 'the beach', can stand up like a man? Isn't it a miracle when a weak frightened guy who's spent years going from one institution to another trying to get cured of alcoholic addiction can hold up his head and look the world in the face?"

"Okay," Rick said, "I'll keep my eyes open for your miracles, Saint Augustine."

VI

BROWNSTONE STOOP

Walking east on the block between Fifth and Madison, Rick was struck for the first time by the incongruously ugly brownstone stoop of his own house. It stood out suddenly like a Victorian whatnot in a display of modern furniture. All the other houses had abandoned the high awkward steps for basement entrances with curved iron railings. Number eight had been plastered and tinted a faded pink. The arch of the recessed doorway was a deep Della Robbia blue and the balcony might have overhung the Grand Canal. Across the street two houses had been transformed by a veneer of red brick and white colonial doorways. Odd that Emily had cared so little about appearances. Odd and perhaps typical. Did her scorn of the Mantons and the cheaply smart make her cling even to the mistaken taste of an older generation? Or had she simply hesitated to spend Gail's money on externals of considerable cost?

It was puzzling. For the moment it made him forget Gail and the problem he and Emily must settle somehow. He stood in the doorway of the long drawing room noting how the pale grey walls and chartreuse curtains, looped over silver arrows at the high windows, gave it an air of serenity and spaciousness. Adelaide had considered the room "difficult." She had run around with little samples of brocade and chintz, her head tilted like an uncertain canary, sighing that the room needed warmth and color and did he think that rose damask would help? Now he recognized how right Emily had been, from the grey-green rug to the yellow roses in a turquoise blue bowl, and he found himself asking her how she could have put up with that damned brownstone stoop all these years. She smiled as if she had followed his thoughts and his question lost its effect of abruptness. Then she gave him the one answer he had not expected.

"I suppose, Avery," she spoke thoughtfully, "that I never really considered this house as my permanent home."

There was no reproach in her tone. It was simply a quiet statement of a fact she had quietly accepted, but it started Rick on his impatient prowling. He had not even put Emily's name on the list of people he had injured. In spite of Joe's accusation that he had shifted his responsibility for Gail, it had not really occurred to him that he had cheated Emily. He jerked the chartreuse curtains back from the long windows and looked out on the narrow, respectable street. What had Emily wanted to see from the windows of her own house? What steps had she dreamed of climbing other than the brownstone flight to a life that was not her own? He could see her slim right hand with the old-fashioned yellow diamond touching the bell-pull of a small, turreted chateau, or lifting the brass knocker of an eighteenth century house in Portsmouth with the smell of the sea in those finely cut nostrils. What the devil had gotten into him today? He seemed to be aware of things, and the significance of things, that he ordinarily missed.

He turned to look at Emily, realizing that he had never seen her before, any more than he had seen the brownstone steps or the chartreuse curtains. She had been Adelaide's older sister, without Adelaide's startling beauty and gaiety. And he had thought only of Adelaide. She had been Gail's aunt, a quiet, dependable, background sort of person. And he had thought only of Gail. Now he *saw* Emily framed in a wide fan-back chair, saw the small proud head with its cloudy brown hair touched into amber lights by the fire, lights that matched the heavy amber beads around her neck and the bracelet on her slim wrist. It was like looking at a grey March landscape and suddenly perceiving a row of willows along a brook turned to a golden dazzle by the sun. Some unguarded relaxation of posture made Emily's slender figure in its grey wool dress seem momentarily expectant and youthful.

Rick was across the room, standing over her, demanding, "How old were you, Emily, when I walked out and left you to look after Gail?"

"Twenty-five. Are you trying to figure out my age, Avery?" Emily laughed and there was a comforting quality to the sound as if she were saying, "Never mind about me. It's Gail we're both worried about. I'm all right. Really I am."

"But I do mind about you," Rick answered her laugh. And again he had the sensation that they could follow each other's thoughts without the need for explanatory words. He strode back to the window, cursing himself for a selfish bastard. It was too late to "mind" about Emily. Nearly eighteen years too late. How could you "make amends," as the A.A. book called it, right something that had been wrong for eighteen years? "I never thought about what I was doing to your life, Emily. I never thought of you at all," he shouted across the long quiet room. "No. All I ever thought about was this fine fellow, Avery Rickham. I was sorry for him. God, how sorry I was for him."

Emily crossed the room and put a friendly hand on his arm. "Don't, Avery. You're just making yourself miserable." She had a curious way of eliding the word, slurring the "er" which made it sound both pathetic and humorous. "Look at me," she insisted. He turned to face clear hazel-grey eyes, firmly lifted chin. "Do I look sorry for myself?"

"No," he admitted, but he noted that the smiling curve of her mouth was too resolute. "But you look as if you deserved something more from life than your sister's child and your sister's house. You should have married, Emily."

"I nearly did ten years ago." Emily's eyes were fixed on the brownstone steps as if she saw a man hurrying up them. Rick could almost see him too—a man in evening clothes and opera hat. A distinguished, prosperous man with a touch of grey at the temples.

"Why didn't you write me?" Rick's voice was loud and accusing. It was her own fault because she had never let him know. "I'd have taken care of Gail somehow. Christ, did you think I was such a damned heel? There's no point in apologizing for swearing when I've so much else to apologize for," he added.

Emily laughed. "It sounds natural to me. Nicky used to talk like that. He was always saying Gail was a hell of a cute kid and you must be a complete bastard." The dignified gentleman with the opera hat and the touch of grey at the temples retreated hurriedly down the brownstone steps.

"Who the hell . . ?" Rick asked and Emily laughed again.

"Nicholas Ellwood. I don't suppose you read his *Devil's Advocate*?"

Rick stared at the straight quiet figure beside him. Nicholas Ellwood had written one of the most sensational of the best-selling "personal histories," featuring his adventures both archaeological and amatory in the four corners of the world. It seemed incredible that he had been attracted to a woman like Emily—and still more amazing that she had refused him. "And you gave him up because of Gail?"

"Not entirely," Emily admitted. "I did hesitate at first on her account. It would have been a precarious and unsettled life for a child. But don't worry, Avery, in the end it was my own choice."

Rick felt a quick sense of relief. Emily had had her chance at romantic adventure—and funked it. Had chosen the dull security of the brownstone house. He had not cheated her after all. "I suppose it would have been a precarious life for a woman too," he agreed. "Adventure reads better than it lives pretty often. I've seen American women go to pieces in the tropics. Fast." The Winged Victory had always complained about the dreadful climate, covering her face with creams and lotions, wearing heavy veils and dark glasses. "They can't stand the heat and the ticks."

"Oh no," Emily protested, color coming quickly to her high cheekbones. "It wasn't that, Avery. Nicky's way of living fascinated me. I always wanted to see . . . ."

"'Strange lands from under the arched white sails of ships,'" Rick quoted softly, almost to himself.

Emily nodded, her face alight with the magic of Masefield's words and her own memories. "Nicky would sit on that couch by the fire and talk about the hot fragrant winds of India, and snow on the domes of Moscow. There was a poem I cut out of a magazine—'But I would go to Timbuctoo if anybody asked me to'. I kept saying it to myself and thinking of Nicky. I was sure I felt that way. But I didn't. 'Anybody' wasn't good enough. I was pretty miserable," she slurred the word again and Rick smiled, finding the effect infinitely touching, "trying to figure it out. Finally, I *knew* that I wanted to see snow on the domes of Moscow—but not with Nicky. I suppose I just wasn't in love with him after all." She pulled the cord of the chartreuse curtains, closing out the darkening, commonplace street and Rick, in spite of his curiosity, accepted her gesture as symbolic.

He followed her back to the fire and when she rang for tea found himself exclaiming, "Thank God there's still one house left in New York where you aren't automatically offered a cocktail at five o'clock."

Emily lighted the flame under the heavy Georgian silver urn. "Didn't you say you were on the wagon?" she asked.

Rick knew she was remembering the night he came back from Central America, when she had brought out a bottle of 1918 champagne to celebrate and he had turned down his glass, explaining that the company doctor had advised him not to mix liquor and malaria.

"I was." He had laughed at Joe for making such a point of *not* being on the wagon, but the book had given the idea validity.

Evidently Emily took the past tense of his statement at face value for she said, handing him a Spode cup and offering him English muffins and jam, "When you want anything stronger than tea, Avery, you'll find Scotch and Rye in the decanters on the sideboard."

The tall crystal bottles had belonged to Adelaide's grandfather. Rick thought of them now as the relics of another age, another way of drinking. It was hard to imagine a man getting "stinko" with one of those fine old decanters in his hand.

"I suppose your father drank like a gentleman," he observed bitterly.

Emily gave him a quick look but her tone was light as she said, "We always had wine with dinner when we were children. I remember the first time Adelaide was allowed a sip of sparkling Burgundy she said it made her knees feel like a pin cushion. Father thought it a great joke—you know the way families treasure silly things that don't seem funny to anyone else." Rick could see the two little girls in their smocked Liberty silk dresses and the long candlelit table with pink roses in a silver vase. It was a portrait by Sargent, a novel by Henry James. It was port and gout and a frock coat and a lost security. It had nothing to do with him. It was more remote than the Odyssey, more alien than Dostoievsky.

"I suppose you could say that father drank like a gentleman," Emily smiled, "but Nicky didn't."

Thank God for Nicky. It should be easier to make Emily understand his own alcoholic problem because of the unknown Nicky. And he had to make her understand because of Gail, because this quiet, surprising woman knew more about his own daughter than he did. He watched the circles of light thrown by the lamps on the high ceiling, not knowing where to begin.

"Gail should be home any minute now," Emily looked at her wrist watch and then at Rick. "Perhaps you'd rather talk to her alone."

"No," Rick shouted in near panic. He wasn't ready to face Gail— yet. He needed Emily's approval first. "We've got to get her away from that fool Manton boy and his ridiculous mother." He plunged into an account of his first impulsive plan to take Gail with him to South America, watching Emily's sensitive face, alert to her quick frown of disapproval, and then went on to Joe's suggestion that they take his house in Riverside for a couple of months. "If we could get Gail to promise not to see Paul. . . ."

"What would you say if anyone asked you to make such a promise?" Emily interrupted.

"To hell with it, probably," Rick admitted.

Emily laughed. "That's what I thought. And that's exactly the way Gail would feel. She's very like you, Avery. Temperamentally, I mean. Even though she looks so much like Adelaide—all gaiety and uncomplicated gentleness."

Emily picked up a khaki helmet and Rick watched the quick, steady, flick of her steel needles. The Winged Victory had started a muffler just before he left Belize and he remembered now how the impatient and somehow disorganized motion of her hands had infuriated him. There was a reassuring certainty of accomplishment about Emily's knitting. Rick could visualize the helmet smoothly finished and folded. He could see it fitted snugly over the forehead of some young aviator. Not a particularly happy prospect but at least the guy would be warm. It gave Rick a feeling of confidence.

"I've been stupid about the whole business," Emily said. "I've made my dislike of Paul and his family too apparent. It has turned Gail into their champion. But when you came home, Avery, I hoped that Gail would see the difference between Paul and a man like her father."

Rick put his hand over his eyes, shutting out the circles of light on the high ceiling. Shutting out the Mantons' crowded, over-decorated room, the phony notables, The Russian Princesses, the high martini-chatter, and Gail's shrill, excited laughter. He had had his chance—and muffed it like a fool. "Not as stupid as I was," he groaned.

Emily gave Rick's averted face a quick, compassionate glance. "We must give Gail time," she said gently. But it was to Rick that she seemed to be granting an extension. A chance to undo the thing Emily did not know he had done. In our despair the old phrases of remorse return to us. 'We have left undone those things which we ought to have done; and we have done those things which we ought not to have done; and there is no health is us' . . . words worn smooth by generations of repetition. Regret need not be a lonely business—nor a hopeless one, Rick thought. That was the secret of A.A. . . . sorrow shared is sorrow miraculously light-ened. Time and Time and Time and Time . . . but there was no time in New York. Only clocks and mirrors. Time had been a tangible thing out fishing with Hank Frost on Long Island Sound. The same wide, unending dimension Rick had known in the bush. If Emily were right, if Gail were really like him, she would feel it in her bones too—the need as strong as the body's need for calcium or iron. Chemical as well as mental.

"Cos Cob harbor isn't exactly Timbuctoo," he lifted his head and grinned suddenly at Emily.

"But better for Gail," Emily agreed with a smile.

VII

A ROUND PEG IN A SQUARE HOLE

The offices of Manton, Manton and Manton surprised Rick. He had expected something out of Hollywood—yards of blonde broadloom, chromium and pale wood furniture complete with supercilious blonde secretaries, ready at any moment to leap into a dance routine with Fred Astaire. He looked around the dark, narrow reception room, noting the worn but valuable Persian rug, the shabby leather-covered chairs, the heavy mahogany tables, the old-fashioned paintings in carved gold frames. It had the dignified, reputable air of a well established lawyer's office. Funny setting for a smart promoter, Rick thought. He located a small grilled window bearing the sign INFORMATION and handed his card to the woman behind the desk. She was neither blonde nor beautiful. A neat, middle-aged female with the manner of a family retainer, Rick half expected her to refer to Manton as "Mr. Paul." As if the three brothers had been dear little fellows in Peter Thompson suits when she first came to work for their father. Only, of course, that wasn't the right picture. According to Joe, Manton senior had been in the paving business in Jersey City. It was the three sons who had embarked on this ambitious and ambiguous business.

"Just a moment, Mr. Rickham," the secretary had not even given a second look at his card, "Mr. Manton is expecting you."

Rick had come prepared to hear that Manton had been held up by an important conference. He was all set for an argument. Ready to insist that he had an appointment at four and he wasn't going to be brushed off. What he had to say to Manton was important. Damned important. Now he felt the angry bluster running out of him like sap out of a chicle tree.

He had waited less than five minutes in one of the man-sized chairs when a page said, "This way, Mr. Rickham." Someone in Manton, Manton and Manton certainly appreciated the psychological value of using a visitor's name. He followed the boy down a long corridor past small partitioned offices with glass tops, through which Rick could see a great many filing clerks busy at deep steel cabinets; dozens of typewriters clicking "noiselessly"; men and women feeding columns of figures into adding machines and comptometers, or holding telephones to their ears and doodling nervously on scratch pads.

At the end of the corridor, three closed mahogany doors made Rick feel like Goldilocks in the house of the three bears. The center one should by fairy-tale logic belong to the middle brother. It was the only one with a brass knocker. Odd place for a knocker—and a fine antique eagle at that. Rick was right. The boy lifted the handle reverently and let it fall. A voice called, "Come in."

The man at the desk looked up as Rick entered. "With you in half a second," he mumbled. "Sit down. Have a cigar. Over there in that knife box on the Sheraton table. Had it fixed up as a humidor." His voice trailed off and he continued to peer intently through a magnifying glass at two letters on his desk, holding the glass first over one, then over the other. Rick watched him curiously. He was a thick-shouldered man with a broad, good-natured face. Thinning brown hair, brushed straight back. Brown eyes. Brown suit. Brown shoes. A well-kept soft brown look, but his stubby hands seemed dexterous. The kind of hands that would be quick and strong, reeling in a trout.

"Got it," Manton exclaimed triumphantly. "Damn forgery. Here, take a look at those Ss." He thrust the magnifying glass into Rick's hand and pointed excitedly. "This is a letter from Alexander Hamilton to his wig-maker. Bought it several years ago from a reliable dealer in Philadelphia. This," he picked up the other letter scornfully, "is supposed to be a note Hamilton wrote Burr just before the duel. Valuable as all get out, of course—if authentic. Ss wrong. Watermarks wrong. Rubbish. Fellow playing me for a sucker. Claimed it had just turned up in a family attic. Oldest dodge in the world." He blinked suddenly and held out his hand. Typical that he gripped hard with his stubby well-manicured fingers. He does hard things the easy way, Rick reflected, remembering that the man-who-knew-the-inside-of-Washington had told about Manton's fancy sportsman's life—hunting grouse with beaters, catching tarpon from the dais of a fifty-thousand-dollar yacht.

"Sorry, Mr. Rickham," Manton apologized, "I must have seemed damned rude. This Hamilton stuff has got me. Started it as a hobby. A man has to have hobbies when . . ." He hesitated and Rick noticed that the round eyes in the square good-natured face were baffled. Odd. Square pegs in round holes were the familiar tragedy, but this variation seemed somehow infinitely more pitiful.

"Business, you know. Nervous wear and tear," Manton went on, but Rick could have sworn that Manton was actually thinking of his wife and son. "I've tried fishing. Tried hunting. Collecting is the best bet. Started with the inkwell from Hamilton's desk set, then decided to furnish this office with original contemporary stuff." He gestured toward the Duncan Phyfe lyre-back couch, the Adams mantel, Chippendale chairs and Savery desk. "You ought to see my brothers' rooms—full of chromium pipes and plate glass. They got their decorator over to fix up the reception room in the same style, but I threw the fellow out on his ear. Picked up things in junk shops along Fourth Avenue. What d'you think of it?"

"It looked like a lawyer's office to me."

"Right," Manton chuckled triumphantly. "Exactly what I was aiming at. You hit it on the nose, sir. Gave you a feeling of confidence, eh? Worth a million dollars in our business. Brothers are all for it now. Funny thing, I got the idea from a lawyer's office in Jersey City. Went there with my dad when I was a high school kid. Some damn citizen's committee or other thought they had something on the old man, paving scandal probably. He took me along to show me the ropes—maybe he wanted to show them that he was a family man, I don't know, but you should have heard him, Mr. Rickham. Talked circles around those lawyers. Shot 'em full of facts and figures. Can't argue with facts and figures—but you can fix 'em." Manton chuckled again. "Office impressed me though . . . solid . . . incorruptible."

Rick studied Manton as he had seen ethnologists examine a poisoned Goajiro arrowhead. The man was shrewd all right. He had probably chosen his broad good-natured face for its disarming aspect. He had a sudden absurd vision of Manton turning down all the slick, clever, suitable faces in some fantastic warehouse and selecting this candid mask.

But this was not getting him anywhere. Yesterday he had gone home early from his office to talk to Emily about Gail—and had been sidetracked by brownstone steps. He seemed fated to run into digressions—to waste time puzzling over the deceptiveness of appearances. What was the point of sitting in one of Manton's museum chairs, smoking one of Manton's imported cigars and listening to the guy sound off on his hobbies? He had come with a purpose but the purpose was not clear in his own mind now. It had been an impulse rather than a reasoned project actually—a feeling that if he could see for himself what manner of man Paul's father was he might be better able to cope with the problem of Gail and Paul. A vague sense that in some masculine way they might reach an agreement. But had he really imagined that he could approach the subject directly? It was becoming increasingly difficult and yet he was determined not to leave without at least giving Manton an idea how he felt about things.

He leaned forward and tried to catch Manton's eye, but the man darted across the room and whirled a drum table around, opening one of the small drawers. He must suspect why I came, Rick decided with growing irritation, he must be stalling. If he pulls out another collector's item I'll ram the damn paper down his throat. When he turns around I'll say something.

But it was Manton who, pushing the drawer back, said abruptly. "You have a lovely daughter, Mr. Rickham. I only saw her once when Paul brought her to lunch with me at my club. Keep away from the shindigs my wife gives as much as possible. Hear you tore into things a bit the other afternoon. Can't say that I blame you," he laughed. "Often wanted to myself. You picked the wrong person though. Gail's a lovely girl. I suppose you don't think much of my son?"

Rick looked into the baffled eyes. He could not put Manton off with a polite evasion that Gail was too young to think seriously about any boy and he hadn't the heart to blurt out the truth.

"My dad would have known how to handle Paul," Manton

confessed. "It's mostly my own damn fault."

"I'm not finding this parent business an easy job either," Rick admitted, surprised at his sudden feeling of kinship with this man whom he had regarded only a moment before as a dubious specimen of *homo sapiens*.

Manton gave Rick a grateful look and then denied the likeness of their situations with unhappy honesty. "Your Gail's all right," he insisted. "Her aunt must have had good sense. Better than Daphne. I gather Miss Willard doesn't care much for Daph. Silly woman, Daph." Manton was obviously enjoying himself now. The hurt look had vanished from his eyes. "Good looker, though. Knows how to dress, eh? Wish she'd quit putting that blue stuff on her hair. Thinks it makes her look French. She's as French as a McGuire from Jersey City could be. Talks about the Celtic strain. Celtic strain, my eye. Her dad and mine were a couple of tough micks who pulled some fancy deals together in the good old days. Prettiest girl in High School, though." He rummaged through the lower drawer of the Savery desk and handed Rick a photograph. "Daph won't let me keep this out any more, says the dress is impossible."

Rick studied the picture. He could see why Mrs. Manton was ashamed of it. It was a large, shiny and unmistakable product of a cheap studio, located at the top of a long flight of wooden stairs, with tin signs advertising a beauty parlor, insurance agent, chiropodist and portrait photographer, tacked hopefully on the risers. In spite of the artificial pose and a bridal bouquet which was obviously a dusty studio prop, Mrs. Manton had been an extremely pretty girl. But there was no soft wonder in the upturned eyes. Even the lips seemed set in an ambitious smile.

"Don't get me wrong." Manton put the photograph back in the drawer. "I'm not sentimental about Daph. I know her too well. Smart woman in her way. But a fool. What gets me down is that I've been a worse fool letting her have her own way in bringing up Paul." His eyes clouded again. "I tried taking him hunting and fishing with me when he was a kid, but his mother always said he was too delicate and he never seemed to get much fun out of it anyhow. Easier to let her alone. I thought boarding school would do the job. Then I figured New Haven might help, but it's too near New York, too many weekends with his mother and her pals." Manton seemed to be talking more to himself than to Rick, trying to convince himself that he had not been a complete failure as a father. "I'd have gotten out long ago if it hadn't been for Paul," he admitted with embarrassing candor, "but I get a chance to take him to baseball games once in a while, try to talk some sense to him. Not that it helps much . . . but at least I've stuck."

"At least I've stuck." The words hit Rick. Hard. But what could he say? Tell Manton he'd been a worse flop himself? He hadn't stuck. No, he could not equal Manton's frankness. Could not really understand how any man could let his hair down the way Manton had. It was like a crying jag. Rick's hangovers were often haunted by fears of what he had said as well as what he had done on a bender—but Manton was sober.

"I'm sorry, Mr. Manton," Rick kept his eyes on his cigar ash which he flicked carefully and unnecessarily into a silver tray, "but everything you've been saying adds to my feeling that I don't want my daughter to marry your son." He had finally said what he had come here to say. Said it awkwardly and as sententiously as a father in an 1890 melodrama.

Manton jerked to his feet like a sleeping air-raid warden at the sound of an "alert." He put a stubby, capable hand on Rick's arm. "Not a penny."

"What?"

"I said not a penny and I mean it. If they want to get married it's their funeral," he chuckled. "Daphne hasn't a penny except what she makes at her shop and I'm always having to fork up for that. She'd help 'em if she could just to get even with Miss Willard—I don't mean that she doesn't like Gail. She does, but you don't need to worry about their getting married."

Rick was relieved . . . and oddly angry. "You mean *you* don't want Paul to marry Gail?" He could not keep the incredulity out of his voice.

Manton laughed again. "You've got me wrong, Mr. Rickham. All wrong. Your daughter is the first attractive 'nice' girl Paul has ever fallen for. He was running around with one of Daph's Russian Princesses before he met Gail. I was mighty pleased that day he brought Gail down to lunch, but marriage is not the answer for Paul now." He spoke with the authority of a man accustomed to handling difficult business deals. "You can count on me, Rickham . . . and I am counting on Uncle Sam. The Army is Paul's best chance. It may make a man of him. I've seen it happen before."

Rick nodded. He had seen it work in the last war. He looked at Manton with genuine admiration, "You don't think the uniform will just make things worse?" he asked and realized how completely selfish he was being, how obvious it was that he was thinking only of Gail and the romantic appeal of a uniform.

"Paul won't elope, you can bet on that. Not on a private's pay. He's like me in one thing—his respect for money. And he'll be Private Manton soon, thank God. Daphne has been trying to wangle a soft spot in Washington for him through a friend of hers, one of those behind-the-scenes guys, but I'll say this for Paul—he isn't having any of his mother's talk for once. He wants to get in the Air Force and I've been standing him to flying lessons on the sly all summer. You're sure," he looked at Rick doubtfully, "that you won't let Gail get around you?"

"No," Rick said positively, not adding that Gail would have money of her own in three years. Still, three years was three years.

"Good!" Manton sounded as if he had concluded a five-million-dollar deal. He evidently had complete faith in the power of money.

Rick did not trust it as much. He suspected that Gail might disregard finances quite unconcernedly. He had never let money affect his own decisions and if Gail were like him, as Emily had suggested, she might throw her hat blithely over the fence—he pictured her silly little white flower with its wisp of black veiling sailing recklessly into the air and smiled. The whole situation seemed somehow less perilous. He felt cheered and told Manton so as he reached for his hat and coat.

"Hold everything!" Manton exclaimed. "I never offered you a drink. Can't imagine what got into me. Come on back, sir, and we'll do a bit of quiet celebrating together. None of that bilgewater my wife serves. Bottle of Irish in my wine cooler. One thing the Irish can beat the Scotch at, eh? Smell of peat moss. Smoky. Like it?"

"Sure," Rick agreed, realizing that it had been years since he had given a damn about the taste of a drink. It was the effect he had been after. "Not today, thanks," he added, hoping Manton would not insist, hoping he would not bring up the wagon. He was relieved when Manton gave him a knowing grin and a friendly slap on the back and ushered him to the door.

"Some other time then, Rickham. Good to see you, sir. Good talk. Always believe in coming right to the point."

Rick had a knowing grin himself as he went down the hall.

VIII

PROMETHEUS

Joe's kitchen was filled with the pleasant, old-fashioned smells of gingerbread and coffee. Emily checked over the tray which Gail was about to carry into the living room—eight blue and white cups, eight teaspoons, sugar bowl, cream pitcher. She was not sure how many A.A.s Avery would be bringing back from the Greenwich meeting. It had been her idea to invite them, when she learned from Joe that the group often stopped at the local dog-wagon for coffee or cokes. It had struck her as a rather dreary procedure and she had hoped that having the crowd here would be an easy way for Gail to meet these new friends of her father's. Now suddenly she was afraid it would not work out. And it would be her own fault if it didn't. In the rush of packing and arranging for Beulah to take a long deserved vacation, she had had no time to talk to Gail about her father's problem.

She heaped gingerbread on a round pewter platter, hoping Joe was not one of those tiresome collectors who never wanted to use his treasures. He seemed like the least fussy person in the world but you couldn't be sure. She must remember to ask him about the large Royal Doulton soup tureen and get Emerald to make a fish chowder. Strange how country living brought back memories of country food. She had not seen a soup tureen since she was a child, or tasted a New England chowder—without tomatoes. She was glad Joe had suggested that they take over his house. Avery looked better already, less tense. If only Gail could be happy here . . . she had not protested about moving to Riverside, but she had been stand-offish with her father ever since the Mantons' cocktail party. Emily pushed the memory away with a worried frown. She was not a believer in direct questions—they always seemed to produce evasive answers. Whatever that trouble was it would have to wait, but she must say something to Gail about the A.A.s before they came. Now. Quickly.

"Gail!" she called.

Gail poked her blonde head through the pantry door. "I've been hunting for napkins. We forgot all about them. Do you think these paper ones would do, Aunt Emily? They're rather sweet." She held up a bunch with gay red and blue sailboats printed in the corners. Emily nodded absently. "And oh, look what I found!" Gail put the white and gold Father cup in the center of the kitchen table. "Isn't it a riot, Aunt Emily? Do you think Mr. Kelly would let Daddy use it?"

Emily wanted to say, "Of course,"—to take Joe's consent for granted, but there was an off-chance that the ridiculous cup might have some special meaning for him. Her conscience struggled with the warm quick sense of relief that Gail was actually thinking about her father—and her conscience won. "Better ask him," she advised and added, keeping her voice light, "Darling, do be nice to these new friends of your father's."

"Naturally, Aunt Emily." Gail's soft mouth tightened at the corners and her eyes had a wary look.

Emily sensed that she had made the wrong approach, but she had to try again. "I know, Gail, but what I mean is try to understand them. They aren't the sort of people you'd meet at the Stork Club," she couldn't resist saying, "but they mean a lot to your father. They all help each other in their fight against liquor. I don't mean prohibition. They aren't reformers—except of themselves—because drinking makes them sick and miserable." She was floundering badly. Avery had asked her to read THE BOOK and she had felt that the chapter on wives applied to any relative deeply concerned, but now she was finding it difficult to translate into terms of Gail's experience. She went on anxiously, "It's hard for us to understand what alcohol does to some people. They say that only a drunk can help another drunk."

Gail laughed, the quick, brittle laughter of a world Emily could not understand. "Daphne Manton says the best way to handle a drunk is to make a joke of it. She says all men act like fools when they get tight and you shouldn't take it too seriously."

"But it *is* serious," Emily protested. She was shocked by this spurious, flippant wisdom. She looked at the girl, perched on the kitchen table with one long slim leg dangling in its scuffed saddle shoe. Her pale blue skirt and oversized matching sweater were touchingly youthful. The cigarette she had lighted with the flick of a kitchen match on a scarlet fingernail, the scarlet nail itself, and the Daphne Manton philosophy seemed nothing but playacting. A child's game of grown-up mimicry. But were they? Could she be sure? She wanted to cry, "Pooh to your Daphne Manton. She's worldly wise and sublimely foolish," but that would only antagonize Gail. Any criticism of the Mantons always put her on the defensive.

"Drink isn't a joke to your father—or any of these men," Emily said earnestly. "It's a disease. An allergy. They are sick people, Gail, fighting for their lives. And we've got to help them. Especially your father."

Gail gave her a startled look and slid off the kitchen table, stubbing out her cigarette. "I'll try," she promised. "You're nice, Aunt Emily." She snuggled her head against Emily's shoulder the way she had when she was a child.

The front door opened and they could hear voices and laughter in the hall. Emily gave Gail a quick hug. "You're pretty nice yourself, darling." She started for the stove, grabbing the pewter coffee pot.

"Hi, women!" Joe came into the kitchen sniffing like a pleased setter. "Smells good in here." He put a friendly arm around each of them, nearly upsetting the coffee pot. "You've got a great father, infant." He patted Gail's blonde head and Emily wondered with a sharp stab of indignation how his wife could go traipsing off to California, taking her son with her and leaving Joe alone. He was a family person for all his wild gaiety and bluster. Avery wasn't. Avery was restive under ties and responsibilities. Lone-wolfish like Nicky.

"Rick made the funniest damn speech," Joe went on, "all about . . ." He spotted the Father cup on the kitchen table and released them both abruptly. "What the hell . . ." He picked it up and carried it carefully into the pantry. They could hear him muttering that he had told Emerald to be sure to put it away. Emily glanced at Gail's disappointed face. It was too bad. People were always making life complicated. She said briskly, if ambiguously, "Come on, Gail, grab the gingerbread. We can probably find one for your father at some little shop on Second Avenue."

There were more than eight people in the small living room. Emily counted noses quickly and sent Gail back for extra cups. Evidently their entrance and Joe's introductions had interrupted a discussion of a speech someone from the Mount Vernon group had made on the all-out importance of the religious angle in the A.A. program. As she busied herself pouring coffee, Emily gathered that he had backed up his contention by some personal experience of Divine aid. She heard Hank Frost's Yankee drawl.

"Seems like it musta happened all right. I've known this Griggs for quite some time and I don't doubt his word."

"Neither do I—but I don't accept his interpretation." Rick, standing with his back to the fire, pointed out with vehement logic that the whole thing could be explained as coincidence, pure and simple.

"Is anything ever pure and simple?" Joe asked with a grin, "except a baby—or an equation in algebra?"

Rick shook his head impatiently. "I'm serious about this. I'm not questioning the existence of God. I simply maintain that any drunk is a fool to expect God to snatch a bottle out of his hand. We've got to depend on ourselves and not on any screwy miracles."

He's like Prometheus, Emily thought, studying his angular profile and understanding with sudden clarity why the ancient Greeks had made a legend out of a man who, chained to the rocks, had defied the Gods and trusted Man.

"How about you, Tony?" Rick appealed to the big jolly-looking Italian whose rubber boots, windbreaker and Block Island cap Emily had found in the garage. She remembered now that Joe had said very few Latins became alcoholics because they were weaned on red ink. But Tony had learned to drink hard liquor at political clam bakes and softball games and felt this made him "an honest-to-God American." Sorting out the various scraps of information she had picked up about the members of the local group, Emily wondered why Rick had appealed to Tony. It seemed quite obvious that although Tony had doubtless exchanged his native wine for gin and Rye, he would not have changed his religion. Miracles would be as natural to him as to any Italian peasant who paused to kneel at a wayside shrine in Tuscany.

"Well, I tella you." Tony held out his blue and white coffee cup dramatically. "This a-here you maka believe like is one cut-aglass punch glass filled up with the besta wine made from the Muscat grape. My cousin he very special about his wine and this a very special party he give for the wedding of his youngest girl . . ." Tony rambled on and Emily half listened to his long account of how his cousin "aska Tony to maka the toast to the health of the bride." He had all the A.A.s laughing at his predicament and when he ended triumphantly that he "no toucha the drop and no getta in the fight," they all agreed that was a "miracle" and Avery, with a twisted grin, gave up his argument.

A large woman in a navy blue and white print dress moved over next to Emily. "I'm Mrs. Watson," she said. "My husband thinks Mr. Rickham is a great addition to our Greenwich group." She nodded her rigidly waved grey hair in the direction of a small, inconspicuous man in a brown suit and Emily remembered Joe's saying at dinner, "Poor Hugh, the only outstanding thing about him is the fact that there is nothing outstanding about him." Emily smiled; he did look a middle-aged, middle-class, middle-of-the-road sort of person. Mrs. Watson was going on in a confidential tone, "I do think it helps for the women to get together, don't you? I never could understand why Mr. Watson couldn't drink like other men. And it's been so hard on the children. We have two boys and one girl. The boys are at Scouts tonight. They used to be so ashamed of their father. Especially the older one. And the boys at high school would kid them. We lost all our friends, nearly. I'd have to call up and make some excuse when they asked us out for supper. Of course, they saw through it and you can't blame them for not inviting us anymore. We live over in Old Greenwich. It's a nice family section and we've got a nice home. Only it did seem so queer at first to have men like Hank Frost and Tony What's-his-name coming over to see Mr. Watson. Not that I'm snobbish. But you know what I mean. . . ."

Emily tried to interrupt—to say that she liked Hank Frost—but Mrs. Watson chatted on. "The MacKenzies are nice people, but they live way down in Greenwich and she's had a dreadful time. They had to sell their house in Jersey and she's working in a store now. Then there's been all that trouble about Dick Spencer and his wife and that Mrs. Bentley-Young.

I suppose you've heard but it does give the A.A.s a bad name. . . ."

Emily looked across the room where Gail was perched on the window seat next to a lean, tanned young man in a worn but good tweed jacket. His clear-cut features looked English. But he wasn't English. Emily had heard Rick and Joe talking about him. He had started out as a caddy and picked up manners and a way of dressing from the men at the club. His older brother used to fight with him and call him a sissy and once, when the brother had driven by on a garbage wagon, he had spotted Dick just starting off from the first tee and yelled, "Hi, there, Vanderbilt-Rocke-feller-Astor." The man Dick was caddying for had been amused and Dick had said, "That's one of those smart guys at school." He had been ashamed to admit that the boy was his brother. And then more ashamed at not having admitted it. You didn't need to be a psychologist to see how an episode like that would start a conflict in a man's mind. Emily watched him filling his pipe, noted the leather patches on the elbows of his tweed jacket, the nervous frown between his eyes. Gail probably reminded him of the girls to whom he had given golf lessons at the club. From caddy to caddy master, to "Pro," wasn't an unusual success story, but the tough part for Dick Spencer was that the club had closed down after gas-rationing started and he was now reduced to driving one of his brother's garbage trucks. Small wonder he had started drinking. The men at the club had probably treated him from the bottles in their lockers after successful sessions of "getting that slice under control." He seemed to have alcohol under control now, but the old conflict had taken a new form. And the A.A.s didn't like it. Not just this gossipy Mrs. Watson with standards as hard as the waves of her grey hair. Hank Frost had said that Dick was a fool not to shake the Bentley-Young female and enlist. "How can he," Joe had protested, "with a wife and two kids?" "He had ought to bring his wife around to the meetin's then," Hank had insisted. "My old woman used to come regular at first. Just to see I wasn't gettin' into no bad com-pany." "Maybe he's ashamed of her," Emily had suggested, but Hank had pooh-poohed that. "She was a right nice girl, assistant in a dentist's office, down to Port Chester. Cut above his own folks if you ask me. Them Spencers always was no account around these parts. She kinda let herself go, though," Hank added, "Got fat and naggish. Don't hold with his goin' to meetin's all the time neither. 'T'ain't just Greenwich. He's over to White Plains and into New York most every night in the week. Don't get time to take her to the movies no more. Guess she enjoyed him being drunk better. Some women don't know when they's lucky." "Well, I might take the Bentley-Young off his hands," Rick had volunteered. "Sounds as if you were offering to buy his car," Joe had laughed. "Better wait till you see the dame. She's poison if you ask me. And I don't believe she's an alcoholic either. I'll make you a small bet that she comes to meetings to get her man. Her being from the right side of the Post Road seems to have gotten Dick, though. The poor dope."

In another group Emily would have put this down as gossip—and she didn't like gossip. But the A.A.s had a way of discussing each other that was different. Different motivation. That was it. They really cared about the problems of the members—not alcoholic problems alone—because, of course, you couldn't separate them. A man's drinking was all mixed up with his life. You couldn't cure one without the other.

"She's after all the men," Mrs. Watson was saying, "with her baby face and her helpless ways. Even Mr. Watson. He tells me I'm not being fair about her. Fair . . ." she snorted, casting a scornful and determined look at the inconspicuous little man.

Emily fled with a murmured apology that she had been neglecting her duties as a hostess. Mrs. Watson offered to help, but Emily was too quick for her. She escaped to the kitchen with the empty pewter platter. She heaped it with gingerbread and was starting back when the telephone rang. Hurrying into the hall she nearly collided with Gail, who had evidently made a record-breaking dash from the living room.

"I'll take it, Aunt Emily," Gail said breathlessly, grabbing the receiver. "Yes, yes, of course, it's me."

The excited, happy tone in her voice meant Paul. Emily went slowly back to the living room, disturbed that he had called tonight—of all nights—hoping Gail would make it brief and that Avery wouldn't notice. But she didn't. And he did.

When Gail finally came back the A.A.s had gone and Avery glared at her. "You were extremely rude to my friends, Gail," he said in a cold, angry voice.

Gail stopped in the doorway as if he had struck her. Her cheeks flamed. "I'm sorry," she said with a proud lift of her chin.

They stood staring at each other interminably. Emily searched frantically for something to say—something, anything to break the tension. She made a great clatter, picking up cups, hoping Gail would notice and offer to help, but neither Avery nor Gail moved a muscle. The line between their eyes was almost visible, taut as a wire. I could walk on it, Emily thought hysterically, in a white tulle skirt like a circus performer, taking little mincing steps and balancing a pink umbrella.

"I'll fix some hot coffee," she offered at last, feeling like a Jane Austen character, as if any conflict could be averted by the timid amenities of the tea table. The theory appeared to depend on the assumption that you could not do anything disastrous with a fragile china cup in your hand, but Avery and Gail looked quite capable of hurling cups—or pianos—at each other. There must be some way of stopping them. Emily looked from one tense angry face to the other and suddenly laughed.

"I wish you could see yourselves. You're the spitting image of each other." Identical expressions of surprise crossed both faces and then to Emily's infinite relief Avery and Gail joined in her laughter.

IX

"A WORLD TURNED UPSIDE DOWN"

When the call came from New York at ten-thirty p.m., Rick said, "Sure, I'll take it." But as he hung up the receiver he wished Joe were around. He was tired and he wasn't at all sure he could handle a case on his own. He'd been out twice with others on A.A. calls—once with Joe to see a woman at High Pines, once with Hank to the town jail. Maybe he could get hold of Hank now . . . hell, no. Ten-thirty was too late for Hank, who had to be at his boatyard at seven sharp every morning. He stood in the back hall staring at an old framed chart of Cos Cob Harbor without even seeing it. Why the devil did this Manfred Schuyler Pell have to go and get himself plastered at ten-thirty? And why did the New York chapter, answering a distress telegram from a relative of Pell's in Cincinnati, have to pick on him? There must be some member nearer Darien than he was. He had a good mind to call Pell and say he'd be over tomorrow. Joe would be coming out for the weekend and they could go together. He leafed through the directory and looked up to see Emily.

"I'll make you some coffee before you go, Avery." She smiled at him with such serene confidence that he felt suddenly alert and determined. "I couldn't help overhearing your side of the conversation," she added, "and I do think it's wonderful of you to go out at this time of night."

"Thanks, Emily." Rick was thanking her for more than her offer of coffee and he knew that she somehow understood. He was coming to depend more and more on her quick understanding, her quiet companionship. Thank God she hadn't guessed how near he had been to quitting on the job. Suppose Joe had let him down when he had phoned from jail! And Joe had said that friendship was beside the point, that any A.A. would go to bat for any drunk who wanted help.

Pell's house was difficult to locate. Rick remembered gratefully that

Joe had said the Ration Board gave extra gas for A.A. work. Rick followed a road branching south of the Post Road, trying to keep his mind on the left and right turns and directions he had picked up from a garage near the railway bridge in Darien, and at the same time struggling with the problem of what to say to Pell when he got there—if he ever did get there. Hank believed in the direct approach, "So you want to quit drinking, brother? Okay, we're here to help you, that is, if you're sincere and honest in your intentions. If you'd rather drink yourself to death that's okay by us too, brother." Rick grinned and took a left fork through deep hardwoods, mostly white oak with dark, scattered spruce. Pell's wife was in the Norwalk hospital with her first baby, the New York secretary had explained, giving him what facts she had. Pell was a fool. Rick's mind backtracked eighteen years. He could tell Pell what a damn lucky fool he was—or could he? Could he force himself to talk about Adelaide's death even if it meant the best way to get at this unknown drunk?

Rick pulled into a driveway, seeing the name Pell in white letters on a green mail box. A dim light in the house made him realize that he had been more than half hoping to find it dark. The man who had answered the phone when he called, while Emily hurried to make coffee, had urged him to come, but he felt more dread of the unknown as he climbed the steps of an old-fashioned porch than he had ever experienced going into the bush. He barked his shin on something and discovered two broken hobby-horses beside the front door. What the devil were two hobbyhorses doing on the Pells' porch? He had understood this was their first child.

From inside the house, Rick heard a thud, followed by another thud and another. He hesitated and then pushed the doorbell, not feeling happy about it at all. The thuds stopped and Rick thought he could hear steps coming uncertainly down the stairs. The front door opened an inch. A dark eye peered curiously at Rick.

"Could this be General Light-Horse Harry Lee arriving with reinforcements?"

"Could be," Rick ventured.

A youngish man in a dirty brown dressing gown over a grey flannel shirt and slacks flung open the door and thrust out his hand with a grandiloquent gesture.

"Captain Pell, reporting, sir. We attack at dawn."

Under the feeble light of the hanging lamp in the shallow entrance hall, Rick tried to get a good look at Pell. A pale, handsome face in spite of a three-day growth of beard. The mouth wide but weak, facile. The nose inconsequential. The eyes, however, notable. Large, brilliant for all their reddened lids and dark puffy bags.

Pell took Rick's overcoat and threw it on a chair. Stepping forward, Rick stumbled on a large book, and in an attempt to recover his balance his left foot slipped on a small volume. He went down heavily and rather painfully on his knee.

"Did they get you, sir?" Pell's solicitude was accompanied by a salute.

A light was snapped on in a living room and Rick saw that the floor of the hall was littered with books. A figure rose from an armchair and came toward them. "Good evening. I'm Warrenton Thraves. You're Mr. Rickham, I take it. I spoke to you on the telephone. Sorry you had a tumble. Mr. Pell has been rearranging his library. These volumes were in his study upstairs." Thraves, a portly fellow in well-tailored riding clothes, stooped and picked up the small red leather book on which Rick had skidded.

"Cornucopias for Carlotta's Coming of Age," he read the title scornfully. "Bilge-water. Stuff and nonsense. Dangerous, too. Throw a man's mind over the fence." He tossed the book with surprising accuracy into the fireplace across the room.

"You horse-whoring Virginia bastard," Pell squeaked in a high falsetto of rage. He retrieved the book, wiping the ashes off carefully on the hem of his dirty dressing gown. "I'll deal with this insubordination later," he threatened. "My apologies, General. May I offer you a noggin of brandy, Sir? Mulled wine . . . shandygaff . . . I have some excellent Madeira in my cellar."

"Nothing, thanks."

"Have you joined the Quakers, Sir? I hadn't heard. Our communications have been cut. You've had a hard ride, a tough gallop from Trenton. Let me make you some coffee, Sir. General Washington has done me the honor to praise my coffee." Pell seemed to be walking straight enough toward a door behind the stairway, but just before he reached it he lurched into a small table and a yellow vase crashed into fragments.

"Egad, that was a close one. Their musket fire is confounded near, sir." Pell straightened his shoulders and with an air of great bravery marched on toward the kitchen.

Damn little use in trying to talk A.A. to Pell in this state, but as long as he was here Rick decided he might as well stick around and give Thraves a hand. Perhaps together they could get Pell to bed. He took the chair Thraves indicated and accepted a cigarette. The Southerner reeked of liquor but he seemed to be carrying it pretty well.

"How long has he been like this?" Rick asked.

"Let's see. Today's Thursday. Sky—he hates the name Manfred—his mother fell for some German actor and ruined the fine old name Schuyler Pell. That's why we call him Sky—anyhow he phoned me Tuesday morning about eleven. Said he was having a baby and needed help. I live a couple of miles down the road, so I came right over. He was well started by the time I got here. Took his wife to the hospital Saturday. The baby was born Monday morning. He's been drinking ever since."

"Hasn't he been to see his wife since Monday?"

"Hell, no. Too busy drinking the kid's health. Tuesday it was 'Mad Anthony Wayne Pell on to Stony Point, my lad.' Today it's been 'Here's to you Light-Horse Harry Lee Pell and keep out of debtor's prison, you little bastard.' I've been trying to duck out, but every time I head for the door he screams that he can't stand being alone. I reckon he's right. Might set fire to the house." Thraves shrugged and reached for a half-filled glass.

"Anyone cooking for you two?"

Thraves shook his head. "Wife does her own work. I've tried a spot of cooking but I can't get him to eat—says whiskey's a damn fine food. Full of vitamins."

Rick pulled himself reluctantly out of his chair. The least he could do was try to get some food into the guy. After a preliminary banging of pots and pans the kitchen had been ominously silent.

Thraves was listening too. "I reckon Sky must have passed out again," he observed unconcernedly and led the way to the kitchen. Empty whiskey, rum, beer and soda bottles covered the floor. Rick stepped warily, noting the greasy pans on the stove and the stack of dirty dishes in the sink. Thraves' cooking had not included much K.P. from the looks of it. On the floor in the far corner near the door to the garage, Pell was asleep, one arm lovingly encircling a closed garbage pail. His face was flushed but his breathing was regular.

"Pretty picture." The sight of Pell seemed to give Thraves a certain satisfaction. He slapped his jodhpurred thigh. "Told him he couldn't get by without eating, been living on egg sandwiches myself."

"Better get him to bed." Rick stooped and got his hands under Pell's shoulders. Get him to bed and get the hell out. That's what Hank would do. He could hear Hank saying, "A.A.s ain't wetnurses, nohow."

"Waste of time, Mr. Rickford." Thraves grabbed Pell's legs. "I've been dumping him on the daybed off and on, but he just bounces up again." Thraves backed out of the kitchen, through the door to the hall and into a small sun-room. It was cold and the rows of plants on a wide window ledge looked dry and neglected. Rick threw a heavy army blanket over Pell, thinking of Mrs. Pell coming back from the hospital with her baby. He had the odd feeling that the withered plants and the stack of dirty dishes in the sink would be harder for her to face than her husband lying on his back with his mouth open. At least he could clean things up a bit before he left.

"Usually snores, groans, and belches. Very considerate now. Company manners," Thraves chuckled, following Rick back to the kitchen.

The shining aluminum kettle was boiling dry on the stove. Rick snatched it off, filled it with cold water, saw that Pell had put coffee in the dripolator, found eggs in the icebox and broke four into the cleanest frying pan.

"Mighty glad to have you take over, Mr. Rickton." Thraves rummaged around and produced a loaf of bread and a couple of bottles of beer. "Got an appointment in New York tomorrow. If you hadn't turned up I was going to call the hospital. Couldn't leave Sky alone. He's bats right now. Scared too. Always scared of something. Pack rats lately."

"Pack rats?" Rick flipped the eggs onto the stale bread and handed Thraves a sandwich.

"So help me, suh, I saw 'em with my own eyes. Bigger than house rats. They've been running round the clearing for three days."

"Squirrels?" Rick suggested with a sharp look at Thraves. This must be a new kind of D.T.s. He wasn't surprised that Pell was seeing things, but the hard-bitten Southerner had acted fairly normal. He was sitting astride a kitchen chair now wolfing his sandwich.

"Too big for squirrels. Don't leap like squirrels. Sky's been shooting at 'em with a Revolutionary musket. Not much of a shot. Not like my old granpappy. Many's the time my granpappy and me had no breakfast till we shot us a brace of squirrels." As if he sensed Rick's incredulity, he added stiffly, "My parents had some property in the state of Virginia, suh. Brought me up like a southern gentleman . . . put me on a horse at eighteen months . . . I was riding to hounds at four. But when I was nine they lost everything. Year later they both died. Granpap was a horse of a different color." Thraves chuckled. "Stayed in a cabin up in the hills. I've always wanted to write about Granpappy . . . great fictional character . . . but all these northern editors want is pink coats and champagne. . . ."

It could be true. Rick recognized the name Warrenton Thraves now. He had seen it signed to a syndicated column on horse racing and the activities of famous hunt clubs. Evidently Thraves had capitalized on his nostalgia for the hard-riding, hard-drinking life of his early boyhood. Thraves went on to describe the sort of stuff he turned out for the slick sport magazines and the pulps, with a cynicism that didn't quite ring true. He tilted the second bottle of beer to his mouth. "Have to make this my last," he declared, "I've got a date with an editor tomorrow morning—or do I repeat myself? Bad sign, that." He tossed the half-empty bottle in the general direction of the garbage can and the smell of spilled beer rose above the odors of coffee and burned grease. Through the partly opened window came the scent of marsh grass. "Smells are surer than sounds or sights to make your heartstrings crack." Rick's nose twitched from the sudden memory of the aromatic marches behind Belize. If he drank again would it be from nostalgia for the Tropics—a pull as strong as the tug of Thraves' memories of Virginia?

"Mighty glad to have you take over, Mr. Rickley." Thraves flung one leg over the back of the kitchen chair and dismounted neatly.

"Ham," Rick spoke with sharp annoyance. He was sick of hearing Thraves call him Rickton, Rickley, Rickford, but he resisted the impulse

to retaliate with Mr. Threves, Thrives, Throves—or even Thieves. Joe had said to watch out for gripes . . . typically alcoholic . . . gripes, grudges and resentments.

"Ham?" Thraves shook his head. "No ham. No bacon. Nothing but eggs. Feel like cackling myself. How about taking Sky home with you?"

Rick hesitated. He didn't like the idea of having a drunk, and a crazy drunk at that, around the house with Gail. Emily would be all right. He knew he could count on Emily. Perhaps when Pell sobered up he could talk to him about A.A. . . . "Ever hear Pell say he wanted to quit drinking?" he asked.

Thraves slapped his jodhpurred thigh emphatically. "Never heard him mention it. Funny guy, Pell. Pet theory is that he needs alcohol to loosen his brain. Maybe he's right at that. Dull fellow sober. Funny as hell when he's *half*-tight, though. Usually overshoots the mark, like tonight. Ever see one of his plays?"

"No. But I haven't been around New York."

"*Savage in Bed* got a Broadway production a couple of years ago. Only ran six weeks. Damn amusing show. Sort of Rip Van Winkle idea with a Thorne Smith fantastic kind of logic. Pell's noble red man was one of King Philip's warriors, who ate some herb for the pox and slept three hundred years; turned up at the Algonquin Hotel—the Wampanoags always hated the Algonquins, according to Pell, thought they were sissies. I wouldn't know, but Sky is hipped on American history. Anyhow, the Savage sets up a wigwam on the roof and all the guests make a great fuss over him. There's a blonde actress who thinks he's 'cunning' and he *is* but not the way she means. He develops a phobia about beds, climbs down the fire escape and pulls them to pieces, is terrified of radios, throws the magic-boxes out of windows and has a passion for gadgets; rides on Fifth Avenue buses and steals the conductor's coin doodads, collects compasses and barometers by the simple process of swiping 'em out of shopwindows, but says they aren't nearly as accurate as the Indian way of taking directions—only he can't find any moss on the trees in Radio City. Lots of junk like that. Finally he goes on a whale of a binge, drinking 'firewater' from the Algonquin cellar, conks a copy over the head to get his whistle, tries to direct traffic, has the whole police department chasing him and ends up in showcase at the Museum of the American Indian to sleep it off. The flatfeet think he's an exhibit. Curtain." Thraves started for the door. "Curtains for me too. Got to be shoving along. Luck to you, suh. Don't think you'll have much more trouble with Sky tonight. I'll give you a ring when I get back tomorrow. See how you're making out."

"Hold it," Rick said, following Thraves into the shallow hall where he stepped carefully to avoid skidding on the litter of books. "I guess I didn't make myself clear on the phone, Mr. Thraves. I came over because someone in Cincinnati wired the New York headquarters of the Alcoholics Anonymous and they called me, but I didn't. . . ."

"Hell for leather, that's fast work," Thraves interrupted, "Must be a great organization. The Green Hornet to the rescue, what!"

"Not exactly." Rick despaired of explaining to Thraves that he had expected to find Pell in a state of remorse, ready to listen to the A.A. program. He'd been played for a sucker, all right. His pride in belonging to such an efficient outfit had turned to resentment. Why the hell hadn't the New York secretary investigated further before sending him out on a fool's errand. In a minute Thraves would swagger down the front steps and he'd be left holding the bag. "Hasn't Pell any friend we could call up to come over?"

"Not a friend. Not a friend in the world. Except me. Arranges their furniture."

"What?"

"Just one of his little habits when he's tight. Barges in on people he knows—when he knows they're out—moves things around. Puts the piano on the porch and the icebox in the living room. Goes to a lot of trouble, but no one appreciates his efforts. Got a lawsuit on his hands now for breaking and entering." Thraves chuckled and opened the front door. "Got to be toddling along. Hold the fort against the pack rats, Rickley."

"Woodchucks." Rick was annoyed that Thraves' parting shot had revived the old argument.

"Ask the Zoo, if you doubt my word, suh. Matter of fact, Sky phoned 'em. Zoo man mighty interested. Said there was a food shortage out West—some crop failed—gave it as his scientific opinion that Pell's description tallied with the western pack rats."

"Why's Pell afraid of 'em?"

"Scared of everything. Scared they'll gnaw through the kitchen floor and eat his rations . . . thinks we're besieged . . . Indians one minute, Redcoats the next. Says Simon Girty's with 'em. Girty's his devil, Dan'l Boone his hero. Don't be surprised if you're Boone when he wakes up."

"Fear's a devil," Rick said, thinking of his own alcoholic terrors and wondering what genuine dread Pell was hiding behind these childish, imaginary panics.

"Must be." Thraves shrugged. "Never been scared but once in my life. Rattler reared up at me. Granpappy shot it in the head. Gave me a whale of a licking for being a coward. Scared the scares plumb out of me. Reckon Sky's afraid of having a kid. Wanted one more than Diana did in the first place. Scared now. Scared of the responsibility. Raved last night that having a son was like shooting your own youth in the head."

"No joke being a father." Rick was thinking of Gail, remembering that he'd made the same statement before . . . in Manton's office. That was it. Pell, Manton, himself. Men wanting children, but not knowing how to take them sensibly, like a bear with a cub. You never saw a Papa bear getting neurotic.

Thraves kicked a hobby-horse out of his path on the darkened porch. "Only kind of horse I don't go for. Sky's nuts about 'em."

"Baby's a bit young for one," Rick laughed.

"Baby, hell. Sky's been collecting 'em for years. Says the hobby-horse is a symbol of life in a mechanized world—or some such bilge—likes to give it a shove with his foot and watch it run in the same place."

Hitching his jodhpurs, Thraves swaggered down the steps, refusing Rick's offer to give him a lift with the warning that Pell couldn't be left alone. Rick observed the typical rolling gait of the horseman afoot and wondered uncharitably how much of it was affected. He closed the front door quietly so as not to wake Pell and tiptoed into the cold sun room.

Pell was sitting on the edge of the day bed, loading a Revolutionary musket from a brass powder horn.

"I wouldn't." Rick moved quickly. To his surprise, Pell handed him the weapon.

"Use it on yourself first, Dan'l. Better than Pawnee torture." Pell rose shakily to his feet and saluted. "Thraves, did they get him? Insubordinate cuss, but a damn fine horseman." He went down on his hands and knees and dragged out two small hobbyhorses. "Been hiding these for us, Dan'l. Horses is his hobby. Hobby is my horses . . . horses hobby . . . hobbyhorses." Pell gave Rick a beatific smile which was followed by a loud belch.

Better get some food in the guy. Rick started for the kitchen again, followed closely by Pell. There was still some coffee in the pot. He turned on the burner, deciding not to take the time to make fresh. Pell wouldn't notice the difference. He opened the refrigerator to get some eggs, conscious that Pell was watching every move he made with a curious expression in his brilliant dark eyes—was it apprehension or craftiness? And why craftiness? What could the guy be up to now?

Pell spilled large old-fashioned matches on the kitchen table. "Ever seen this trick, Dan'l?"

Rick had, but he pretended interest.

"Show you another." Pell fumbled in the pocket of his grey slacks and held out an empty hand. "No keys. Need keys for this trick. Bet you never saw this one, Dan'l. Wonnerful trick. Wonnerful."

Rick tossed his key ring on the kitchen table, with the keys to his office, to Joe's house and to his car outside. The coffee had started to boil. He turned off the burner, cracked eggs in the frying pan. When he looked around Pell had vanished. "Hey, you," Rick called. "What's the idea?" His first thought was the musket. He had thrust it behind the plants on the window ledge, while Pell was dragging out his hobbyhorses. If that was what Pell was after it would be easy to find—too damn easy. Rick cursed his own carelessness and rushed into the sun room, but Pell wasn't there, nor in the living room. The front door was wide open and a cold breeze ruffled the pages of the books on the floor of the shallow entrance hall. Holy Catfish. That accounted for the crafty look. Rick had visions of a wrecked car and a badly damaged driver. Then he managed to spot the dark bulk of the Buick on the right of the driveway. He ran down the steps, shouting, expecting to hear the whirr of the motor. The car was empty. A rustle of leaves startled him. Around the opposite corner of the house he made out Pell's wavering figure. Must have been chasing pack rats. Rick grinned with relief. "Come in, you idiot." He took a firm hold on Pell's arm and led him into the house, turning the key in the old-fashioned lock and dropping it into his pocket. "Hey, you, give me my keys."

Pell teetered on the heels of his thin, damp slippers, giggling.

"What's so funny? Give me those keys."

"Keys in leaves. Nobody leaves. Keys in leaves. . . ." Pell laughed with shrill malicious pleasure.

H. Peculiar Henry. So that was that! Not a Chinaman's chance of finding them in the darkness, even with a flashlight. Better wait till morning and go after them with a rake.

For a short time Pell was as docile as a child who has played a successful prank on a watchful adult. He sat on the kitchen table downing coffee and egg sandwiches, singing *A World Turned Upside Down* and expounding, between lusty belches, his theories on the general upside-downness of American civilization. When Rick turned his back to attack the pile of dirty dishes in the sink, Pell made a sudden dash for the telephone. Rick dropped a plate, ran after him and overheard Pell carefully spelling out a message to Western Union: "Do not let your footsteps in the snow behind you turn your head."

"That'll fix him," Pell chortled. "Sells Young Love to the women's magazines. Thinks he's Shakespeare."

Rick remembered grimly all the crazy telegrams he had sent when he was drunk. There had been a cable to George W. Bustard, an important official in the chicle company: "Bustard—Bustard—Bustard—Bustard—Bustard—Bustard—Bustard—Bustard—Bustard—*bastard*." He had counted the ten words meticulously. No wonder this little habit and the telephone calls he had made at three or four in the morning, waking men to explain to them in slow, clipped accents what stuffed shirts they were, had cost him several promotions. "Rickham's a terrible souse, but no one can beat him in the bush." He had known that was his reputation and he had been proud of it. Proud and angry and ashamed.

Pell was studying the Norwalk phone book, holding it upside down and moving his finger from line to line. "Can't find it. Wrote it down on a gin bottle. Thraves must have thrown bottle away. Insubordinate cuss." He fumbled for the O on the dial and shouted, "Norwalk Hospital. Norwalk Hospital. 'S'matter of life and death. Got to call my wife."

"No, you don't." Rick put a quick finger on the hook. "Call her tomorrow. You're going to bed now." He was surprised that Pell allowed himself to be propelled upstairs without any argument.

Rick went into the sun room, took off his shoes, pulled up the heavy army blanket. It smelled of stale liquor, but he must have slept because another smell woke him. An acrid, pungent smell—like burning paper. Not even stopping to put on his shoes, he made for the stairs. A thick smudge was rising from the waste basket where Pell evidently had thrown a lighted cigarette. Fortunately, he had also knocked over a glass of soda-water so that the damp papers had not ignited into a real blaze. Pell lay on his back, sound asleep in spite of a mingled coughing and snoring. Rick snatched the basket, flung it in the tub of the bathroom and turned on the faucet. The smudge died out quickly and Rick returned to Pell's room, opening the windows and letting in a rush of damp, cold air. Light filled the eastern sky. Rick looked at his watch. Seven twenty. Better hunt for his keys while Pell was still asleep.

Rick turned to the left off the driveway about where he judged Pell had emerged from the darkness last night. "Needle in a haystack," he muttered, kicking at a heap of wet leaves. Small cedars stood ahead of him. Heavy drops of dew dripped off a lighter, brighter something at the tip of a low cedar branch. Rick stepped nearer. The brighter something was the long, flat key to his safety-deposit box. The keyring must have caught miraculously on a twig when Pell had tossed it. Thank God. Maybe it was a good sign. Maybe his luck had turned. Rick grinned, thinking that Tony and a lot of the A.A.s wouldn't call it "luck." He felt better anyhow. Last night he had been cross and depressed because he wasn't doing anything for Pell that a nurse couldn't have done just as well. Now, he knew that Pell had done something for him. There was sense to this twelfth step of the A.A. program. The process of seeing yourself as others see you was like a dose of calomel, strong but cleansing.

It was Emily who suggested that he take Pell to High Pines when he called her to apologize for not phoning her last night. Her voice came to him with its special quality of quiet confidence. No, she hadn't been worried—but Gail had. She had come into Emily's room at six, fretting because Rick wasn't home, afraid he'd gone out and gotten drunk. "Not a chance." Rick felt more confidence in the statement than at any time in the last six weeks.

He wasted no time calling High Pines, arranging for them to take Pell in, getting Pell dressed and bundling him into the back of the car. He was filled with a fine, alert competence.

Going into second on the steep hill between the tall dark trees which gave High Pines its name, he was assailed by his first doubt. Pell was still sleeping when Rick looked back at a red traffic light in Stamford. Suppose he woke up now and raised hell about being taken to a strange place?

A side door opened and two hospital orderlies came out, followed by a big man in a blue suit, who stopped on the steps to look them over. Rick recognized Dr. Wales from MacKenzie's description of his thick white hair and lean youthful face.

Pell jerked awake, shielded his eyes with his right hand and peered out of the car window like a sentry caught napping at his lookout. "Gad, sir, we made it," he congratulated Rick as an orderly opened the car door. Pell stepped out and, spotting the commanding presence on the steps, assumed an exaggerated military stride. Behind him Rick winked at Dr. Wales. Pell stopped abruptly, clicking his heels and saluting.

"General Washington, I presume."

Wales returned the salute. "At your service, sir."

"General Lee knows this terrain, sir." Pell indicated Rick with a sweeping, commendatory gesture and hiccoughed loudly.

"My men will attend to your wants, sir." Wales nodded to the grinning orderlies and Pell, with another salute, marched off majestically between them.

Rick looked at Wales admiringly. "You certainly caught on fast, Doctor. I've been Light-Horse Harry Lee or Dan'l Boone all night." He followed Wales into a small office, gave him what information he could about Pell. "Sorry I don't know much about his finances," he concluded, "but I'll stand back of his expenses for a week if there's any difficulty. You'll call me if he gets in a state to talk sense, won't you?"

"Right." Wales shook Rick's hand. "Great organization you belong to, Mr. Rickham."

Thraves had used the same words—but they hadn't meant the same thing. Rick felt pride in the doctor's approval of A.A. Pride in his own power to stick through a long, exhausting night. Only he wasn't exhausted. He had never felt better in his life. As he turned the car down the steep hill between the tall dark pines, he was filled with an immense contentment.

X

DIVING ROCK

Rick could never get to sleep the night before going duck shooting. In addition to a Night-before-Christmas anticipation, he was possessed by a dozen adult anxieties. Had he set his alarm clock? Would the damn contrivance go off? Would he hear it? He got out of bed to make sure and then his mind started to fumble over the contents of his duffle bag. Had he forgotten his flashlight? It would be dark when Hank came by for him. Had he rewound the line on the anchors of his decoys? Had he put the extra heavy load in the left pocket of his hunting coat and the medium in the right? He had worked out a system, due to the shortage of shells—using a medium load when the ducks were close to the blind, saving the heavy ones in his left barrel for long shots. God only knew when you'd be able to buy twelve gauge again. H. Peculiar Henry. If he mixed the shells in his pocket . . . he better go look. He threw back the blankets, slid into his slippers and pulled on a flannel bathrobe.

Moonlight came through the window at the top of the stairs, enabling him to feel his way without turning on a light. The worn Brussels carpet muffled his steps. No point in being so quiet—twenty burglars could romp through the house without waking either Emily or Gail. The only way they ever knew when he had been up and about at all hours of the night was by the traces Emerald found in the morning on the kitchen sink—opened cans of crabmeat or sardines, jars of big green olives, the dried skeleton of a bunch of grapes or the last piece of meat from the bone of a steak. "What's we-all going to eat for our lunch today?" Emerald would ask Emily after breakfast. "Isn't there enough of that steak to do something with?" Emily would counter and then laugh, realizing that Rick must have been foraging again. Emerald would shake her head over Mr. Rickham's extravagance. "Likely that man he goin' to eat us outen house and home."

Crabmeat, sardines, olives, even a piece of steak were cheaper than liquor. Rick justified his substitute cravings, but they were not as soporific. He had always been an uncertain sleeper, always depended on a stiff nightcap, but since he had quit drinking he had hardly had a decent night's rest. Anything and everything seemed to keep him awake—A.A. meetings particularly. He would come home over-stimulated, his mind full of other people's problems—and his own. The night after his call on Pell had been the only exception. Then he had fallen asleep like a two year old.

His knapsack and two thermos bottles stood ready on the kitchen table. Emily insisted that he take hot soup as well as coffee when he went duck shooting, convinced that the gallons of coffee he drank daily were to blame for his restlessness. But you had to drink something—or did you? A highball would be the answer now, a long tall drink he could carry upstairs and sip slowly with a cigarette, feeling the warmth quieting, relaxing him. He might just smell it anyhow. There was a small supply in the pantry cupboard which Emily kept for guests. He pulled out a bottle of Scotch and sniffed. Surprisingly, it was disappointing. He tried Rye . . . m-m-m . . . n-n-n? He put it down. He studied the label of another bottle—maybe Bourbon would small better. He unscrewed the cap. Better, but still not what he wanted. Suddenly he knew he wanted rum and lime and the scent of the Tropics. And there wasn't any rum. To hell with it then.

In the front hall he checked the pockets of his hunting coat with the aid of his flashlight, found that the shells had been correctly arranged, picked up a couple of apples from a pewter bowl on the table and climbed the stairs. Had he been kidding himself about only wanting to smell that liquor? *Would he have taken a drink of rum if he had found it?* He didn't know. He honestly didn't know. Hank said "slips" were deliberate. Hank would tell him he had been playing with fire . . . fire-water could raise more hell than fire—the Indians had named it well . . . he had called it "fear-water" himself when the black, faceless terrors of a hangover had pursued him like the hounds of heaven. . . . Thank God he would be out on the harbor with Hank in a few more hours, coping with wind and tide.

A moderate nor'wester was blowing when Hank and Rick passed the Power Plant and saw their first duck in the edge of the marsh grass near Park Island.

"Drop your oars and grab your gun," Hank whispered.

"Your bird." Rick pushed on his oars, propelling the boat stern-first so that Hank in the middle seat would face the duck and be able to shoot without blazing over Rick's head. "But we'll never get in range before he flies."

Rick kept the skiff close to the high bank, then let it drift quietly with only an occasional flip of an oar to keep it stern-first. Nearer and nearer they coasted, bent low, trying not to move their heads or their bodies. Now they could see the duck plainly, a large "blackie." Now they were in range but still Hank didn't shoot. "Get nearer," he whispered. Rick eased along noiselessly another ten feet till he could see the bird's right eye watching them, bright as a brown shoe button. "He must be crippled already."

"Bit nearer."

"What do you want me to do, run him down?" Rick could not understand either Hank—or the duck. Why didn't the black fly, or swim? Unless he thought the few wisps of grass hid him sufficiently and his safest course was immobility. They were now too close to shoot without blowing the duck to pieces. Rick waited for Hank to clap his hands to startle the bird into flight, then shoot at a more respectable range. To his amazement, Hank was raising his automatic shotgun—at less than ten yards—and taking careful aim. Bang!

The big duck exploded off the water, straight upward twenty feet. Then the strong northwest wind seemed to catch him and hold him fixed for a second. Probably he was bewildered and studying his course. Hank let go another shot. Not a feather dropped, the bird wheeled and hurtled down wind.

Hank was muttering and sputtering that the blasted barrel of his shotgun musta gotten bent. Rick could not keep from grinning behind Hank's back, but he managed to hold his tongue about Hank's odd behavior in shooting a sitting duck. Funny damn thing. Hank had acted like a regular sportsman about fishing, refusing to use ganghooks for bass because they didn't give the fish a fair chance, and now here he was violating a fundamental rule of hunters.

Still muttering, Hank pulled on his oars and headed toward the north end of Brush Island, where they beached the flat-bottomed skiff high in the marsh grass. On a narrow point, sheltered by a crescent formation of rock, Hank had built a rough blind. He waded out now in his rubber hip-boots and arranged two broadbill decoys in the shallow water to the east, putting three broadbills and two blacks just off the marsh grass to the south. "All set," he grinned and offered Rick the better eastern spot in the blind. Rick refused. He was more interested in watching Hank than in shooting himself. They had waited nearly half an hour in the cold wind when Hank whispered "Mark, East!"

A lone whistler was stooling in from their left.

"Your bird," Rick whispered again.

The duck was stooling in perfectly, yet Hank waited. Waited. Even when the drake offered the easiest shot, just as he braked his wings and seemed to stand still before dropping into the water, Hank did not shoot. Rick was torn between indignation and amusement. What in the hell was the matter with the guy! The duck was paddling up to the westernmost decoy when Hank finally drew a careful bead—and missed. The bird scrambled out of the water and was pulling off to the west, when Rick knocked him down.

"Your gun spreads the shot more'n mine," Hank mumbled.

Rick reached over for Hank's automatic, aimed at the flapping golden-eye. The pellets kicked up the water in a fine circle, and the circle had a center—the golden-eye stopped flapping.

"Nothing the matter with your gun, Hank. What did you have to drink last night?"

"Five or six cokes."

"No wonder, five or six cokes would make my hand shake like a leaf."

"You mean that?"

"Sure, a friend of mine, who's a doctor, told me that a man came to see him with what looked like a fine case of alcoholic jitters, but the fellow swore he never touched a drop. The doctor couldn't account for it till he finally found out that the guy was in the habit of drinking ten to twelve cokes a day."

"Holy Jumpin' Catfish, is that right?"

"I guess it's the same as a coupla beers," Rick pondered, "a coupla cokes won't hurt you either, but moderation seems to be a hell of a hard word to learn. It is for me, God knows."

Hank cocked one eyebrow at Rick. "Reckon a guy has to hold on to a few bad habits, though. Can't expect to reform himself all to one fell swoop. Speakin' of which, how about breakin' out that there thermos o' coffee while I retrieve Mr. Whistler. Too bad we ain't got no dog along."

It *was* too bad, for it took Hank nearly ten minutes to go back across the island, launch the skiff, pick up the duck, hide the boat again and return to the blind. During which time one bunch of six blacks heading for the stool flared off as Hank rowed around the point, and two broadbills coming dead upwind sheared off toward Sunken Rock when they sighted Hank stowing the boat in the marsh grass.

Two mergansers, a reddish brown female and handsome black and white drake, swam up to the decoys, leisurely inspected them and leisurely swam away. Rick watched to see if Hank would shoot.

"Feller up to Darien says you can make merganser breast edible by soakin' it in vinegar and parboilin' it. Hell, you could make an old shoe real tasty with that much trouble."

Rick laughed. "Reminds me of the time I shot a cormorant in Quintana Roo. Gave it to a Mexican who cooked it with lots of garlic. Said the garlic kept you from tasting the cormorant and the cormorant kept you from tasting the garlic." Rick emptied the dregs of his coffee, screwed the top back on the thermos and studied the oyster grey sky. Not a duck in sight. He moved his long legs restlessly in the cramped blind. "Joe and I found plenty of birds at Diving Rock last week. How about it, Hank? Let's shove off and try our luck over there."

"Nope."

There had been plenty of birds at Diving Rock when Hank had gone out there late last December—and plenty of memories. Too damn many memories. One of the men at the boatyard had just heard that his son was in a Nazi prison camp and that had set Hank to cursing this blasted war and worrying about his own son. Steve was in the Pacific and the Japs didn't go in for prison camps. It wasn't a happy thought. Hank had come home early in a state of depression which had put the idea of a drink into his head for the first time in months, but a drink wouldn't do any good, he told himself, he'd just pull out of a hangover and there'd still be the war and his worry about Steve. A piece of daylight remained. He would go out and take a crack at some broadbills. He climbed the curved stairs, thinking of all the other Frosts whose feet had worn the steep treads, seeing Steve the first time he had managed to reach the top by himself, hanging on to the fluted railing and looking down at his father with a triumphant baby smile. In his bedroom he took down his heavy twelve-gauge shotgun from the rack where it lay beneath Steve's lighter twenty. He had promised Steve a twelve for Christmas . . . Steve flying over some swampy, stinking island shooting little yellow devils instead of ducks.

His rubber boots creaked against the stern seat as he leaned against the oars. The tide was too high, no cover on the reef off Greenway's. He'd have to go on to Diving Rock even though he would have scant time to shoot after he got there. Two broadbills winged across his wake, long range. He tried for the rear one. Missed. But the report brought more ducks than he had ever seen off the water westward of Red Nun Buoy #2. They were canny critters, all right, seeming to know how short the season was now-a-days. He could remember when he and his father used to go after 'em in January off Diving Rock.

Remember too the icy nor'west morning when Steve shot his first duck with that little twenty gauge. Hank had been behind the rock bringing over the knapsack with cocoa and sandwiches when he heard Steve shoot twice. Then he heard Steve yell, "I got one, Pop, I got one."

Steve had joked about that duck ever since. "I got my first shot at a duck, anyhow," he would laugh after a miss and Hank would say, "That bird practically climbed down your barrel, Son," and Steve would recognize the pride in his father's voice and grin.

Hank landed on the windward side of the same beach. Keeping the water below the leak in the knee of his left boot, he dropped the lead rectangular frames which served both as anchors and reels for his decoys. He had brought only two blacks and three broadbills. He agreed with some fellow in *Field and Stream* that "large flocks of decoys mean hunters to wild ducks." They sure were canny critters, but these decoys would fool 'em. Sitting with a brown, barnacle-covered boulder between him and the sharp wind, he watched the decoys tacking first southwest, then northwest, in and out of his sight. Mighty lifelike. Mighty pretty, too, against the darkening water of the Sound.

He had waited less than five minutes when a big black drake came straight at his eastern-most decoy, coasting in not fifteen feet high. Straight at him. He held his fire until it was almost over the decoy, hoping to drop it there so it would drift against the reef and save getting out the boat. He had figured it right. By walking only twenty-five yards and wading to mid-calf he could just reach it and rake it in with the barrel of his gun. It was a big bird. An ample meal for two. Only him and the old woman to eat now. Steve could always wolf a whole duck himself. Six broadbills whipped across the far edge of the reef. He might just reach them, but he let them go. No use wasting a cartridge.

He poured coffee from the thermos into the outer red cap, set it down on the pebbly beach while he re-corked the bottle and screwed on the inner white cap. Reaching for the red cup, his eye fell on a small metal object, about the size and shape of a thimble. He picked it up—a copper cartridge butt—and twenty gauge. One of Steve's. Left here last year, or the year before. How long would copper stand salt water? His grandfather's ships had been sheathed in copper, not just covered with copper paint to the waterline . . . his grandfather, Stephen Frost, master shipbuilder; his son, Stephen Frost, bomber pilot.

Taking off his light wool shooting glove, he slipped the copper shell-cap into his trouser pocket with his keys, his lucky Spanish-American War silver dollar an uncle had brought back from Manila when Hank was a small boy, and a quartz pebble he had picked up at Mount Tom when he was courting the old woman. Oblivious to the leak in his left boot, he waded out and began gathering in the decoys. He worked fast, not bothering to wind the marlin onto the anchors, just twisting it anyway across the body of each balsa bird. He couldn't stay there thinking of Steve. He loved this rock. But his love was, he calculated, five percent for the rock itself, twenty percent for his father, and seventy-five percent for Steve.

He would never come to Diving Rock again until he could come with Steve. And that might mean . . . he would never come to Diving Rock again. His heart was heavier than the bag of decoys he lugged over the saddleback beach. Fumbling with the oars in his blind misery, he started to row home. Over his right shoulder the sun was setting—long yellow streaks under dark masses of clouds. Gulls settled on Diving Rock like white snowflakes. As they had done in his grandfather's time, as they had done when the first Frost came to Cos Cob harbor in 1640.

He remembered gulls following his troopship across the Atlantic in 1917. Gulls that had seemed a symbol of the home to which he might never return. Gulls that had flown out to welcome him off Sandy Hook in the spring of '19. "Gulls!" he cried, "Bring Steve back. Bring Steve back."

"Nope," Hank repeated.

What the hell was the matter with the guy? Rick was all set for an argument, then he took one look at the closed agony in Hank's half-averted face and said quickly, "Guess you're right at that. The wind seems to be dying down pretty fast."

But he was puzzled. Puzzled by Hank's sudden aversion to Diving Rock and his peculiar habit of shooting "sitters." It was the end of the season before he got any answers.

A week of cold, rainy weather had driven Joe out of his unheated garage and Rick, Emily and Gail back to New York. Joe had urged Rick to come out every Friday for the Greenwich A.A. meeting and spend Saturday shooting. They had had a couple of good ducking days together, then Rick had spent a weekend with Manton at a fancy shooting club on Barnegat Bay and kept thinking of Hank. H. Peculiar Henry, it would be fun to see Manton and Hank in the same blind. Manton, of course, would regard shooting a sitting duck as outright murder. He was such an extreme advocate of Sport for Sport's sake that even the other members of the club kidded him about refusing easy shots and called him the fanatical fusilier. Rick knew what Manton would think of Hank. He wondered what Hank would say about Manton.

The question finally came up on a cold December morning. Hank wanted to try Great Island in Greenwich Cove, which meant nearly a two-mile row and an extra early start. The setting moon was meshed in the pine trees on the Greenway estate as they rowed southward over the ruffled muddy waves. With the setting of the moon the weather changed abruptly. The wind backed from easy to northeast and stiffened.

"Good sign." Hank was jubilant, "When the wind backs agin the sun that means dirty weather—and dirty weather's what brings them ducks inshore."

"Which," Rick laughed, "is about the only simple rule in duck shooting around here." He was envying Hank his intimate knowledge of the winds and tides along the Sound. You had to consider the wind first of course, not only in calculating your aim, but in setting out your decoys, putting them to leeward so that you could shoot at the breasts of the ducks as they came slowly upwind to land, rather than at their armored tails as they hurtled over. First, last and always, however, you had to consider the tide. The tide was the big complication. Rick had done most of his shooting near La Cienaga Grande, west of Santa Marta, Colombia, where the difference between high and low tide is only about eighteen inches, and in the waters around Belize, where the rise and fall is two feet—sometimes less. But Cos Cob harbor has six or seven feet—sometimes more. "Figure that the ducks will hug the windward shore on a day like this," he said. "Figure on setting your decoys to leeward . . . and if you don't figure on the tide you'll find yourself on a mud flat!"

Hank grinned. "Figgerin's half the fun, ain't it?"

"Right." Rick enjoyed the challenge of the tide as much as Hank did, but you could never convince anyone like Manton that the fishing and hunting around Cos Cob harbor were anything but tame. He looked at the black windy sky and the black choppy water. "Wish it would snow."

"Wouldn't wonder if it did before we get back." Hank stuck his hand in the water. "Water's warmer'n the air, now. And the flood's runnin' good. I calculate to set our stool on the sou'west o' Great Island. She'll flare both ways round the point and make our ducks swim real lifelike."

Rick was amused by Hank's collective use of the old word "stool," which came from the early days when live ducks were used as decoys and rested on small wooden perches. And he was amused by Hank's calling a single decoy a "duck"—although that was often confusing.

"Never did much figgerin' about where to set the stool in my drinkin' days," Hank admitted with a reminiscent grin. "Used to go out with a feller by the name of Bill Daly. All the figgerin' we did was how many pints o' liquor we had along with us. Wonder is we never blowed our fool heads off."

Rick had not missed liquor when he was out shooting with Joe and Hank. Not even on the weekend with Manton, when everyone had hurried in from the blinds to sit around a fire with highball glasses in their hands. But now he saw himself on the porch at the Polo Club in Belize after a day on the salt marshes, saw cormorants and pelicans riding the waves, and smelled the sweet lime sharpness of a rum collins.

"Think we'll ever get liquor out of our heads, Hank?" It was out of his body now—he felt stronger, younger than he had in years—and his nerves were steadier, less jumpy, but he was still quick to anger and his mind still played the same old alcoholic tricks on him, always seemed ready with the old answer, "A drink would fix it." After that night, when he had stuck it out with Pell, he had felt a fine confidence that he would never drink again, but the confidence ebbed when things went wrong at the office—when Driscomb got in his hair, when Gail . . . she was still playing around with Paul, still resentful of any criticism. He couldn't get at her. Maybe if he had had a son like Hank—

"Liquor's bin in our heads maybe twenty-thirty years, can't rightly expect to git it out too fast. Alkies is funny people anyhow. Tide kinda puts me in mind of an alky's nerves. Most fellers feel high some days and low the next, but an alky has regular perigee tides o' feelin'—way down in the mudflats, and then way up in a big flood when you think you gotta make whoopee all over the shoreline to show how high you feel."

"Good metaphor," Rick said, surprised at Hank's figure of speech, surprised that Hank understood the violent ups and downs of emotion which he had thought peculiar to himself. A.A. certainly got you over the notion that you were an odd ball. At nearly every meeting some speaker told some personal experience which dispelled Rick's sense of desperate and grandiose isolation. Hank was right—alkies were funny people. And he, Avery Rickham, was one of them—"one of them" was a new feeling. A fine, belonging, herd-instinct feeling. "Group therapy"—the cold phrase had turned warm and alive with meaning.

They were coming in close to Great Island now, a scant half an acre of rocks and grass, with the wind freshening every minute and a curtain of cloud delaying the visibility. Hank pulled out his father's hunting-case silver watch which served him as both timepiece and compass—if he had the right time he could always check on the tide and find his way even in a fog, by the feel of the water, the action of weed and driftwood and the depth and nature of the bottom which he measured with a six-ounce sinker on a blackfish line. "Forty minutes to sunrise," he announced with satisfaction. "Plenty o' time to git our dunnage unloaded an' our stool set."

Hank used the flashlight sparingly, arranging two small but solid wooden boxes as seats on the wet, slippery grass which was tall enough to hide everything except their brown shooting caps with furred ear flaps. Both men wore waterproof trousers and heavy sheepskin coats. Rick started to open his collar—after the long row and the first swallow of coffee Hank had handed him he was almost too hot—but a sudden grit-grit sound, like sand thrown against a wire screen, made him button it up again in a hurry. He had gotten his wish all right. It had started to snow. Hard dry particles were striking the blades of marsh grass with a sharp grating sound.

A whistle of wings and a cautious quack told them that birds were already passing overhead or mingling with the decoys. Faintly, they could make out two moving shapes—or was it three? Hard to tell, for the decoys themselves tacked back and forth in the northeast wind, "swimmin' real lifelike," as Hank had predicted.

"Three," Rick whispered. He had finally managed to count twelve shapes and there were only nine decoys. Then the three extras paddled away toward Sand Island.

"Don't worry," Hank whispered back, "plenty more's a-comin'.

Conditions is just about right. We'll get our limit today, or my name ain't Henry Cotton Frost, the Third."

With the increasing light three more blacks landed on the water and swam slowly into range. Rick watched Hank raise his gun, lower it, raise again and lower it. All his admiration for Hank's knowledge of winds and tides vanished and his former incredulous irritation burst out in an angry whisper, "What's the matter, want to catch 'em with your hands?"

"Waitin' for 'em to cluster."

Rick could hardly believe his ears. He saw the three ducks swim into a straight line, saw Hank fire, hitting two with his first shot and actually knocking the third with his next as it rose into the air. Hank waded out and retrieved the blacks. When he came back his manner was tense. He laid his automatic against a dead cedar stump and looked at Rick, his thick eyebrows pulled into angry half-circles over his owl eyes.

"So, you wouldn't shoot a sitter, is that what's ailin' you? 'Specially, you would refuse to shoot if three ducks was clustered. Holy Jumpin' Catfish, Rick, would you pick three berries in one bunch, or wouldn't you?"

"That's different." Rick tried to keep from laughing. Hank would have to think up a better one than that.

"Not with me, it ain't different. I'm out for food. 'Specially now, what with meat scarce and rationed." He took off his hunting cap and scratched his thick black hair, his eyebrows moving into a puzzled scowl. "On the other hand, must say I wouldn't shoot one o' them tame mallards under the railroad bridge."

"Not really? Why wouldn't you shoot a tame mallard?" Rick's tone was good-humored but mocking. He was finding out what he had wanted to know ever since the first day he had shot with Hank. Now that the argument was out in the open he felt better but he watched Hank's face anxiously to see how much kidding he could take.

Hank started to say, "Shootin' a tame mallard's too easy," but saw the trap in time. His eyes crinkled. "Easier to toll one in with bread and wring his neck."

Rick laughed, "Would you shoot a sitting rabbit—or a partridge?"

"Sure."

"I wouldn't."

"But you'd shoot a standin' deer, or a moose?"

"Sure."

"Hell's bells, what's the difference?"

"Difference is—I'd use a rifle."

"You got a point there, Rick," Hank admitted, "but you're playin' a game. I'm after meat. You think I should crawl through the muck and the weeds and get my ass half froze and then give Mr. Whistler a warnin' so's he can get up and fly? Hell, if you aim to make this here duckin' a game, why not go to a shootin' gallery and pop at clay pipes?" He had taken Steve over to the State Fair in Danbury when Steve was so small Hank had to hold him up to the level of the pipes and a crowd had gathered to watch the kid knock 'em down. The memory cheered him— Steve ought to have pretty good luck shootin' at them pesky Japs.

"Atta boy, Hank! Talk about *reductio ad absurdum*. You sure knocked the stuffing out of the sportsman's code." Rick pounded Hank on the back. There was sense to Hank's point of view. As much sense as to Manton's—probably more.

The rest of the morning Hank seemed hell-bent on proving to Rick that he could make the hardest, fanciest shots if he had a mind to. As the blacks swung toward the decoys Hank, who usually held his fire until after their preliminary circling, would let go. He got two, then one, then two. All of them long shots, none of them easy, and two distinctly circus performances. He could not seem to miss. The last of the five shots was made at a duck a good sixty yards behind him, crossing at right angles to the northern tip of the island. He fell backward off his box, but the duck fell too. Hank picked himself up and winked at Rick. "Ain't such a waste o' ammunition as I thought."

Rick was pleased at the result of his criticism of Hank, but he wasn't pleased with his own record. He had missed a whistler with his right barrel, crippeed it with his left as it towered over his head, and had to use a third shell to finish it off. "Talk about wasting ammunition," he muttered. The first time Rick had gone ducking with Hank he had discovered that although Hank knew more about fishing, more about winds and tides, he could give Hank pointers on guns, loads and angles and was a better shot. When he knocked down a black pulling straight over him he felt better, for this shot, which looks easy to a beginner, is never easy. He made three doubles in succession and by early afternoon each man had his limit of ten birds, plus mergansers.

The snow had stopped, but the wind was rising ominously.

"Shouldn't wonder if the glass is fallin'," Hank said sharply. "Snow stoppin' makes me suspicion this wind. We'd better grab a coupla sandwiches and make tracks for home quick as we can."

But it was a slow and ticklish chore getting in the decoys. Ice had formed on the wooden backs and on the anchor lines, so they had to abandon the practice of winding the lines and loop them around the heads, hoping to avoid snarls. When they finally got to the boat, only three oars were to be found.

"How the hell did that happen?"

"Musta fell overboard when one of us was retrievin' dead birds," Hank muttered. "No use cussin' at our carelessness now. No use wastin' time lookin' for it, neither. Git in the stern, Rick, I'll row." His voice was steady but urgent.

Waves, short and eager like stormy lake waves, gnawed at the weather gunwale as they headed across Greenwich Cove toward the shelter of Indian Head. That is, they were aiming toward the shelter, but the wind threw them off the course so much, in spite of the tide which was with them, that Hank shouted maybe he'd better head upwind and land, where they could leave the boat and walk home.

"You're the doctor," Rick shouted back.

Hank turned the boat, bringing his back three-quarters to the wind and Rick nearly facing it. Rick jabbed his forefinger to windward. "Squall," he shouted.

A sheet of spray, white as swirling snow and twenty feet high, was coming toward them down the channel from the northeast, traveling at a terrific speed.

Hank spun the bow to face the squall. It was the only thing he could do. There was no time now to reach land.

The first line of the squall seemed to lift them and fling them back ten feet, but miraculously the bow stayed into the wind, although for a few seconds the oars were almost useless.

If it keeps up, Rick thought, we're goners. No boat could survive and certainly no man could steer in this blow. But after the first freakish blast the wind steadied into a regular gale, about twice as hard as when they had left the island.

Hank settled to the grim struggle of keeping the bow into it. He seemed to be managing when one oar jumped the oarlock. No sooner had he recovered it, than the other oar jumped. With the jerky seas, the tide running strongly at right angles now on their altered course, and the battering of the wind, it seemed impossible for Hank to keep the oars in place.

Quickly, Rick pushed the two guns and the stern anchor behind him to counterbalance the forward shift of his own weight as he dove flat with his belly on the middle seat and reached a hand over each of the oarlocks. His grip would hold the oars in place—if he could hold it.

Neither of them tried to speak now. Both knew that so long as they could keep the skiff's nose into the wind they had a prayer, though even in this position the waves might prove too big and swamp the boat before they could reach the shore a mile or more to leeward. Rick lifted his head cautiously; he was still clutching the oarlocks, a wave hit him in the face but, shaking the water out of his eyes, he could see Murderers' Island and Diving Rock ahead. There was a house on Murderers' Island—shelter—if they could reach it. If. . . . But the way the tide was setting them sideways the likeliest chance seemed to be Diving Rock. Would the tide set them enough to the northward to fetch the Rock, or would the natural direction of the wind drive them between the Rock and Murderers' Island . . . and out into open water, running higher and higher up the lee shore? The idea that the wind might be strong enough to *flatten* the waves flashed through Rick's mind.

Hank well knew it was not—the first blast had been strong enough but if that had kept up they would be swimming now—or drowned. He was trying ever so carefully to swing the bow to the east of the wind's eye. He nearly turned it too far the first time . . . the wind seized the bow and tossed it through east toward south. Hank dug in his left oar and, thanks to Rick's grip which held it from jumping the oarlock, managed to bite the blade into the vicious, white-crested water till the bow was back in the wind's eye. Mostly, he would have to trust to the tide to pull them in, but he tried once more to easten the bow a bit. This time he was even more cautious. And now the wind seemed to be losing its steadiness and coming in gusts with small lulls of lesser violence.

He yelled at Rick to watch to windward and coach him so that he could take advantage of any slackening. This way he managed to make a distinct bit of westing—turning the stern westward toward the Rock—twenty feet now, perhaps, ten feet a minute later.

Suddenly the water was breaking only two boat's lengths off their north side. "This is it!" Rick thought, but Hank knew the reef, knew that if he could edge in still closer to the smashing line of water they would either be thrown tail first onto the Rock—or at worst be a dozen swimming strokes away.

He edged the boat closer.

"She's going to hit hard," he yelled. "When I holler, jump on the Cos Cob side. I'll jump on the outside."

"Okay."

"Jump!"

Rick, covered with frozen spray, his joints stiff from his cramped posture, his hands numb, his fingers seemingly bent into a permanent clutch, managed to slide over the side just as Hank went over the opposite gunwale. The boat shipped water. The gunwale banked Rick's knee against a rock—his shrapnel leg—pain shot through him. It was almost good to feel pain, to know that you could still feel. He hung on grimly, water up to his waist, and helped Hank push her in and around behind the main rock.

"Let go!" Hank shouted. "Take care o' yourself and let the boat go!" Hank had miraculously retrieved the bow anchor and as the wind blew the boat out of their half-frozen hands, he threw it ahead of him into a deep fissure.

They crawled and fell, slipped and clawed over icy boulders till they reached a natural niche on the west side, half protected against the wind.

"Swing your arms," Hank advised, looking at Rick's blue face, "Rowin' kept my blood a-goin'." Rick tried to swing his arms. He felt like a frozen windmill.

Hank went back to the boat twice, returning first with the thermos, lunch basket and one oar, next with two oars and their guns. He succeeded in getting the top off the thermos and held the cup for Rick who was still unable to move his fingers. "Look kinda frost bit," Hank said. "Mustn't heat them fingers too fast."

"Heat 'em fast on what?" Rick managed a feeble grin. He watched Hank plunge into the leeward boil again, bringing back two floorboards from the skiff, getting down on his knees and starting to whittle shavings off one board. Rick knew a few tricks about making a fire in the bush, but how to do it here, in this small lee under icy rocks with the tide only a foot below them? Still, there was no other place. Rick could wiggle his right hand now. He fumbled for his knife, got the blade open with his teeth, found a cartridge in his pocket and was cutting off the top when Hank looked up.

"Good. Four oughta do it. Keep the casin's. They'll burn too."

Hank had saved the wax paper from the sandwiches they had eaten at noon, because he was conscientious about salvage and because, being in the Harbor Patrol, he didn't like littering up the Sound. He spread these now on a flat rock, carefully spilled the powder from the four shells, and laid the cases around the pile after throwing the shot into the water. Rick watched him moving silently, purposefully, unwrapping the remaining food, rolling the paper into loose balls, adding the newspaper which had fortunately lined the basket, except for a piece which he twisted into a tight train, or fuse, into the powder. Hank knew a few tricks too. The chips and slivers went onto the pile next and then the upturned wicker basket. When Hank took a big kitchen match out of his water-tight emergency match safe, Rick moved to the north side and held his coat as a shield. The match scraped against the corrugated surface of the safe—and flamed. Holding it in cupped hands, Hank stooped to the fuse of newspaper. It caught. Both men stepped back quickly. The gunpowder went whoosh and the pile of paper under the basket burst into flame. Hank grabbed the floor boards and struck them savagely against the sharp edge of a boulder. Then he balanced them tepee-fashion over the burning basket and a bright cone of fire shot into the murk. Big flakes of snow whirled in the light, faster, faster.

"Ought to do a war dance." Hank grinned, holding his hands cautiously toward the fire.

"Arrows through the window," Rick muttered.

"What?"

"Oh, just a crazy notion of mine—at least that's what Joe calls it." Maybe Hank would understand—he seemed closer to his ancestors than most people nowadays. "I used to come out of the bush, where there's always plenty of danger, and whenever I got to New York—which wasn't any oftener than I could help—I'd keep wondering what the hell was wrong with the place. It seemed too damn safe. I'd walk around wishing arrows would come through the windows the way they did in our forefather's time."

Hank nodded. "One of my great, great aunts moved out west to Arizony. She used to write her sister how she never dast to sweep her cabin in the middle, always started from the corner so's to keep in reach of her rifle in case a redskin come."

"That's it," Rick said. "And that's why I don't feel too badly about this war. Bombs through the roof—instead of arrows through the window. We had it coming to us. You can't expect luxury without lifting a finger for it. I swallowed all the fancy phrases in the last war, but I can't stomach 'em this time. We're fighting to keep the U.S.A. top dog in the world. Period."

"I get what you mean," Hank exclaimed, his face illumined by the flare of the fire. "Darned if I don't. And if my Steve has to die shootin' them Japs, I'd ruther it 'ud be for somethin' practical like his ancestors done grabbin' land from the Indians." He turned his head and his face was in shadow as he added, "Reckon I owes you an explanation, Rick. Reason I refused to go to Divin' Rock that other time was—I uster come out here with Steve. Made a vow not to set foot on this here Rock till Steve come home. And look at me now. Wind and tide sure made a monkey outa me."

Rick was aware of an old partridge whir in his head, which he recognized as the sound—or sensation—he always experienced in a tight spot. He'd been in plenty before, but this looked bad. Now that the first relief at landing anywhere, the first cheer of the fire, had worn off, it seemed pretty ironic to freeze to death in the mouth of Cos Cob harbor, within sight of the nearest houses—but the nearest houses were all closed for the winter. Hadn't he seen a caretaker a couple of weeks ago burning garbage at one of the big places to the northeast? If he happened to notice their fire . . . if they could signal to him . . . if. . . .

It was darkening fast now, in spite of daylight saving. Storm clouds heavy with snow were hurrying the dusk into night. Hank straightened suddenly.

"Reckon Joe would think we was both crazy, standin' here gabbin'. Got to make up our minds what we're goin' to do."

"You're the doctor."

"Way I see it—we got two courses open to us. Stay here an' try to keep above the tide and likely freeze to death, waitin' till we can get the boat out; or make on hell of a big blaze and hope the police down to the Power Plant or the Coast Guard'll spot it. In which case we gotta burn the skiff."

"I guess that's our best bet," Rick said, knowing what it meant to Hank to sacrifice the skiff.

Hank was already half way across the rock, pulling in the anchor. Between them they got the boat ashore and with heavy stones stove in one side. Then they wrenched off splintered sideboards and piled them on the fire. When these caught they dragged the battered hull and leaned it against the rock, its stern on the fire, its bow pointing skyward.

They stood back with grim satisfaction. Hank found the sandwiches, handed a couple to Rick and took a swig of coffee. Then, as the flames swirled up the outline of the skiff, Hank crawled to the highest boulder and stood there waving his arms against the spray.

Bang, bang, bang. Bang, bang, bang. Rick had picked up Hank's automatic and with stiff fingers was sending salvos of three shots into the air. He would keep it up as long as the shells lasted. He grinned at the irony of using all their treasured ammunition.

Outside the circle of fire, black night surrounded them now. The flames from the skiff's bow were flattened by the wind, waving like an orange pennant. Surely someone would see it . . . but who would be looking out on a night like this?

Hank kept dancing and flinging his arms about till Rick feared he was fall either into the fire—or into the sea.

Bang, bang, bang . . . bang, bang, bang. The orange pennant was drooping now. The fire was dwindling fast. Rick had used all his own cartridges and all of Hank's but nine. He was saving these for a last signal.

Hank crawled down off the rock. "They musta seen it," he said, but Rick knew he was whistling to keep up his courage.

"We've got five more sandwiches, half a thermos of coffee and nine shells." Rick tried to make it sound like a full larder and Abercrombie and Fitch's stock.

The fire was embers and the tide, swollen by the wind, was licking the edges with little, cruel hisses.

"If it weren't for the tide, we could keep ourselves warm in this niche quite a while yet. But up top there, don't figger we could last till the water falls agin. Well, we can always try swimmin' for it."

It was a feeble joke, but Rick managed to laugh, then he shouted, "Hey, look!" There was no need to point. A scimitar of yellow light was waggling back and forth over their heads. They leapt to their feet and waved their arms. The light settled directly on them. Hank pulled off his coat and tossed it about in the wind.

"They seen us," he said. "That's the Patrol boat from Indian Harbor." But he sounded depressed.

"In the nick of time." Rick pounded Hank's shoulder. "Boy, oh, boy, Hollywood couldn't have done better."

"Yup," Hank agreed, still in his dismal tone, "an' I'll never hear the last of it. I've knowed most o' them Harbor Patrol boys since we was kids. Hank Frost, who thinks hisself the most weather-wise guy on the Sound, caught out in a storm an' yellin' for help. I can just hear 'em. Holy Jumpin' Catfish, I'd most ruther o' froze to death!"

The yellow light steadied, cutting a sure path through the darkness like a narrow trail between the living green walls of the bush. "Are you never afraid of *yourself, hombre*?" "No!" Rick's mind shouted in swift confidence. Fear of a squall swamping a small boat, yes. Fear of freezing to death on a rock in the sheltered area of Cos Cob harbor, yes. But the alcoholic terror of himself, no.

"Holy Jumping Catfish!" Rick shouted, his laughter booming out to meet the yellow path as they scrambled down the rock.

XI

DRINKING HORSE

Emily looked from Gail to Rick and back again. It was becoming an habitual gesture. She felt like an umpire at a tennis match, her eyes going anxiously from one side of the net to the other—and there *was* a net, a net they sometimes tried to reach across—a net that more often seemed to turn into a solid wall.

She was sitting between them now in the second row of caterer's chairs at the New York A.A. clubhouse, agitated by their tenseness like an electric battery being charged simultaneously with direct and alternating currents. Gail was nervously opening and shutting her purse, a miniature red leather hatbox, fiddling with her lipstick and compact. Every time she snapped the catch Rick would jerk his head as if a shot had been fired. He was talking in a loud, unnaturally jovial voice to Kidd Whistler, standing in the aisle beside him.

Rick had wanted Gail to come—he was to make his first speech at a New York meeting—and Gail had seemed eager to hear him. But perhaps it had been a mistake. Rick might be self-conscious talking in front of his daughter and Gail's limited experience might keep her from understanding the tragic but heartening sincerity of these alcoholics. Instead of bringing them closer together, as Emily had hoped, tonight might push them still further apart.

They had been far enough apart all Fall. When they first moved back to town, Emily had suggested that they really ought to make some plans for Gail's debut—a small affair, of course, because of the war. Perhaps a tea at home for older people and then a dinner at the Junior League before one of the Assemblies.

Gail had snorted, "But I don't want any party, Aunt Emily, really I don't. Debuts are terribly silly and old-fashioned. Besides, I've got a job."

Rick had looked pleased for a moment. Emily knew that he considered debuts archaic survivals of the tribal youth ceremonies his anthropological friends talked about. But instead of agreeing with Gail for once, his face had darkened suddenly and he had jumped on her last statement with ironic emphasis. "I suppose you consider modeling hats for your precious Daphne Manton a career."

Gail had flushed angrily and Emily had felt like shaking him herself, but tonight it was Gail who had been at fault. Again, Emily felt like an umpire at a tennis match watching the white lines of the court. They had gone to dinner with some other A.A.s at a rather dreary hotel in the neighborhood of the clubhouse. Gail's new black wool dress with its scarlet top and her small black velvet toreador hat had made the whole place seem even drearier, the *table d'hote* food lukewarmer, Mrs. Hank's ancient sealskin shabbier and even the lovely oval of Sylvia Landon's face tired and lined. Gail had been sitting next to Sylvia, who was trying desperately to get into the Waves. "Why don't *you* enlist?" Sylvia had asked and Gail had tossed back her shining bob and laughed, "I'm too young." She hadn't added, "and you're too old, aren't you?" but the very fact of her youth was somehow tactless. An unhappy shadow had crossed Sylvia's sensitive face; Rick had scowled and Emily had blamed Gail for her insensibility—she might at least have worn a plainer, less conspicuous dress. Then with characteristic fairness Emily had shifted the blame to herself—she should have made some suggestion to Gail, but Gail had run downstairs at the last moment and, anyway, Emily had about given up trying to cope with Gail's wardrobe. Daphne Manton's ideas were definitely in the ascendant there.

Kidd Whistler was giving Rick rapid thumbnail sketches of new arrivals. "See that tall guy with the sandy hair, near the door? That's Cubby Burman, the greeter card man, made a fortune in 'em but his wife swears he never wrote her a letter in his life. Drank to forget sex, apparently."

"Maybe the greeting cards tie in with sex too," Rick suggested, thinking of their nauseous sentimentality.

"Could be." Kidd Whistler was obviously not much interested. "Two guys Cubby's talking to are average alkies of the big city nervous type, one's a lawyer, one's a bond salesman, both of 'em started out as social drinkers. And that distinguished-looking gent, looks like an ambassador, see him?" Kidd's flute player's mouth widened into a grin, "He's an undertaker. Ought to hear him tell how he used to drink embalming fluid!"

The narrow hall was filling fast now. As members continued to crowd through the door, Kidd pointed out Ben Kletch, a longshoreman who "could lap it up plenty. Doing a good job though, been dry more than a year," and Milton Kesselberg, that rare thing—a Jewish alcoholic. "Not that we got anything against Jews. Don't misunderstand me. Jews just don't seem to become rum-hounds. Funny thing, but it's true."

Rick wondered if years of persecution, years of living in ghettos, could have anything to do with it, could make the Jew afraid to lose his watchfulness even for a moment in the oblivion of alcohol. Emily was speculating about the Jewish religion, which prescribed in such detail the ways of cooking meats, the feasts and the fasts, could there be any ancient law that had given the Jew an inherited attitude of moderation toward alcohol?

"Be seeing you, folks." Kidd Whistler bounced up and down on his toes and went off toward the speaker's table.

"He ought to wear a white turtle-neck sweater with a big blue Y on his chest," Rick whispered.

Emily smiled. "I notice you didn't say a big red H."

Rick laughed and saw Whistler elbowing his way back. "Harold's about to start. He's putting you in the second slot, okay?"

"Okay." Rick knew that at A.A. meetings the second position was usually given to weak, or unknown speakers, but he didn't care. At a Monks Club or Harvard dinner he would have been insulted, now to his surprise he told himself reasonably that most of the men in this room had been dry longer than he—hell, it was an honor to be asked at all. "Is Bill Griffith speaking first, or last?" He hoped it was last so he could listen and not be worrying about what he was going to say himself. "I'd like to meet him afterwards."

"Hey, haven't you ever met Bill? Gosh, that's a darned shame. Bill's down in Washington tonight."

Rick made an impatient sound in his throat.

"Easy does it, boy." Whistler teetered up and down on his toes. "You'll meet him. Bill's a great guy. Every chapter in the country is after Bill. Can't be two hundred places at once. Not even Bill."

The small frail man behind the speaker's table gave a sudden vigorous rap and then looked around like a startled chipmunk. He had a sallow skin, dark circles under somber brown eyes and a slight, nervous impediment in his speech. "This is the regular Tuesday night meeting of the New York group of Alcoholics Anonymous," he said hurriedly, without giving the crowded room a chance to quiet. Someone in the hall outside which was packed with standees yelled, "Louder," and with a distracted effort he continued, "and the first time I have led a meeting. That may not seem remarkable to the rest of you but to me it is almost as amazing as the fact that I have not had a drink for eleven months." The applause seemed to surprise and disconcert him and again he did not allow time for it to die down. "A year ago it would have taken a quart of gin to get me up here. I used to depend on gin a good deal because I hated small talk and any kind of a party, but in my business, which was real estate, I had to go around to get acquainted with possible buyers and I was always conscious that any woman I happened to be trying to talk to seemed to be looking around at other men. If I joined one of the men and started to make conversation he would invariably say, 'Sorry, Harold, excuse me a jiffy. So-and-so just came in. Got something important to tell him. Be right back.' Only he would never come back. I was a bore. That's what I was. One day after my hostess had asked me if I liked to play bridge or poker or word games, and I had said No to each, I looked her in the eye. 'I'm just a bore,' I stammered. 'In fact, I am the President of the Damn Bore Club.' Three shy guys who overheard me looked at me in relief and edged over. 'We're members of that club, too,' they whispered. After that I used to amuse myself picking out other members. Secretly, of course."

The A.A.s were smiling now, and Harold Parsons, sensing that they were with him, seemed to lose his stammer. "There was never enough to drink at those parties, so I got the habit of liquoring up before I went. It worked fine for a while. I don't know whether I actually stopped being a bore, or whether the gin kept me from caring whether I was or not. The trouble was I didn't really like the taste of gin. I didn't like being a drunk, either. I was afraid of losing my job but by this time I couldn't stop. If I didn't drink I was a damn bore—if I did I was a drunken bum. I wanted to find some way out. I thought of religion. Henry C. Link's books were the first help I got. He gave me an idea—not religion—bridge. Nobody cares what kind of a conversationalist you are the bridge table. All they want to hear is six spades. I took lessons, I studied a system, I subscribed to a bridge magazine, I turned to the bridge column when I opened the newspaper instead of the war news or the stock market or the baseball scores. I became the best bridge player in Jackson Heights—but I couldn't stop drinking. Sometimes I'd bid six spades and not make 'em. But it was bridge that got me into A.A. A fellow I met at a duplicate club in New York brought me to my first meeting. . . ." He stopped abruptly, looking around in bewilderment, and said apologetically, "Sorry, I guess I'm still president of the Damn Bore Club. The first speaker is Carl—tell them your full name, Carl." Harold Parsons wiped his forehead with a crumbled handkerchief, but the applause brought a shy smile to his chipmunk face.

A rotund, blond man with a look of easy humor in his round blue eyes and at the corners of his rather small mouth, waited for the applause to stop. "I guess Harold, here, was being generous—my last name is always good for a laugh, drunk or sober—and I trust you fellows are sober. It's P-e-h-l-e-h-l," he spelled it out, "usually mispronounced Pale Ale. Not that I think my name accounts for my drinking. I'd be an alcoholic all right if my name were Carl Jones. I have been off pale ale and stronger booze now for two years, six weeks, and four days. But I am not going to talk about myself tonight. When an alcoholic doesn't talk about himself—at least that's something original, isn't it? Seriously, I've been thinking a lot about us alcoholics and I have an idea. It's just my own idea, mind you, but I think there's something to it. I've got a theory that there may be such a thing as occupational drinking. Harold mentioned being in real estate and having to go to parties to meet potential buyers or sellers. I hadn't put real estate on my list but I'm going to add it right now." He pulled out a card from his left-hand top pocket and scribbled on it. A ripple of interest went through the audience. A middle-aged woman in the front row nudged her husband and started to whisper. He shushed her impatiently.

Carl Pehlehl looked up from his list. "I don't mean that all the men in the following professions are rummies, but I do believe that all these occupations encourage drinking. First, newspapers. I've never been a reporter myself but I've seen plenty of front-page movies and I guess you've seen 'em too. The boy that makes the scoop is always plastered, isn't he? And in real life there seems to be a tradition of drinking among reporters—maybe it isn't considered as much a part of the game as it used to be—but Joe Kelly . . . I guess everyone of you in A.A. knows Joe Kelly. He's sure helped a lot of us. . . ."

Rick kicked the back of Joe's chair and Joe squirmed uncomfortably—what the hell was Pale Ale going to tell about him?

"As I was saying, Joe told me that when he was on the lobster trick of the old *Sun*, there were six of them and it was understood that one man could be 'sick' and one drunk every night—sick usually meant drunk, didn't it, Joe? And the trouble was they sometimes lost track of whose turn it was to be drunk or 'sick'. One night Joe was the only one to show up—but the wonder of it was, not that Joe showed up, but that there never seemed to be a night when everyone forgot to show up.

"The next occupation on my list here is not . . ." he paused, "bartending!" Pehlehl knew how to get his laughs and wait for them. "No sir, the man behind the bar sees too many of us rummies making fools of ourselves on the other side of the counter. Far as I know there is only one bartender in A.A."

He looked at his card again and went on in his loud, cheerful voice, "Advertising. I'd put a big danger sign on that one. You just about have to drink in agency work. Luncheons are a favorite time for conferences and I gather they're always wet. I've known a lot of smart fellows in advertising and publicity, but if they've got any tendency toward alcohol they're not smart to stay in that business. They are always making excuses and telling you they have to drink because they work under such terrific pressure—a lot of that pressure would strike a sane man as pretty phony—getting all steamed up about selling some damn product, putting good minds to work on copy for soap or nail polish. No wonder those guys drink—not just to speed themselves up but to keep from puking at themselves."

Pale Ale was right. Rick was glad to hear someone else take a crack at advertising, but he refrained from kicking Joe's chair again. It was too sore a subject between them. Recently, when Rick had been riding Joe about wasting good hunting weather working all weekend on a new canned soup account, Joe had admitted that he sort of squared things with himself by taking on nonprofit accounts—churches, educational institutions and charities. He was especially proud of a campaign he had laid out for a negro college. But the depth of Joe's cynicism about the whole advertising business was contained in what he called "Kelly's Law," i.e., the quality of the product varies inversely in proportion to the size of the advertising appropriation. Rick had agreed. In his own field the best gum to his taste was an unknown spruce gum peddled from a two-room factory in Maine—and it wasn't all boyhood recollection either, Rick still chewed it whenever he could locate a package.

Rick missed several categories mentioned by Pale Ale. He was wondering how he could tie this in with his own talk, wishing he had not urged Gail to come. Hell, think of the A.A.s, not of Gail. He looked across at her now. She had stopped fiddling with her purse and was leaning forward, listening intently.

Pehlehl was saying, "Any kind of salesmanship seems to me a tough spot for an alcoholic, where you're supposed to be a 'good fellow,' and being a good fellow seems to mean drinking with the other guy till he practically passes out and signs your order. I know because I sold farm machinery all over the country. If the war hadn't turned reapers into jeeps I'd probably still be drinking my way through the corn belt. It wasn't any intelligence on my part that made me change jobs, but now that I am in one of the non-alcoholic professions—yes, there are some, teaching and farming are two—I know what a help a job can be to a man who has made up his mind to stay dry. I said I wasn't going to talk about myself but I guess I've got to break that promise to show you what I mean. When I saw that my farm machinery selling days were about over, I happened to be calling on the dean of a State agricultural school. I always used to visit the faculty and students of agricultural colleges on my regular rounds, to get acquainted and make lists of new customers. Very often the professors would ask me to address their classes. You have to know quite a bit about the latest methods of scientific farming, soil erosion, crop rotation and so forth, to sell a new piece of machinery. Farmers aren't exactly spendthrifts—not that I blame them. Well, I was talking to the dean of this college and saying this would be my last call and what did he do but suggest that I try my hand at teaching there. Several of their younger instructors had already been drafted. It sounded sort of screwy but I thought hell, if he's willing to take a chance at least I'll be getting away from bars in strange towns and all my drunken pals. I had been trying to cut down liquor for some time; I might as well try getting away from it. The teachers I had met didn't seem to drink much and certainly my students would have to be sober in the classroom and they wouldn't be apt to ask a prof to join their Saturday night shindigs.

"I had been used to getting pretty well liquored up every night so it was a hell of a struggle to confine my drinking to weekends, but I managed to do it and get to classes Monday mornings—bleary-eyed but technically sober. I was scared though, haunted by the idea that sooner or later a bender would carry over to Monday and I'd miss a class. I could picture an inquiry and the loss of my job which I was beginning to like better than anything I had ever done.

"Sure enough, it happened on the worst Monday in the whole year, a Monday when my favorite class was having a final exam and I was supposed to proctor and write the questions on the blackboard. There was a hell of a blizzard that Monday too. It got me down and I had a small hangover anyhow. One drink would fix me up. It did, all right. By three o'clock, when the exam was scheduled, I was blind drunk. When I came to the next day I was appalled, disgusted, suicidal. Luckily my married sister happened to be visiting me. She phoned the college, said she was my nurse, and that I had had a heart attack on my way to the exam. It got by with the college but not with my sister—nor with me. She told me about A.A., and my remorse, at letting those students trudge through the snow and then have to spend another hour another day taking an exam, made me determine to go to a meeting. I had done a lot of stupid, crazy things when I was drunk but I was more ashamed of letting those kids down than anything I had ever done—and still am.

"With the help of A.A. and by the grace of God—and yes, thanks to being in a non-alcoholic profession—I haven't had a drink since my first meeting. The point I am trying to make is simply this—if you're in a business where drinking is—or seems to be—part of your job, why not try to change the job? But whether you can change or not, stick to the A.A. program."

Emily watched Rick walking up to the platform and thought irrelevantly, Why, his nose is like an Arab chief's—the haughty bridge, the wide flare of the nostrils—he ought to be wearing a burnoose, or whatever they wore in the desert, instead of a light tan tweed. Gail leaned over and whispered, "Oh, dear, Daddy's got on *green* socks with that reddish-brown tie. Why didn't we notice in time?" Rick was slightly colorblind and was always mixing up green and red, even reddish-brown, and appealing to them for help.

They missed the chairman's introduction and heard Rick saying, "I'm an alcoholic. My friend, Joe Kelly, who brought me into A.A., says I am an alcoholic with a high bottom." He looked down from his full six-foot three and grinned. There was an immediate response of laughter. "Seriously," Rick continued, "I suppose I *have* a high bottom in the A.A. sense. I have never been in an institution, never drunk 'smoke' on the Bowery, but I spent a night in the hoosegow last September for 'disturbing the peace' and I have done plenty of things I am ashamed of. . . ." He looked straight at Gail, who flushed and tried to smile back, but dropped her eyes in quick embarrassment.

"Things I'll never forgive myself for. The bottom I hit was low enough, God knows, and certainly unpleasant enough for everyone around me, and I am convinced that I never could have come up for air without the help of A.A. I tried for three or four years on my own, but no dice. I could never get beyond the fifty-ninth day. And usually the twenty-first day was a regular jinx when I was on the wagon. Now, I've been dry a little over three months—which is a short time compared to the rest of you—but a record for me." Rick waited for the applause to stop. The A.A.s were a responsive audience, quick to give a fellow member a hand and encouraging laughter.

"I've been thinking about what Pale Ale, here, had to say on occupational drinking and I believe he's got something. You can add engineers and archaeologists to your list, Mr. Pehlehl, and I'd like to suggest that there may be such a thing as geographical drinking. I believe there is more alcoholism in big cities than in small towns, villages and farming communities. I don't believe human beings were ever intended to live in rabbit warrens like New York. Years ago I was happy in New York. . . ." His face darkened and Emily knew he was thinking of Adelaide. "But since I got back from the Tropics I haven't felt at ease in this terrible, terrifying town—until tonight—and I am sure that is because I am with our group. A group that seems to me unique in a big city—something like the old New England Town Meetings, where everyone knew everyone else and could speak his mind.

"I've got a lot of things on my mind now and I don't know whether I can sort them all out but going back to that idea of geographical drinking, the Tropics, where I've spent a good deal of my life, is a swell place to become an alcoholic. There's a tradition of drinking south of the border just as Pale Ale says there is in the newspaper game. The climate usually gets the blame—it makes white men so languid that they claim they need a lot of pepper-uppers. That's the theory but I think loneliness has a lot to do with it too. You see, engineers like me and archaeologists like the guys I met around the bars in Belize, go out alone into the bush with a native mule-driver—and you can't get much conversation out of one native, or out of the bunch of *chicleros* I used to have with me. You work hard and you get damn lonely and when you come back to a town the first place you head for is a bar.

"I knew one archaeologist who was so lonely that he . . . I nearly gave away the point of the story. Have to start over again. I was in a saloon in Progreso one time when an old archaeologist I just knew by sight came in and lined up beside me. Pretty soon we fell to talking, bought each other a couple of rounds of drinks, and before long were swapping stories and bragging a bit—you know how I mean. I forget what I was boasting about, but it seemed to make the old fellow sore. Suddenly he started yelling at me, 'I've got something I bet you've never seen.'

"'What's that?'

"'I've got a whore that drinks with me!'"

A woman in the audience tittered.

"I started laughing. 'What's so damn unusual about that? Plenty of them have drunk with me.'

"'Have they indeed?' he sneers. With that he sticks two fingers in his mouth and lets out a shrill whistle. And in trots a beautiful bay mare—right into the barroom. Then I realize that he has said, 'I've got a *horse* that drinks with me,' not a *whore!*"

Laughs interrupted Rick. "The chink who ran the joint seemed to know just what to do," he continued. "He hauled out a big tin washtub, emptied a coupla dozen bottles of beer into it. And that mare lapped it all up."

The laughter was so loud that Rick could not be heard for a minute. Then he went on, "Seems he had trained this horse to drink with him when he made camp after clearing bush from Maya temples all day, and digging out shards of pottery and carved whistles that had belonged to high priests who knew how to multiply and divide before the barbarians of Europe and Asia could do more than wield a stone ax—which is about all their descendants seem to know how to do even now in 1943. . . ."

Gail's grey eyes were wide with interest—this was the father who had sent her funny little carved figures and odd beads from a mysterious jungle, precious items she had treasured through her childhood. This was the man she had daydreamed about as an adolescent, the man who would some time come back and tell her tales, better than Mr. Nicky's, of strange places and strange people. Not the angry man who always jumped on her for everything, who seemed to hate the sight of her.

"The old bird used to win a lot of bets on that horse," Rick was saying, "because she'd drink practically anything. But I was glad to hear him get a hell of a bawling out once from a vet in San Pedro Sula for giving her champagne on top of her usual beer. The poor mare had a hell of a hangover and the vet treated it just like a human hangover with ice strapped to the head and spirits of ammonia.

"It was soon after I met up with the drinking horse that my own hangovers began to get too bad for ice packs and spirits of ammonia.

Booze was catching up on me in a big way and what scared me most was that my hangovers changed from physical to mental—or maybe I should say psychological. Anyone can get through the usual headache, thick tongue and upset stomach, but I didn't see how I could survive the dreadful depressions that would last for days and days and were followed by terrific, unaccountable fear. I can't explain that fear. It was not fear of anything in particular, but fear of everything. It was not fear of dying, it was fear of living. It made me want to die—the way a seasick man wants to die—but I didn't have the guts to kill myself. I was afraid of fear. I knew it was caused by alcohol but I couldn't stop drinking. I've since been told by a doctor that this state of depression and fear was a sign that I was becoming allergic to alcohol. He said that some sort of chemical change like this often hits heavy drinkers in middle age.

"If you've never had the kind of fear I'm talking about, you're lucky. It's hard to explain. It simply paralyzes you. I remember one day in Guatemala City. I was using a red Chevrolet that belonged to my company, I'd left it out in the patio with the top down when it started to rain. A regular tropical rain that lasted two days—and I just sat in my room with my arms crossed and my back against the wall, trying to get up courage to go out and put the top up on that car! I wasn't drunk—don't get me wrong—I wasn't even drinking, but I had been on a bender two or three days before. It was afterwards that the fear always hit me. Maybe some of you remember the Muskrat in Kipling's *Jungle Book*, I think his name was Chuchundra, who was afraid to leave the wall and come out into the middle of the room. That was me.

"I knew alcohol was responsible for this fear that was making my life intolerable, but I could not stop drinking on my own. I could not be responsible about liquor. I tried. God knows I tried. But there's no use going into my attempts to stay on the wagon—here. It's a pretty familiar story to all of you. You've all tried the wagon and failed the way I did. Joe Kelly was right when he told me, on the way to my first A.A. meeting at White Plains, that the wagon is the wrong dope psychologically. I've learned a lot from A.A.—and I guess I've still got a lot to learn—but that was one of the ideas that helped me. Another was the slogan, 'Easy does it,' but most of all I think it's the feeling these meetings give you that you are not alone with your problem—or what the doctors call group therapy.

"Speaking of a group not-drinking together reminds me of a funny example of group-drinking I ran into once in Colombia, South America, on a trip with an ethnological pal of mine who wanted to see the annual fiesta of the Kagaba Indians, when they celebrate getting in their harvest. They drink a vile concoction like vinegar, called *guarrapo*, made from the dregs left over after making sugar from cane. Every man, woman and child over twelve in the village of Palomino was drunk for a week. And it was the happiest drinking I have ever seen. They all had guns and *machetes* but they never used them. If they felt like fighting they would slap each other's faces or pull hair as a challenge to a wrestling match. When one man got another down that was the end of the bout. This didn't prevent the loser taking on the winner again five minutes later. He would make a flying tackle and they'd roll around on the ground, slapping and grunting. But it was all good clean fun. And the drums were beating all the time. Day and night.

"We saw some wonderful connubial drinking too. Husbands and wives drank together, fell down together and went to sleep in each other's arms—right in the pouring rain one afternoon—then got up and began drinking again. Maybe if some of you A.A. wives had drunk with your husbands, instead of scolding and nagging at them, they would not have developed 'guilt complexes' and hidden bottles all over the house and sneaked drinks on the sly. It's just an idea.

"Anyhow, the whole week we were there I never saw an Indian sick or with any kind of a headache or hangover. But they only drink twice a year, at spring planting and at harvesting. That's probably why they can stand their orgies so well. My ethnological pal talked a lot about the Greek Bacchanalias, which were more elaborate, of course, but had the same motive as this primitive ceremony we witnessed—a religious thanksgiving, a community celebration. Whereas our drinking in the U.S.A. is aimless and individualistic."

Rick paused. "Maybe you don't like being compared to a bunch of drunken Indians, but the point I'm trying to make is that group action means strength—and A.A. has group action. I've knocked around the world a lot and this is the most amazing organization I have ever run into—I certainly did *run* into A.A. as if the devil were chasing me. He was. That old demon, Rum. And I want to thank the guy who founded A.A.—Bill Griffith still seems like Santa Claus to me because I still haven't met him—and all of you who have kept A.A. going, and especially Joe Kelly who took me to my first meeting. Thank you."

Gail leaned across Emily and patted her father's arm impulsively. "You were wonderful, Daddy. Wonderful."

The Chairman was saying, "Before our next regular speaker, I want to introduce a new member, who was with the first contingent of Marines to get ashore at Guadalcanal. He was wounded there and sent home in a hospital plane. Gunnar Nordstrom, will you say just a few words?"

A big man in a Marine uniform with a crutch under his left arm got slowly to the platform. He had thick fair hair, sea-blue eyes, heavy shoulders, and a thrust to his head as if he were used to facing winds and salt spray.

He was younger than anyone Gail had seen at the meeting. Most of the men and women around her were middle-aged, but this man couldn't be much older than Paul. He wasn't like any boy she had ever met, though. His face was rough-hewn, his hands big with strong artisan fingers. He was like the young men you read about in historical novels, like the men who sailed with Columbus—no, they must have been small and dark and agile—but he might have set sail with Leif Ericson. That was more like it. Nordstrom must be Danish or Norwegian. Gunnar was a funny name but it fitted him somehow.

"I haven't got much to say," Gunnar Nordstrom began in a deep, diffident voice, "but I'm glad to be here. If I weren't here I'd be in a flophouse in the Bowery, drinking 'smoke' on the 'beach'. That's where one of your members, Mr. Porter J. Emerson, found me. I was about through. I guess I'd hit what the last speaker called 'bottom,' all right. When I got out of the hospital and the Marine doctors handed me a discharge on account of my leg, well, I was sore but I thought sure the Merchant Marine would take me back. You see, I'd been with them since I was a kid up to the time the Japs hit Pearl Harbor. Well, they turned me down, too, and like I said, I was finished.

"I guess some of you are wondering why I'm still wearing this uniform." There was pain in the blue eyes now but Nordstrom's voice was gruff. "Hell, it's the only suit of clothes I got to my name and we're allowed to keep 'em for three months after our discharge, and you can't buy a suit without a job.

"The first speaker ought to add the guys who get invalided out of the Marines and the Army and the Navy to his list. There are going to be plenty of guys like me who are going to be so damn mad that they can't fight any more that they'll take to liquor sure as shooting.

"I don't know as I can honestly blame my drinking entirely on the way I feel about not getting back in the Marines. I guess I come by drinking naturally. My father, my uncles, and all their friends were hard drinkers out in northern Minnesota where I grew up. I can remember long winter nights and bitter cold winds outside and a big bright fire and a jug passing from hand to hand and big deep-voiced, bearded men shouting and roaring, and sometimes fighting, and always telling great tales of the way their fathers and uncles used to drink in Norway. Men who hardly said a word from sunrise to sunset.

"When a hard drinker like me gets a bad knock-down I guess he can't help becoming a drunk. But I'm trying to help it now. And it's a lot tougher for me to fight liquor than to fight Japs but I'm glad Mr. Emerson brought me to this meeting. Nobody'll have to bring me next time. I'll be here." Gunnar Nordstrom limped back to his seat in the front row and Gail joined in the warm applause.

Gail could not keep her mind on the next speaker, an earnest, bald-headed man who read the Twelve Steps from a pamphlet and explained the A.A. program carefully, if somewhat pedantically. Her mind was skipping with a fine flaunting of geography from hot green jungles to cold blue fjords.

A soon as the meeting ended with the customary saying of the Lord's Prayer, Hank Frost turned around from the seat next to Joe. "That young Gunnar's the kinda feller I'd like to have workin' at my boatyard," he said to Rick. "Took quite a fancy to him, ought to know somethin' about boats, bein' around 'em all his life. Goin' to offer that boy a job right now."

Mrs. Hank nodded, the velvet pansies on her black toque bobbing in agreement, her round, placid face alive with motherliness. "He could maybe have our Steve's room for a while." She looked questioningly at Hank. "I'd like to feed him up a bit, put some meat on his bones."

Gail trailed along as the Frosts went to locate Gunnar Nordstrom. Then hung back, suddenly shy, unable to move nearer, unable to leave and join her aunt and father who had been surrounded by members laughing loudly about the drinking horse.

Hank was handling it well. Gail watched the first look of frozen pride on Gunnar's face at taking a job from a stranger—even an A.A.—thawing in the warm honesty of Hank's offer. Hank explained about his boatyard, *his* even though he had lost it through drinkin' like a crazy coot all over the town of Greenwich, told what a hard time they were having to get men who had a feel for boats.

"I guess Nordstroms got boats in their blood for centuries," Gunnar said in his slow diffident voice, "boats and liquor more than money—or women. . . ."

He turned and saw Gail in her black and scarlet dress with her tore-ador hat and her shining yellow hair. Their eyes held until Hank turned too.

"Well, say. I been forgettin' my manners. This here is Rick's girl—the fellow who told about that drinkin' horse," Hank chortled. "Had to come traipsin' all the way into New York so's my old woman could hear him. Glad we come now, Gunnar. You git your duds together, young feller, and make tracks for my place, you hear."

XII

HOTEL ROOM

Medicinal. . . . Whiskey was medicinal. . . . Whiskey was good for a cold . . . Rick took another turn on the thick grey carpeting between the bed and bureau of Grand Rapids maple. He had been pacing his narrow strip for twenty minutes. He had a cold. A cold in his head. A cold in his eyes. A rawness in his throat. Must have picked it up on the train. If he were at home now Emily would be bringing him a tall glass of hot lemonade, Beulah would appear with hot water bags, Gail would pop her yellow head in the door—but he wasn't at home.

He kicked a velour-covered chair out of his path and jerked gay flowered curtains back from a small window. H. Peculiar Henry, you couldn't make a hotel room gay with flowered curtains, or homelike with Currier and Ives prints. No point even in opening the window when the air blew out instead of in and all you could see was a dark, blank courtyard . . . Sylvia Landon had stood at a hotel window and wanted to jump. . . . He didn't want to jump now—he wanted a drink. And it would be Bill Driscomb's fault if he took one. Driscomb should have been in this "home-away-from-home" in Pittsburgh, calling on distributors but at the last minute Driscomb had phoned the office that he was down with flu. Damn Driscomb and his flu. . . . Whiskey would keep *his* cold from turning into flu. . . . Whiskey was medicinal.

The bathroom was hot, white, glaringly impersonal. Rick shook bicarb into a glass and punched the ice-water tap. He had seen a bar across from the drug store as he entered the lobby—a nice crowded, jolly-looking bar. He gulped the soda, swallowed another aspirin and looked at his wrist watch. Only five thirty. Too early for dinner and you couldn't tramp the streets with a damp, smoke-laden wind blowing down your neck, or sit in a stuffy movie house full of other people's germs as well as your own. What the hell could you do then?

Habit answered for him. What did you always do in a strange town between five and seven from Lima to Hong Kong to Moscow . . . dropping your bags in a strange lobby, swinging out into a wide, brightly lighted avenue, or turning into a narrow twisting street with sunshine still slanting on pink and white stucco houses? Hunt for a bar, that was the answer—not just any bar either—there was always some spot where the real gang gathered, sometimes in a hole-in-the-wall, a dump, but *the* bar nonetheless.

He could see himself striding into the *cantina* in La Ceiba which the banana cowboys called the "club," shouting, "Life is hard but I am harder" . . . and the bartender, a superstitious half-breed with an Oxford accent, looking at the ceiling in terror as if he expected a thunderbolt to strike Rick, imploring him not to say such things in this place . . . Rick and his friends roaring with laughter, shouting in chorus, "Life is hard but I am harder."

Oh, the wonderful, confident, world-conquering feel of liquor!

"He who conquers himself is greater than he who conquers a great city." . . . Why the hell did he have to remember that now? His mother's quiet voice . . . his mother's steady, challenging look. . . . Rick sat on the edge of the bed and dropped his face in his hands. His mother had died when he was ten . . . why did the old misery sweep over him now? The cool, frosty touch of her cheek when she came into his room late at night after dinner and the theatre with his father in Boston . . . the warm, protected feeling when she tucked in the blankets and whispered, "Now you're as snug as a bug in a rug." . . . Long days of lonely agony after her death lying in the grass near the fox runs at his Uncle Walton's farm in Wrentham, watching the foxes' sharp knowing snouts and thick jaunty brushes . . . days that gradually, gradually lessened the bewildered pain . . . summer days that slowly turned into fall and the forgetful excitement of making the scrub football team at a new school . . . but never entirely forgetful . . . first his mother . . . then Adelaide . . . no wonder he could not pray. . . . "Pray not for easier lives, pray to be stronger men"—again his mother's quiet voice seemed to fill this room she had never seen . . . pray—but he could not pray.

"Ask God to help you to stay dry for twenty-four hours," the A.A.s were always saying . . . but how could you unless you were a Catholic like Joe? It was easy for Joe—Joe had never lost the habit of prayer . . . MacKenzie had though. MacKenzie was a Presbyterian who had grown away from the Church as much as Rick had. Mac had been skeptical too—but Mac had told at a meeting about sitting alone in his cheap two-room flat when he first got out of High Pines, remembering the pleasant house he had owned in East Orange—the pleasant house he had lost through liquor, thinking of his wife at work in a store in Greenwich, cursing himself for letting her down, pitying himself because he had been turned down when he had applied for a job with a hick law firm in Stamford—a job he would have scorned a year before. Mac made it very vivid—the old alcoholic mind working around with inevitable logic to the idea of a drink—a drink that would make him forget the mess he had made of his life. Mac had gotten his raincoat from the closet and an old felt hat and started for the door. "Don't let me open that door, God! Don't let me." The words had come into Mac's mind with a click like a light switched on in a dark room. He had turned around and walked back to his chair. He was still sitting with his hat and coat on when his wife got home—but he had not had a drink. He had sat there not daring to move, saying over and over to himself, "Thy will be done, Thy will be done," singing all the hymns he could remember from the prep school he had been kicked out of as a boy.

"Pray not for easier lives . . ." Mac's desperate cry, his ludicrous hymn-singing had been prayer as truly as these words of Phillips Brooks Rick's mother had repeated . . . but he couldn't sit on this Grand Rapids maple bed in this damn hotel room and ask God's help to be a "stronger man" . . . he could fight to be stronger though—fight for the strength not to let Mac and Joe and Hank down . . . if he got drunk now it would make it tougher for the rest of them—weaken their faith in A.A.

He lifted his head—and the telephone mocked him. A small utilitarian instrument of the devil waiting for his hand to reach out. Patiently, tauntingly waiting for his voice over the wire asking the desk to send up a pint of Bourbon. It would be so easy—so safe . . . not going downstairs to a bar—a bar and another bar and another bar. . . . Time and Time and Time and Time. Just a pint in his room—a pint to make him forget a hotel room. . . . Bourbon was good for a cold—medicinal . . . ten drops of whiskey on a lump of sugar when he was a child, sick in bed with a cold. . . . "He who conquers himself. . . ."

This was it. This was the battle for himself—more important than conquering a great city . . . harder than anything his mother could have dreamed he would have to fight . . . tougher even than his earlier skirmishes with John Barleycorn after joining A.A. . . . They had been mere outpost engagements. . . .

The first cocktail party; he had gone with Emily, wanting to try it out, rather anticipating the test of his resolution, confident in himself and A.A., and spent the afternoon refusing drinks, his conversation seeming to consist of repeated, "No, thanks, I'm just not drinking today." Monotonous but not too difficult.

He had learned the trick of coping with insistent hosts now. "Look," he would ask, "would you like it if I urged you *not* to drink?" He had enjoyed their puzzled replies, "Why no, I suppose not," and his own terminal retort, "Okay, turn the tables and see how I feel." It usually worked—unless the host were drunk himself . . . your drunken host was usually easier to handle though, than your insistently hospitable one— "Not even a beer—or a glass of sherry?"

The first dance; he could no more imagine dancing without liquor than dancing without music, but he had tried that too. A group of Joe's married friends held a series of subscription dances during the winter at one of the country clubs and Joe had asked Emily and Rick to go with him. Rick had expected Joe to invite Sylvia Landon out too, he had been seeing a good deal of her all fall, but Joe had tugged at his red forelock and hesitated. "Oh, I don't know—this is sort of Monica's crowd." Joe, however, had not hesitated about wanting Emily and Rick—it would be a hell of a lot easier for him if Rick went—they could stick together—it couldn't be too hard for the two of them to get through a dance without a drink.

But it was. Middle-aged women are seldom good dancers. Middle-aged men are apt to be worse, but at least the men had seemed aware of their ineptitude. Dancing was incidental to the really important occupation of pouring out drinks from the row of bottles they had each deposited in the center of the long tables where everyone gathered. Rick had been puzzled as to what the women got out of the evening—certainly not sex. He had never known an American woman who was not shocked by the suggestion that sex had any connection with dancing. . . . Music—Liquor—Dancing—Sex—was it a memory of youth that impelled these smartly dressed females with their pathetic eagerness toward gaiety? Three hours of heaving buxom torsos around the dance floor—three hours of getting hot, tired and—what was worse—being hit by that sudden "fed-up" feeling which had preceded so many of his binges in the past. . . . Boredom could be blamed for a good percentage of his drinking. Emily was slim and danced well enough but he'd a hell of a lot rather be talking to her in front of a fire in Joe's living room. He had caught her eye across the table, together they had fled through the ballroom, past a knot of recalcitrant husbands shaking dice at the bar who had watched their escape with envious, glazed eyes. It had been a close call. Too damn close. Another hour and Rick would have been pawing the bar rail himself.

The first company report; in the tropics he had always knocked out his reports with a bottle of rum parked next to his typewriter. Last week he had tried to get one done without a bottle. He had put it off till the last possible minute and finally gone out for a large thermos of coffee from a neighboring drug store and settled down in his deserted office to complete agony. In an hour and a half he had emptied the thermos and not been even half way through the report. Crazy, that he could only stay away from liquor by substituting another drink! Was he never going to get to the point where he would not think of a drink—any drink? Would every damn situation where he had always depended on "Dutch courage" have to be faced separately?

Cocktail party . . . dance . . . office report . . . he had managed to survive them all without a drink. But this was a double-header—a double feature. Suddenly he saw himself in scene IV *and* V—Avery Rickham Alone in a Hotel Room *with* a Cold . . . he couldn't get by that combination . . . but he could get the hell out. What was keeping him? Driscomb's appointment tomorrow morning with the Bonham company manager which he had tried to change . . . he could have been on the train home if the manager had been willing to see him this afternoon. To hell with him. Wasn't it more important for him not to take a drink than to finish up Driscomb's job in Pittsburgh? If he took a drink the job would be finished—and how!

He jerked his suitcase open, pulled a shirt and sock out of the maple bureau. The other sock fell to the floor. He stooped to pick it up. . . . God damn it, he was running away. If he ran away from scene IV now, wouldn't he just have to go through it all over again the next time he landed in a strange hotel. . . ? "He who conquers. . . ."

He slammed the shirts and socks back into the bureau drawer. . . . "Pray to be stronger men."

He would not catch the next train back to New York . . . but he could not sit here stewing and sniffling in this "home-away-from-home," either . . . there must be an A.A. chapter in Pittsburgh . . . if he could just locate one A.A. to talk to . . . they were always saying at meetings that if you got in a tough spot and felt like drinking the thing to do was to call up another member . . . but he didn't know anyone in Pittsburgh. He grabbed the phone book and searched it frantically. The phone was still behaving maliciously—before he had finished thumbing the pages the bell rang.

"This is Bob Dickson," a jovial voice spoke. "Just heard you were in town, Ken Morley told me you called at his office this morning. Like to see you, old fellow. Buy you a drink right now."

Rick twisted the telephone cord around his fingers as if he were tying a knot in his will power. Dickson had been a likeable guy in college, but the biggest drunk in their class. "Sorry, Bob," Rick made his voice hoarser, "got a terrible cold. Hit me like a ton of bricks. I'm in bed right now, chuck full of aspirin."

"Tough luck," the hearty voice boomed back. "Tell you what I'll do for you, Rick, bring you a pint. Do you good. Nothing like liquor for a cold."

He had heard that one before—a thousand devils had been chanting "medicinal" at him for the last two hours. He managed to cut Dickson short—rude or not, what the hell did it matter—grabbed his hat and overcoat and rushed out of the side entrance of the hotel. Walking wildly, head down in the cold, smoke-filled air, he bumped into a man, muttered an apology. The man turned and started after him. "Too many drunks in this town." Rick laughed crazily and plunged on, confirming the man's worst suspicions. Buildings seemed to hurry past him like a motion picture montage, but he didn't notice—didn't notice anything until a "Bowling" sign swung in front of him. He went down a dark flight of steps, found an empty alley, rolled five strings as fast as the pin boy could set them up. He named the king pin Bill Driscomb and his curve slid into the right hand pocket with an accuracy and bang that attracted a score of shabby admirers.

Wet through from the exercise and the aspirin, he taxied back to the hotel, hurried through the side entrance again, just in case Bob Dickson might be hanging around. The room looked different—almost endurable—no longer haunted by the ghosts of his battle with himself. . . . "He who conquers . . ."

He wolfed two more aspirins, fell asleep, tossed and dreamed. Got up at six-thirty, dressed, packed feverishly, gulped grapefruit juice and coffee at the drug store across the lobby from the bar. He reached Bonham's office as the secretary was unlocking the door, paced for fifteen minutes, a cigar clenched in his teeth. The business was silly—could have been finished in two minutes yesterday afternoon. He reached the station twenty minutes early, plumped down in the smoker, tossed his bag in the rack over his head, his teeth still clamped on the unlighted cigar. "I won," he said out loud, "but God, it was close." A man across the aisle looked at him curiously as if he must be drunk.

XIII

MRS. CÉZANNE

Gail stood disconsolately at the front window of the house in the East Sixties where her father had prowled three months before. It was not the street that depressed her; if she had known that he had labeled it, "dull and respectable," she would have defended it eagerly. It was a wonderful street. She leaned her forehead against the cool glass of the window-pane remembering how only a few years ago her eyes had been just level with the center catch, so that she had to stand on tiptoe to look above it, or steep to peer at the yellow, orange and green taxis whizzing by, whirling girls in bright evening dresses and young men with flying white scarves off to unknown gaiety. Gail had watched with an entranced, impatient confidence, telling herself that soon boys and boys and boys would dash up her brownstone steps, seeing a strange and glamorous Gail step proudly down the stairs in fur boots over golden slippers and pause for a last look in the hall mirror at orchids pinned on her shoulder and a spangled wisp of tulle in her hair.

She pinched the blue wool of her Motor Corps uniform and brought herself back to reality. Dreary reality. Daphne Manton's shop was always arrogantly closed on Saturday, her customers being the sort who never spent weekends in town, and for once Daphne and Aunt Emily had agreed that Gail ought to join the Motor Corps. People were always urging her to do things—Sylvia Landon the other night talking about the Waves. Even if she were old enough Gail knew she would hate the uniforms and the discipline and the mobs of females herded together like boarding school, only worse. Of course they were doing a fine, patriotic job—everyone was . . . Aunt Emily working at the Red Cross, all the girls she knew getting up benefits for French Relief, Polish Relief, Chinese Relief—everyone pitching in, doing something. She was a hateful, selfish, frivolous person with people dying all over the world, but—you spent years dreaming about being eighteen and look at it now. All she wanted was a little fun—harmless fun—dances and dates and falling in love and meeting new men and wondering about them the way her mother must have wondered about her father, and along tulle veil and bridesmaids and a tiny apartment and lots of silly fat babies. It was a simple thing to ask of life, but she didn't seem likely to get any part of it, when every boy she knew was off somewhere flying a bomber, or pushing a jeep through the desert, or at some dusty camp in Kansas. Even Paul was stuck in New Haven this weekend. He had been taking private flying lessons besides his regular A.S.T.P. training and expected to be inducted soon and sent to Miami if he made the Air Corps. He wanted her to marry him first. . . . Maybe she would in spite of her father and Aunt Emily. Daphne was all for it. . . . She might call up Daphne now. There was always something going on at Daphne's apartment—but the men Daphne assembled were mostly ancients who made fancy speeches and tiresome passes at girls. Gail jerked the chartreuse curtains across the long window and flung herself face down on the couch in front of the fire.

"Mr. Nicky" used to sit here talking to Aunt Emily and sometimes he would hold Gail on his knee and show her pictures of naked black children with fat stomachs and gold rings in their noses, and little thatched houses and high blue mountains. He had made the world seem full of funny exciting things. He had made her remember her father and how he had lifted her to his shoulder when she was five so that she could touch the twinkling glass drops of the chandelier. Her father had told her about stalactites hanging from dark caves and once she had dreamed about his carrying her through a thick green forest—thicker, greener than the woods of Hansel and Gretel—a pink and yellow bird had flown over their heads and suddenly a terrible animal, with a head like a lion but white and shaggy as the polar bear in the zoo, had stood in their path and her father had put the little whistle carved like a man, which he had given her, to his lips and blown three clear notes and the terrible animal had rolled on the ground like a kitten. It was a silly dream but some of that childish wonder and pride had come back to her during her father's speech Tuesday night—only to vanish.

The very next morning he had hurried home to pack his suitcase and Gail had shown him some proofs of herself modeling Daphne Manton's latest hats. They had just arrived and Gail thought they were marvelous. Even Aunt Emily said they were lovely, but Rick had been furious when he found they were intended for one of the fashion magazines. "Not with your name," he had shouted. "You hear me, Gail, if you want to sell your face I suppose that's your own damn business, but Abigail Avery was your grandmother's name. It's a fine name. You are not to cheapen it."

Gail twisted the corner of a sofa cushion in desolate, baffled resentment. Why couldn't her father ever approve of anything she ever did? Why couldn't she manage to do anything to please him? Why were they always flaring up at each other, driving Aunt Emily crazy with their tempers and their hurt feelings?

The front door bell rang and Gail could hear old Beulah going slowly and correctly down the hall, probably with the silver salver ready to receive calling cards from a white-gloved hand. Beulah belonged to the old school. She had never accepted the deplorable fact that ladies no longer went calling and that what she was apt to receive nowadays were packages over five pounds or charity tickets—"A dollar apiece, if you please, Mam—for the firemen's ball." It might be fun to go at that. Gail jumped up from the couch thinking how horrified Beulah would be at the ridiculous notion.

"A person for you, Miss Gail." Beulah's tone indicated her disapproval. "He did not have a card, but he asked me to say his name is Gunnar Nordstrom. Shall I tell him you are not at home, Miss Gail?"

Gail patted Beulah's stiff back. "It's all right, Beulah, he's a friend of my father's. Run along now and I'll let him in." She flipped her hair back from her shoulders and tugged at the jacket of her blue uniform. "Beulah, Beulah, do I look all right? Do I look like the Princess at the top of a glass mountain?"

"You look like your mother, Miss Gail," Beulah said with a rare smile of praise, "and that's good enough for anyone. Don't go bothering your head about Princesses on glass mountains," she added with a sniff.

Gail opened the door to the hall and called, "Hi!", proving the complete irrelevance of language, for the casual word rang out in gay, excited welcome. Hold everything, she warned herself quickly. This thin, tired Norseman in a cheap suit which was too short in the sleeves was her father's friend, exactly as she had told Beulah.

His first abrupt words confirmed this as he limped behind her into the living room and sat on the edge of the fan-back chair.

"All the A.A.s in Greenwich are worrying about your father."

"I know," Gail said quickly, "Aunt Emily and I were worried to death when we heard about the storm. I wish he wouldn't go out in one of those little boats."

"That isn't what I mean," Gunnar smiled, and his strong mouth became gentle, but his eyes were stern. "A man has to take risks to be a man. I guess we need danger to feel we're alive. . . . War's like that. Not that I like war . . . but I don't like peace much either. Not the peace of cities. Your father was a lot safer on that little island in the storm than he is walking around this town every day. It's a hell of a place for an alcoholic or for any big guy." Gunnar looked toward the long front windows. "Take that street out there. I kept wanting to push all those houses out of my way as I came along just now." He stretched out his arms and Gail could see the red brick colonials, the pink stucco and their own brownstone tumbling down like the pillars of Samson's temple. "Even then there wouldn't be anything worth seeing," Gunnar added.

Gail did not interrupt to defend her street. She sat on a footstool in front of the fire with her head tilted to one side wondering what this strange young man with his deep, hesitant voice had seen and what he most wanted to see again . . . horizon-touching fields of yellow grain or horizon-touching blue oceans.

Gunnar took a corncob pipe out of his pocket and knocked it on the brass fender. "Your father's got to get out of this town. And you've got to help him."

Gail turned her head to look at him. "But what do you want me to do?" she asked like an obedient child questioning a nurse.

Gunnar laughed, a big laugh that filled the quiet, dignified room with the boisterous sound of the quarterdeck. "You *are* an infant, aren't you?" And suddenly he found himself wishing she could stay that way. It was a rugged world for a girl like this to grow up in. The girls he had known could take it, but he didn't think any too highly of them for that—for their hard, shallow adaptability. Hell, he was being soft about the kid. You damn well had to take war and the world in your stride. And if you happened to have an alcoholic father you had to face that too.

"You saw those men at the meeting last week. You heard what they said." All through his own speech Gunnar had watched the girl with the shining hair and the intent grey eyes under the toreador hat, wondering what she was doing there. "Drink is your father's problem and it's one hell of a problem. He was doing fine according to Hank and Joe when you were all living out at Joe's place, but he nearly had a slip in Pittsburgh. They all feel he'll take a nose dive if he has to stay in New York. Weekends help, I guess, but the duck season is nearly over and anyhow it's not like being in the country all the time. You wouldn't think a little place only forty miles from New York could give a man a feeling of living in the wilds like the bush your father's been in and the places I've seen—but it does. Joe tried to talk to your father last night and Hank said he was 'aimin' to speak to Miss Emily,' but I decided to put it straight to you. I didn't tell any of them I was coming, just hopped the first train after my shift at the boatyard was over. Never entered my head that you might not be home." He leaned back and ran his hand through his thick fair hair. "You seem to be the stumbling block."

"Me?"

"Your father told Joe he couldn't coop you up in the country all winter. He said you had friends in town and a job. Like it?"

"Sort of."

"Is that a uniform you've got on?"

"Motor Corps," Gail said, wishing she had had time to change.

"Like that?"

"Not much. I don't mind driving but it seems sort of pointless taking officers and people around—only I guess I'd hate nursing more and you've got to do something." She must sound like a fool to this man who had been around the world in the Merchant Marine and wounded on a distant beach. "I'm sort of a useless person," she added in a small voice. "Daddy thinks so."

"He thinks a hell of a lot of you," Gunnar said positively. "That's part of this trouble, according to Joe. Joe says your father blames himself for running out on you when you were a baby." How the devil could you make this girl understand the darkness of alcoholic remorse, the despair and desperation? But she damn well had to.

"Would you like tea now, Miss Gail?" Beulah's brisk presence filled the room. She snapped on lights and pulled a table nearer the fire. Gail jumped up from the footstool and seated herself in the fan-back chair opposite Gunnar. "You'll stay, won't you?" she asked. This was a new Gail. This was evidently the elderly servant's idea of how a young lady should behave.

Gunnar grinned and pulled out an old-fashioned gold watch with a closed case. This wasn't a girl he could talk to about her father—or himself. "There's a picture I've been wanting to see," he said. "I guess I'd better be shoving along." But how could he go without trying again, without at least telling Gail about the place he had seen in the woods back of Greenwich? The doctor had told him to walk as much as he could, the shattered bones in his knee had been put together with bits of wire—it would probably be stiff for a long time—but the muscles must be exercised. He had spent last Sunday trying it out and come across a big remodeled barn with a "For Rent" sign, the sort of place he liked himself, a place he had felt suddenly that Rick would be able to breathe in. "How about coming along?" he asked Gail. It might be easier to talk to her away from Beulah, away from this correct untroubled room. "I could buy you dinner too. Hank lent me some dough till pay day."

Gail dashed into the kitchen, told Beulah to "skip" tea and to tell Aunt Emily she'd be back early but not for dinner, raced up the back stairs, warning herself not to be excited—the picture would probably be one she had seen and they would eat at Child's or the Automat. But she didn't care. She tossed her uniform on a ruffled taffeta chaise lounge. Gunnar had said to hurry. Gunnar had said could she wear that black and red dress with the toreador hat.

He was waiting for her in the front hall, a shabby reversible coat over the cheap suit, a crutch tucked under one arm, but she gave no thought to the fur boots over golden slippers and the boy whose white scarf would fly toward unknown gaiety.

They hurried through the early December darkness to Fifty-seventh Street, where Gunnar stopped and pulled a clipping out of his pocket.

"There isn't any movie in this block," Gail said.

"Movie?"

"You wanted to see a picture, didn't you?"

Gunnar's quarterdeck laugh brought curious stares from passers-by and a quick flush to Gail's face. She lifted her chin. She'd show him that she wasn't a silly movie-hound, that she knew something about painting—she had been to several Varnishing Days with Paul. On the way up to the gallery in a small lift she started asking him glibly if he didn't think Dali's revolt against the machine was really counterrevolutionary?

He shook his head as if her words were buzzing flies. "I wouldn't know," he said in his deep, hesitant voice, "but I guess Dali annoys me. He can paint, but his ideas get in the way of his painting . . . like a comic strip artist . . . only you have to hunt in a catalogue for his captions. I don't want to *read* pictures. I want to *see* them."

They shouldered their way through the crowd, which always seems to pop out of nowhere into galleries. Gail wondered why you never saw any of these people on the streets, or in theaters or restaurants. She felt sure she would recognize their rapt, cynical faces and disparagingly eager voices. Perhaps the art dealers kept them in storage and brought them out, carefully dusted, their automatic tones set with the correct records.

Gunnar ignored them. He found the Van Gogh he wanted and stood in front of it, absorbing its hot yellow sunlight. He made no comment except to point out how Van Gogh put his paint on, the thick angular precision of his brush strokes. Then, with hardly a glance at any intervening pictures, he located a grey-green street of Cézanne's solidity, his sure geometric balance. With a sudden flash of insight Gail thought Paul talks about Art and Gunnar talks about painting. She smiled to herself as if she had made a vital discovery.

"Don't look any more." Gunnar propelled her toward the door. "I sometimes got so hungry for pictures after a long trip on a freighter that I'd try to swallow the whole Brooklyn Museum in one gulp. The damn Japs have one sound idea, they never unroll more than a single scroll at a time."

Out on the street Gunnar hesitated. There was *Le Matelot*, a small French restaurant, over near the docks where he used to go with a gang off his ship and get drunk on red ink and brandy. They had called it *"Le Matelot Ivré."* How could he stand it sober? It would be tough all right, but it was the only spot he knew in New York where the food was good and cheap. He had eaten in too many places the world over to savor the taste of American chain-eateries and he couldn't take a girl like Gail to any old dive. Madame, as he well knew, kept a sharp eye on her customers. She didn't allow any rough stuff and her caustic tongue was more effective than any bouncer he had ever run into. Okay. He'd give it a try. There were some guys in A.A. who bragged about going into gin mills with their old pals and drinking cokes at a bar. He ought to be able to manage this.

Gail had never been so far west of Fifth Avenue except when she and Aunt Emily had sailed for Europe but *Le Matelot*, with its noisy sailors, its babel of foreign tongues, its red checked tablecloths and smell of garlic and wine seemed gay and exciting. She found herself saying that her father would like it here, and Gunnar grinned at her.

"That's the way to talk," he said. "Your father needs *you* to think about him. I was trying to tell you back at your house but I got sort of sidetracked by that old servant of yours. You think Rick doesn't half try to find out what you're like—what your ideas are?"

Gail nodded.

"Well, maybe he doesn't. Maybe he can't. I guess it's a hell of a job for one generation to talk to another. My old man and I could never say two words to each other without getting angry. He'd curse me for a no-good sissy because I was always fooling around with paints in the cupola of our barn where I'd fixed up a kind of studio. Once he caught me taking a small tin-full of the red paint he'd bought for the silo and he threw a bucket of it at me and threatened to wallop me good. I was fifteen and as big as I am now, so I lit out that night and never went back. Three or four years later my sister wrote me that he'd died. I was in Panama when I got the letter and I went out and got drunk but I didn't really give a damn. I never thought anything about him till a boat I was on happened to put in at a port in Norway and I got shore leave and hiked along the coast and saw the old wooden houses the fishermen live in and the nets they drag up from the sea and got the feel of the dark skies and the mysterious fjords and knew why my father had been a melancholy, angry man in the open sunny fields of Minnesota. I knew why my father and all his big bearded brothers were silent, hard-drinking guys when winter came and there were no mountains to shelter them."

He had tried to paint it once—a man standing in the narrow rectangular shade of a great red barn looking with somber eyes at stretching acres of yellow corn. Only he had not been able to make the yellow clamorously alive the way Van Gogh did, nor convey the men's lonely need for the dark green of pines and the cold blue of a fjord. Crazy to try. Crazy to tell this girl about his father when he had never told anyone else—not even himself in so many words. He pulled a crumpled pack of cigarettes out of his pocket and offered one to Gail, leaning across the red-checked tablecloth to light it.

"Thank you, Gunnar Nordstrom," Gail said in a soft voice that turned the syllables of his name to magic. Back at her house she had said, "But what do you want me to do?" like a child questioning a nurse, now she seemed to be thanking him for more than a cigarette, more even than the things he had just told her.

Madame herself brought a great brown pot of *bouillabaisse* and lifted the cover proudly. *"C'est ça!"* she said, sniffing the fine aroma. *"Eh bien,* my big sailor, at last you have found *la petite."* She turned to Gail with the mischievous directness of the French, "He walk always alone, this man from the north, *là-bas.* He loses the best part of life, *n'est-ce pas, Mademoiselle?"*

Gail laughed and Gunnar flushed.

"And me, I miss the red buttons, Madame."

"Ah oui, les pauvres petits—without their ships, without any country." Madame's fine dark eyes were full of sadness. "It is always the same thing, *la guerre."* She lifted her head and patted Gunnar's shoulder. "But we do not lack *le vin rouge.* I go for a bottle to make a little *fête.* We will drink together."

"No!" Gunnar shouted, the word exploding above the clatter of the small room. Madame shrugged and lifted sharp eyebrows.

"Sorry," Gunnar muttered. "I am not drinking today."

"*Eh bien, eh bien, alors*. One does not make such a fracas for a little thing *comme ça*." Madame bustled away.

But it wasn't a little thing. Not to him it wasn't. God, how a drink would help! A drink might make him forget. "This place used to be full of French sailors with funny red buttons on their caps," he told Gail, "And we'd get together and sing—men off boats of every country singing together."

"I wish I could have heard you," Gail said. "I wish I could have been here."

"Look," Gunnar said and his blue eyes were sad and hard as Madame's dark ones, "we weren't any pretty musical comedy chorus singing to amuse a bunch of bored, stupid people. We were drunken sailors and merchant marines singing to forget long lonely days at sea and short brutal nights in port." He looked at Gail and hesitated. Why had he ever set himself this job—this cruel, impossible job of showing a girl like Gail what life was about. Again he was tempted to let it go, to protect the curving gaiety of her smile, the young eagerness of her grey eyes. But he had to go on. He had to be relentless. The memory of Rick's dark, tortured face at the last meeting came between him and Gail. Rick was a guy worth helping—and he'd be drunk in a week—or a month—unless somebody did something.

"It isn't any fun to grow up, Gail Rickham, but I guess you've got to. Your father knows what life is like and it isn't any Hollywood picture. That's why he drank. That's why I drank. You could help him if you'd try to understand. I know it's tough for anyone who has never been drunk in a bar and gotten in a fight and cursed himself for a fool. The A.A.s will help him—especially Joe and Hank. They've both made the program work for themselves, but I've got a hunch Rick needs you." He hesitated again. "Do you look like your mother? Is that it? Joe thinks that's the trouble."

"Beulah says I do. But Aunt Emily says Daddy and I are too much alike. Maybe that's why we get so mad at each other the way you and your father did."

"Hell, I'm a fine one to set myself up as if I knew all the answers."

Gunnar tore off a piece of French bread from the basket in the center of the table. "I guess I just feel more like your father than any of the other guys in the group who've stayed put all their lives. I know how cities get him down. No elbow room. No air. Could you stand going back to the country? Or would you hate it too much?"

"I think I'd like it," Gail said softly with a slow bemused smile, but she wasn't thinking about the country.

"There's a shack I found in the woods back of Greenwich that had a 'For Rent' sign. I'd be willing to bet your father would be happy there. Maybe you'd let me bring my paints out some Sunday. It's got a big north window and the light is wrong at Hank's place."

"Do you still paint?" Gail could see a fair-haired boy in the cupola of a red barn—a fair-haired sailor sheltered by the funnels of a great ship.

"Some," Gunnar muttered. They had given him charcoal and stuff in the Marine hospital, they had told him he was good—but he wasn't good—he never got things down the way he saw them—the way he saw Gail now in that red and black dress with the long gold hair. The flaming Latin bravado and warmth of the costume and the completely un-Latin coolness and innocence of the grey eyes. Could he ever get it on a canvas?

"I'd like to try you in that outfit and call it, 'The Blonde Toreador'," he grinned at her. "I'd put in a terrifying, ugly bull rushing at you—that would be Life, see? Symbolic. And you waving a red scarf and looking as untouchable as you did a few minutes ago."

"Don't tease me, please, Gunnar," Gail begged. "I used to say to Aunt Emily when I was little 'I'll tell you if you promise not to laugh.' I'm still that way. I can't bear to be laughed at. Were you just kidding or would you really paint my portrait?"

"I wasn't kidding," Gunnar frowned, "but I'm no good. I'm just a damn fool drunken sailor with a bum leg who thinks he's Cézanne—or something."

Gail looked at Gunnar the way Emily had looked at Rick the night he had made his first A.A. call, the way Ruth must have looked at Boaz when she followed him through alien corn. "Nonsense!" she laughed. "I bet Mrs. Cézanne had to tell Mr. Cézanne how wonderful he was every morning at breakfast." Then she blushed and added hurriedly, "Tell me where the 'shack' is—I'll talk to Aunt Emily. Maybe you could show it to Daddy tomorrow. He's out at Uncle Joe's, you know. Maybe Aunt Emily and I could meet you. I think there's a train at ten fifty-five."

Gunnar took a big swallow of bitter French coffee. Women—even this girl—or perhaps particularly this girl—seemed to change with baffling rapidity from childishness to maturity, from the romantic to the practical, before a man could catch up with them. No wonder Rick was puzzled by his daughter. No wonder Rick cared how she felt about him.

XIV

SARSAPARILLA

Rick was stewing around the huge studio living room getting in everyone's way. He carried in another armful of logs, more than he could possibly manage, and dropped two down inside the front door where they shed bits of bark and drops of dirty water just after Emily had swept the Navajo rug.

Gail, running down the narrow balcony stairs, tripped over a log, caught at a small table and knocked over a heavy pottery jar full of ground pine. "Oh Daddy, why *must* you leave logs just where people have to walk?" She looked at the run in her last pair of nylons with despair.

"Why don't you look where you're going?" Rick picked up the two logs and flung rather than dropped them into the woodbox beside the already blazing fire, so that they struck the raised cover and tore off one hinge.

"Another little job—which I suppose you'll wish on Hank Frost," Gail remarked.

Rick glared at her. Then his look softened. Gail in her scarlet jersey dress with its wide gilt belt was like a modern angel on a Christmas card, and Gail had surprisingly turned down a date with Paul Manton to celebrate New Year's Eve at the Stork Club. "It was nice of you to stay here tonight," he said awkwardly.

"I wanted to." Gail stooped to pick up the ground pine and stick it back in the jar which had fortunately not broken. Gunnar would be here soon. She had not seen him since the day after he had taken her to dinner at *Le Matelot* when they had all driven up Cognewaugh Road in Joe Kelly's car.

Joe had recognized the place as belonging to an erratic sculptor who had gone to Mexico, and he had easily located the real estate agent and the key. The "shack," an enormous remodeled barn, stood on a wooded hillside overlooking a deep ravine and an elliptical pond formed by damming up a brook.

"We can go skating, Gunnar," Gail had exclaimed and then in quick contrition added, "Oh, I'm sorry, I forgot all about your leg."

Gunnar had laughed, "That's what I'm trying to do myself. I used to be able to skate on one toe when I was a kid in Minnesota."

Rick had paced the big room triumphantly. It was a good sixty by thirty feet, open to the rafters in the center with great hand-hewn beams and a narrow balcony on two sides. "I guess I won't bump my head here," he had grinned.

Emily had smiled, remembering how Rick had had to duck at every door in Joe's house. "When do you want to move in?" she had asked, catching his enthusiasm, knowing as Gunnar had known that this was the right place for Rick.

"Tomorrow!" Rick had challenged. "But of course it isn't possible." And Gail would probably hate being out here, he had thought.

Gail had hung over the balcony railing, her hair like a spot of sunlight in the darkness. "Come and see the bedrooms," she had called. "There are four of them. Two on each side with a bath between. I've picked the one I want. It's the smallest but I can see the pond from the window."

Gunnar had been standing in front of a huge sculpture which blocked the corner of the room near the big north window. It was a life-sized group of a man, a woman and three children fleeing with terror on their faces, their clothes lashed by a wind that you could almost feel. "I suppose it's refugees escaping from the Nazis," Gunnar had said, "but they don't look French or Polish . . . they look like Americans."

Joe had ambled over, "You're right, Gunnar, they are Americans. I read a piece about it in the paper. It's supposed to be our 1938 hurricane and that's a tidal wave behind them."

"H. Peculiar Henry," Rick had exclaimed. "You don't suppose we've got to live with that thing, do you?"

"Yup," Joe had grinned, "that's what the agent said. Reason the place hasn't rented. Fellow won't have it moved. Some museum out West is considering it and it stays here till it's sold. He calls it *September Remember*."

"Why?" Emily had asked.

"Old mariner's proverb about hurricanes. 'June too soon. July stand by. August you must. September remember. October all over'," Joe had quoted.

"But I like it." Gail had joined them. "It frightens me but it reminds me of that Greek thing—the man and his family all twisted up with snakes."

Gunnar had smiled at her approvingly. "Good for you, Mrs. Cézanne," he had teased and they had both laughed in the special joy of a shared memory, unaware that love was up to his old tricks of accelerating the tempo of recollection so that two people who have in reality just met may seem to have accumulated an attic full of precious souvenirs and keepsakes.

Gunnar would be here soon. Gail dashed to the kitchen for a mop, blessing Aunt Emily for having achieved the impossible in moving out, not "tomorrow" as Rick has proposed, but the day after Christmas, and Joe for his suggestion that they switch the A.A. New Year's Eve party from his house to the "shack."

Joe came through the dining room now carrying a case of coke.

"Are you sure we've got enough?" Rick asked for the fourteenth time.

"It's just too bad if we haven't," Joe laughed. "It's after eight and the stores have been closed since six. Easy does it, Rick." He was stowing the bottles into a Brittany cupboard opposite the fireplace which had been converted by the sculptor into a complete bar, including a concealed electric refrigerator. "How about bringing the ginger ale and sarsaparilla?"

Rick went through the pantry where Emily and Sylvia Landon were busy stacking chicken sandwiches and doughnuts on the largest platters they could find.

"I hope we have enough doughnuts," Rick worried. Reaching toward one cake box he upset a package on the top of another tin. It slipped to the floor, emitting a crackling stream of pretzels. . . . Pretzels without beer . . . hell. How could you have a New Year's Eve party without liquor? Last year he had been at the Polo Club in Belize with the Winged Victory. He could hear the native Marimba Band, its rhythm growing wilder and more emphatically sexual as the guests plied the musicians with drinks; could feel the rum and the music running through his body, making him capable of great Mordkin leaps; could hear the hilarious laughter. . . . "How the hell can we celebrate tonight on cokes and ginger ale?" he asked dejectedly.

"Oh, but we do," Sylvia smiled at him reassuringly. "Just wait and see. It really is fun. You can get that sense of abandon without liquor. Did Joe ever tell you about the time we tried it out last summer? It was an awfully hot night. We were sitting around the A.A. clubhouse in New York, Joe and Kidd Whistler and Jane Post and I, feeling let-down and restless. Suddenly Joe said, 'Let's all go up to Boston . . . Boston has a sort of sporting quality like New Orleans and San Francisco.' The four of us trooped down to the night boat and had an absolutely cockeyed weekend, going to ball games and dances, following any crazy notion that came into anyone's head, such as calling on Professor Hooton of Harvard and suggesting that he feed chimpanzees and gorillas liquor to see if any of them became alcoholics. It was wonderful. We went through all the psychological motions of a bender—without liquor!"

"Good for you," Rick applauded and went on into the kitchen to get the sarsaparilla. Hank had told him about drinking sarsaparilla at the New Year's Eve party last year and how it took him back to swimming in the old Mianus River above the dam when he was a kid and the bottles of pop they would buy at a "Wop" grocery store afterwards. The trouble with me, Rick thought now, is that sarsaparilla always reminds me of the castor oil my mother used to mix in it . . . but you could get back to habits that antedated the liquor habit if you tried. And God knew he was trying.

In the kitchen Emerald, who had been lent by Joe for the evening, and her girlfriend, Benzadrina, a slender pretty mulatto, were washing the dinner dishes. Emerald, as always was unflurried. She had an abiding faith in Mr. Kelly, them A.A.s, God—and Emerald. Rick overheard her now twitting Benzadrina who was worried about her husband in the

Army being faithful to her. "Them no-account Creoles ain't nothin' to fret your head 'bout, chile, they couldn't hold no man not effen you give 'em flypaper bedsheets."

Rick joined their rich Negro laughter. "Got a gallon of coffee ready for us, Emerald?" he asked.

"Don't you worry none about that coffee, Mr. Rickham." Emerald used the same comforting tone she had to Benzadrina.

Rick shouldered two cases of non-alcoholic beverages and dumped them beside Joe in front of the bar. "How many do you think will show up?" he asked for the third or fourth time.

"Ten-twelve, maybe fifteen." Rick's apprehension about the party was getting them all down. Joe was hoping that Pell, who was coming over from High Pines, would not turn up drunk. He shared Hank's distrust of Pell. The guy was a screwball. A.A. could not hope to cure a man whose main problem was something other than liquor, but he was Rick's first case and Joe was worried about the effect on Rick if, as Hank predicted, Pell turned out to be hopeless.

"What'll you bet that Hank is the first?" Rick went to the front door and peered out into the bright blustery night.

Gail, who had gone upstairs to change her stockings, paused and her hand tightened on the balcony rail. If Hank came first that would mean Gunnar. Gunnar would surely come with the Frosts.

"I'm betting on Cricket Chester." Joe squeezed the last bottle into the bar. "He loves parties, especially at the houses of people he considers his social superiors."

"Who's he?" Gail asked. His name sounded young. Maybe he'll go skating too. She hoped Gunnar had not forgotten to bring skates.

"A busboy of forty," Joe laughed. "He became an alky through drinking the dregs left in glasses at cocktail parties. Nice little fellow with a wry, nimble wit. Great friend of Porter J. Emerson's."

"Oh," Gail said quickly, "that's the man who found Gunnar on the 'beach'."

"Right, infant." Joe gave Gail a speculative glance and went on, "Emerson's a bank president and director of more companies than you could shake a fountain pen at, collects Chinese pottery and Bowery drunks. Knows more about New York's 'beach' than the Chatham Square cops—used to drink 'smoke' there himself. Used to be at some of those same cocktail parties where Cricket learned to drink the dregs—only Emerson never left any dregs. He's got a houseparty of ex-alkies up at his place on North Street now, including Cricket. Bet you Cricket'll come in that door ahead of the bank president. Cocky little guy, Cricket."

"You lose, Joe," Rick called from the door. "Here comes the first bunch and it's not Cricket and Emerson, it's the crowd from High Pines."

A sleigh with a gay clatter of bells and a protesting squeal of runners on gravel had rounded the driveway and stopped with a flourish which was somewhat marred by the driver's grumbling, "Told you there ain't enough snow on the roads for a sleigh, ruin my horses' hooves, ought to a charged you folks triple 'stead of double to bring you over here."

"There, there, my good man, where is your holiday spirit?" Pell leapt out of the sleigh and lifted a pretty dark-haired girl from the back seat, carrying her through the doorway and depositing her carefully in a big chair near the fire.

"Diana has a varicose vein in her right leg from childbirth," he announced. "The doctor says she must keep her foot elevated, but he does not share my theory that all sufferers from varicose veins could be cured by the Pell method of walking on their hands."

Diana gave him a smile that was half-vexed and half-amused. It was her characteristic attitude toward her husband. The solid fabric of her commonsense had been adorned—or weakened—by a stray strand of whimsicality. It was this weakness for the absurd that had made her fall in love with the screwball writer in the first place. "He was drunk when I met him," Diana told herself repeatedly, "and I thought he was terribly amusing." But it was becoming increasingly difficult to find him amusing now. She slipped her arms out of the new mink coat Sky had given her in a fit of remorse to atone for his drinking bout when the baby was born.

"What a lovely coat," Sylvia said, touching the soft dark fur enviously.

Pell picked up the coat and carried it off with a proud strut. Diana watched him and her smile was more vexed than amused. Some women, she knew, enjoyed the extravagant presents which were the inevitable aftermath of their husband's benders; enjoyed too, she suspected, the exaggerated moods of repentance, their female egos inflated by masculine abasement. But Diana's commonsense was revolted when Sky proclaimed that she was an angel from heaven and he was unworthy to touch the hem of her garments. She kept thinking about the unpaid bills for the baby, trying to confront the dismal fact that to depend on Sky either as a husband or a father was such a precarious business that not even an angel would attempt it. "He ought to be married to a trained nurse," she told herself grimly.

Pell returned bearing an old-fashioned gout stool and set it before his wife, placing her swollen leg on it with ostentatious tenderness. He had found the stool in an antique shop and, nothing daunted by the price, had expended the last thirty-five dollars of the sizable sum he had begged from his publisher as an advance on his next book. The advance, Pell had explained dramatically to the harassed editor, was an investment in the future. He was having a baby. Being a father would bring maturity to the writing of Manfred Schuyler Pell. The money, as Diana knew only too well, had almost all gone for the mink coat, but the gout stool, instead of increasing her sense of Sky's irresponsibility had curiously touched her. She had canceled her train reservations to Virginia where, in desperation, she had decided to take her baby back to her family's big ramshackle house near Charlottesville.

Mrs. Bentley-Young, in a fluffy pink evening dress which showed off her plump pretty shoulders, and Mr. Junior, as the A.A.s called Cornelius Van Nostrand Riggs, the Fifth, had been the other occupants of Pell's sleigh. They were both staying at High Pines for "rest cures" and Mrs. Baby said it was "really the most diverting place, much more fun than Palm Beach."

She must be slipping, Joe thought, if she sticks around Greenwich to be near Dick Spencer. It was easy enough to see why Dick had fallen for her Junior League accent and her childishly worldly ways, but you'd think she'd have better fish to fry. . . . Joe let out a hoot of laughter at the picture of Mrs. Baby in her long pink dress standing over a smelly frying pan.

"What's the joke?" Rick asked.

"Nothing," Joe said hastily.

The big room was filling fast now. The MacKenzies and Watsons had arrived together. The tenseness had gone out of Mac's face, even the crease in his trousers seemed less precise and whereas, in another man, this might have been an indication of carelessness, even deterioration, in MacKenzie. Rick recognized it as a symbol of a new ease and confidence. People were always stopping Rick and telling him how much better he looked, but you could not see changes in yourself. MacKenzie had become his yardstick. Mac had been "dry" only a few months longer than Rick so the miracle of personality transformation which Joe had talked about was a visible and, Rick hoped, comparable fact.

Mrs. Watson had headed straight for Emily, dragging her inconspicuous husband after her. Her social ambitions were as set as the rigid waves of her grey hair. Rick could hear her sharp middle-western voice and Emily's courteous but aloof rejoinder. Emily had real breeding. She made Mrs. Watson, who was always telling people that she was the daughter of lawyer Sanderson in Chillicothe, Ohio, seem cheap.

Rick was thankful to see the Frosts, Gunnar, Dick Spencer and Tony. He much preferred the humorous gaucheries of Tony Trombetta and Hank's ungrammatical Yankee drawl to Mrs. Watson's middle-class snobbery. Hell, he was being a snob himself.

Mrs. Hank in her shabby sealskin was holding on to Hank on one side and Gunnar on the other. Her round placid face seemed determinedly calm as if she were exerting all her will power to keep from thinking of her son tonight. Hank had told Rick that they had had a letter from Steve last week written in October and saying how homesick he was for Connecticut in the fall. He had stood everything else so far without a single complaint but the unchanging green of the Pacific islands had seemed more than he could stomach when the trees were turning on Cos Cob Harbor. "If I could just get one good look at the beeches and maples Grandpop planted along the road in front of our place I'd die happy." The elder Frost had set out maples and beeches alternately so that his descendants could "pleasure themselves with alternate splashes of red and yellow come fall."

Gail jumped gracefully off a window seat and started toward them but was intercepted by Mr. Junior.

There was a loud stomping on the porch and Rick opened the door again to admit Porter J. Emerson and his party from North Street. As Joe had predicted Cricket entered first, followed by two dark, exotic-looking females and a broad-shouldered, stocky man with thick grey hair and a patronizing manner, masked by ebullient affability.

The taller of the two females was batting her eyelashes at Rick.

"I met you at Daphne Manton's cocktail party," she challenged.

"H. Peculiar Henry," Rick roared, "if you aren't the Princess who lost her rubies in the Bronx Zoo!"

The eyelashes batted more rapidly, then a laugh came out of the wide scarlet mouth. "You make the joke, yes? Now I will tell you the funny one." She crossed her arms in her Russian sable coat and tossed back her curly black hair. "I am the Princess Sonia Ivanovna Tragodiev— but in Mike's bar they call me 'Battling Annie'."

"You're a good egg, Annie," Rick laughed. "How did you happen to come here?"

"My very good friend, Mr. Porter J. Emerson, he bring me."

"Picked you up on the 'beach,' eh?"

"Beach? But it is too cold for the swim. . . ." The Princess, shivered and the eyelashes batted in inquiry. "You are the big man for the joke, yes? I come to the A.A. one week ago and already I meet more of the attractive men than at the Daphne Manton cocktail party."

So that was it. Another Mrs. Bentley-Young. Rick looked across the room where *she* was perched possessively on the arm of Dick Spencer's chair. Spencer had not brought his wife in spite of Emily's special telephone call. "There's someone I want you to meet, Annie," Rick grinned. It would be fun to watch them slugging it out—Sonia the Slugger vs. Mrs. Baby.

The Princess had followed his look. "If it is the woman, no. Women I do not like. If it is that young Englishman, but yes. Young Englishmen I like. He is perhaps the remittance man, yes?

Rick did not trouble to deny it. "Go to it, Annie," he clapped her on the back. "I'm betting on you."

As soon as he had introduced them Rick ducked out, hoping to
locate Emily and help Joe pass the drinks, but he was immediately waylaid by the smaller of the two women who had come with Porter J. Emerson. She was young, with a homely, quizzical face which was somewhat
redeemed by the look of compelling alertness in her bright shoe-button
eyes. Her smooth purple-black hair was parted in the middle and folded
along her high forehead like a grackle's wings. Her costume seemed to
consist of green and magenta scarves and as many heavy silver necklaces
and bracelets as a gypsy fortune teller. "Where's your tent?" Rick was
tempted to ask her, but she got in the first word.

"What is your name?" she asked him.

"Smith."

"Your first name?"

"Smith."

"I asked what is your full name."

"Smith Smith."

"Have you a middle name?"

"Smith."

"You mean to say your name is Smith Smith Smith?"

"You don't mean *I* mean to say—you mean *you* mean to force me to
say."

She gave him a peculiar look. It seemed to start west of the meridian
and slant toward Ursa Major.

"Who are *you*, you small questioning woman?"

"My name is Corva."

"Related to corva, the crow, no doubt. You love to collect small shining objects like names—like Smiths. Please note that I do not ask what
is your first name."

"Please note that I insist on telling you. My first name is Avroc."

"Corva backwards, eh?" Rick laughed.

"Quick," Corva's black eyes sparkled approval, "you may sign the
circle." She opened a large hand-embroidered bag and took out an
address book of paper so thin that it could be used to roll cigarettes—
and was. Corva explained that to avoid stagnation she tried to make more
friends than she smoked cigarettes. If she could not remember a name

and address it meant they were not meant to manifold. "Here, sign the circle."

"The circle and the cipher are dissimilar masks," Rick said, scrawling the name Smith Smith Smith in the tiny book.

"You speak my language." Corva's look was like the slanting flash from the type of lighthouse marked on charts as "occulting." "You could give me parents," she added.

"I fear you are not rounded enough for my hammock."

She patted her rump. "Not so rocky. And my nipples are introverted, though my mind is full of mollusks."

Rick was getting bored. He looked around for a way of escape and saw Pell standing just behind him, listening with an expression of envious amusements.

"How the hell can you talk like that sober?" Pell stammered. "Or are you sober?" he asked more hopefully.

"Yup." Rick nodded. He had been surprised himself at the surrealist lingo that flowed out of his mouth in response to—or defiance of—this small crowlike poseur. Pell was a dull guy without a drink. Pompous and dull. He had come to call on Rick one night from High Pines and Rick said afterwards to Emily, "No wonder he drinks since all his wit seems to come out of a bottle." And Emily had smiled. "He's probably shy, Avery. Some people who are witty on paper are tongue-tied in conversation." Here was Pell's chance. Corva would peck at his words and turn them into bright shiny objects.

Rick turned to go but Corva clutched his arm and her bracelets jangled discordantly. "I know you don't like me but I just want to ask your merchandising advice, then obviate. I am a small working woman, what would you suggest for bread-getting?"

"You remind me of Chopin. Why don't you whore out as a music critic?"

The small ugly face puckered into sadness like an old gypsy woman's in the shadow of her tent. "I too despise the tinkly triviality of Chopin."

"Rickham is wrong," Pell declared bombastically. "Quite wrong. You have the impudent gaiety of Schostakovich's Polka."

Rick made his escape with a grin. Pell and the little crow-woman spoke the same language—but it wasn't his language. He wanted to find Emily. Shouldering his way through the crowded room he saw Gail and Mr. Junior playing gin rummy on the window seat. Gail was as bad as he was—always getting involved with undesirable creatures. Cornelius Van Nostrand Riggs, the Fifth, was another Paul Manton. Maybe Gail liked the type. The suspicion sent anger pounding through Rick's veins.

Easy does it, he told himself. He'd been exaggerating as usual. Going off the handle again. Over what? Over a few screwballs in a bunch of swell people. The trouble was screwballs always stood out, the others were the sort you'd meet at any party. Nice. Friendly. He liked them. Hell, he was thankful to be here in his own house on New Year's Eve instead of whooping it up in some noisy club where everyone was trying to hide boredom with liquor, where noise was taken as a synonym of gaiety.

There was laughter in the big studio now. Cricket Chester was doing an imitation of Porter J. Emerson picking drunks off the "beach" and Emerson was applauding with good-natured guffaws. Six or eight men who had come in late were watching, holding glasses of sarsaparilla in their hands. There were strong faces among them. Happy faces—faces that had not always been strong or happy. Only Sylvia did not look happy.

Sylvia was standing with Joe in front of the fireplace. She had changed to a bright emerald dress and had pinned a small bunch of red berries in her soft blonde hair. It was a festive gesture but the hard color of the dress made her pointed Madonna face look as pale as a mural on the walls of an old convent. Would Joe marry her if Monica didn't come back from California? Rick knew that Joe had expected Monica and Jimmy for Christmas. He had shown Rick a letter from Jimmy: "Dear Mr. Red, Mother says we can't go home for Christmas because I've got a cold and the change of climate might be dangerous. But gosh it isn't a bad cold and Christmas is no fun here. There isn't a smitch of snow. I had planned to go sliding and skating and gosh I thought you might even take me duck shooting with you. I am getting big fast. Mother says I am outgrowing all my clothes. Have you still got that Father cup I gave you or did Emerald let it fall to pieces in her hands? Gosh, I couldn't find anything decent for you out in this place but I wish you would send me a baseball mitt and maybe a small gun. . . ."

Rick was sure that Joe would never ask Monica for a divorce . . . but what about Sylvia? They were seeing more and more of each other. . . . "Who am I to worry?" Rick shrugged. The spiral galaxy in Andromeda was a great help.

Joe was looking at Sylvia with concern in his red-brown eyes. "What's wrong, Sylvia?"

"The Waves turned me down." The abrupt statement was filled with quiet desperation.

"They'd turn down Joan of Arc!" Joe protested hotly.

"You're a wonderful person, Joe." Sylvia smiled naturally for the first time in hours of forced gaiety. "I can always count on you to cheer me up." She threw back her head in a gesture of renewed faith in herself and the world. "I'll make the Waves yet. I just have to gain ten pounds and toughen up a bit. I'll get Bill Griffith to write them. I didn't want to bring alcoholism into this . . . but I'm afraid someone must have. They wanted a letter from my home town so I asked the minister of our church. Do you think he. . . ?"

"Could be. The old so-and-so." Joe's voice was indignant. Still, you couldn't exactly blame the minister. The public didn't know what A.A. was doing. Once a drunk always a drunk to a conscientious pastor who would regret the necessity of mentioning the deplorable fact but feel it his duty to . . . Joe tugged at his wild red forelock. "I'll see you in uniform yet, me darlin'." The confidence in his voice was infectious. Sylvia smiled again.

Emily was not in the big studio living room. She was becoming as elusive as Bill Griffith. Rick still had not heard him speak at an A.A. meeting. Bill had been in White Plains the night Rick had gone to Pittsburg. He had spoken several times at the New York clubhouse and Webster Hall but Rick had always just missed him. Joe kept saying, "Bill wants to meet you. He's heard all about your high bottom and your drinking horse. We'll all get together for dinner soon, Sylvia and Emily too. I know Emily will like Lois Griffith. She's a great person. Bill could never have done what he has done without Lois."

And *he* could never have gone as far as he had on the road to sobriety without Emily, Rick thought gratefully. It was amazing to him the way she managed to pick up and move at the drop of a hat—his hat, he grinned to himself. First Joe's house for two months and then, when they had just settled down for the winter in town, back to the country again at a moment's notice. And wherever she lived the place seemed to become effortlessly and intrinsically her own. Was it because, as she had so surprisingly told him nearly four months ago, she had never really considered the brownstone house in the east Sixties as her permanent home? He remembered the poem she had quoted that day, "But I would go to Timbuctoo, if anybody asked me to," and could see Timbuctoo becoming over night Emily's special province. He was still puzzled by her turning down the chance at an adventurous, migratory life with Nicky. Puzzled but thankful. He had reached the dining room door in his search for her now, when he was waylaid again. This time by Hank Frost.

"Say, I been aimin' to ask you what kinda ducks you got down to Quintanaroo—or whatever you called that place."

"Oh . . . shovellers, redheads, blue-winged teal, golden-eyes and even your broadbills—in March," Rick reeled the names off, reminding himself of the way Emerald had listed the fish that Mr. Frost caught.

"Broadbills down there in March! Why we got 'em right here in Cos Cob Harbor at the same time o' year." Hank cocked an owl eye at Rick. "Say, was they mostly one sex more nor t'other?"

"That's funny," Rick said slowly. "Come to think of it they were mostly female broadbills, or scaup, as my British pals in Belize called them."

"Holy Jumpin' Catfish, that checks! I been keepin' count on 'em and the way I figger, we got ten males to one female 'round her in March. Looks like the gentlemen sent their wives down to Florida for the winter, don't it?" Hank chuckled. "Just keepin' a few broadbill cuties on hand to amuse 'emselves with."

Emily came through the dining room door dragging two bridge tables. Rick jumped to help her. "I've been looking all over for you," he said accusingly.

Emily smiled. "You found me at just the right moment. Here, put these over near the window and I'll get the cards. The MacKenzies and Watsons want to play bridge, and Joe and Sylvia are going to take on Mr. Emerson and Cricket. I hear they're practically champions. What about poker? Do you think you could get up a game, Avery? I've cleared the dining room table and Joe brought some chips."

"You're a wonderful hostess—because you're not too much of a hostess."

"You had me worried," Emily laughed. "There's really no more poisonous creature in the world, is there?"

The two bridge tables were quickly arranged, but the poker game was harder to round up. Poker without liquor . . . pretzels without beer . . . hell, they might as well try it, the party would bog down if they didn't do something. Rick found the Princess and Dick Spencer in the kitchen concocting a Russian drink, *kvass*, out of cranberries and spices.

"You win, Annie," Rick laughed. "How about a game of poker, you two?"

"We are very busy," the Princess shook her head and stirred the spicy mixture on the stove. "I am telling Dick about my husband. He raises silver fox and ginseng in New Hampshire. He is not known as the Mad Russian and he does not wear the beard." Laughter came out of the wide scarlet mouth.

Hank and Mrs. Hank were already seated at the dining room table stacking red, white and blue chips in neat piles, and Emily had enlisted Tony. They could use two more. Rick went back to the studio and bumped into Mrs. Bentley-Young, who was trying to teach Gunnar a new rhumba step. "Poker?" he suggested not too hopefully.

Mrs. Baby looked coyly up at Gunnar. "I'm too stupid about cards but you'll help me, won't you?"

Gunnar broke away. He had been trying to break away all evening. "Sorry, I've got a date to go skating." He was across the room before she could clutch the sleeve of his navy blue sweater.

Gail saw him coming. She was still sitting on the window seat playing gin rummy with Mr. Junior. She had lost over four dollars and was growing more and more depressed. The evening to which she had looked forward for over a week was being slowly but completely ruined. She had watched Gunnar being ensnared by Mrs. Bentley-Young the moment he entered the room and thought, in a moment he'll escape. But as the moment passed she had decided forlornly that he either did not know how to escape—or did not want to escape. The latter was worse, of course, but if he were too inexperienced socially, too stupid to get away from the tiresome, flirtatious female. . . . It was almost better to have an indifferent man than an inept one . . . almost.

"Have you forgotten that you promised to go skating with me?" Gunnar asked in his deep, hesitant voice.

His words changed everything—put the stars back in the sky—righted the world on its wobbly axis. Gunnar had thought that she wanted to stay on that window seat playing a stupid game. Gail smiled a warm, radiant smile and Gunnar put out his hand and pulled her to her feet.

Rick, followed closely by Mrs. Bentley-Young, took in the situation and came to Gail's rescue. "We need you for poker, Riggs."

Mrs. Baby looked coyly up at the dark saturnine face of Mr. Junior. "I'm too stupid at cards, but you'll help me, won't you?" she quoted herself.

Rick winked at Gunnar and led his victims off to the dining room. A few minutes later he threw in a poor hand and wandered back to the studio. Gail was running down the narrow balcony stairs again. She had tied a black velveteen dirndl over her red jersey dress and flung her short white fur packet over her shoulders.

"Where's your muff?" Rick asked.

"Muff . . . but I haven't any muff, Daddy."

"I'll get you one," Rick said, seeing the flare of bonfires around a big lake, hearing the buoyant notes of a waltz on the clear cold air, "a small white round one to match your jacket."

"Daddy, how marvelous!" Gail stood on tiptoe to kiss him.

Gunnar watched them happily. This was as it should be. This was what he had hoped for. His skates clicked together as he swung them like a small boy who needs to make a noise to confirm his pleasure. Gail turned and grabbed his hand and they ran together out of the door into the bright, blustery night.

Rick headed back toward the poker game. For once his sudden memory of Adelaide at Lake Placid, his confusion of Gail with her mother, had not made him antagonistic to Gail. Pell, Corva, and Diana Pell were sitting together in front of the fire. He supposed he ought to do something about them. "How about a game, you people?" he asked. "We could split up the poker table . . . or one of us could drop out and make four for bridge."

"Cards. Cards. Cards." Pell waved one hand in a grandiloquent gesture of scorn. "The 'weary, stale, flat and unprofitable'—I am quoting Hamlet—'amusement of small minds.' We three are content to sit before your fire, sir, and revive the long-lost art of conversation."

"Go to it!" Rick grinned. "And more power to you." It was typical of Pell to show off his pompous pyrotechnics, which seemed to be making such an impression on the small crow-woman, in front of his wife, as if he got an extra kick out of having Diana witness his success with Corva.

Diana looked up from the afghan she was knitting and gave Rick her half-vexed, half-amused smile. "It was nice of you to think of us, anyway," she said in her soft Southern voice.

"I was just telling Corva that I met a most significant man recently." Pell paused and fixed Rick with his large luminous eyes.

Rick was caught. "Yeah?" he asked, hoping it would not be a long story.

"Yosuke Ichigama, who won the bowling championship of Japan—with the help of the 1923 earthquake!" Pell doubled up with mirth.

Corva leaned forward with her look of compelling alertness. "Go on, Manfred," she cawed.

Pell, hating the name Manfred, was flattered by her passionate intentness. "Ichigama had made eleven strikes. He needed one more to make a perfect score and win the tournament. His first ball on the twelfth round curved way over to the right and was heading toward the gutter. Groans went up from Ichigama's partisans, he was reaching for the dirk in his belt to commit *hara-kiri* . . . when. . . ." Pell paused dramatically, "the earthquake cut loose. The first tremor pulled his ball away from the brink of the gutter and sent it careening down the alley, right into the one-three pocket for Ichigama's twelfth strike!"

Rick gave a perfunctory guffaw and Corva pushed the purple-black wings of her hair back from her small quizzical face. "Where did you meet this Magic Mountain?" she asked enviously.

"In a psychiatrist's office. Dr. Wales sent me into New York to take the Thematic Apperception test," Pell proclaimed, "and I met Yosuke Ichigama in the waiting room. Curious character, Yosuke. He thinks he is the son of the Earth Monster, who makes earthquakes according to Japanese folklore, and that his father is angry at him. He hasn't been able to hit the king-pin since 1923. Interesting neurosis. Significant. You must take the Thematic Apperception test, Corva."

Porter J. Emerson had told Pell that Corva was an unsuccessful composer who had drunk to get inspiration, and become a bad alcoholic. She had been "dry" for nearly two years but was worrying because she feared that her creative vein had dried up too. Pell considered this "a most significant bond" between them. He had not been able to write a line on his new play since Rick had taken him to High Pines. He glared resentfully at Rick's departing back now. Rick must have wounded Corva cruelly, if unconsciously, when he had advised her to "whore out as a music critic." According to Porter J. Emerson, she earned a semi-living as a music critic for one of the politically radical, artistically contributed vindictive criticism. He had seen her articles, signed with her real name, Catherine Burbank. Another bond. Another significant something.

"And you, Manfred, must go to a numerologist!" Corva retaliated. "To find the correct rhythm for your personality, Manfred." She dropped the name in disgust as a crow spews out a dull object.

Diana Pell looked up from the pink afghan. "All his friends call him 'Sky'," she suggested in a suspiciously sweet voice.

Back at the poker game Rick found Hank's owl eye cocked at a big stack of chips in front of Mrs. Baby. "Don't know nothin' about the game," he grumbled in a low tone to Rick, "and look at her, will you!"

Mrs. Hank was grimly placing her bets as the Bentley-Young went on raising. "I can't seem to remember what they're all worth. Are the blues twenty-five or fifty?" Mrs. Baby would complain, picking up a pile of chips, not even bothering to count them and shoving them into the center of the table with her small, scarlet-tipped fingers. "Oh, do look at my hand Mrs. Riggs, please. I'm so stupid at cards. Do you think I ought to bet any more?"

"Make up your own mind," Mr. Junior said indifferently. Indifference was his characteristic attitude, but he wished vaguely that the pretty girl in the red dress had not gone off skating with that big bruiser.

The pot was growing fast now. Everyone had dropped out except the two women. Hank, watching "the Missus" anxiously, whispered again to Rick, "Plays like a man, same as she fishes. Never seen her flustered nor flamboozled yet."

"Okay, I'll call." Mrs. Baby yawned and threw down her hand. It was more fun to bet against a man than against the placid, elderly female.

"Holy Jumpin' Catfish! A natural royal straight flush!" Hank helped the "old woman" to gather in her chips.

Tony was pounding the table in excitement. "That'sa good. That'sa God-damn good."

Everyone was obviously and vociferously delighted at Mrs. Hank's luck, but Emily turned to Mrs. Bentley-Young and said sympathetically. "Too bad. You had four kings, didn't you?"

Emily's kindness was amazing, Rick thought, and then Gail was rushing into the room like a whirlwind, flinging herself at him, screaming, "Daddy, Daddy, come quickly. Gunnar's hurt his knee. Oh, Daddy, hurry. Hurry!"

Rick put his arm tight around Gail's shoulders. "Get some blankets somebody and flashlights. Emily, you telephone the doctor and get the downstairs room ready. Come on, Gail, we'll take care of him."

Pell appeared in the doorway carrying the gout stool which he had snatched from under Diana's leg. "Here, use this. You can put his leg on this."

Rick shoved Pell out of his way. He had been wanting to shove the guy to hell-and-gone all evening.

"How'd it happen, Gail?" Rick asked as they headed for the front door followed by Joe and Hank with steamer rugs and flashlight. "Stand back everyone." Rick spoke with the authority of a man who has lived long in the bush. He was the sort of person who goes to pieces over trifles but is calm and efficient in emergencies.

The firm pressure of her father's arm around her shoulder, the quiet competence of his tone, was steadying Gail but there was still an edge of hysteria to her voice as she answered, "It was all my fault, Daddy. I wanted to try waltzing and Gunnar was skating backwards and I slipped and hit his bad knee and he fell and I couldn't get him up and his leg is all bent under him."

The big studio living room was full of confusion after they left. Everyone except Pell, Corva and Mr. Junior had studied first aid and everyone had a different idea of what to do.

"Better get him some brandy," Mr. Junior suggested brightly and everyone roared.

"A fine idea for an A.A.," Porter J. Emerson shouted. "Better make some coffee, one of you women." He looked with less than his customary affability from Mrs. Baby to Corva, to the Princess who was sitting on the window seat with Dick Spencer drinking kvass out of a tall glass.

"I'se got plenty a good hot coffee on my stove." Emerald appeared carrying a tray with a small silver pot, and Porter J. Emerson decided that the world could be divided into two groups—the competent and the incompetent. Emerald, Rick, Emily, Joe, Hank, Mrs. Hank and himself he placed in the first category, the rest he swept aside.

"Bring it in here, Emerald," Emily called. She had had a hard time locating the doctor. Mrs. Hank, leaving her winnings on the table, had followed Emily to the telephone and given her the name of the man Gunnar had been consulting, but even doctors seemed to spend New Year's Eve celebrating. When Emily finally caught up with him and obtained his promise to come over immediately, she and Mrs. Hank had hurriedly made up the bed in the small back room off the kitchen which, since Benzadrina "slept out," arriving sleepy-eyed every morning by bus, they had fixed up as an extra guest room.

"I'm all right." Gunnar had tried to grin through set lips when they had settled him into bed and given him a cup of hot coffee.

"I'll sit with him till the doctor comes," Mrs. Hank volunteered, as Emily shooed out everyone but Rick and Gail.

Fire whistles, church bells, irrelevant hoots combined with inharmonious singing from the studio. "Happy New Year to you. . . . Happy. . . ."

"Poor Gunnar," Gail said softly. "It isn't a very happy New Year for you!"

Gunnar smiled and this time the effort was successful. "It's the happiest New Year's Eve I've ever had!"

Rick looked at Emily and Gail. "My God, it's the happiest I've had in eighteen years."

XV

THE MAN IN THE MIRROR

"God damn it, Gail," Rick bellowed, standing at the foot of the narrow balcony stairs in his hat and heavy overcoat, "we'll miss the train."

"Just a minute, Daddy, please," Gail called back frantically. "I can't seem to find anything this morning and I've lost my trip ticket . . . it must be in my red purse. . . ." Her voice trailed off and Rick shouted, "Take the red purse then for Christ's sake but HURRY!" Why the devil did women make such a fuss about matching purses and gloves and things anyway? Why couldn't they have pockets in their clothes like a man? He was working himself into a fine lather when Emily came out of the dining room, a coffee cup in her hand.

"Go ahead, Avery," she suggested. "I'll call a taxi for Gail. She can take a later train."

Rick tore through the kitchen, backed the car out of the garage, nearly taking a piece of the door with him, yelled at Benzadrina to close the garage, swung around the circle in front of the house and pounded the horn furiously.

Gail raced down the steps, clutching a small fuchsia hat and two purses, the new silver fox coat Rick had given her for Christmas flying off her shoulders. She spilled the contents of both purses in her lap and began to transfer lipsticks, compact, cigarette case, keys, scraps of paper, loose change, a tiny vial of perfume, a gold clip which held crisp new bills and finally the commutation ticket from the miniature red hat box to a large black suede envelope.

Rick, keeping one eye on the road, glanced at her in baffled annoyance. "For the love of Mike, why couldn't you take that red bag in the first place?"

"Oh, Daddy, not with this hat!" Gail put the two clashing colors together and smiled. Then she reached over and took the key out of the ignition.

"Now why did you do that?"

"To open the glove compartment," Gail explained patiently, cramming the red purse into the small littered space and snapping the aluminum lid shut.

"H. Peculiar Henry!" Rick stopped the car with a jerk. "Where in hell's my brief case? Look in the back seat, will you, Gail?"

Gail suppressed a desire to say, "Now who's missing the train?" as Rick turned the car in the middle of Valley Road and headed back for the house. Ever since the night of Gunnar's accident she had been filled with an admiring devotion to her father. He had been wonderful afterwards too—taking her to see Gunnar, first at the Greenwich Hospital and later at Hank Frost's. The surgeon who had re-set Gunnar's leg had said he would be all right if he took it easy for a while. "No more skating till this knee gets stronger." Gunnar was back at Hank's boatyard now. "Plenty a things a guy can do settin' on his tail," Hank had laughed.

Gail laughed suddenly now at the memory and at the sign of her father's angry face as he ground the gears changing to second on Cognewaugh Road.

"You're a fine one to laugh," Rick said indignantly. "If you hadn't stayed out half the night chasing around New York night clubs with that fancy playboy of yours, you might have gotten up at a decent hour this morning and not made me go off without my brief case," Rick wound up with devastating logic.

Gail flushed. "I'll get your Goddamn brief case." She jumped out of the car before it had stopped and raced into the house. It wasn't fair of her father, she thought resentfully, to blame her and then take a nasty crack at Paul. She had not seen Paul in over a month and she knew he had been hurt because she had turned down his invitation for New Year's Eve. He had written and written and kept telephoning her from New Haven. Besides, she had wanted to find out how much she liked Paul now after meeting Gunnar. It was natural to compare two men, wasn't it? . . . Only they were so different you couldn't actually compare them at all. . . . Life was getting awfully confusing lately. She found the brief case in the dining room where her father had left it under the morning paper, grabbed it and ran back to the car.

Rick had been taking himself abruptly to task. Words he had read in the A.A. book that foggy morning in Joe's living room came back to him with specific warning. "If we were to live we had to be free of anger" … "resentment is the number one offender." This was the first time Gail had been late. It had been fun commuting together, driving to the station in the cold, pale light of winter mornings, standing between her and the wind at the front end of the platform while she jumped up and down in her silly slippers to keep warm, climbing into the smoker where Joe, who got on the train at Riverside, could be holding a seat for them, seeing all the men look up and smile the way men smile at a pretty girl, feeling proud and happy because Gail was his daughter.

"Thanks, infant," Rick said as Gail tossed the brief case into the back seat and scrambled into the car. "Sorry I was cross."

"You ought to be," Gail snapped—and then was sorry herself. Why couldn't she be like Aunt Emily? Aunt Emily never tried to get the last word—or the first word either. You simple could not quarrel with Aunt Emily. "Mr. Manton sent his best to you, Daddy. I saw him yesterday. Daphne took me back to her apartment when we left the shop and Paul met us there and his father said you were a great guy and a great shot and to be sure to tell you that he was counting on you to go salmon fishing with him this spring at Tadoussac. He belongs to some club there."

Gail was trying to make amends but the memory of Daphne Manton's cocktail party came into both their heads and reduced them to an embarrassed silence. If her father had gone on drinking the way he had that dreadful afternoon, Gail thought, and acting the way he had, she would surely, surely have eloped with Paul. Joe and Aunt Emily kept telling her how remarkable it was that Rick had stopped drinking without a single "slip" in five months, but Gail was still baffled by her father's sudden tempers and his persistent dislike of Paul. The Mantons were always saying nice things about her family and her family was horrid about Daphne and Paul. It had been fun dancing with Paul at the Stork Club last night. Paul danced like nobody else in the world.

A train was pulling into the Greenwich station as they drove up. Rick tossed a quarter to the man at the parking lot and boosted Gail up the rear steps.

"A Goddamn local," he swore, seeing that the car they had entered had an off-center aisle and that all the smaller seats were occupied.

Gail picked one of the benches which had been unkindly designed to accommodate three people and slid in next to the window. "Here, Daddy, spread my coat out. We ought to be able to take up all the room between us if you put your brief case next to you."

"Not a chance, infant. I know how these damn trains fill up at every station." He pulled out his watch and then a time table, "H. Peculiar Henry! If we had waited nine minutes we could have caught an express."

Rick opened his brief case and tried to concentrate. He had a hell of a lot of reports to go over and a directors' meeting coming up in the afternoon, but as he had predicted they had gone no further than Mamaroneck when an enormous powdery female crowded in next to him, and every time Gail turned a page of her newspaper she flipped it against him. "Why the devil can't women learn how to fold a newspaper?" he asked in exasperation. "Here, let me show you."

The day that had started badly enough grew steadily worse. Rick had arrived late at the office, to find two important men waiting for him. He had lunched at one of the downtown clubs where everyone else had an old-fashioned or a martini and several men had ordered highballs afterwards. Now, he fumbled with the papers on his desk, trying to keep his mind on the reports he had been unable to read on the train. Facts and figures blurred together and he kept thinking that a drink would help and then hearing Hank Frost's voice.

Hank always contended that there was no such thing as a "slip." When one of the members had gone off the beam, he would slouch up to the speaker's table at the Greenwich meetings, cock his owl eye at the crowd and say in his ironic, Yankee drawl, "So you had a *slip*, brother? You're tellin' me you couldn't help yourself and I'm askin' you, you been sober since you come into A.A. ain't you? In your right mind? Nobody held a gun at your head, did they? Nobody put that drink in your hand and poured it down your throat, brother."

Hank was right. The word "slip" was too accidental. It suggested a banana peel or ice on a doorstep. Something you could not control. There was certainly a moment of decision when you made up your mind to take that drink . . . or not to take it. It involved the whole business of free will. William James had been a champion of the individual's power to determine his own destiny. . . . "An adventure in autobiography of which the conclusion is not determined in advance" . . . or something like that. If you denied free will what the hell did you have left? . . . Man driven by the gates and the furies. A sorry spectacle. Not to be endured. When you talked about a "slip" you robbed man of his birthright.

Okay. So this was NOT a "slip." He was going out deliberately to get *one* drink. Not twenty. This wasn't the start of a bender. This wasn't like that time in the hotel in Pittsburgh when he had had to fight like hell to keep from ordering a bottle. He could handle the stuff now. He had been dry over five months. Joe would say, "You haven't got alcohol licked in five months—or five years." The A.A.s were always talking about the danger of the first drink.

He'd show them. He wasn't heading for trouble now. He knew what he was doing. And he had to have one drink. He felt like hell. His eyeballs ached, a sure sign that malaria was hitting him again. A United Fruit Company doctor had been treating him with atebrine and plasmochin, which seemed to be working better than the quinine he used to carry in his pockets like candy in the bush, but this afternoon there was the familiar blurred feeling in his head, the old dull pain in his anklebones. He shoved the papers back on his desk, grabbed his hat and topcoat from his locker and told his secretary he would be back in half an hour to meet Mr. Driscomb.

Damn Bill Driscomb anyhow. He was a regular Jonah. Every time Rick had anything to do with Driscomb a drink seemed to be the only answer. He had been dreading this conference all week. Driscomb would try to sell his scheme to the directors—and he was a damn good salesman. The trouble was he didn't know a thing about the bush. It was up to Rick to convince the Board that Driscomb was all wet, that his program of war-time economy wouldn't work, no matter how feasible it sounded on paper. Rick thought of his friends in Carmen—swell guys.

Driscomb would make life hell for them by just not knowing what they were up against. Rick had to out-smart Driscomb—if he could. But he had to be on his toes to do it. One drink would fix him up. Ease his tension. Give him self-confidence.

As he came out on the street he shivered and pulled up the collar of his coat. It was a raw nasty February day. Dark masses of clouds scurried over the Battery. His hatred of New York struck through him as violently as the wind that whipped around the corner. A regular nor'easter all right. Rick looked with contempt at a man scurrying before the breeze like a badly handled sloop. The poor dope, he probably didn't even know the direction of the wind. City people were all fools. They had never sailed a small boat in a tricky breeze or followed a compass in the bush. To them weather was just a thing to complain about. They were not even sufficiently aware of it to cross the street and walk on the sunny side—when there was a sun.

Rick turned into Sam's Place, where the men from the office were always stopping by on their way to the subway for a couple of quick ones. Hot stale air and the familiar mixture of liquor and cheap tobacco and sawdust struck him. Two seedy customers, who looked as if they had been propped on the bar stools all night, turned their heads as the gust of fresh cold air hit them. "Shut it, brother," the nearer one muttered. *"Brother."* The word stirred a protest in his mind . . . Hank.

There was a phone booth at his left and Rick headed for it on impulse. He'd call Joe and tell him he was in a bar and about to take one drink. Not twenty. It seemed suddenly important that Joe should know. He didn't want to put anything over on Joe. He wanted to explain to Joe how he had figured things out, to tell Joe this wasn't a "slip." If Joe said, "You're nuts, boy. It can't be done," maybe he'd walk out. Maybe. He dialed the number and heard the automatic solicitude of the receptionist's voice. "Sorry, Mr. Kelly just stepped out. He is expected back in an hour. May I have him call you?"

That tied it. Rick threw the receiver back on the hook and pushed out the glass doors impatiently. It was an omen all right. If you had worked with natives and Indians as much as he had you came to believe in their instinctive reliance on signs and portents. Probably just the subconscious pointing out the way you actually wanted to go. Well, he wanted a drink. He crossed to the bar, picking a stool as far from the seedy incumbents as possible. It was a short bar.

He had been to some of the "longest bars in the world"—Tiajuana, when it had been a wide open town and women in trailing evening dresses came down from the Casino in Agua Caliente to explore the night life. He remembered the expression of envious contempt on the face of the blonde whore for whom he had been buying drinks when one of the non-professionals had tried to pick him up.

And the time a couple of the engineers' wives had wanted to see the cribs behind a big dance hall. The manager had come around to their table and suggested it like a tourist guide and Harry Andrews had been furious. Wanted to sock the guy. But Molly had said it might be "fun." Molly had wild brown hair and wild brown eyes and was always looking for a new thrill. She had been pretty tight. They all had. Luckily neither of the girls had understood Spanish. They had kept begging Rick to translate the obscenities the other "girls" had hurled at them as they walked down a long narrow corridor.

It had been damned funny. And disquieting. Harry had looked sheepish and Mrs. Norton had hung on to her husband's arm as if she were afraid he might leave her for one of the dark lusty wenches in brightly flowered kimonos.

The thing Molly hadn't been able to get over was the pictures of the Virgin tacked to the white plaster walls in nearly every cubicle. She had grabbed a stiff drink when they got back to their table and she kept saying over and over, "Did you see those prints of the Virgin Mary, Harry? I went to a convent in France the year mother was trying to get a divorce in Paris and the nuns thought she was *vraiment une grande dame* because she had an accent as atrocious as the British nobility and a chinchilla coat. They didn't know that mother was running around with a Georgian Prince and that he made a fortune out of selling her that coat which he claimed belonged to his aunt. Oh my God, Harry, did you see those pictures? They reminded me of the convent. I mean they actually did." She was almost crying. Mrs. Norton had not said a word. She had put an over-generous amount of lipstick on her thin mouth and peered desolately in her compact mirror at her fading blonde hair. Christ, what a night it had been!

The bartender stopped polishing glasses with a damp grey towel and came over to Rick. He looked like a mortician. Why did people expect bartenders to be jolly fellows? This guy had a damp grey forehead to match his damp grey towel. Most of them looked like men suffering from stomach ulcers. Rick couldn't remember any jolly bartender except old Angus at the Monks Club. Angus was straight out of the Pickwick Papers or Punch. Genial . . . but Scotch. He knew how much every member was good for in drinks and credit. There had been a bartender at one of the recent A.A. meetings who hadn't had a drink in two years. . . . Handling the stuff every night. . . . Smelling it. Most of the members seemed to think he was remarkable but probably Pale Ale had been right. A bartender saw what liquor did to you if you drank too much.

Hell, he'd better order his drink now and get going. One drink. Not twenty. Rum was no good on a day like this. A tall cool glass with the smell of lime and the hot fragrance of a tropical breeze and the sharp bright glitter of magenta and white and saffron on a plaza in Rio.

A Pernod in Paris. Little stacks of coasters and the garcon totting them up till it took all the francs in your pocket to pay *"l'addition."* "No good for you. No good for me," Aleece had said. The shrill gay clatter of a sidewalk café and the soft lavender mist of Notre Dame. Paris must be hell with those clumsy, guttural, un-witty Germans swarming over the place.

This wasn't getting him a drink. He looked along the bar and noticed with disgust that one of the seedy customers seemed to be pouring straight gin into a thick tumbler. The other one had beer with a Rye chaser. That had been Hank's drink. He was always boasting about the number of beers with Rye chasers he had downed in the old days, telling his favorite story about the time after he had been in A.A. nine months— "long enough to have a baby and to know better than to take a drink," he invariably added—he had gone into New York for the "sole and express purpose of getting' me a jag on." He had brought a bottle of Rye in his overcoat pocket and gone to the hotel near Grand Central where he used to stay with his father when he was a boy. He wasn't "aimin' to waste any time goin' round to bars and gittin' tight gradual. No sir, no nonsense about this." He had it all planned out how he would go up to his room, deposit his bag and his bottle, order up a case of beer, turn the key in the lock and start drinking himself into insensibility. That was the way he wanted it, see? He had signed the register and had the key in his hand but the clerk had started "hemmin' and hawin' as to how some folks ain't moved their duds out o' the room yet and the maids got to clean up. Would Mr. Frost mind waitin' in the lobby, or might he suggest that there was a real nice cocktail lounge and he would send one o' the bell hops to call Mr. Frost just as soon as the room was ready?" Hank had tossed the key on the desk and walked out through the revolving doors. He had caught the next train back to Greenwich, Hank always made it sound like a miracle. Miracle—hell. It was some perverse streak in Hank, some Yankee cussedness. Certainly God had not made him toss his bottle of Rye out on the N. Y., N. H. & H. railroad tracks when he reached Port Chester. God was not going to stop Rick from ordering one drink now. One. Not twenty.

But not a martini. That was Daphne Manton's drink. He could hear her over-emphatic, "But I do like my martinis DRY, don't you, Mr. Rick-ham?" Hear the shrill voices of women in all the prettified chromium and red leather bars in New York insisting like bright, well-taught parrots, "Make mine a martini. Very DRY, please!" Most of them could not tell the difference. It was the smart thing to say and they repeated it endlessly in their smart Café Society accents in their smart Café Society clothes. What they really liked were the small green olives on toothpicks. He could see the greedy dark red fingernails that looked as if they had never been scrubbed with an honest brush, that looked like Lady Macbeth's hands dripping with the blood of Duncan. They had spoiled martinis for a man.

An old-fashioned might do. Or a whiskey sour. There was a list of drinks and prices on the wall behind the rows of display bottles like *Specials Today* of sodas and sundaes in a drug store. And a long mirror. He caught the eye of a man looking directly at him. A big man with a clear, healthy skin. No dark pouches under *his* eyes. No frightened nervous twist to *his* mouth. Not a drinking man, obviously. You could always tell.

Rick stared into grey eyes as a cat stares at itself in a mirror. He felt his skin prickling. The man was himself. This was an Avery Rickham he had not faced in years.

"What's yours" The bartender sounded as if he had grown tired of asking the same question, as if he thought Rick must be deaf or crazy, staring at himself in the mirror like he was seeing a ghost. You sure ran into a lot of queer ducks in this neighborhood. But it wasn't good for business to have a guy sit at a bar as if he were in a railroad station waiting for a train and had forgotten to look at a time table. That was a pretty good crack. The bartender was pleased with his unusual notion. He must remember to tell Sam when he came on at four-thirty. Sam had the best hours. The men from the coffee importers' offices and the big Chewing Gum building would stop by on their way to the subway. Good tippers too. Never made any trouble. This big fellow dressed like them but he acted funny. The bartender tried a louder tone, "What can I get you?" and added a "sir," with a tip in mind.

"Gimme a coke," Rick heard his own voice saying. It was not what he had planned to say. He didn't know what made him say it. *Made?* That was a queer way to put it. Nobody *made* him ask for a coke. Or had something put the words in his mouth? What had William James said about "saving powers" which one can "in a crisis make contact with and be saved?"

The man with the beer and Rye turned on his stool and gave Rick a bleary, derisive grin. "He orders a coke, he does! Walks right into a bar like a kid with a nickel in his pants and orders himself a coke!"

"That's right," Rick said. He downed the sweetish brown liquid and stood up. "Want to make something of it?" When Rick stood up at a bar men were apt to lose rather rapidly any idea they had had of "making something of it." His six feet three inches had saved him from plenty of fights in plenty of bars. He got a kick out of seeing little blustering men crumple suddenly into apology or silence. This one did now. Rick threw a dime on the bar and opened the door. "Shut it, brother." The Rye-and-beer called out with belated spunk. Rick grinned.

He had been right about the nor'easter. It was driving small sharp particles of snow down the darkening street. H. Peculiar Henry, how long had he been in that bar? There would be the devil to pay if he were late meeting Driscomb and the Board. He pulled his watch out of his vest pocket, cursing the awkwardness of layers of buttoned clothing and feeling the wind stab at him maliciously as if it had been waiting for the chance. His watch must have stopped. In the shelter of a jutting doorway he shook it and held it to his ear, surprised at its warmth. Surprised that it was ticking. He had been gone only twenty-eight minutes. Time and Time and Time and Time. Emily said Proust was the only person who understood Time. She talked about Proust's agility in going back and forth in Time and Memory. But this was the damnedest thing. He could have sworn that he had spent at least three hours in that bar. Three hours without a drink. There had been time to remember a lot of things. Time for a miracle? That was what Hank would call it. Joe too. Rick did not know. He honestly didn't know. He didn't believe in miracles. But how could you explain it? He had gone into Sam's Place for a drink. One drink. Not twenty. And he had heard himself ordering a coke! No matter how you looked at it, it was queer. He was being rational about it. He was a rational guy. But it was damn funny. He supposed you could put it down to his seeing himself in that mirror—but why had he happened to look at just the moment when he was about to order a drink? And one drink *would* have been twenty. He admitted that now as he rang for the elevator in his building. The A.A.s were right—the first drink was the big danger for an alcoholic. He would never have shown up to meet Driscomb.

When he opened the door to his own office his secretary fluttered toward him. "I was afraid you were going to be late, Mr. Rickham," she said in the over-solicitous voice which had always annoyed him.

Afraid? Rick threw back his head and laughed. She didn't know what cause there had been for fear. But he did. He picked up the reports from his desk. Facts hurried through his mind and assembled like parts in a complicated mechanical line-up. He had not been thinking about the flaws in Driscomb's program but the necessary data to disprove it had slid down some subconscious track and turned into a finished argument. He was all set, thank God. He grinned, wondering how near that casual phrase came to a prayer.

XVI

CROW TALK

The softening breezes of early April, scented with burning grass from inland fields and nearby salt marshes, found the Pells back in the small house in the Darien woods where Rick had first tried to practice the Twelfth Step. An aunt with a modest income had refused to let Rick pay for her nephew's first week at High Pines and, "touched by the talented boy's sorry plight," had advanced enough money to keep him there for three months. He had gone home hopefully the middle of January, but the February blizzard had so depressed and infuriated him that he had started to drink again and finally, in a fit of solicitude for Diana—"how could a delicate girl brought up in Virginia endure New England's snow-slough-despond?" he had asked himself—he had sneaked into the garage, siphoned gasoline out of his car, poured it on a patch of snow under the spruce trees next to the porch and, lighting the hated snow, had nearly set fire to the house. Diana, terrified, had called the fire department and Pell, protesting, "It's nothing. It's nothing. I'm just a little manic today," had landed not in jail, where the irate firemen had planned to dump him, but back in High Pines.

He had stayed on as a "charity patient" until Dr. Sam Wales' private fund for such cases was seriously depleted. Then Diana, who had taken the baby to stay with a friend in Poughkeepsie, had written that she would give him one more trial, but that this was his last chance. Positively his last.

"Mrs. Sweet Jasmine. Have missed you indecently. Am completely new character. Driving Poughkeepsie to get you and the Colonel Wednesday morning," Pell had wired back with characteristic optimism regarding both his own shortcomings and gasoline rationing.

"The Colonel" was Pell's name for the baby whose Great Uncle,

Colonel Randolph Davis, had come through with a timely check for a thousand dollars after receiving Diana's tactful announcement that she had named her first child for her favorite "kin."

The day before he drove up to Poughkeepsie Pell had taken Lassandra, one of Emerald's seemingly inexhaustible supply of friends, to clean house. She was a large, almost white woman with dark brown freckles, dark brown horn-rimmed glasses and a mincing walk, evidently intended to inform all and sundry that she was light on her feet. When they entered the house it was cold and smelled of mildew. Thraves had loyally kept an eye on the oil tank and set the temperature just high enough to prevent the pipes from freezing, but not warm enough to keep a damp chill from striking at their bones now. Pell had turned the thermostat up and hurried Lassandra toward the kitchen where she began to grumble that she didn't like "the state of things nohow." Pell had shushed her with a lofty statement that his wife would be home tomorrow and would expect a good dinner, Lassandra better order soft-shelled crabs or lobster and asparagus. Lassandra, knowing quite well that "them things wasn't in the market," had nevertheless been impressed and had docilely taken brooms, mops, carpet-sweeper and cleaning rags out of the kitchen closet, revealing an array of half-empty whiskey, gin and beer bottles. Pell had pounced on them in a frenzy of righteousness. He was not only the kind of husband who hired a maid and got the house in order for his wife, he was a sober man—a man who could not bear the sight of liquor around his place. The smell of mingled gin, beer and whiskey had filled the kitchen as Pell emptied the bottles resolutely into the sink. But was that all? Hadn't he hidden bottles all over the house where Diana was least likely to discover them during the "snow-slough-despond" in February?

He had stalked determinedly through the living room in a whole-hog, shoot-the-works spirit, locating one full quart behind the Encyclopedia, two more back of the now dead plants on the window sill in the sun room and a final pint in the lower drawer of his typewriter desk. He returned triumphantly to the kitchen but the quart of Bourbon was giving him twinges of regret and he was relieved when Lassandra, who had watched him in consternation, suggested that "effen he was goin' to waste good liquor like that she had a friend who would sure appreciate it."

Pell's "completely new character" of model husband and sober citizen had continued happily after Diana's return from Poughkeepsie. He had even scrupulously put Corva out of his mind, in spite of the attraction he had felt toward her on New Year's Eve and the flattering adulation she had shown him the following week when she had persuaded Porter J. Emerson to drive her to High Pines to call on Pell. She had sat in the cluttered Mid-Victorian waiting room, twisting her slim artistic hands. Corva's fluttering, helpless hands, which reminded Rick of the Winged Victory and consequently annoyed him inordinately, were strangely exciting to Pell. Perhaps it was just the hands themselves, "white serpents of love . . . or should I say servants . . . pale deer slipping through a scherzo wood," he had written her after his return to High Pines in February when the snow still lay thick under the tall dark trees and the impulse to burn it in a ritualistic defiance of winter had persisted in Pell's mind.

It had been a long letter. And all the time he was writing Pell had kept wondering why he did not go to the telephone and call her and ask her to come out from New York to see him. She would come. Of that he had felt certain, but at the same time he had realized, for ignorance of self was not one of the defects of his character, that he did not really want to see her. He wanted to use her as "something to write against." And how he had written! Fifteen typed pages, mostly in the surrealist double-talk they both relished, but with one simple lyric passage, describing his early morning walk to the harbor and the snow goose he had seen. It was a local rarity, so unusual in the region that no one at High Pines had believed he had seen it. They had even skeptically suggested that the bird must be a large gull or possibly a belated heron, but he had believed in the snow goose and he had counted on Corva to believe in it too. The goose symbolized something to him—something like "independence, indifference and high white pride." When he had finished the letter, which he had started as he usually did without a date or salutation, he had reinserted the first page and typed in the upper right hand corner,

"High Pines,
Snow Saturday of the Snow Goose."

Now the snow as an April shower at the roots of the new April grass, the snow goose had been superseded by a confident bluebird, and Pell was going to New York with Diana to buy her a spring hat. Gail had told Diana that Daphne Manton had promised to give Gail's special friends a discount which would bring the price down to only twenty or twenty-five dollars, and that made them "really marvelous bargains" and Daphne had "the most marvelous hats this season." Diana had smiled, her smile that was half-vexed and half-amused. Gail was a sweet child but she, Diana, had never paid that much for a hat in all her born days. Pell, over-hearing this conversation, had proclaimed in his most lordly manner, "Of course, you shall have a new spring bonnet, Mrs. Lovely," and had proceeded to make a festive occasion of it. They would not only buy a hat, they would further celebrate by going to lunch and a matinee. He would order the tickets through the Yale Club at once.

Pell drove Diana to the early train, she had some shopping to do at Best's for the "Colonel." Sky had objected disdainfully to the hideous knitted garments his son wore and insisted that Diana buy the poor, helpless infant some proper clothes, pulling out old photographs of himself in ruffled, hand-embroidered dresses to demonstrate how a son of Manfred Schuyler Pell should be clothed. He kissed Diana uxoriously at the station, reminding her to pick up the theater tickets at the Yale Club and to meet him not later than twelve-thirty at Daphne Manton's shop.

When he drove back to the house, determined to finish the scene he had been working on before starting for the eleven something train, he was greeted by a fraught-with-important-news Lassandra. "Western Union say you is to call her as soon as you steps foot in this house."

The message was a desperate plea from Corva that he come at once—"Today"—to see her.

Joe Kelly had been telling him the same night, after the A.A. meeting when Gail and Diana had talked about hats, that Catherine Burbank had had a "slip" and was in a nursing home in Ossining. Joe had tried to tell him why—but Pell knew why. For nearly two years Corva had been "dry" and for nearly two years she had not written a bar of decent music. She had been following the A.A. principle of "first things first." Then she had decided that if she could compose nothing but the bloodless, academic stuff she had written before liquor thawed out her creative arteries, she would rather not live at all. With that decision she had reached for a bottle. She was "putting first things first" in her own way. She had written the opening of a fugue—and passed out. The fugue was good so far as it went, but Corva, wretchedly trying to "taper off" in the nursing home, had sent word that she desperately needed to see some of the A.A.'s, especially Pell.

Pell, putting "first things first" himself, had decided that at the moment Diana and her spring hat were more important to him than Corva. Now he didn't know. God in heaven, he didn't know. He told Western Union to hold the line a minute, he wanted to send an answer . . . but what answer? Finally he spelled out two messages, one to Corva saying he would be there today; one to Diana trying to explain in ten words that he had to go away on an A.A. case—matter of life and death—she must buy the prettiest hat in the shop and get Gail to go to the matinee with her. He had sent this wire in care of Gail at Daphne Manton's shop.

Then he had gone upstairs feeling confused and elated. The tame crow he had discovered and purchased at an exorbitant price from a small boy in the village of Darien fluttered and cawed in greeting as he opened the door to his work room. He had acquired the crow as a sentimental symbol of Corva, but Diana had not cared for the crow any more than she cared for Corva. She had been afraid the bird would fly around and peck at the baby, so Pell had bought an elaborate cage and never let the poor crow out except in his own work room. Now he filled his corncob pipe with dried kernels of corn and held it in his mouth. The crow flapped to his shoulder and then with accustomed, but remarkable daring, nipped a bit of corn out of the pipe and flew off triumphantly. Corva would be amused by that trick. He would take the crow with him to call on Corva.

Catherine Burbank was paler and thinner than ever, her small quizzical face more compellingly, feverishly alert. She seemed hysterically amused by the crow and touched by the "image of the image." Pell was glad he had come. He had made the right decision. Diana would be solaced by a new hat; this small female in the purple coat with big silver buttons had a more desperate spiritual need. They walked for two hours along the bank of the Hudson and Pell foresaw that the afternoon would always be memorable for some crystalline, purgatorial quality in the malefic spring air, some sense he got from her talk, or the lambent weather—or both—that made him aware of time-flow as he had never been before. Aware of the continuity of each instant and its growth, acutely aware of the truth of Bergson's statement, "time is inventive."

He left Ossining in a state of mental intoxication. Absentmindedly, he boarded a through express which had been stopped by track trouble. Absent-mindedly, he sat down in the diner and ordered a beer; quickly caught himself and changed it to coffee. The waiters were cleaning up the car prior to reaching New York and were not particularly pleased to see him, but one elderly Negro, fascinated by the crow and overcome by the size of Pell's beforehand tip, agreed to bring a club sandwich with the coffee.

Coffee might calm his nerves. He was starting a "dry" jag, he knew the signs, he had had them before. But this was a special one. A lallapallooza. A *finis coronat opus*. It had been building up for some time, the strain of behaving like a dependable husband and the certain realization that Diana would leave him forever if he drank again had begun to tell on his nerves. Now guilt tweaked at his conscience the way the crow was tweaking at the bars of his cage. He had been a fool to let Diana down on the first festivity they had planned together since the baby was born. His egocentric excitement over Corva's adulation suddenly nauseated him. His mouth and hands were twitching. He watched his hands, seeing Corva's slim twisting fingers, "two pale deer slipping through a scherzo wood."

"It is fascinating how characters emerge from crannies in one's life . . . approach tentatively, waving feelers like—grasshoppers, not cockroaches, my dear—then recede with the vagueness of an early Chaplin movie or advance and attain the solidity of the first thirty-one theorems of Euclid. . . . That dim half-moment when one does not know whether they are destined to recede or advance—that is a crisis of more than campophagine import."

Pell addressed these remarks to his trained crow—and to himself—

as he ruminated on the pellucid encounter with Corva. Pellucid was the word for it, the gravity of a cameo and the fixity of seaweed dried into sand. Disgusted as he was by his own actions, he was still enthralled by the vision of Corva standing in midcourse . . . flight or foray? . . . on the worn stairs of the railway station at Ossining-on-Hudson . . . "Sing-Sing-on-Muddy-Water, that is . . . God is the sun on a muddy river. Hudson, however, did not discover this river, but some remote-in-time far-foraging dolichocephal, circa, centripetally, 25,000 B.C."

The crow blinked superciliously and Pell opened the door of the cage and let him out. He perched on Pell's shoulder and began to peck contentedly at his tweed jacket, snatching out one thread and snipping his pleasure in mechanistic precision. Pell pulled out his fountain pen and began to write, appropriating the back of a dining car menu.

"You are like a small bowl of rationed oleomargarine before the coloring has been added. I like to write on trains, to the stimulating sense of the body being moved in space through no effort of my own, leaving the mind to its own travels, free to idle hither and yon. . . . What is yon? Or rather *where* is yon? *Cherchez* this female word, you small indefatigable etymological bloodhound. Yon is Saxon, I think, but could be Pict? . . . or Teutonic, i.e., Indo-European, via the cold northlands of the Big Eaters.

"Anyway the mind is now yon—and yon means you—Corva. That snow Saturday of the snow goose I was almost horribly in love with you . . . approximately . . . that is roughly speaking . . . according to folk sayings February is the month to fall in love. Beware the banal, but beware also bewaring the banal. All geese understand the in-love-fallingness of February. Also, mongeese, or mongooses.

"February is dim-gone, but you are seen clearly if tenuously as you alertly examine the footprints of the creatures which have trod before you along the periphery of humor. Do not lose your notes, my little mango, in the river of prairadox—compound of paradox and prairie dog—but report your findings at the next regular meeting of the Greenwich group."

Pell had now exhausted the backs of three menu cards and the patience of the waiter. "I'll autograph one for you," Pell flourished his fountain pen. "You have heard of Manfred Schuyler Pell, the playwright? My next play is to be laid in a dining car." The waiter, entranced, carried the baffling oleomargarine paragraph in his wallet until one night when he lost heavily in a crap game and his adversary accepted his valuation of twenty-five dollars for the famous writing of a famous writer.

The other two cards Pell stuffed in his pocket. He would send them to Corva. Better make a copy when he got home. Pell made carbons of all his letters; Diana had been amused and shocked to hear a particularly charming passage from one of Sky's love letters to her issuing from the mouth of the Indian in *Savage in Bed*.

Poor Diana. Lovely Diana. He must think of Diana now. They were pulling into Grand Central. Pell maneuvered the crow back into its cage. Diana did not like the crow. On impulse he thrust the cage at the startled waiter. "Here, take this impudent small bird with the compliments of Manfred Schuyler Pell. My wife does not care for Corva." He plunged into the crowded anonymity of the station before the waiter could stammer a refusal. Diana would be pleased by his fine, thoughtful gesture. He must please Diana. He could picture her waiting in the small hall where he had thrown the books six months ago, waiting to show him her new hat.

The train from New York to Darien moved with aggravating indifference to Pell's impatience to get home, but at last he turned his car into his own driveway. . . . The shadow of a windsome cedar, bending blowing cedar shadow . . . grey-blue on the light grey pebbles of his own driveway . . . the tip of the shadow angled across grey pebbles to the greening lawn . . . a confident bird flew its own pointed shade out of its unshadowed nest.

Closing the garage doors Pell saw the darkening marshes of Scott's Cove.

> "As the marsh hen secretly builds on the watery sod,
> Behold, I will build me a nest on the greatness of God."

He congratulated himself on remembering the lines of Sidney Lanier, but the sod of his resolution was watery and unstable, indeed.

"Hi, Mrs. Lovely!" he yelled hopefully as he opened the door.

"Miss Pell she ain't comin' home till later on," Lassandra called from the kitchen from which the smell of cabbage came in unappetizing waves. "She phone and say for me to look after the baby good." Lassandra, whose cooking left much to be desired, had proved to be a "treasure" with the Colonel. She spent hours measuring his tasteless formulas, sterilizing bottles, testing them on her thick wrist, washing diapers and toting the baby carriage in and out of the sun in the backyard. She was also becoming a Cassandra of evil news, Pell decided.

"You wants your dinner now, Mist' Pell?"

Pell growled assent, beginning to feel very sorry for himself, forgetting with typical alcoholic disregard of facts that he had brought this on himself by ditching the matinee date with Diana.

His hands were twitching with rage as he washed them. In his work room the corncob pipe half-filled with dried kernels was an ironic reminder of Corva. He rummaged in the bottom drawer of his desk from which he had so nobly extracted the pint of liquor and pulled out a bottle of sedative tablets. "Dose, one tablet in emergencies," the semi-quack East Side New York druggist had told him. This was an emergency. He wolfed four.

"Yo' dinner is coolin' itself," Lassandra called. And so it was. The corned beef and cabbage were tepid by the time Pell reached the table.

He was growing more and more sorry for himself. Hadn't he gone to the trouble of hiring a cook for Diana? The least she could do was to see that the cook cooked. Lassandra could be taught if Diana would give her simple instructions. Southerners had a reputation as gourmets. Corned beef and cabbage. Ha! Even the coffee was cold. Angrily he ordered Lassandra to heat it while he gulped a slice of soggy, pasty cherry pie. The coffee returned, burned now.

"Damme," he exclaimed, pushing back his chair and stalking over to the fireplace in the living room with his best military strut. He was Washington at Valley Forge. No, he was Grant in the "Wilderness." He would hammer his way through all these obstacles, damn 'em. He had lighted a cigarette, now he hurled it into the un-laid fireplace. Grant always smoked cigars. Cigars usually made Pell sick, but his picture of himself in Grant's "hammering campaign" called for a cigar, and he knew where there were two in a blue bowl on the mantel. He had brought them back from a fraternity dinner several months ago intending to give them to Hank Frost. With shaking fingers he yanked off the cellophane—"God damn invention of a nation scared of bacilli." The cheroot was much too dry. He coughed on the first puff . . . but . . . Grant smoked cigars . . . and Grant was at bay, at bay but *not* retreating. Grant would be having a drink now . . . wasn't Grant always half-drunk before a battle?

Suddenly, craftily Pell started for the cellar stairs. He knew where one bottle was still hidden . . . had he forgotten purposely to throw it out when he had emptied all the others? Months ago he had concealed a quart of Rye in the grandfather's clock which he had taken down to tinker with when Diana had complained about having a clock in the hall that didn't run. Not bothering to switch on the light he reached inside the clock and his fingers closed on the smooth roundness of a bottle of *Old Grandad*.

He tucked the bottle under his jacket and carried it furtively and exultingly up the two flights to his work room. Opening the tinfoil with a penknife he took two big swigs—why fuss about a glass which he would just have to rinse out before Diana found it? He had tried to cut out drinking for Diana, he had given the crow away to please Diana and what did she care? But Corva cared. Corva would understand that liquor was essential to an artist. He pulled the crumpled menus out of his pocket, regretting that he had handed one to the waiter—something about a bowl of margarine. He took another swig out of the bottle to down the sting of Grant's cigar which he was hoping would go out in the ashtray where he had just laid it. He was feeling better. Much better. He put two yellow sheets with a carbon between—like sunlight on each side of a blue cedar—into his machine and started to type.

> Catherine is a lovely name,
> Catherine is a lovely catholic name.
>   My beloved nurse when I was a thin small boy was a lovely
> fat catholic catherine. . . . Note, this line spoils rhythm? No, it

is just not what I thought of when I woke up this morning. Forget that.

Cathexis is on Catherine and not her unlovely antonym.
My lovely lost antonia—see, what made me think of that is that
catholic is like cather . . . not only that antonim is like antonia.
See, what great shadow on the cave wall is the Freud-man
shadow?

Now, if I could only damn it think of what I had when I
woke up . . . some swell four lines on catherine-cathexis-the-
catholic . . . a groundswell of loveliness . . . there was more play
on the word-sound. I mean now *word*—a teacher's word—sound,
a singing noise . . . more play on lovely than on Catherine.

Gone . . . what man invents a machine to write down
immediately when you think it—those clear brain hours of early
light—this man deserving is. No not a dictaphone, if other
sleepers there be, humanitarian-conditioned apes that are we.

Catherine is not the antonim of lovely . . . but Catherine
has antennae waving feelers tentatively in the pellucid air of the
Hudson. No my sweet mango, grasshoppers—not cockroaches.

Still the lost the lovely lines—was your fugue like that?—
tempus fugit—emerging, vanishing, fish-silver, fish shadow—
would Doc Wales be able to catch those four fish lines, pull
them gleaming, wriggling out of my subconscious? Eels he
caught often, long slimey, ugly with bloody heads where we
bludgeoned them Doc Wales and I . . . seaweed also, always seaweed, dark, clinging, cold—

Pell shivered and took another long pull on the bottle. He ripped
the page from his typewriter and then reinserted it and wrote at the
top,

"April is the cruelest month."
Why do white lilacs smell like purple lilacs?

He took another drink, fell asleep in his chair, fell off his chair, crawled to the daybed and was snoring heavily when Diana entered the room.

Gail rushed to the door of Daphne Manton's shop when Diana appeared, promptly at twelve-thirty, looking excited and pretty in her mink coat, her arms full of packages. "Sky here yet?" she asked, and Gail stammered his message, which she had memorized in an agony of apprehension over Diana's disappointment.

Diana stood quite still for a moment, happiness draining out of her face, her eyes widening with hurt—or was it fear? Gail couldn't make out. She had grown very fond of Diana. A fondness compounded of admiration and envy of this girl, only a few years older than herself, who was married and had a baby and a husband who gave her mink coats and wrote brilliant plays. Now Gail felt suddenly more mature, wiser than Diana. She had been going regularly to the Greenwich meetings with her father and aunt, learning about alcoholism and the things Gunnar had talked of that night at *Le Matelot*. She put her hand on Diana's arm protectively. "They have to go on those A.A. calls. Don't worry, please, Diana. Daddy is always rushing off to see someone—in the middle of the night sometimes. . . ."

"I know," Diana said, but she couldn't make her voice sound convinced. Of course, it was Sky's duty to go . . . only she wished it had been anyone in the world other than Corva; could not quiet the suspicion that if it *had* been anyone else, Sky would never have gone. "You're a darling, Gail." Diana's smile was almost a success. "I do hope you can go with me. We'll have fun anyway."

Coming out of her office, Daphne Manton said, "But of course you must go, my pet. And we'll find the perfect hat for your friend." In Daphne's world there was no heartache that could not be cured by a new hat. She brought out a tiny brown sailor with a long yellow plume and tilted it herself at exactly the right angle on Diana's curly dark hair.

Looking at herself in the mirror Diana smiled. The hat did something for her. With the yellow plume curled under her chin, she didn't look like a girl who fretted about bills and a baby. She looked amusing—whimsical. Maybe that was what Sky wanted—what he found in the ugly little crow woman . . . but how could that small person in emerald and purple scarves compete with Diana in this bright, capricious hat? Diana smiled again.

They started off gaily for lunch at the *Algonquin*, where Sky had planned to take Diana. Diana seemed to know everyone in the crowded room. People waved to her and Frank Case stopped at their table to chat, asking what that brilliant husband of hers was up to now. "I have an autographed copy of *Savage in Bed*," he told Gail. "Remarkable play, remarkable wit and—a fine ad for my hotel." He had laughed and ambled over to another table in his amiable, intimate way.

This is the sort of thing Paul would like, Gail thought, and asked Diana if she could bring Paul over to meet Sky sometime. Gunnar didn't think much of Pell. He distrusted Pell's glib pyrotechnics. A serious writer had to go at his work with "blood, sweat and tears," the way a serious painter did. Gunnar could be annoyingly sure of himself sometimes. Superior. Paul was arrogant too . . . but it was a different kind of self-assurance . . . why did she keep comparing them? Gunnar was humble about his own painting—too modest, really, according to Aunt Emily. He had started a portrait of Aunt Emily last week and Gail had been hurt because he had evidently forgotten all about painting her in the toreador costume.

"Is Paul like his mother?" Diana asked and Gail nodded. She hadn't exactly thought of it before, but it was true. Paul and Daphne had the same love of excitement, the same quick, rapacious eagerness for life.

"Don't marry him yet, Gail. You're terribly young, you know, and. . . ."

Gail was tired of being called "infant" and regarded as "terribly young" by everyone—especially Diana, but Diana seemed young and happy herself at the theater and when they came out into the violet sparkle of Times Square she said, "Let's stop at the Ritz for a cocktail."

Gail, with a commuter's timetable in her head, hesitated and Diana went on, "I'll tell you what let's do, Gail. Let's stay in town for dinner and then you come on out to Darien with me and spend the night, please, Gail." There was an urgency in Diana's voice which Gail could not understand. Was she angry at Sky . . . or was she afraid? But why?

Diana propelled Gail into a drug store and thrust nickels at her. Then she went into the next booth and Gail could hear her through the thin partition asking for Mr. Pell and then in another tone giving Lassandra instructions about the baby.

The taxi they took from the Darien station, after a hurried dinner in town, made several stops for other passengers before turning into the deep hardwoods of the Pell's road. Diana sat on the edge of the seat, clutching her packages, stabbed by remorse—Sky had been sweet, really, wanting to buy her a new, extravagant hat, planning a festive day. Gail had been right, it *had* been his duty to go on that A.A. case.

"Sky darling!" Diana called, running into the house. The lights were on and the cellar door, oddly located at the foot of the front stairs, was open . . . burglars? "Sky!" Diana screamed and, receiving no answer, raced in panic up the stairs.

Gail followed Diana uncertainly into the blue and white nursery and stood back watching Diana bend over a crib. Then she tip-toed closer and looked enviously at the sleeping baby. Diana had resisted the temptation to pick him up but had tucked the blue blanket in unnecessarily and motioned Gail toward the door, closing it softly behind them.

The door across the hall was open and from it came loud snores punctuated by groans and belches. Diana stood for a long minute, her hand clutching the frame of the door, the familiar expression of baffled anger—or was it fear—in her eyes. Then she walked into the room. In one scornful glance she surveyed the whole unpleasant scene—Sky sprawled on the day-bed, the almost empty bottle of whiskey on the floor beside him, the thick cigar stub in the over-flowing ash tray on the desk, the yellow page on the typewriter. She leaned over and started to read, her eyes growing darker and angrier. Then she noticed the two wrinkled menus and picked them up curiously; sentences leapt at her—"That snow Saturday of the snow goose I was almost horribly in love with you. . . ."

Diana crumpled the menu and let it fall from her hand as if despair had followed too close on the pounding heels of anger. She gave another different look at the sprawled figure of her husband, snapped out the light, shut the door and leaned against it as if she would never summon sufficient energy to move. "I've got to do something about Sky," she said more to herself than to Gail.

Gail jumped. After one horrified glimpse of Pell she had retreated from the door, watching in apprehension as Diana stood reading the yellow page on his typewriter—suppose he woke up suddenly—suppose . . . if only her father were here, he would know what to do. "I'll call Uncle Joe. He'll come right over. I'm sure he will," Gail said. "Daddy's in Boston."

Diana nodded. She seemed not to hear nor to care, but when Gail asked where to find the telephone Diana pointed listlessly toward the front hall.

Gail clattered downstairs as if she were pursued by banshees. She had never seen anyone "passed out" before. Her father had been drunk and angry and dreadful that day at the Mantons' but not like Sky. Had he ever been like that? Oh dear God, had Gunnar ever been like that? Gunnar with his thick pale hair, his clear direct eyes, his deep hesitant voice.

Joe said, "Okay, I'll be right over, infant," but he didn't want to go. He hadn't much use—or much hope for Pell. Along with several other A.A. members he considered Pell as belonging to the lunatic fringe, he supposed every organization whether political, religious or alcoholic had a lunatic fringe. "Look, Gail," he added, worried about Gail and Diana being alone in the house with Pell after Rick's account of the night he had spent with him. "Lock the guy in his room till I get there, will you? And if he wakes up and starts raising hell and breaking down the door, just sock him in the jaw, baby."

Gail burst into relieved laughter. Joe had cheered her up. He'd fix things . . . but how could anybody fix things for Diana, really? How could Diana stand being married to Sky if he got that way very often? Please God, don't let Gunnar be like that ever. She went slowly, unhappily up the stairs.

Diana was still standing with her back to the door, the cross in the paneling behind her made her look like a very young victim of some ancient cruelty. Rick had told Gail that the crosses in doors had originally been designed to keep out witches, and that although the superstition had disappeared the design had remained. Gail shivered, she couldn't bear to see Diana standing there. She must get her away. Lock the door and get her away.

"I've got to do something about Sky," Diana said again.

"But I've done something, Diana. Joe is coming. He'll be here soon."

"That wasn't what I meant, Gail." Diana slipped her arms out of the mink coat and pulled the small whimsical hat off her head. "I've got to leave Sky," she said.

XVII

"WHEN THE DOGWOOD BLOOMS THE BLACKFISH BITE"

"When the dogwood blooms the blackfish bite"—the phrase ran through Emily's mind like a ballad to Spring. Hank Frost had tossed it into the midst of a discussion with Rick on tides, bait and tackle and the chance of "ketchin' 'em over Tod's Point way." He had quirked his left eyebrow in Emily's direction and she had known that he relished the saying with its characteristic New England emphasis on practicality and its reticent awareness of the green and white enchantment of May. Hank's speech was larded with folk sayings—"When the chestnut leaves are as big as a squirrel's paw . . ."—she could not remember what happened then. Was it that the flatfish started to run? Or was it time to set out your tomato plants? Emily smiled at the realization that her pleasure in these phrases was anything but practical.

"Don't smile, Aunt Emily, you'll spoil Gunnar's picture!" Gail jumped up and looked over Gunnar's shoulder. She had been lying on the grass in a yellow sun-uit, her long slim legs gleaming with a new lotion. Apparently absorbed in the serious business of acquiring an early tan, her eyes behind dark glasses had evidently been watchful.

As a background for his portrait of Emily Gunnar had chosen a spot some distance from the studio where an old shed had been left standing near an open field. The sculptor had used it as a storeroom for bags of plaster and discarded blocks of marble, and Rick and Hank had fixed it up when Emily said she'd like some place to raise chickens. Gunnar has posed Emily in her grey wool dress against the weathered silver of the shed. In his picture dark clouds moved across a wide sky, a wind tossed the shimmering underleaves of a poplar, light touched Emily's blowing amber hair and the warm color was repeated in her amber beads and in three Rhode Island Reds pecking at the ragged grass. Gunnar called it *Escape from the City*. He was painting in a Grant Wood style of hard simplicity but there was tenderness and admiration along with a touch of irony in his depiction of the urban figure looking beyond a rundown farm to distant sloping meadows. You seemed to feel her defiant pride, foresee the order her inexperienced but resolute spirit would bring to the neglected land—the peace the woman had found.

"It's too damn green!" Gunnar threw down his brush and glared at the sharpening emerald of grass and trees. He had set himself the difficult problem of grey against grey and grey-green, the pale moon-washed tones of April, but now it was May and the accents had altered, his color scale had been thrown out of kilter. "I'll never be able to finish it now. . . ." If only he had been free to paint more often than Saturdays and Sundays. . . .

Emily moved quickly. It was good to move again after leaning interminably against the shed. Good to feel the rough humps of grass under the thin high-heeled slippers Gunnar had insisted that she wear. "But it *is* finished, Gunnar," she said with impersonal delight, "and it's fine!"

Gunnar turned to her with his slow grateful smile. "That's the trouble with not being a real artist. I never know when to stop. I can't tell when I've got a thing right." He picked up his brush and wiped it carefully on a paint-smeared rag, his heavy shoulders hunched in discouragement.

Gail watched him with a small anxious frown. She was swinging her dark sunglasses and she stood on tip-toe and popped them on Gunnar's nose. "Now look," she laughed, "that's the color everything was three weeks ago. See, you needed my glasses."

"Thanks, Mrs. Cézanne." Gunnar grinned.

Gail gave him a shy, swift glance and darted toward the house, her yellow sunsuit flashing through the green shadows. "I've got to dress," she called back as she ran.

It was comfortable to be middle-aged, to know what you wanted even if you didn't get it, Emily thought, stabbed by her awareness of the vulnerable, transparent, and unpredictable quality of youth. Gail was going into New York with Paul. He had been inducted last week and was at Devens hoping to be shipped to Miami. He had wired Gail last night that he had managed a twenty-four-hour pass and would get off at Stamford, grab a taxi and pick her up. Gail's uncertainties about Paul, her puzzling attitude toward Gunnar—especially since that night she had spent with Diana Pell—troubled Emily. She looked at Gunnar wondering how much he had noticed, but he was stowing tubes of paints into a small wicker basket.

Emily liked the way Gunnar went at things, his neatness, his capable artisan hands, his patience. She shared his suspicion of the artistic temperament, regarding it as a sign of inadequacy rather than an indication of genius. "That looks like a fishing basket." She smiled at the clever way he had fitted everything in.

"It is." Gunnar slung the strap over his shoulder. "Hank got himself a new one and gave this to me. I'd been carting my stuff around in a shoe box." He stood in front of his canvas and studied it doubtfully again. "Like to see how it looks indoors? Maybe it'll stand up better away from all this green. Do you think you could carry it, Miss Willard? I'll get the frame."

He limped into the shed and Emily's eyes followed him with concern. The doctor seemed sure that Gunnar's knee would be all right in time but Hank complained that he was always overdoing at the Yard, stubbornly refusing to take things easy.

When Emily reached the sloping flagstone path to the house, Gunnar overtook her, carting the easel and a grey wooden frame. "Rick and Hank ripped these boards out of the shed and I saved them and knocked them together," he explained proudly. "Gosh, I was lucky to find four that matched." He smoothed the weathered silver boards with sensitive fingertips. Here was something he knew was right.

Gunnar fitted the picture into the frame and propped it over the mantelpiece in the small dining room which Emily had had repapered in an indefinite pattern of grey-green leaves. Emily stood off openly admiring the effect. Gunnar squinted speculatively. "I had this place in mind while I was painting. It seems to fit, doesn't it? The studio is too big. I always think of that as Rick's room." He was right—a room for a big man, or a big crowd of people. "But this is your place." Gunnar looked at the white organdy curtains, the old-fashioned plants—geraniums, begonia, cyclamen—in the sunny bay window. "Yup, I guess my picture belongs here." There was a sound of relief and deep contentment in his voice.

"It belongs in a museum—or an exhibition," Emily smiled, "and that's where it's going, Gunnar Nordstrom. There's a show of local artists starting next week in the Greenwich library. I read about it in the paper. You've got to take it there."

"But it's yours," Gunnar protested. "I painted it for you."

"Then I'll lend it to them." Emily put her hand on his arm and was surprised at the tenseness of his muscles. "And thank you, Gunnar. It's a very beautiful picture." She had been about to refuse but the relaxing of his arm told her that she had been right in her acceptance of his gift. She wished Gunnar would let her give him the money for a year at some Art School—or even a summer at Woodstock—but she knew his pride would stand in the way.

"I'll make some coffee," Emily suggested. Rick ought to be home soon and he was always ready for coffee. They were going out for dinner so she had given Benzadrina the afternoon off. She started for the kitchen as Gail's heels clicked on the narrow balcony stairs.

Gail stood in the dining room doorway, a smart, slim figure in a yellow wool coolie coat trimmed with black braid. Her shiny black straw hat had an exaggeratedly high peak—"Paint me next, Gunnar," she challenged, "You could call it *Escape* TO *the City*!"

Gunnar laughed. "Fashion magazine stuff!" he snorted.

"But you said you would once," Gail insisted, "don't you remember? You said you wanted to paint me in that toreador thing."

"That was before I knew you so well," Gunnar teased.

"What do you mean, Gunnar Nordstrom?"

He hadn't meant anything except perhaps that she was too pretty—that it would be hard for any painter to catch the unlined, almost impersonally lovely look of youth—impossible for him. But now he found himself saying, "I didn't know then that you were the sort of girl who could be happy selling hats and getting yourself photographed with a war going on and everything."

Gail's grey eyes were troubled. She hadn't been exactly happy about it lately herself, not with Sylvia talking about the Waves and Paul getting drafted. "But what do you want me to do?" she asked as she had asked that December afternoon in the house in the east Sixties. "What else could I do?" she added with an appealing note of self-deprecation.

"You could get a job at the war plant in Old Greenwich for one thing."

"Okay, I will for one thing." Gail's eyes darkened exactly the way Rick's did when he was angry, Gunnar thought, but he wasn't sorry he had aroused her—the war news aroused him daily, he couldn't sleep thinking about the guys he had known who were still in the middle of it—if he ever drank again it would be because of the war.

A car was tearing up the steep grade. They could hear the blast of a taxi horn and quick steps followed by an impatient pounding. Gail raced for the door and Gunnar could hear her gay, "Hi, Paul," and Paul's confident, "Good to see you, beautiful. Nice rags. Very nice. One of the Mater's new models?"

"Oh, Paul, come and see Gunnar's picture. He finished it this afternoon. There's time, isn't there?" She was pulling him after her, calling, "Gunnar, Paul wants to see your picture."

Emily hurried out of the kitchen and greeted Paul with cool cordiality. He looked erect and handsome in his uniform. Too handsome. Too trim. As if Daphne Manton had somehow contrived to have his G.I.s especially tailored. She was being unfair, absurdly unfair.. . . Paul was going to war—and war was a hideous job for any man to face—but Emily was defensively aware of Gunnar, Gunnar in his old plaid shirt and corduroy pants, with the look of stubborn withdrawal on his face and the bleak memories of the realities of battle behind his averted eyes. She had to protect Gunnar. It was stupid—or cruel—of Gail to bring the two men together. She couldn't understand women's flirtatious, vixenish ways—Adelaide inviting an old "beau" up for the weekend that summer at the Cape. Adelaide who had told Emily she had fallen in love with Rick at first sight. Perhaps, Emily thought, it was because she herself had only fallen in love three times, counting the lobster fisherman's son when she was sixteen and the family had packed her off to France, and of course Nicky—in a way—and. . . .

"Nice work. Very nice," Paul was saying and Emily detected the same note of superiority in his tone as when he had admired Gail's costume. "Interesting frame, Nordstrom. I gather you share my dislike of gold— throws a picture out of key. Mind telling me where you had it made? I'd like the address."

Emily could see by Gail's quick smile that she thought Gunnar would be pleased and that she was baffled by his gruff, "Picked the boards up back of the shed, knocked them together myself."

"Swell effect," Paul's irritating air of being a patron of the arts was undisturbed. He said goodbye to Gunnar with the flourish of a young Medici, gave Emily a correctly measured smile and rushed Gail off to the waiting taxi.

"The coffee must be ready," Emily said as Gunnar stood looking at his picture frame as if he would like to tear the silvery boards off and hack them to pieces.

He followed her into the kitchen and stared through the small window over the sink down the road Gail and Paul had taken. "You've been awfully good to me," he said in his slow diffident voice, "you and Rick." He turned and faced her with abrupt decision. "I'm taking a job in Bridgeport next week."

"I'm sorry, Gunnar. We'll miss you," Emily said quickly. Her hand tightened on the handle of the coffee pot. Gunnar must not know that she had guessed the reason of his going. She had been stupid about Gunnar, not really considering him at all—thinking only how good it was for Gail to be around with a man instead of a playboy. Not imagining that anything serious would come of their being so much together. This might be the best way out. Gail was too young. She was still in the childishly flirtatious stage of trying out her attractiveness on all comers—on Dick Spencer and even the sardonic Mr. Junior. She looked anxiously at Gunnar. He was strong. He could take it. He had knocked around the world since he was fifteen. He must have known many other women. He would not let himself be hurt too much—but what was too much? Especially for an alcoholic. She had forgotten that.

"I'm not going to get drunk," Gunnar grinned at her as if he had followed her thoughts. "There's an A.A. chapter in Bridgeport, I'll get in touch with them."

"Good." Emily assumed a briskness she did not feel. She handed Gunnar the yellow tray with three cups and a plate of sugared doughnuts. "Let's take it in the studio and you might light a fire for me. It's always cold in that big room." She wished Rick would hurry. She was certain he had not suspected Gunnar's feeling for Gail and the fact that he didn't would make things easier. She was always complicating situations by her own over-awareness.

Rick drove his car along the Mianus River, blue-silver in lengthening afternoon light. Dogwood drifted suspended in airy motion between the dark pines and spruces of Cognewaugh Road—like *Les Sylphides*, Rick thought, seeing the white virginal figures swaying in the nostalgic ballet on the great stage of the Opera in Leningrad. He had been in love that spring when he had gone with other American engineers to lay out the construction of an enormous dam in southern Russia. He had met Magda in Leningrad—a small passionate girl with a white face like a dogwood leaf. She had been a student at the new Ballet School, a funny intense little creature with her head full of Soviet doctrines, and yet every time she practiced a *pointe* every gesture of her thin, flexible arms was rigidly prescribed. "You are as devoted to tradition as the Czar," Rick would tease her and roar with laughter when she flew at him like an enraged song sparrow.

"Americans are sexually adolescent," the Russian General had said in a high-class bordello off the Nevskiy Prospekt run by a Madame Miroir. . . . "Mirrors are man's worst invention," Rick had told Lucille and her brown stupid eyes had popped with fear . . . but a mirror had saved him—a barroom mirror where a man who didn't look like a drunk had met his own eye . . . he could never feel the same way about mirrors again . . . but he wouldn't mind being sexually adolescent again. H. Peculiar Henry, he had not fallen in love since the Winged Victory. Here it was May and dogwoods were pirouetting on the Connecticut hills like *Les Sylphides* and he was not falling in love.

He had run into the Russian Princess one night at a closed meeting of A.A. in the New York clubhouse and she had hailed him, "Come on over to my place and I'll make you a drink—the best substitute for vodka." They had climbed three flights to her apartment on West Twelfth Street and Rick had been startled by the sense of being in Paris—Madrid—Moscow—the uniformity of Bohemia. Long curtains of brilliantly embroidered stuff hung at the windows, a wide studio couch was covered with a white fur rug and cushions of hard, primitive colors—orange, magenta, emerald. An ancient ikon stood in one corner, a grand piano in the other. The Princess had come back from her small, neat, modern kitchen with two tall glasses of steaming tea and lemon on an inlaid copper tray.

"Wonderful!" Rick had grinned and remembered, oddly, Emily's saying, "snow on the domes of Moscow but not with Nicky." Hot tea and lemon and small white-faced dancer in Leningrad. . . . But vodka too—the white sweet-burning vodka. . . . "You are like vodka," he had told Magda.

The Princess had batted her eyelashes at Rick—he was getting used to it—beginning to like it. "You are the Russian man," she had said. "How is it that you spend the years in the hot countries? That is what I have heard and that is what I do not understand. Misha will not live in New York. The steam heat suffocates Misha. At our farm in New Hampshire he is happy. It reminds him of the Urals where he was born."

Battling Annie had a funny approach, all right. She had been talking about her husband on New Year's Eve in the kitchen with Dick Spencer.

"Me, I love the cities, especially New York," the Princess went on sipping her hot tea. "It is because I grew up in Paris, perhaps—but New York I love even more than Paris. New York I need more than vodka. I am doing very well now about the drinking, also we have the very fine plan, my husband and I. In the winter I am the ski-fashion adviser for Jacques Freres, in the summer I lie on a hillside in the sun and watch my husband and all his silver foxes running about."

The sharp, knowing snouts of silver foxes—the thick jaunty brushes and a boy lying in the grass near the runs—a boy whose bewildered pain over his mother's death had gradually, gradually healed. . . .

"I am the very lazy woman," the Princess had stretched contentedly on the couch next to Rick. In contradiction to her wifely chatter her firm pointed breasts tilted toward him provocatively under her tight black dress. Rick had put out a tentative hand.

The Princess had moved to her feet with the quick one-motion litheness of a cat. "First, I will sing for you." She had opened the top of the big Mason and Hamlin, played a few swift exploratory chords, tossed back her curly black hair and started to sing. Her voice was low, husky and passionate—the kind of voice that had been a dime-a-dozen in Paris after the revolution when Russian noblemen drove taxis and Russian Princesses sang their deep nostalgic songs of gypsies and Volga boatmen at every little café.

After that night they had met fairly often, before or after the Thursday meetings, and Sonia had shown Rick a side of New York he had never discovered himself—a Greek restaurant on West Forty-second Street, where they ate artichoke cooked in garlic and stuffed with lamb, an Armenian place on lower Lexington Avenue famous for its shish-kabab, a dump on Second Avenue with sawdust on the floor, drawings by famous cartoonists on the walls and slabs of roast beef that rivaled Simpson's on the Strand. It was like Soho or Montmartre—not the New York Rick had hated.

Why the hell hadn't he fallen in love with her? Annie was a good egg, as Rick had told her, only half-meaning it New Year's Eve. Was it because she genuinely cared about her husband in spite of her Slavic ways? Or was it that Love and Liquor went together, were an inseparable team—Love and Liquor . . . Beer and Pretzels. H. Peculiar Henry, was he getting too old?

Rick turned the car into the driveway. He and Emily were having dinner at Porter J. Emerson's tonight. He hoped to hell Corva and Pell wouldn't be there. Diana had taken her baby with her to her family's place near Charlottesville. Try to find a southern girl who hadn't grown up in a ramshackle house with white columns! Still, Diana was a nice person and she had had a tough break with Pell.

He took his fishing rod, tackle box and a basket with six blackfish in through the kitchen. Hank had had all the luck today, catching the first fish, the biggest fish and the most fish. Rick had only pulled in three small ones, but Hank, who was always generous, had insisted on giving him three of his. "Only me and the old woman and Gunnar to eat 'em now—and Gunnar don't eat nothin' like Steve uster—kinda off his feed lately, Gunnar is."

Rick wrapped the fish carefully in a newspaper and put them in the tray in the ice box. He'd clean them later—or maybe Benzadrina would. She wasn't as interested in fish as Joe's Emerald was.

"That you, Avery?" Emily called from the studio and Rick felt contentment touching him like the cool feel of his mother's cheek at night when he was a small boy. The sight of Gunnar disappointed him oddly. He liked Gunnar—still he wanted to come home and find only Emily and Gail in the house.

"I'm afraid the coffee's cold but it won't take a minute to make you some fresh." Emily was a great believer in fresh coffee, not the burned and bitter brew Benzadrina was apt to heat up for him.

"How's everything, Gunnar?" Rick asked, trying to be cordial and then added, "Won't you be late for dinner?" knowing the Frosts' habit of early and punctual suppers.

Gunnar pulled out his old-fashioned watch. "Gosh, yes. I've got to be shoving. Miss Willard and I got to talking." He hesitated and then said in his deep diffident voice, "I'm taking a job in Bridgeport next week."

"Hey," Rick said, "whatever for? Hank'll miss you. You ought not to walk out on Hank like that."

"It's Mrs. Hank I hate to walk out on even more than Hank," Gunnar said. "They've both been swell to me—you've all been swell to me but—I've got to go."

Rick shook his head in bewilderment, probably Gunnar had been offered higher wages in Bridgeport—still it didn't sound like Gunnar to put money ahead of other things. "Well, I suppose you know your own mind. Anyhow, Bridgeport isn't Timbuctoo. We'll be seeing you, Gunnar. Better come down for the Friday meetings, boy."

Emily, coming in the door from the kitchen, smiled at the way Rick had picked up her Timbuctoo phrase and at the way, since he had evidently not guessed Gunnar's motive in leaving, Rick had somehow, by his very ignorance, made things easier. "Gunnar finished his picture today," she said.

It was like Emily not to refer to the paining as "my portrait," Rick thought. "Good work, Gunnar, let's see it."

Gunnar paused at the door as Emily led Rick toward the dining room. He wanted to stay, to hear Rick's opinion but—"I better get going," he said reluctantly and closed the door.

Rick looked from the picture to Emily, seeing what Gunnar had seen—the slender woman in the grey dress leaning against the weathered shed had a spirited, subtle beauty. He stopped looking at the picture and stared at Emily, standing near the white mantel, the light turning her cloudy brown hair to amber. The quality of expectant youthfulness he had glimpsed that afternoon in the house in the east Sixties had not been a momentary illusion, a trick of firelight and an unguarded relaxation of posture, it was permanent—his now and forever—because at last he had eyes to see. He had not fallen in love this spring—he had been in love all the time. God, what a fool not to know—but he knew now.

"Snow on the domes of Moscow but not with Nicky," he cried triumphantly, "with me, Emily."

Emily moved toward him with a slow radiant smile. His arms were around her, his hand touching the soft cloud of her hair. "I'm glad I waited, Rick," Emily's small proud head tilted to meet his lips.

XVIII

JUNE TOO SOON

"I know them Eyetalians eat mussels." Hank shook his head. "But I never figgered they was fit for a white man."

"Of all the God-damned ignorant, narrow-minded Yankee snobs. . . ." Joe's voice boomed out over the rocks and Rick, standing in a foot of water washing the blue-grey mussels they had just picked, looked up startled.

Hank spat a long stream of tobacco juice into the Sound. "I was just usin' a manner o' speakin'," he said slowly, "no offense intended. I don't hold none with them narrer-minded folks who looks down on wops— them grease balls could make a stick blossom and they ain't bad citizens but . . . I kinder hesitate to eat somethin' I ain't et as a boy."

Rick hoisted the pail of mussels into the boat, picked a periwinkle off the rock and tossed it to Hank. "Ever try one of these?" he grinned. "There's a 'wop' stall on Third Avenue where you can get boiled periwinkles. You snake the meat out with a toothpick," he explained, amused by the puzzled quirk of Hank's eyebrow, "and they have cuttlefish, baby octopus. . . ."

"Can't say I cared much for that octopus you got me to take a bite of down in Barrios," Joe snorted. "About as delicate as a bicycle tire."

"That was an old fella. You've got to get 'em young and tender. Then they're like . . . well, like. . . ."

"Shredded hot water bottles!"

"I'll get you guys some and I'll bet you'll like 'em."

"I'll try anything *twice* if recommended by that great gustatory explorer, Avery Rickham." Joe laughed, but it wasn't his usual big jubilant bellow.

"Not for me." Hank was turning the periwinkle over in his calloused palm. "Now this here might just be fit to eat—puts me in mind of them snails I et in France in the last war. Hit the spot too, 'specially in cold, damp weather which was all the kinder weather I ever seen in Frogland. But octopus, no thanks."

"Frogland! Wops! There you go again," Joe spluttered. Why the hell did he feel like needling Hank today. . . ? Except perhaps that Hank always seemed so sure about everything—especially A.A., and he himself had felt so uncertain lately about A.A. and everything else. He had cut a couple of the recent Friday meetings in Greenwich because he had gotten so damn bored, hearing Hank and Tony and some of the other members telling the same old stories about their drinking . . . because he was restless . . . because he didn't know what the devil to do about Sylvia—and Monica. Hank had come over to Joe's house one night last week and lectured him for an hour—he was heading for trouble if he didn't stick to the program; if he stayed away from meetings. Hank meant well. God knew, he was grateful to Hank, but Hank couldn't seem to understand that staying "dry" was one thing and going to a meeting every Friday night for the rest of his life was another.

"Hank eats eels," Rick defended him, disturbed by Joe's unfair and persistent picking, "and that's more than most commuters will do. Me, I've eaten iguana—lizard, iguana eggs, and I know a man who ate a rattlesnake at an Indian feast."

Hank's eyebrows were still skeptical. "Well, I'm aimin' to broaden out in the vegetable kingdom leastways. Miss Emily was tellin' my old woman that milkweed is good as sparrow-grass. We always been great ones for a mess o' dandelion and salt pork, no reason milkweed shouldn't be real tasty."

"That's right," Rick said. "But you have to cut it when it's not more than six inches high. We had some the other night—not much like asparagus, really, sweeter but darn good. We're going to try purslane too. You know that creeping, crawling weed that gets in everybody's garden? You eat it raw, like watercress, with lots of 'wop' garlic rubbed on the salad bowl." He grinned at Hank again, stretched in the sun and pulled out a pipe. "Funny thing, we seem to be learning something from all the shortages caused by the war. I sort of get a kick out of it . . . a feeling of getting back to reality . . . I guess a lot of people are finding out that it's fun to use their ingenuity discovering substitutes for things. . . ."

"Too bad we can't use milkweed for gasoline," Hank chortled. "I know a crackerjack trout brook up to Dutchess County but. . . ."

"Hey, you guys." Joe's red-brown eyes brightened for the first time. "I knew there was something I'd forgotten to tell you. I've located an outboard motor!"

Rick felt steep, surprising anger—he hadn't been hit by one of these uncontrollable rages in months, not since the morning when Gail had been late for the train. Liquor had drained slowly out of his body leaving him stronger and steadier than he had felt in years; alcohol seemed to be seeping out of his brain too, freeing him from tensions, but now . . . He started to speak and saw Hank looking at Joe in outraged scorn.

"Holy Jumpin' Catfish, outboard motors sez you! Them damn gadgets has eased the muscles right outa a man's arms and back . . . and they ruins the fishin' with their fool put-put splutterin'. God Almighty, Joe Kelly, what the hell's gotten into you—outboard motors!"

Joe looked as startled as if Hank had struck him in the face. "Why . . . of course . . . I wouldn't troll with the motor going like some of the dubs around here but we could get over to Tod's Point in no time and . . . why, hell, a motor would be damn handy."

"Handy! The sissy says it would be handy! Did you hear that, Hank?" Rick was shouting, his wind-burned skin turning a deep red, his Arab-chief nose seeming to jut out of his irregular face. Joe was even more nonplussed by the phenomenon of Rick's anger than he had been by Hank's. *"Carrajo y cojones,"* Rick banged on. "Here we've just been talking about how the war was bringing us back to first principles and I've taken off twenty pounds of alcoholic potbelly, rowing around this harbor with my own two mits, fishing and ducking with Hank, and suddenly little Miss Kelly says she has located an outboard motor!" Rick's voice squeaked and broke in his effort to make it sound effeminate.

"Don't have a stroke over it," Joe tugged at his red forelock trying to keep his own temper. "I'll never mention the subject again . . . brrr . . . did I ever get both barrels from both of you." He shook himself like a man trying to find out if he is all of a piece after a ground mine blows up in his face. "Explorers—those effeminate creatures—use outboard motors on the Amazon and in the Antarctic, men like Beebe and Dickey and Byrd, but I'll never mention 'em again. Pass the ground glass, I'm hungry."

"The famous Dr. Joe Beebe Byrd Kelly has established an advance base on Diving Rock . . ." Rick mimicked.

"Exhausted by his exploration of the Mianus River and the wild waters o' Cos Cob Harbor, the poor thing," Hank took it up.

"Cut it out, you two. Stop talking like a pair of God damned idiots!"

"Easy does it, brother." Hank's black look dissolved in a shaggy grin under his two-day stubble.

"Okay." Joe jumped into the stern seat of the rowboat and grabbed a pair of oars—he'd show them that he could do his share of rowing. "Now that we've got the mussels, what's keeping us?" Sylvia was coming out on an afternoon train and Emily was to meet her; she would be sitting on his porch now, waiting for him. The thought of her pointed, lovely face gave power to his oars, quieted the uneasy devil that had been riding him all day.

It was mid-June. Orioles rolled their bright song from the nearby shore, yellowlegs threw back a falling piccolo call from the water. The scent of lilacs mingled with the salty smell of the incoming tide. The day had not quite decided whether to be warm or cool; summer had not made up its mind whether it was here or not. Rick didn't care. He felt suddenly young and immortal and immensely strong. Love was in him like a high tide. Love of Emily—but more than the love of one woman— love of life, love of living.

"I know I'll never write anything decent," Joe said suddenly, "but a day like this makes me feel like a great writer."

Rick nodded. "I feel like Cortez today." He laughed and took a long pull on his oars. "As young as Douglas MacArthur at sixty-two. Boy, what a man, MacArthur!"

Hank, perched in the stern, looked from Rick to Joe. Alkies sure was funny critters—down one minute and up the next like a regular perigee tide. Rick was doing okay but he was kinder worried about Joe— Joe's Missus ought to get herself back from California and bring the kid with her if she cared two shucks about Joe. Joe was hankerin' for the kid the way *he* hankered for Steve—a small boy riding his tricycle along the sidewalk of a village street, riding to meet Hank coming home from the boatyard. A June day fifteen years ago and peace and family love and Steve waving at the maple-shadowed corner, shouting, "Hey Dad!" . . . "My dear Dad"—three words at the beginning of a V-mail letter in his pocket and now, right now, perhaps, a boy tensed in the cockpit of a bomber over green foreign islands—or crumpled. . . . Hank's eyes followed a gull soaring confidently overhead. "Bring Steve back. Bring Steve home," he repeated his oddly comforting, silent prayer.

A whiff of bay came across the water and Rick could feel the warmth of the sun on a bayberry patch on the Cape and Adelaide beside him opening a picnic basket, smiling at him . . . Adelaide and Emily . . . different as two sisters could be but alike in a way no other women had ever been in his life. Adelaide had given him gaiety and peace . . . Emily gave him peace and courage. Two different Avery Rickhams had each found his answer. He could see the proud lift of Emily's head, the crinkling warmth of her smile. . . . Peace. . . . "My peace I give unto you" . . . the peace of trusting yourself, of having some control over your tantrums, of knowing how unimportant one was to the universe and yet how truly a part of it . . . liking a woman as well as loving her, and knowing that she liked you . . . the still secret new gladness of their discovery of each other. "What did you think of me when I first came up to the Cape?" Rick had asked Emily the other night and she had laughed. "Oh, Adelaide and Mother thought you were perfect, but Father and I were afraid you were too perfect for our taste—a bit stuffy and correct," she had teased and then added, "I never could have fallen in love with that Avery Rickham. I'm not jealous of Adelaide—she wouldn't have cared the way I do for Rick." Emily had taken to calling him "Rick" now as if that marked the difference between the man who had loved Adelaide and the man who loved her.

They were late getting back to Joe's house—long tranquil shadows and the soft sound of women's voices in the twilight. Joe hung back, deliberately prolonging the process of putting the oars away in the garage, savoring Sylvia's nearness, as Rick hurried toward the steps.

"Why, you look like Neptune." Emily reached up and pulled a piece of dried seaweed out of Rick's hair. It was years since Joe had heard Rick laugh so happily.

Joe followed slowly, Sylvia's white dress a magnet, Sylvia's tired eyes a problem; a problem that wasn't—couldn't be—his, not with Monica and Jimmy. "You've been doing too much, Sylvia," he said with protective anxiety in his voice. "I thought you promised me to turn that case over to someone else."

"I know," Sylvia sighed, "but I couldn't let Sarah Doyle down. I sat up all night with her again." There was pain in Sylvia's eyes and an involuntary distaste in her tone. Sarah Doyle was an ignorant, elderly female who had lost job after job through tippling. She seemed destined to go from bad to worse, but she clung to Sylvia as a repository for long, garrulous, drunken tales of woe. "I'm afraid she's hopeless," Sylvia added despondently.

"Ain't nobody hopeless." Hank put in a sturdy word. "Not to an A.A. they ain't. Not when you seen what happened to Irv Clapp. I said he was hopeless myself after three years of him turnin' up to the Greenwich meetin's more often drunk nor sober. Would a been willin' to bet you good money the guy hadn't the guts to stick to the program and look at him now. Sober's a judge—soberer nor some judges I seen. Not a drink for five months and his wife come back to him and he's got him a good job. If Irv can make it, ain't nobody hopeless."

"You're right, Hank," Rick said, but he knew how Sylvia felt. He had felt completely discouraged himself about Pell.

"Sure, you're right, Hank," Joe shouted, "but I don't give a damn about this Doyle woman. I don't want to see Sylvia working herself into a nervous breakdown."

Sylvia gave him a shocked but grateful smile. "I guess I didn't realize how tired and nervous I was till I got on the train, and I've got a thesis to finish for my degree—it's overdue now." She took a deep breath of lilac-scented air and relaxed a little against the column of the porch. "Let's not think about it. Coming out here today was a lifesaver."

"Think of the poor saps in New York with the Sunday papers all over the living room floor and their minds littered with war and muggings and divorces. God, I'd like to abolish newspapers—what is news compared to mussels on a rock or the tug of a blackfish?" Rick stretched in mighty contentment, long legs propped on the porch railing, straight chair tilted backwards in the precarious balance dear to the male animal.

Emily smiled at him. Unlike most women she had no impulse to warn him that he might break his neck. It was obvious. It would also obviously be an intrusion on her part to break his mood—women never seemed to consider a mood's neck too valuable to break.

"Hiya, Mr. Thoreau," Joe grinned. "Remember where he curses at newspapers, says he never read any memorable news in a newspaper, that if you've read of one man robbed or murdered, one vessel wrecked, one calamity of one sort or another—I can't quote it exactly—anyhow the point is that *one* is enough, you never need read of another. He even contends that a 'ready wit' could write the so-called news six months or a year in advance with 'sufficient accuracy'."

"Good for him." Rick brought the legs of his chair down with a bang of approval. "I guess I'll have to try the old boy again. I used to get sort of lost in his nature stuff."

"Thoreau's like Shakespeare," Joe proclaimed, his voice full of a vast melancholy and a vast humor. "Any man can find what he's looking for— me, I like Thoreau's prejudices—maybe we'd call 'em resentments in A.A.—his hatred of talking to businessmen and farmers, saying sportsmen and loafers make the best companions. He should have met a few advertising men—boy, would he have despised my brethren. He'd have liked Hank, though."

"I ain't no loafer," Hank protested, looking pleased behind his twoday stubble.

Sylvia turned her head toward Joe, her eyes pensive. "'Most men lead lives of quiet desperation.'" She quoted.

"Say Thoreau to me," Emily said a low aside to Rick.

"Thoreau. What is this, a game?"

"Asheville." Emily smiled. "It's the first thing that came into my head when Joe mentioned Thoreau. Not Walden. Not Concord. Not New England, even. I saw a small knoll where Adelaide and I used to climb to find the first crowsfoot violets. Adelaide had pneumonia when she was six and Mother took us South for the winter. I saw scarlet tanagers and wild azalea—not the neat pink plants you send to a friend at Easter but a whole mountainside of pale yellow—orange—flame."

"Adelaide never told me about Asheville." Rick looked at Emily almost accusingly as if he had been cheated of a memory—two small girls running through the woods, their hair the color of azaleas. Adelaide's pale yellow, Emily's. . . .

"She was awfully little," Emily laughed softly in apology.

"And you were an old lady of eight," Rick teased, loving her, loving Adelaide in a warm continuity of emotion.

The others had gone on talking around them. Rick heard Sylvia say, "I hear you threw a monkey wrench into the last Greenwich meeting, Joe."

"That's right," Joe's voice boomed out. "And I meant it, too. We've got too many members who never contribute anything, refuse to get on their feet and speak because they're too shy—or too lazy—or something, so I up and told them I wouldn't say another word till some of them spoke."

Sylvia looked at Joe. "You just don't know what it is to be shy. I was terribly afraid to get up at my first meetings. . . ."

"But you did it," Joe insisted, "and now you're one of the best speakers in A.A. Aren't you glad you made yourself do it? Wasn't it part of your cure as much as the twelfth step? The rest of these guys would be a lot better off if they would stop sitting in the back of the room listening to Hank and Tony and Dick Spencer and Rick and me sound off. I figure we're cheating them by letting them off too easy."

"The Greenwich meetings *are* getting monotonous," Rick agreed, "and I think you've put your finger on the reason, Joe. Whoever happens to be Chairman just naturally falls back on the regular speakers—he knows they'll deliver something." He grinned at Joe. "I thought you were having an alcoholic grouch the other night, but I guess you've got a point, boy."

"But couldn't you let them talk from their seats?" Sylvia suggested. "It's awfully hard for some people to get on their feet and walk up in front of a crowd."

"That's what Irv Clapp did Friday," Hank said. "He looked at Joe kinda funny and leaned forward in his seat and said as how he didn't feel up to makin' a real speech yet but he went on and told how the thing that had helped him most was 'Easy does it.' Irv's the hustler type," Hank explained to Sylvia. "Uster be in the insurance business; 'git up and go' was his motto in the old days—git up with the help of a bottle and go with the help of a bottle—now he don't care how many o' them policies he writes so long as he don't take no drink." Hank chortled suddenly. "Irv's got a lot on the ball; told me the other day that big sloth what hangs upside down in the first cage down to the Museum where we been holdin' our meetin's . . ."—he glanced at Sylvia—"I don't recollect whether you seen it, anyhow Irv says the sloth reminds him of the way an alcoholic lives—upside down!"

"Pell ought to crawl in beside him," Rick said grimly.

"How's he doing now?" Sylvia asked.

"Not so hot. I guess there's a lot more than alcohol wrong with Pell."

Pell was a screwball all right. He had turned the small house in the Darien woods into a Retreat for Retired Alcoholics—not ex-drunks. Pell was very insistent on giving army ranks to his patrons, but the only person who seemed to be profiting by the enterprise, according to Emerald, was her friend Lassandra, to whom the Retired Alcoholics frequently handed half-empty bottles which "a certain party sure appreciated."

"Yeah," Joe said. "I don't want to be a gloom-thrower, but there's a lot more than alcohol wrong with a lot of us. We're neurotics . . . if not psychotics."

"Holy Jumpin' Catfish, there you go again with them four dollar words. Suppose you get 'em outa them books you're always readin'."

"What's wrong with trying to learn something about yourself?" Joe glared at Hank.

Hank sniffed. "The twelve steps is good enough for me. Just foller The Book and you'll be okay."

"'Live and let live' then, Hank," Sylvia cut in. Her right foot in a narrow white slipper, crossed over her left knee, had been jerking as regularly as a metronome. Joe watched her anxiously, glad of her defense, but concerned over her nervousness. "No two people are exactly alike," she went on with passionate intensity. "Some people have to read books, are compelled to try to understand themselves and everything . . . others—maybe they're luckier—can follow a program without question."

"The Book is okay," Joe said. "I never could have stopped drinking without A.A. . . . but we all talk about the need for a personality change—and the Book doesn't tell me what was wrong with Joe Kelly's character in the first place—what caused me to be an alcoholic."

"What the hell do you care so long as you ain't drunk?"

"I care a hell of a lot." Joe turned the end of a cigar slowly in the flame of a match. "It's great to be sober but I want to be happy, I want to. . . ." He threw the stub of the match across the darkening lawn—he couldn't tell them that he wanted to write a novel—scratch a newspaper man and you'll find a novel, scratch a successful advertising man and you'll find a coupla stillborn books. . . . "Maybe psychiatry or psychoanalysis can help me. . . ."

"I've seen A.A. cure a heap o' drunks them doctors couldn't do nothin' with," Hank contended.

"Sure," Rick agreed, and Hank looked at him hopefully, "the medical profession as a whole has been a flop with alcoholism—lots of honest doctors will admit that, but your local doc who thinks the only way to treat a rummy is to fill him up with a mixture of Rye and phenobarbital and let him sleep it off isn't the whole profession, thank God."

"You're nothing but a narrow-minded Yankee, Hank Frost," Joe said for the second time, "afraid of 'wop' food and psychiatry. You better go and see Dr. Wales yourself. Christ, Freud was the greatest man of our age and you probably haven't even heard of him, but you've heard of the Wright brothers and Marconi and Bell. What good are all the telephones and radios and airplanes to the human race if we're turning into neurotic personalities—alcoholics, hypochondriacs, manic-depressives, schizophrenics. . ."

"All them fancy words," Hank shook himself. "Red's a name thrower—an' that's worse'n a flame thrower. Better get goin' before one of 'em burns me." He grinned and started down the path.

"Things are really worse in the Greenwich group than Hank knows," Rick told Sylvia. "They're forming a rival group."

"Who is?"

"Hugh Watson, Mrs. Bentley-Young, Griggs, Pell and a few others. They say some of their alcoholic friends would like to join A.A. but won't come to a public meeting. They're planning to get together at each other's houses."

"The station wagon set of A.A.," Joe muttered. He had been bored at the Greenwich meetings, sick of listening to the others, sicker still of hearing himself but . . . he didn't like the new group's apparent snobbery either. There wasn't any right side of the railroad tracks for a drunk. If these prospective members couldn't face that fact—to hell with them. What got him down was that he couldn't wholeheartedly take up cudgels for either side and how could an Irishman be happy if he was on the fence in a scrap? How could he be happy straddling every situation— Sylvia and Monica? He had started going to Dr. Wales to try to find out why he could not be satisfied as an advertising man, why when he had plenty of time to write the novel he had always wanted to write he couldn't do it. Pell could. Pell, for all his screwball actions, was hard at work on a new play. He had always looked down on Pell but Pell was a success—maybe he was just envious—'just,' that was a puny word to couple with one of the meanest, most soul-souring of human emotions. Wales was helping some. He liked Wales, but he hadn't told anyone, not even Rick or Sylvia, about his daily visits to High Pines. He was taking the 4:15 every afternoon and telling everyone that he was knocking off early to play golf.

"I was surprised when I heard Hugh Watson was with them," Rick was saying. "He seems like a well-meaning little fellow, meek but well-meaning."

"His wife must have put him up to it," Joe said sarcastically. "She just can't stand mixing with people like Tony and Hank."

"Who's barking up what tree now?" Rick roared with laughter. "You were certainly jumping on Hank with all fours yourself only a minute ago."

"That's different," Joe said—and it was, somehow.

Sylvia looked at Joe. "I know how you feel," she said. "Snobbishness has no place in A.A." Her lovely, pointed, medieval face was lifted in challenge. "A.A. is as democratic as Christianity. . . ." She paused, and for a moment her fatigue and her nervousness disappeared and Rick heard again the ringing certainty in her voice that had filled it the night she spoke at White Plains. She was telling Joe not to worry now.

"Other groups have split up in other cities. Maybe it's a good thing. It doesn't matter where you get A.A., or how, so long as you get it, so long as men and women learn how to live without alcohol, even if some of them learn slowly, even if some of them fail." Her voice dropped and she seemed to be talking to herself now. "It doesn't matter."

XIX

JULY STAND BY

A fresh salty breeze came across Greenwich Harbor as Rick got off the 4:15. He had ducked out early from his office to escape the heat that steamed up from sticky pavements and was reflected and enclosed by high buildings. New York was becoming a tropical city but not learning how to live with tropical ease—no midday *siestas*, only the unnatural icebox cold of air-conditioning, which sent you shivering into the street like a man struck by the chills and fever of malaria.

Rick took a deep breath, feeling as if the breeze was even taking the wrinkles out of his white linen suit, which Manton had admired extravagantly at lunch. Rick had laughed when Manton asked who his tailor was, remembering the big Negro in Belize who had made him a dozen white linens. He had taken in an English tweed as a model and the Negro had looked at the Saville Row label with an expression of disdain—he didn't think much of English cutters—material, yes, but not the fit. Manton had been amused by the anecdote, but Manton had obviously had something on his mind. He had a cellophane face when you got to know him, and Rick had grown to know and like the guy after shooting with him in New Jersey in the fall and salmon fishing with him in Maine, but their friendship—if it could be called friendship—had a wary, parental character. Neither of them ever quite forgot Gail and Paul.

In the big chilly dining room of Manton's Downtown Lunch Club with its airplane view of New York, Manton had order a rum collins and Rick, refusing, had suddenly said, "Give me a lime ricky without the rum, waiter." The smell of the lime, the pleasant sight of the small chartreuse fruit floating in the tall glass, the sharp-sweet, nostalgic taste— hell, he didn't miss the rum—not too much.

Manton, watching him, said abruptly, "Daphne's drinking herself into a stupor, worrying over Paul. You'd think she was the only mother in the world who had a son in the war. A.A. be any good for her?"

Rick's reaction had been anything but charitable—he could see Daphne's pale blue hair whisking around the New York clubhouse, see her trying to turn the meetings into social events. He'd be damned if he'd be the one to talk to her . . . still, she might really need help—perhaps Sylvia could tackle her. Rick had seen Sarah Doyle with Sylvia recently— a thin, pale woman with a damp hand and a tearful blue eye. No wonder Sylvia was depressed. Daphne might be a diversion. "I could get one of our women members to call on Mrs. Manton," Rick had said finally. "That is, if she is serious about wanting to stop drinking."

"Oh, Daph is never serious about anything." Manton had waved his wife aside much to Rick's relief. "Except about Paul," he had added.

This is it, Rick had thought. Paul had been behind the cellophane.

"She's reining Paul's chances in the Air Force; hanging around Miami, starting to look for a house there while I was off fishing in Key West. Put a stop to that, I can tell you. Dragged her back to New York with me. Now she calls him up long distance every night. Can't leave him alone. And he's sick of it, too. For the first time in his life Paul is sick and tired of it. Asked me to keep her out of his hair. . . ." There was triumph in Manton's voice. For the first time in his life he had established a man-to-man feeling with his son.

Rick had thought of the day he had gone to Manton's office, the day he had said, "this parent business isn't an easy job," and the sense of kinship he had had for this guy who was making as much of a mess of things as he was. They were both learning—late and hard—but learning.

"Wish you could see Paul," Manton had gone on. "Uncle Sam did the job. Told you he would, didn't I? Paul's a real man now, not a night club playboy. Hopes to get his wings soon as he's through his basic training. Only thing that gets him down besides his mother—and I'll fix that—is Gail."

So now you're planning to fix Gail. Rick had grinned at the broad, good-natured face across the table—Gail might not be so easy for Manton to fix. "What's the trouble?" he had asked.

"Paul never hears from her any more—you know how they count

on letters at camp. He writes her all the time, I gather, and she . . . know anything about it, Rickham? Funny thing to ask you, but Lord, when a man's in the army he needs to be sure of his girl. Don't get me wrong, Paul didn't put me up to this. I just got a hunch that you and I could talk things over. Any other man in the offing, so far as you know?"

Rick had shaken his head. He didn't know anything about Gail. Period. They hadn't quarreled lately—God, that was negative—he had missed commuting with her, but he had been pretty preoccupied with Emily, and Gail, when he saw her, had seemed busy and affectionate. "Gail is working in a war plant in Old Greenwich," he had said slowly. "She seems to like it. Maybe she's tired. Maybe that's the reason. She's been doing a bit of weekend entertaining of soldiers and sailors down at the Riverside Yacht Club, but I don't think she's interested in any of them." The Army, Navy and Marines had been swarming over the studio on Sundays but Gail seemed to like them all, her laughter was bright and impersonal—or was it? Had he missed something special?

From the vantage point of his new understanding with Paul, Manton had looked at Rick, commiseration in his round brown eyes. "Easier for a man to get close to a son than a daughter," he had said generously. "If there isn't anyone else, what would you think. . . ." Manton had pulled a monogrammed handkerchief out of the pocket of his brown and white seersucker suit, touched his receding hairline, put the handkerchief carefully back and looked at Rick. "You know how I felt about their marriage, Rickham, you know I was as much against it as you were. Wouldn't give them a penny, remember?"

Rick had remembered, remembered his own incredulity and anger.

"Well, now I've got a proposition to make. Want to be on the up and up with you. Wouldn't mention it to Paul till I had a chance to put it to you straight . . . but here it is—if your Gail will marry Paul now and you're willing to change your mind, I'm ready to support them. Yes, sir, and I'll take care of Mrs. Paul Manton if anything happens to my son."

"Fair enough." And it was—according to Manton's standards. Funny, that a man could be both shrewd and stupid. Rick had tried to keep down his irritation. "I'm quite capable of looking after Gail," he said rather huffily, "and she'll have money of her own when she's twenty-one, but that isn't the point. It's up to Gail." "Live and let live," the A.A. slogan, had come into his mind. . . . Die and let die—Christ, you couldn't see the casualty lists every day in the papers and not feel that youth had a right to grab what it could of life.

"But you wouldn't oppose their marriage now?" Manton had insisted.

"No, I wouldn't oppose it," Rick had said reluctantly, "but I honestly don't know how Gail feels. And it's up to her," he had repeated.

In the end he had promised Manton he would sound Gail out, tell her he wasn't against it if Paul was the person she really wanted to marry.

As Rick crossed over the bridge to the north side of the tracks where he had parked his car, he recognized Joe's red head halfway down the steps. "Hi Joe!" he shouted.

Joe turned, looked as if he wanted to duck, hesitated and waited for Rick to catch up with him.

"So, this is the train you take, you old loafer. Pretty hot for golf, isn't it? Come on up to our place and have a swim in the pond."

"Can't do it." Joe seemed curiously embarrassed and Rick thought, hell, if he's got a golf date, why doesn't he say so? "Be seeing you." Rick started toward his car, but Joe still loitered. Suddenly he slapped his folded newspaper against his leg with an air of decision.

"That golf business is just an alibi," he said. "What I've really got is an appointment with Dr. Wales up at High Pines. Been going to him for about a month now."

"Good idea." It explained a lot Rick hadn't understood about Joe lately. "But for Pete's sake, why do you act as if you had a date to rob a bank?"

Joe shook back his red forelock and laughed in relief. "Gosh, I'm glad you take it that way, Rick. I've been scared the A.A.s would think I was going nuts or something—don't tell Hank. He'd have conniptions."

"Hell, I can't see why you can't work A.A. and psychiatry together if you want to." Rick unlocked the door to his car, rolled down the windows hurriedly and let the air into the closed interior which was hot enough to roast a pig.

Joe stood with his foot on the running board. He pulled a cigar out of his breast pocket, struggled with the cellophane wrapping, bit off the end, struck a match . . . *Clockwise. Counter-clockwise.* Rick could see the windshield wiper moving its absurdly efficient arms against the storm, see the flame of a match die and darkness come back over Joe's strong, humorous face with its high beak of a nose, hear Joe's voice telling him about A.A., bringing him words of hope."Wales is sold on A.A.," Joe said now, tossing his match into the gravel. "That isn't the trouble. I wish some of the A.A.s weren't so damned narrow-minded about psychiatry."

"Bill Griffith isn't," Rick said, "and Mac. There are a lot of guys in A.A. who are going beyond the fact of sobriety. Not that it isn't a big fact. Not that you damn well couldn't go anywhere if you didn't lick liquor first." Joe had helped him. Why the hell couldn't he say something that would help Joe now? Words came and sounded like words. He tried again. "I guess I'm lucky. A.A. seems to be the answer for me, pure and simple, the way it is for Hank." A.A. and Emily—but Joe was the last person he could tell about Emily. It would be like flaunting his happiness in the face of Joe's lonely and anomalous state. Maybe Dr. Wales could get Joe straightened out on Sylvia and Monica; that must be half his trouble. Maybe. . . . "I'll bet Wales'll get you going on that novel you were going to write in college." Rick slid under the wheel of his car and turned the key in the motor, watching Joe's face brighten into its familiar grin.

"Be seeing you." Joe ambled off toward his own car, his shoulders lifted.

The smell of salt diminished on the breeze, but pines scented and shaded the hill of Cognewaugh Road. Rick drove his car into the garage and cut across the grass toward the terrace. Gail was stretched out on a steamer chair in a white lastex bathing suit, her yellow hair pinned on top of her head, giving her the look of a Gay-Nineties belle who had skipped a generation and forgotten her black alpaca and long black stockings.

"Hi, infant," Rick called. "Where's your aunt?" Emily was always the first to greet him when he came out from town . . . Emily in a thin crisp dress with a tall pitcher of lemonade in her hand.

"Oh, you and Aunt Emily. . . ." Gail put her yellow head down on a brown arm.

"What's the matter, Gail?" Rick looked at her with awkward tenderness.

"I think it's wonderful, Daddy. Honestly I do." Gail lifted her head and gave Rick a quick, tremulous smile. "I'm happy for you and Aunt Emily and me only. . . ."

"We were going to tell you first, infant, but. . . ."

"You don't need to *tell* anyone," Gail laughed, "only it's awful seeing you all the time and being in love myself and. . . ."

Rick pulled a wicker chair close to the steamer chair and patted Gail's hand.

Her fingers tightened around his like a child's and there were tears in her eyes. "I thought it was going to be fun to be in love—but it isn't, it's hell."

Rick laughed. "That's better, infant. Keep your chin up. And it won't be hell any more. I had lunch with Paul's father today and we talked about you two . . . I guess I was wrong about Paul."

"Oh, Paul!" Gail threw the name away from her like an old letter crumbled into a ball and tossed into a waste basket.

"But I thought you wanted to marry Paul. I thought that was what you were talking about," Rick said patiently—as patiently as a man sitting on the edge of a dock at Falmouth watching a small boy practice bowlines. "I'm sorry I've been so nasty about Paul. I want you to be happy, Gail."

"Oh Daddy." Gail put her head down on her arm again and her shoulders shook with desolate sobs. "You don't know anything about anything. Couldn't you see it was Gunnar . . . ?"

"Gunnar?"

"What's wrong with Gunnar?" Gail faced her father, her grey eyes dark with anger. "Just because he grew up on a farm in Minnesota and works in a factory—I didn't think you were a snob, Daddy. Are you going to get mad at every boy I like and spoil everything?"

"Gunnar," Rick said again, remembering Gunnar's way of teasing Gail, of treating her like a kid sister. "Gunnar's a fine man, Gail. I like him a lot, but I just never thought of you and Gunnar somehow."

"What's wrong with that?" Gail shouted.

"I just didn't know," Rick said humbly, "but what *is* wrong with it, Gail?"

"Everything," Gail said desperately. "Everything. Gunnar went to Bridgeport to get away from me, but he couldn't do it. He can't do it . . . and I feel awful about Paul. We were sort of engaged after that cocktail party last fall. Not exactly—just sort of. I was mad at you and I guess I did it to spite you in a way, but I wasn't ever really in love with Paul. It wasn't like Gunnar. The first time I saw Gunnar I knew. Only I hated to hurt Paul. And I've tried to tell him it was all off . . . and I've tried to write him and I can't and I don't know what to do and Gunnar won't marry me."

"The hell he won't!"

There was a shrill peak of hysteria in Gail's laughter. "Oh, Daddy, you make me feel better. Gunnar keeps saying you'll agree with him. He says he's only been 'dry' eight months and that I've got an alcoholic father and he'll be damned if I have an alcoholic husband and . . ."

"He's got a point," Rick said slowly. "I don't think Gunnar'll go off the beam. He's got plenty of guts and he's done a swell job in A.A. but an alcoholic isn't any fun to live with, Gail, even when he's sober. You've had a bad enough time with me and you're pretty young. . . ."

"I'm older than Abigail Avery when she married my Great-Grand-father," Gail challenged him, "and you're always talking about what a woman she was."

"But her husband wasn't a drunk. . . ."

"I was scared," Gail admitted in a small voice, "that night I stayed with Diana and saw Sky passed out—I was scared to death." Please God don't let Gunnar be like that, she had prayed that night, but for weeks afterwards whenever she looked at Gunnar she had seen Sky's puffy face, heard his snores, groans and belches.

"Gunnar isn't like Pell," Rick said, "but couldn't you wait a while?"

"Wait—and have Gunnar go off some place further away than Bridgeport? Minnesota, maybe . . . or California, or . . . don't you see, Daddy, I can't wait? I can't let him go off without me."

"Your mother and I waited."

"Did you like it?"

"No," Rick grinned. "It was hell." All one long summer taking the Friday night train to the Cape—when he could get away from New York—going to dances and picnics with Adelaide, trying to hurry her, trying to get her to set a date for their wedding, and Adelaide laughing, "But Avery, it's such fun being engaged."

"I guess I'm like you," Gail said. "Waiting spoils everything. I want to get married and start having babies—fat blond babies with Viking eyes. It was funny about Paul. I could never imagine having a black haired child."

Good Lord, Rick thought, Adelaide and I never talked like that. Why the hell didn't Emily come home. "What does your aunt think about it?" he asked.

"I don't know," Gail said. "I haven't told her. . . ." Rick felt a warm, incredulous pleasure in Gail's confidence in him—this was being a father. This was the terrifying, priceless thing he had almost missed.

"I guess," Gail was going on. "Aunt Emily thinks Gunnar's too good for me. She says he has the makings of a fine artist and I suppose she looks on me as a sort of silly, unsensible child. But I'm not. Not any more. I've got everything all planned out. I can keep on with my job. They think I'm good over at the plant and Gunnar can go back to Hank's boatyard. He likes it a lot better than the work in Bridgeport and he wants to make boats as well as pictures, and as soon as he sells a few paintings he could work part time, don't you think? And I'm going to buy this house if I have enough money when I'm twenty-one and some-time we're going to Mexico for a year so that Gunnar can study with Orozco." Her words had tripped over themselves like children racing out of school at recess, her face had been radiant with the future, now it drooped into sadness and she clutched her father's arm. "You've got to help me, Daddy. You've got to talk to Gunnar. He'll listen to you. He thinks you're a great guy."

"I'll get my shotgun," Rick promised, putting his arm around Gail's shoulders, feeling her relax against him as she had on New Year's Eve when Gunnar had hurt his leg and Rick had said, "We'll take care of him, Gail."

XX

AUGUST YOU MUST

The heat wave was turning Joe's brain to liquid wax. He could almost feel the grey cells melting, running together like a badly molded candle. New York was a stew pan. An oven. A double boiler. Offices all over town were closing early, particularly the advertising agencies, Joe remarked with surprise. "Just because we make our living pulling other people's legs we don't have to pull our own, do we?" Joe's senior partner had clapped Joe on the back. "Go on home, Red, and get a swim and build yourself a long cool drink. Do you good."

But nothing did any good. Joe hadn't tried the drink, but he had tried nearly everything else. One morning when the Weather Bureau had predicted, "Continued heat. No break seen. Temperature expected to reach 96 degrees Fahrenheit at noon," he had appeared at the Riverside station in a white sport shirt, white slacks, white buckskin shoes—no socks. No tie. No coat. No hat. Plenty of other men were *carrying* their coats, but they all looked askance at Joe.

"Where's your coat, Joe?" Kibitzer Crunden broke away from a group of men on the platform and picked on Joe's most obvious deficiency.

"You win," Joe laughed. "I was betting who'd be the first to ask me that. Thought it might be Dick." He glanced at the smooth-looking young broker in a brown tropical worsted, with a wide panama hat. "God Almighty, women have more sense than men when it comes to clothes." There they were—girls in sleeveless cottons with bare legs going to jobs in Greenwich or Port Chester, women in sheer black or navy with wide transparent hats, bound for New York. "Hell's delight, men are nothing but slaves to convention. I'm doing this in the spirit of scientific inquiry as well as for personal comfort. Here you are, Crunden, here's a six-cent cigar as a prize for being the first to criticize me."

Crunden had waved the cigar away, reddened and walked off, his head in the air, but two men behind Joe had chuckled and one of them had pulled off his coat with a grin of approval in Joe's direction.

It had been a moment of rather puerile triumph, but nothing satisfied Joe. And the heat went on. It kept him away from two Greenwich meetings of A.A. The very thought of the stuffy room in the Museum with the smell of monkeys and parrots coming through the open door was enough to make him vomit. He had cut a couple of appointments with Dr. Wales for no good reason but the heat and the claustrophobic feeling of the small office and the familiar stiff chair across the desk from the doctor.

Gas shortage—or no gas shortage—the heat had projected him like a rocket bomb into his car one afternoon, had propelled him all the way to Bridgeport in search of a bordello where he had been taken years before by a bartender pal. What the hell could you do about sex anyway? Joe often looked at the placid facades of his fellow commuters and wondered what they did. He was dead sure they were bothered, even the married ones—especially the married ones, maybe. What in hell did Rick do—Rick, who had spent so much of his life in places where a brown-skinned female was easily available? No one would care what a man like Joe, whose wife had been away for a year, did so long as he left his friends' wives alone—wives who often did not act as if they wanted to be left alone, Joe reflected with a wry grin. Still, there was not much of that sort of meaningless flirtation going on around here.

Why in the name of God wouldn't Sylvia have an affair with him—what a stupid, pussyfooting, piddling euphemism—"affair!" Why wouldn't she go to bed with him—sleep with him—live with him . . . he spewed out words in a torment of wanting her. It would have been so easy. So natural. So beautiful—Sylvia was beautiful. Beautiful—but afraid. "Of what?" he had asked her a hundred times. They wouldn't be hurting anyone. Her husband had married again. She had no children. Her mother and father were living in a small upstate New York town. Who would know? Who would care? Not Monica. She needn't think of Monica. But had she? Was that the trouble, the reason she always found some trivial excuse—the apartment hotel where she lived was very conservative, very strict—someone might find out—it might hurt A.A. if it were known—she hated hole-and-corner things. "Your damn fastidiousness gets in the way of your living," he had told her angrily—but you couldn't be angry with Sylvia. If you fell in love with a medieval saint instead of a woman, what the hell could you do about it? Nothing—nothing except the unromantic, unsatisfactory thing he was doing now.

Bridgeport was unromantic, ugly, hot. A jerry-built town. He drove through the narrow, crowded streets in an increasingly restless depression. He had passed a few fine colonial houses on the outskirts and there was one lovely elm-shaded street he remembered in Stratford, but he couldn't find a decent piece of architecture anywhere in the rest of the city. How the devil could Gunnar stand it after living in Hank's snug, solid old place? Gunnar had brought a bunch of young fellows down to one of the Greenwich meetings, guys who had been discharged from the Army or Navy, guys like Gunnar who had tried liquor as an answer to the hellish problem of readjustment. He might look up Gunnar now . . . but Gunnar would be working. The town was jammed with war workers, men and women pushing through the hot streets looking for something, herding in and out of cheap movie houses, filling the pool rooms, bowling alleys, bars, drug stores; buying chewing gum, lipsticks, condoms, razor blades, ten-cent magazines—Westerns, Love Stories, Detective Thrillers.

He was looking for something himself. The unpainted frame building was battened up, a large "For Sale" sign nailed on the rickety porch.

Joe wandered into a nearby brick tavern with a big plate-glass window and a sour smell of cheap beer. The Irish bartender recognized him and began bewailing the good old days in a mournful sing-song.

"Closing 'em up here. Closing 'em up there. And all them sailors and war workers picking the girls up on the street. Drove 'em out of this section entirely, ruint my business on me—and the other end of town you can't hardly walk a block without being accosted."

"A fine moral distinction!" Joe gulped a sweetish brown cola drink and handed the bartender a cigar. He wanted someone to talk to—someone with as big a gripe on the world as he had.

"Sure and 'tis a fine moral country, America, and you're lucky if you don't get led straight into a den of thieves by one of these dames and rolled, or conked on the bean, or slipped some knock-out drops in your beer these days."

"It's a great world," Joe agreed, his voice taking on its exaggerated intonation of vastness. "Hush-hush and hypocrisy are flourishing like the green bay tree. New York is the same as Bridgeport. Flatfeet hounding 'em away under the orders of the puritanical Mayor. La Guardia closing burlesque shows, shutting up dance halls, jerking out slot machines with the fanatical fury of a Cotton Mather!" Joe pounded the small empty glass on the bar.

The bartender's mottled red face took on a started expression of shock. "'Tis pretty far you're going with them words, Mister. I'm a fair-minded man meself and I've always heard tell as how this here Little Flower has done a fine job for the great city of New York."

"Sure," Joe agreed, "he's cleaned up a lot besides vice—graft and dirty politics, sure. I'm just sour on the world today."

"And who wouldn't be with that bilgewater you're after drinking? And the heat and all. There's bottles aplenty that will put the soul back in your body, Mister, and one on the house for the sake of old times. An ice-cold beer now . . ."

Joe pushed back his stool. He'd commit any foolishness he liked, from wenches to gambling, but he wouldn't take a drink. He didn't actually want a drink. Before he realized it he was out of the crowded ugliness of Bridgeport, sliding up and down the beautiful roller coaster of the Merritt Parkway. It was like sailing through green islands, a cool breeze against his face. He passed a car and the driver gave him a queer look and a quick warning blast of his horn. Joe glanced at his speedometer and saw the needle pointing at sixty-five—and the speed limit was now forty. With great difficulty he slowed down, held his foot back from pushing the accelerator to the floor. He wanted to shoot the works some-how. Blow his top. But the only dissipation he could rout out that night was a game of bridge with some neighbors in which he overbid with deliberate recklessness and dragged his bewildered partner down for a five-thousand-point loss.

Nothing was any good. And the heat kept on. He couldn't sleep at night. The only cool spot was his back porch where he had had Emerald make up the wicker couch. And the dawn woke him there. Morning after morning the red ball of the sun would rouse him and the heat haze would shimmer over the harbor. "No relief in sight." He didn't need the morning paper to tell him that.

He didn't need the newspapers to tell him anything. Thoreau was right. Montaigne was right—sitting in his sturdy tower in Bordeaux with civil wars raging around him, writing his timeless comments on the curious behavior of mankind. But Thoreau and Montaigne had not had to contend with radio commentators, with endless diagnoses of war news. You had to forget the war if you wanted to write a novel—but how could you with headlines shouting at you morning and evening? Somewhere in New England a squirrel was reported as having attacked a woman and a boy, in Maryland a squirrel had chased a dog. That struck Joe as important . . . it threw light on the fundamental terms of human existence—maybe the heat was infuriating the squirrels—what would it do to ants who really could challenge human civilization?

One night he had thrown himself on the wicker couch determined to sleep—but he couldn't sleep. He knew the signs. No use tossing and sweating any longer. He had looked at the radium dial of his wrist watch. If he hurried he could catch the 12:15 to New York. Coming into Grand Central he had realized that New York was a day town, not a night town to him. He hated the spurious imitation of nocturnal joy, the frantic determination to be "gay" after dark, the folly of thinking that gaiety meant throwing money around the Great White Way, paying twice as much for a drink, or a woman, or anything, as you would in Paris or any city that loved gaiety for itself.

The Yankee Stadium was the only place he cared about in New York. It meant Jimmy to him. He could see Jimmy jumping up and down on the bleachers, waving his school cap and shouting when Lou Gehrig hit an enormous triple with the bases full. The last time, just before Monica took Jimmy off to Pasadena, they had been rooting against the Yankees. They had talked it over man to man and he had explained to Jim that the fan who always rooted for the home team was a dope, like the man who always voted a straight party ticket—the game was the thing. And it was good for baseball not to have the same team win the pennant year after year. Jimmy had quoted it word for word to Monica when they got home, along with a play by play account of Chet Laabs' home run.

No one could ever understand how especially Joe cared for his stepson. Every time he looked at the boy's profile, a replica of his father's, Joe was tortured by a sensation of pleasure and pain. He knew it was morbid—maybe Wales could help him separate his emotions about Jimmy, help him forget the guilt of his accidental shooting of Jim Bradway and remember only the boy himself with Monica's eyes and a smile that was so individual, so definitely his own that it always made Joe think of the amazing fact of evolution—that no two human beings in all the generations of man had ever been exactly alike.

New York had been hot even in the dark hours of early morning. New York had pleased Joe no more than Bridgeport. He had thought of calling Sylvia and been deterred by the idea of the night operator in the strict and conservative apartment hotel as well as by the foregone conclusion of their argument if he did manage to see Sylvia.

The next night he had gone to bed even earlier, taking the precaution of switching off the telephone in the downstairs hall. He was in no state to be called in the middle of the night on an A.A. case. If anyone chose to get drunk, let him. It was no skin off Joe Kelly's nose tonight. Blame the heat wave if a guy went on a bender, or landed in the town jail, or put a bullet in his head.

Miraculously he slept, woke at dawn to the faintest stirring of a breeze across the harbor. The tide was high enough for a dip off his own dock and Joe loped up to his room in slightly better spirits. But the sun seemed to flatten the breeze and by the time he had finished shaving and dressing he was perspiring again. "You look like hell," he said to his reflection in the mirror, "but not so bad as if you had a hangover, my lad. Remember that. And thank God for it, too."

Emerald was singing in the kitchen as Joe came downstairs and hurried out on the front porch, over which red and white hollyhocks peered, to get the morning papers. Damn it, they were late again. If Emerald could get in on time from Stamford every day why the devil couldn't the paper boy be prompt? He'd call up the dealer and tell him to cancel his subscription. It was lousy service. He'd buy his newspapers at the station after this, the way lots of other men did. He strode into the hall, hunted up the number in the book and took the receiver off the hook. A long steady brrr hit his ear. He'd forgotten to turn the phone on. Probably someone had been trying to get him. As he snapped the switch the bell screamed raucously, like a baby that has been howling all night.

"Yes," he shouted. "Stop ringing so I can hear you."

"Hey, Joe, is that you?" Rick's voice came over the wire. "I've been trying to get you for twenty minutes. The damn fool said your line must be out of order. How are you?"

"Hot," Joe said, "and hungry. I haven't had my breakfast yet."

There was a strangely long pause and Joe thought the wire must have gone dead, then Rick said, "Look, Joe. I'm coming over. I'm ready to start now. Wait for me."

"Sure, we'll give you another cup of coffee."

Funny, Joe thought, going into the dining room. He always sat with Rick on the train anyway. Something must be up, for him to drive all the way over from Greenwich now. Maybe Rick had had a slip—but he'd sounded all right on the phone. Maybe he'd had a row with Gail. Joe hoped it wasn't that. Gail was a sweet kid. Growing up fast, too, and she and Rick had seemed to be hitting it off lately. Joe ate scrambled eggs listlessly, drank half a cup of coffee, lighted a cigarette.

Emerald brought in three New York newspapers. For a guy who hated reading about the daily blunderings of the world he certainly was a fool for trouble. It was a habit like alcohol, he reflected, and acquired at about the same time. He had started his serious drinking on the old *Sun* and his pernicious absorption of long columns of print at the same time. It had developed into a compulsive routine—he would start the *Times* at breakfast, save the *Tribune* for the train, but first of all glance at the tabloid which he always left for Emerald. Emerald thought it the world's greatest newspaper and in some respects he agreed with her. In a melodramatic age people seemed to need the sensational approach of yellow journalism.

Emerald laid the tabloid on top of the other papers as usual. The usual war head screamed across the top but below it was a picture—a lovely, pointed medieval face. Sylvia Landon! Even as he recognized the bad photograph, his eye took in the caption:

JUMPED OR FELL?
Body of Beautiful Divorcee Found in Courtyard
Story on Page 2.

Four minutes later Joe was sitting at the table frozen, unable to turn the page, his cigarette butt burning a hole in a green doily.

Rick rushed up the steps. "I wanted to get here ahead of the papers," he panted.

Joe didn't look up, didn't turn his head. He was holding one hand over his eyes like a man blinded by an explosion. "Tell me what it says—I can't seem to. . . ."

Rick picked up the paper, stubbed the cigarette in an ashtray, turned the page, his own hand shaking. He poured a cup of coffee, gulped it down, his eyes traveling down the small print. "They don't know anything, Joe, but I'm sure she fell. I'm sure it was an accident." He wasn't sure. Christ, if he was sure of anything he was sure Sylvia had killed herself. Sylvia standing in her blue linen dress at the White Plains meeting, Sylvia saying, "I stood at a long window looking down into a narrow courtyard lined with neat rows of garbage cans—I wanted to jump . . . A.A. has held me back from that window. . . ." Joe would be remembering that too.

"Read it," Joe said, his voice as hoarse as if he had had a tonsil operation.

The story gave Sylvia's name, age, the address of the apartment hotel where she was living, her ex-husband's name, her father's name and the name of the small upstate town. Details they both knew, details that meant nothing, such as the name and address of the passerby who had found her. Rick read on, then stopped abruptly.

"Read it," Joe said. "For Christ's sake keep going or give it here."

"The night telephone operator told the police that Mrs. Landon had tried several times to reach a Mr. Joseph Augustine Kelly at an out-of-town number. Mr. Kelly is a well-known advertising man and a prominent member of the Harvard Club. The police were unable to locate Mr. Kelly last evening."

Still Joe didn't move—didn't seem to have heard. Rick watched him. It would be better if Joe would curse himself for having failed Sylvia—anything would be better than this frozen, paralyzed silence.

"Look, Joe," he said. "We ought to get into town as fast as we can. There are things we can do. It says here that Sylvia's mother and father are on their way to New York. That her mother is prostrated. We can probably help. . . ."

"Help!" Joe laughed, a sound that was like the laughter of all the creatures in hell. "Help! Now?"

Somehow Rick managed to get Joe into his car and drive him to the train. He felt as if he had pulled Joe out of the middle of Long Island Sound, as if he were pushing with all his weight to bring the breath into Joe's lungs . . . but what kind of artificial respiration could you use to force life back to a man's mind?

Sylvia's apartment, when Joe and Rick arrived, was full of people, each with a different theory about her death. The house physician, a disillusioned-looking man with a neat grey mustache and the manner of a Park Avenue doctor who has come down in the world, was telling a woman reporter that Mrs. Landon had asked him for some sleeping tablets two days before. He had given her a mild sedative and thought she must have gotten up in the night to open the window and, confused by the effect of the drug, leaned too far out. "The heat was enough to make anyone sleepless and depressed," he added. The reporter glanced at him shrewdly, as if she thought he was contradicting his own verdict of accident.

Jane Post, the woman who had gotten Sylvia into A.A., pulled Rick and Joe aside and spoke in a low voice, keeping a wary eye on the reporter. "The police called me last night, found my name in Sylvia's telephone book. I had to identify her." Jane's shoulders shook in an involuntary shudder, but she steadied herself and took a long drag on a cigarette. There were dark circles under her fine eyes and the white collar of her thin navy blue dress was twisted as if she had pulled the dress over her head in frantic haste. "I think it was deliberate. I think Sylvia's friends might as well face that. We can keep it from the papers and her family but I . . . it almost seems worse to me if it was an accident. I know Sylvia was unhappy—she was more upset by being turned down by the Waves than most people realized and she didn't get her thesis finished for Columbia and they held up her degree and Sylvia was afraid she'd start drinking again. She didn't want to let A.A. down. I'm sure this was her way out—a terrible way for us—but *her* way."

Joe still didn't say anything—didn't shout, "There's another reason. A reason only Joseph Augustine Kelly, that fine fellow, knows," but the words were pounding in his brain so loudly that he looked around to see if Jane or Rick had heard them.

Rick was saying, "God, Jane, I admire your courage—looking at it like that." Jane must have spent hellish hours trying to figure it out, not being able to say what she thought to anyone till he and Joe got there. "But I don't suppose we can ever really know what happened. I don't suppose there are reasons—or any sort of logic—for suicide." He was watching Joe, choosing his words carefully. The surgical sharpness of Jane's analysis had evidently helped her, but it might be too much for Joe. "That is, *if* it was suicide," he added. "I don't see how anyone can be sure."

Across the room a man in a morning coat, with the unmistakable professional solicitude of the undertaker, was talking to a large handsome woman in black and a tall stoop-shouldered man. Sylvia's mother was almost a caricature of Sylvia—complacency had blurred the lines of the pointed, medieval face.

"That must be Sylvia's mother and father," Rick said. "I suppose we ought to speak to them."

Joe followed like a man in a nightmare walking naked down a crowded street. The lines of his face still set in a mask of withdrawal.

Mrs. Burton put a capable, jeweled hand on Joe's arm. "You were my daughter's dear friend, Mr. Kelly. She wrote me about you often. Oh, my poor lovely Sylvia. All her life has been sad and I wanted to give her everything. I wanted her to be happy. Did she tell you about her marriage—such a tragic mistake? Sit here beside me, Mr. Kelly, I want to talk to you." She gestured to a couch in the far corner of the room.

The undertaker moved away with a bowing assurance that everything would be taken care of.

"We can't take care of Sylvia now," the tall stoop-shouldered man said grimly, "but we couldn't seem to do the right thing for her when she was alive." He took two cigars out of his pocket, handed Rick one and went on as if satisfied that Rick was the sort of man he could speak his mind to, "Sylvia was like her mother. You might not think it, but she was. Only Sylvia always wanted something no one can find and her mother always gets what she wants. I've been able to help Myrtle and she's helped me, too. Knows as much about my factory as I do. President of the Woman's Club, first woman to be elected to our School Board, Director of the Girl Scouts—Myrtle's got a finger in every pie in our town. Only thing she never used her head about was Sylvia. Spoiled her. Sided with Sylvia against her husband. Myrtle was never fair to him. He was a decent young fellow, would have stuck by Sylvia even after she started drinking—but I guess the divorce worked out better for him. Married again, has a nice happy wife and two kids. I wish Sylvia had had a child. Might have been the answer for her. Certainly would have helped us now. I'm worried about Myrtle. She's taking it awfully hard. Blames herself for not getting Sylvia to come home to live. The way I see it— there isn't anyone to blame except Sylvia."

Jane Post and this tall, stoop-shouldered man had reached the same conclusion for different reasons but with the same healthy ability to look at facts without fear. "I wish you'd say that to my friend, Joe Kelly," Rick said. "He's talking to Mrs. Burton now. He's pretty cut up about it. Sylvia tried to reach him last night. I know he's blaming himself, thinking he might have saved her."

"You can tell him what I said if you think it would be any help." Mr. Burton's eyes followed Rick's to the couch across the room. "Tell him he might have talked Sylvia out of it last night, but it wouldn't have done any good—not really. At least that's what I think, Mr.—sorry, I didn't get your name. I just knew you were a friend of Sylvia's." Exhaustion was turning the man's face grey. "I've got to get Myrtle home. Got to look after her."

And I've got to look after Joe, Rick thought. Coffee—coffee seemed to be the A.A. answer to almost any situation in which liquor would have been the crutch in the old days.

Rick, Joe and Jane Post went down to the coffee shop in the hotel, where a few late breakfasters lingered over their morning papers. It was in all their minds that Sylvia must have eaten here, perhaps at this very table near an open window with a view of the arch of Washington Square, where top-heavy buses swooped up the Avenue and the life of a great city hurried on.

Jane was doing her best to get Joe to talk. "Did Mrs. Burton tell you she simply couldn't understand how Sylvia could have lived in those two dreary hotel rooms when she had a lovely home and such a pretty bedroom that was just the way it had been when she graduated from college. . . ?"

"The place was pretty awful," Rick agreed. "I thought women always fixed things up, put pillows around—or something. . . ." He was remembering the way Emily gave every room she lived in a subtle, personal touch, fumbling in a masculine way to express what exactly Emily did to a house. "It looked so impersonal. As if Sylvia had just moved in yesterday and might move out tomorrow."

Joe forced himself to swallow the hot weak coffee. Rick was right. When he had first met Sylvia she had been living up near Columbia University in a furnished apartment that had had the same curiously uninhabited look as her rooms off Washington Square. He had never noticed it particularly before but his mind, which had been closed with horror all morning, opened a tentative crack, like an oyster cautiously lifting its shell for air. This small odd fact touched him, puzzled him, suddenly reminded him of the brilliant crimson curtains Monica had hung in the blue-grey dining room of Jim Bradway's house.

Jane Post reached for the pot of coffee. "Sylvia was a transitory person, I guess. I don't think she ever had the feeling of living anywhere after her divorce. She told me once how she fixed that house up after she was married—it sounded sort of pale and monotonous to my taste, but I'm crazy about wild color."

Crimson curtains waved before Joe's eyes. Monica seemed nearer, realer than she had in a year. It didn't make sense—or did it? He couldn't think—couldn't figure it out, but he had to pull himself together somehow.

"Well, this isn't running the chewing gum business," Rick said, reaching for the check. "I've got to shove." He studied Joe's strong profile, in which the lines seemed to have been altered in one stroke by a macabre artist from humor to despair. He was thinking of Joe more than Sylvia, he realized, but he couldn't help it. He *had* to think of Joe now. "Look, Joe, how about going back to the country? I'll call up Emily and get her to meet you." Emily would know what to do, what to say to Joe. Emily could apply artificial respiration to a man's mind. "Plan to stay with us for a while. We've got plenty of room."

Joe pushed his chair back slowly. "Thanks, I'm okay. I better get up to the office."

Jane hurried into the lobby ahead of them. "I promised Mrs. Burton I'd be right back. There are things to pack and telegrams to send. I'm going up with them tonight to stay till after the funeral. You two will come, won't you? It's an awful trip. You have to change trains at Albany but. . . . Oh, and will one of you call Kidd Whistler and let the rest of the A.A.'s know? It's to be Friday at four at the Burtons' house. Here, I'll write the address down." She pulled an envelope out of her blue snakeskin purse and scribbled directions. "I'll call you later when I find out about trains. There'll be someone to meet you." She disappeared into the elevator and Rick marveled at the way women could go at things, pushing their grief down, telling sorrow to wait like a child while they did the things that had to be done.

"See you on the five-fifteen," Rick had said as he stood with Joe in the broiling sun looking for Joe's bus.

But Joe wasn't on the train. Rick, sitting in their usual seat in the rear smoker, watched the legs of men hurrying down the ramp. Brown seersucker legs, blue seersucker legs, tan Palm Beach cloth legs, short legs, long legs, slow-striding legs, double-timing legs—but not Joe's legs. The door opened and closed, hot underground station air came into the artificially refrigerated car, but no Joe.

Rick stopped in the Cos Cob station and called Joe's house. Emerald said he had not been home and had not telephoned. Maybe he had taken an early train and gone to see Dr. Wales. Rick leafed through a torn telephone book, located the number of High Pines and found another nickel. "No," Wales said, "he skipped his appointment again. Call me when he turns up and I'll come out to see him. I might be able to help." Another nickel for another idea. Rick dialed his own house—Joe might have taken his advice and gone to see Emily. Again the answer was no. Rick changed a dollar at the ticket office and called Joe's office on the chance that someone might be working late—didn't advertising men always brag about working overtime? But evidently not when you needed them. A long metallic buzzing and the operator's voice: "They do not answer, shall I call you back in twenty minutes?" Rick put the receiver back on the hook, picked up his change from the small slot, remembering how he had shouted, "Hell no!" the night of the White Plains meeting when he had been trying to reach Gail and the operator had asked her automatic, stupid question, how he had pounded in a fury up the stairs. There was no fury in him now, only a despondent sense of helplessness. Joe's partner lived in Rye—maybe he could reach him, maybe Joe had gone home with him. "You're asking me?" an indignant voice boomed over the wire. "Hell no. Joe isn't here. Thought he was sick. Never showed up at the office all day."

So that was that. Rick walked out of the booth, looked at a timetable, debated with himself as to the advisability of catching the next train back to New York . . . but where would he start looking for Joe? Better get home. If Joe wanted him, that was where he would call. Besides, Emily would be at home—Emily with her gifts of courage and peace.

"Do you think Joe went back to Sylvia's apartment to help her family?" Emily asked.

That must be it, Rick thought, reaching for the phone again. Again he was met by disappointment. Jane Post's competent, tired voice told him that she hadn't seen or heard of Joe since they had left her at the elevator in the morning. "Are you afraid he's drinking?" she asked, facing the A.A. fear with the same abrupt courage with which she had met Sylvia's death. "Not that I blame the guy," she added. "I'd have taken a shot myself only I knew it wouldn't do any good. Look, Rick, don't let it get you down. I'll call the clubhouse. Someone will find him and we'll let you know."

Rick sat by the telephone all evening while Emily and Gail played gin rummy, the sight of the yellow head and the cloudy auburn hair bent over the cards steadying him. God, he was lucky. Joe had nobody . . . Joe.

It was Kidd Whistler who telephoned long after midnight, when Emily and Gail had gone to bed and Rick still sat with a book on his knee, not reading, not thinking, just waiting in a coma of anxiety. "We found him," Kidd said. "Jane said to let you know. Sure, he was plastered. Must have been drinking all day. The bartender at the Saint Thomas Hotel called A.A. instead of the police. Yup, they're doing that now in quite a few places—one bright spot anyhow. Phil Weber and I beat it up there. Took him over to Towne's. What? No, he's drawn a blank. They'll fix him up. Better get some sleep yourself, boy. Joe will be okay. He knows what it's all about."

XXI

BOOMERANG

Kidd Whistler had been optimistic about Joe. All the A.A.'s were positive Joe would snap out of it. "Sure, he'd had a slip—so had plenty of other members—but Joe had been in the group too long to go off the deep end—and stay off."

Emily was confident too. "Give him time, Rick, he's had a terrible shock, but Joe's a strong person. Don't worry, darling, or you'll start me worrying about *you*." She had put her arms around Rick's neck and pulled his head down level with her eyes and he had felt her quiet strength going through him. God, how had he ever managed to live without her all these years! How did Joe manage without . . . and there he was back in the old fretful puzzle of Joe's binge.

Hank maintained that Joe had been heading for trouble for a long time. "Seen it comin'," Hank said, "the way you can feel a storm blowin' up on the Sound. It weren't only Sylvia—he was as full of the jitters as a porkypine is of quills afore that." But Hank couldn't explain why, couldn't see how completely Joe's continued drinking knocked the props out from under Rick. Joe had helped him—he had to help Joe now. Not only for Joe's sake but for his own. And he didn't seem to be getting anywhere—except deeper and deeper into a feeling of hopeless uncertainty.

Rick had brought Joe out from Towne's Hospital in New York to the "shack," as they called the house on Cognewaugh Road—a sick-looking, self-cursing Joe. But being with Rick and Emily—seeing their evident happiness in each other—had only seemed to make matters worse. Joe, after a few sober, moody, irritable days, had walked out of the house one morning, headed for a wop joint in Mianus famous for good beer in big steins, and had been picked up late that night by Hank Frost. A cop friend of Hank's had called him and Hank had called Rick. "Reckon we better pop Joe into High Pines," Hank had suggested, much to Rick's amazement. "Seems like that Doc Joe sets such store by could do somethin' for him now." Rick had agreed, had telephoned and made the arrangements, remembering Wales' tall figure in a blue suit standing on the steps and returning Pell's exaggerated military salute. Wales had caught on fast to Pell's absurd playacting. Wales was a real guy. Emily had been driving Joe over to High Pines every afternoon, but this way Wales could really keep an eye on Joe.

Still Rick went on worrying and the heat continued. At the Cos Cob station the next afternoon he looked at the tide. It was high. A swim in salt water would be a hell of a lot more refreshing than a dip in his own pool which was now only a few degrees cooler than the air.

Swimming out to the raft with long lazy strokes, he pulled himself up, shook the water out of his eyes and saw a broad brown back against the upright of the diving platform. The back turned and Rick recognized Wales' thick white hair and lean, humorous face. This was luck, especially as the raft was deserted by its usual mob of kids.

"I don't suppose you remember me. . . ." Rick began, squatting on the edge of the raft, his long legs dangling in the cold water.

Wales smiled—it was a wide, generous smile. "Of course I do. You're Light-Horse Harry Lee," he laughed, "or you were when I first met you. And what's more important," he added, "You're Joe Kelly's friend."

Rick nodded, his eyes squinting from the hot glare of the sun on the water. He jerked his head to face the doctor. "God, I hope you can help Joe—and fast."

Wales studied the emphatic, angular features, noted the twitch of Rick's left eyelid. Here was another one headed for trouble if he didn't watch out—all alcoholics seemed to be driven by the same frenzied impatience. "In my business," he said with deliberate slowness, "we learn not to hurry. You can't go fast when you're trying to get at things that have taken a long, long time to grow and a long, long time to be concealed, buried under layers and layers in the unconscious. . . ."

He grinned suddenly and pointed across the harbor at the steeple of a Greenwich church rising serenely against the orange and violet sky. "Hell, this is no time or place for a lecture on psychiatry. Tell you what you do, Rickham, if you're interested. Come on up to New Haven with me tomorrow. I'm giving a speech at the Yale School for Studies on Alcohol. You might learn something," he said in his humorous, lazy voice. "Or if that doesn't tempt you, this might—your Bill Griffith of A.A. is scheduled for the closing talk."

"I'll bet he won't turn up," Rick said. "There's some sort of jinx on Bill Griffith and me. I've been in A.A. nearly a year and I still haven't met the guy, but I'd like to hear you." Rick had made the same complaint to Kidd Whistler at the New York meeting in February. He had been peeved then; now he found it hard to get in a rage, sitting on the float surrounded by orange-green water with this big reposeful man.

The next morning Rick sat in a rattly day coach beside Dr. Sam Wales. It was noisy, dusty and NOT air-conditioned. As midsummer heat and cinders poured through the open windows, Rick took back all his former diatribes against air-conditioning. Both men had folded their coats and put them on the rack over their heads, but even in shirtsleeves they were perspiring constantly, constantly mopping. Rick wanted to question the doctor about Joe but he hesitated, thinking that Wales probably needed time to go over his speech, not knowing how to begin anyhow.

"Go ahead and ask me about Joe Kelly," Wales said suddenly, putting down his newspaper. "I gather he's pretty much on your mind."

"Well, sure," Rick stammered, "but I don't quite know what I can ask—or rather how much you can tell me."

"But I do." Wales laughed and looked at Rick with his large, humorous blue eyes. "Of course, a psychiatrist, like any doctor—even more than any other doctor—keeps his patients' confidences. But in dealing with an alcoholic who is a member of A.A. there are some things I like to talk over with other members. You belong to a remarkable organization, Rickham."

Two large colored women in the seat ahead got up and waddled to the door as the train pulled into Bridgeport, Rick reached over and pushed the seat back, getting his long legs out of the aisle and stretching them out on the dusty plush. "What puzzles me about Joe is . . . well, he isn't half as up-one-minute and down-the-next as I am. What Hank Frost calls the Perigee tides of an alky."

"That's good," Wales said. "Damn good way to express it. Tell you how one of my colleagues puts it. Look. . . ." He took his big saddle leather shoes off the seat and ran his hand along the horizontal edge. "We'll call this line the normal tension level of a normal person. Your so-called normal guy may go a few inches up when he's high," Wales' strong brown hand rose slightly above the plush seat, "or a few inches down when he's low, but an alcoholic goes way up—several feet—and way down to the floor. Erratic curve, see?"

"Like my fever chart when I had malaria," Rick nodded.

"Same idea," Wales agreed. "You're sick people. Only you're apt to forget that fact when you stop drinking. The pattern is still there, see? The big swing from high to low," Wales gestured again, "is always in the alcoholic—or neurotic—personality. And alcoholics *are* neurotics. Liquor exaggerates the swing. Some people drink when they are on the up-curve—to celebrate, others when they are hitting bottom—to drown their sorrows. That's fairly obvious, but the thing that a lot of you guys who quit drinking may not understand is that even after you've cut out alcohol you haven't changed your emotional pattern."

"That's right." Rick nodded again. "I'm not quite as bad as I was when I was boozing but I still get unaccountable elations and damnable depressions—sometimes over nothing. And I've been 'dry' nearly a year."

Wales was fanning himself with the folded newspaper. The motion was leisurely, soporific. "You'll probably have to guard against those moods for more than a year. Maybe the rest of your life. But knowing about them usually helps and there are ways to cope with them when you feel them coming on—call up an A.A. friend, go to a ball game, read a mystery, go for a swim the way you did yesterday and sort of keep that normal level of tension in mind." He drew his finger along the edge of the dusty red plush seat again.

Rick took out a pack of cigarettes, offered one to Wales. He felt more relaxed, more at peace with himself and the world, than he had since he had turned the knob of the radio over a week ago to the horror of Sylvia's suicide. Joe was in good hands.

"Another thing my colleague says—as a matter of fact he hasn't said it publicly yet, but it is to appear in an article in the December issue of

Quarterly Journal of Studies on Alcohol—he calls alcoholism 'a disease of growing egocentricity.' How does that strike you?" Wales' humorous blue eyes studied Rick.

"Hits me below the belt," Rick laughed. "That's the kind of a guy I am—or maybe *was*—but it's not so true of Joe. At least I don't think it is."

Wales didn't answer directly. He went off at what seemed to Rick a sudden tangent. "Ever meet any of Joe's family?"

"You mean Monica and Jimmy?" Rick asked. "No. I was in Central American when that happened."

"I was thinking of his mother and father and an older sister he seemed to be pretty fond of."

"You mean it goes back that far?"

"H-m-m." Wales didn't pursue it. "I was talking to Miss Willard when she drove Kelly over one day. She has a theory that Joe is over-romantic about women. A Galahad complex. Wants to do great deeds for them. Feels he's let them down. Could be. Fits in with his childhood picture. Very perceptive person, Miss Willard. Good thing if Joe fell for her."

"Not on your life!" Rick shouted and then laughed at his explosion.

Wales threw back his white head and laughed too. "Congratulations, Rickham. And I mean it. I've only met three women who have her quality—one of them is Mrs. Wales, thank God, and the other is Lois Griffith."

The platform of the New Haven station was unrolling under their window. They grabbed their coats off the rack, found a taxi and drove through the overgrown town to the red brick buildings of the Yale Divinity School.

The hall was well filled with social workers, ministers, and temperance lecturers who constituted the bulk of the enrollment. Rick recognized several A.A. members from various chapters and joined them as Dr. Wales made his way to the platform.

Two men were already seated there. One, "a long, lean, humorous, intelligent Vermont Yankee," must be Bill Griffith from Joe's description. The heavier man, Dr. Jellinek, Director of the School, spoke briefly and introduced Dr. Samuel Wales of High Pines, a pioneer in the psychiatric treatment of alcoholism.

Rick liked what Wales said about the stupidity of the ordinary physician and the old-fashioned psychiatrist in regard to alcoholism. He was a damn honest guy, admitting that the medical profession had blundered pretty badly, on the whole, until A.A. came along. Then, the doctors and psychiatrists had sat up and taken notice—here was a new technique—here was an astounding percentage of cures—well, call them arrested cases—whatever you called them, they were a challenge. Again he quoted his colleague, this time on what he termed the "secret therapy" of Alcoholics Anonymous. In other words, the conversion angle, the religious experience. That was where A.A. had it all over the medical profession.

Rick was sunk. It all boiled down to that. It always boiled down to that. It was the crux of A.A. all right, not only according to the A.A. members but according to this psychiatrist whom he trusted, for whom he had developed a genuine admiration. But, hell, it was still the stumbling block to him—Avery Rickham.

Dr. Jellinek was talking again, introducing Bill Griffith. Rick watched the lean Vermonter unfold himself, look over the audience, walk down the steps from the rostrum to the main floor and say with a grin and a slight drawl that he welcomed the spirit of informality and would like to talk as if this were an A.A. meeting. "Some while ago," he began, "a few of us from A.A. met with a group of distinguished physicians who were studying what they called 'recovered alcoholics' and 'unrecovered alcoholics'—medical terms. They mentioned a third group—'normal people.' Maybe some of us who had been 'dry' several years were hurt to find that we were still not considered 'normal.'

"The doctors were very humble—like our good friend Dr. Sam Wales, here—they admitted that medicine has not done much for the alcoholic. They seemed to think that alcoholics are more sensitive, more emotionally childish than normal people and this hurt us—we had always considered ourselves intellectually precocious.

"In other words they were describing the alcoholic character much as I would have put it. Let's say—the alcoholic tends to the grandiose.

"I was that way myself even as a child on a Vermont farm. I can remember the day my Grandad told me about the boomerang of Australia which came back to you if it missed the animal you were throwing it at. Grandad concluded with the dogmatic statement that nobody but an Australian could make a boomerang. That made me mad. You see, I had grandiose ideas. I determined to show him that I, Bill Griffith of Vermont, could make a boomerang. I neglected my lessons. I forgot to fill the woodbox. I spent all my time reading all the books on Australia in our own library—except for the time I spent with drawshave and saw on every likely piece of timber I could lay my hands on. My Grandad got good and mad when I sawed the headpiece out of my bed.

"As luck would have it, this turned out to be the right piece of wood for a boomerang. I threw it around the Congregational Church steeple and it came back to me. Then I called my Grandad out for a demonstration. I threw the boomerang, it went around the steeple, came back and nearly decapitated Grandad."

Bill paused while the audience laughed. "Now there was an example of the grandiose. I had spent an utterly unreasonable amount of study and exertion for no useful purpose—simply to prove my own importance.

"I could give you other examples that might look as if I had been developing some admirable quality, such as persistence—actually I was developing my ego. In school and in the war. It was during the war that I made the great discovery that a few drinks released me from self-consciousness.

"After the war I went to New York. I was overcome by the vastness of the place, the numbers of sophisticated people. I felt a great urge to show these city folks that a Yankee from the Vermont hills could hold his own with them. I went to night law school. My wife and I lived in cheap rooms to save money—we had decided that money was all-important in getting ahead. My social drinking increased. Little did I realize that I was building a boomerang that would come back and nearly decapitate me.

"From a legitimate means of relaxation and release, liquor was becoming a necessity to me. And I was pouring it into a body that was very sensitive to alcohol. We have a way of stating in it A.A.—alcoholism is an allergy of the body combined with a compulsion of the mind. That was what was happening to me. My hangovers became worse, each time I drank I got drunker than I intended. But my business career was going ahead. I was making money in Wall Street, getting the social recognition I craved. Only I couldn't seem to live without liquor—or live very happily with it. I was a drunk by 1924.

"By the time the depression hit I was being mainly supported by my wife, Lois, who is down there now in the fourth row." He waved a long arm toward a grey-haired woman with a gentle face, gentle and strong, and with the same look of serenity his own face had.

"Then came my big chance. I was offered a job as manager of a large syndicate. I had succeeded in staying sober during the preliminary talks—six or eight weeks, I guess—but they all knew about my drinking and before the deal was closed one of them came to me and said, 'Bill are you sure you can stay off liquor; not take one single drink?'

"'Oh sure,' I said, 'of course I can.'

"'Well, would you mind if we put that in the contract?'

"'Not at all, not at all.'

"So they wrote in that if I took one drink my job as manager was ended."

Rick knew what was coming—it was the same sort of thing that had happened to him when he'd tried to go on the wagon on account of an important job—and landed behind the eight ball. The A.A.s around him were all grinning reminiscently as Bill Griffith went on to tell how he had gone out to New Jersey to inspect the plant and gotten into a poker game afterwards at his hotel with some of the company engineers. They had had a jug of "Jersey Lightning" and offered him a drink. He had refused repeatedly, but late in the evening he had gotten to thinking that in all his long drinking career he had never tasted "Jersey Lightning." So he had had a drink. Three days later he had come to on his bed in the same hotel. The phone was ringing. It was his new boss, telling him his job was ended.

"Now I submit to you," Bill undid the buttons of his coat and pulled at a dark blue tie with white curlicues, "that is *not* the habit of drinking. That is an infinite projection of habit which might well be called an obsession."

From then on things had gone from bad to worse pretty rapidly. Bill had been in Towne's Hospital in New York, where Kidd Whistler had taken Joe. Even his doctor and his wife had about lost hope for him. Then one day an old friend, a former drinking pal, had come to see him. Bill had offered him a drink and Ebbie had refused. Ebbie had looked different. He said he had got religion. He had talked to Bill about it.

"Now I never thought much of the God business," Bill smiled, "but Ebbie called it simply 'a Power greater than ourselves' and I had always believed in such a power. After Ebbie left I began to ask myself, 'Can beggars be choosers? Does a cancer patient quibble about cures?' No, he goes to the best physician in utter dependency.

"This thought kept sticking in my mind through two or three more weeks of drinking. Then suddenly I cried out in abject desperation, 'I am willing to do anything. *Anything*. If there is a God, will He show Himself?' I had no faith at all but suddenly I was overcome with a feeling of being surrounded by Something. I felt transported to a mountain top . . . I had a sense of light and ecstasy, followed by great peace.

"'Oh, so this is the peace that passeth understanding,' I told myself. But I became cautious. Scared. I called the doctor. I thought I was going crazy.

"'No, boy, you're not insane,' he said. 'Whatever it is you've got hold of, you'd better hang on to it. It's a lot better than what you had before.' I did hold on. . . . That was ten years ago and I haven't had a drink since."

He looked around the solemn gathering and grinned. "Some of my irreverent friends in A.A. call my religious experience 'Bill's hot flash,' but it is very similar to several described in William James's *Varieties of Religious Experience*. You could call James a founder of A.A. although he never heard of it, and Ebbie, certainly, and a man in Akron, Ohio who believed that what had happened to me could help other drunks.

"I am not saying that every man and woman in A.A. gets this sudden type of 'conversion,' as our doctor here called it. As a matter of fact," and here Rick felt as if Bill Griffith were looking directly at him, speaking to him, "most of our members approach the spiritual angle of our program tentatively—some of them skeptically—but it comes. Slowly often.

Unobserved by the person himself, perhaps, but the personality change is just as much of a miracle.

"It may come through faith—or it may come through works. You see we get people both ways. The twelfth step of our program is helping other alcoholics. That is religion too.

"Our program has been borrowed from both religion and medicine. For instance," he raised his left hand," the doctor recommends analysis and catharsis." He raised his right hand. "The priest, or minister, advises examination of the conscience and confession." He looked at his left hand again. "The psychiatrist says, 'You have stepped out of the herd. You are an introvert. You cannot be happy unless you can make contact with your fellow men.'" He turned to his right hand. "And what does the religious man say? 'Think of others and you will be at peace. Practice the Brotherhood of Man.' The medical man tells his patient to 'find a hobby, some new compelling interest,' and the religious man talks about the 'expulsive power of a new affection.' They are saying the same thing in different words, and we have found that what they say is true.

"So . . . A.A. is a synthesis of religion and medicine—plus our own experience. We have added two main things: first, transmission by alcoholics—we've proved that only a drunk can help another drunk, second, group therapy—membership in our society takes away an alcoholic's feeling of being a pariah and gives him a new, compelling interest in life. A newcomer feels more important each day that he does *not* drink. And we've been told pretty often that we are all the type that *has* to feel important. That's another reason for A.A.'s success."

Rick was impressed by the way Bill Griffith handled the questions which followed the enthusiastic applause. A spinsterish female asked if he approved of the work of Temperance Societies. The A.A. next to Rick nudged him. But Bill met the issue squarely.

"I realize there are many temperance workers in this audience," he said, "but I must say frankly that we A.A.s are not out to reform the world. We are just trying to reform ourselves. We know that there are many fortunate people who enjoy liquor and are not harmed by it. So we say, 'More power to them,' but it does harm us and that is what we are interested in." He paused. "I guess I might as well add that the average alcoholic doesn't like reformers. It only makes his own resentments worse when people preach at him and scold him. It is vitally important for anyone who deals with a drunk—especially his family—to remember this."

A priest asked if the news of Pearl Harbor had caused many "slips" among the members of Alcoholics Anonymous.

"I was afraid it would bring them wholesale," Bill answered honestly, "but it didn't. Probably the reason is that each one of us has had his personal Pearl Harbor with full measure of humiliation and defeat."

A Canadian social worker, a stout, serious man, got up and thanked Bill Griffith for showing the value of tolerance. "I must say," he ended, "that it seems to me unfortunately true that the besetting sin of most reformers is self-righteousness."

"That reminds me," Bill Griffith grinned, "of something that happened at one of our meetings. We had invited a minister to attend, and after the usual A.A. speeches which described some pretty tough drinking in Bowery dives and some pretty irresponsible conduct ending up in alcoholic wards, the minister was asked to say a few words.

"'I have been deeply impressed,' he began, 'by the remarkable evidence of the way this movement has helped so many dissolute persons to stop drinking. It is splendid. I congratulate you. I must, however, confess to one reservation in my mind. Isn't it likely that people as dissolute as some of you claim you have been may have another sin as yet to be cured?'

"The leader of the meeting jumped to his feet. 'That is perfectly true, sir,' he said. 'Many of us do have another sin. But it is not sex. It is intolerance.'"

When the audience swarmed around Bill Griffith, Rick moved forward and joined Dr. Wales. Suddenly Bill detached himself from the persistent questioners, his arms outstretched.

"Well, Rick. I'm glad to see you at last."

"How the devil did you know me?"

"Wales whispered to me on the platform that you'd come with him. But I guess," Bill laughed, "I'd have recognized your famous high bottom anyway. Joe's talked a lot about you. You're his prize case."

Joe. Rick's face darkened.

"Joe Kelly will be all right." Bill Griffith put his hand on Rick's arm. "Joe has come too far along in A.A., helped too many other people to fold up permanently now. Right, Doctor?"

It wasn't a question, really. Rick felt that Bill Griffith's confidence would have stood up even to a negative answer from Wales.

Wales smiled. "Doesn't the Bible say that faith can move mountains, and Kelly is just a man—a man who's had a bad blow but who has your faith. It's the thing that will help him most now. And I'm speaking as a psychiatrist," he added.

"It didn't help Sylvia," Rick said. "Joe didn't help her. None of us helped her."

Bill Griffith looked at Rick's dark, unhappy face. This was harder than any of the questions he had had to answer after the meeting, but he faced it with the same honesty. "Maybe we did help Sylvia for a while. She said she was happier in A.A. than she had ever been in her life. Maybe we failed. Look at it this way, Rick, A.A. may fail once or twice—or a dozen times—and we may be sick at heart and full of self-reproach, but that isn't a healthy attitude. It isn't even statistical. We've got to keep our minds on the hundreds of men and women A.A. has helped—the hundreds more it is helping every day. Sylvia was a lovely person, but Sylvia was one and we are many."

Rick could see Sylvia in her white dress leaning against the column of Joe's porch, her lovely, pointed medieval face lifted in challenge, hear the ringing certainty of her voice. "A.A. keeps on—men and women learn how to live without alcohol, even if some of them learn slowly, even if some of them fail. It doesn't matter."

XXII

DRAWING A BLANK

You drew a blank. And then you came out of it. Dazedly. Reluctantly. The thing you could not endure was still there. The thing you had poured liquor down your throat to forget was there. Sylvia's lovely pointed face. But with Monica's dark hair and your sister's eyes. Sylvia's face, which was not Sylvia's face any more but the face of all the women you had ever known looking at you accusingly.

He was going crazy. He was having a new kind of D.T.s. Whenever he snapped out of it he felt as if his neck had literally cracked with the jerk of coming back to reality. Crimson curtains wavered in front of him. Crimson curtains hung at the window of a dreary apartment near Washington Square—curtains Sylvia must have pushed aside the night . . . no, he was getting it all wrong. The crimson curtains had been in Jim Bradway's house.

Joe sobered up intermittently. He sat across a desk from Dr. Wales' calm, wise face and tried to tell him about it, but he didn't make sense. Not to himself, he didn't. People talked to him. Rick. Hank. Gunnar came down from Bridgeport to talk to him. They told him he was a good guy. But he wasn't a good guy. He ought to know. Joe Kelly ought to know Joseph Augustine Kelly.

He must have been able to function all right. Walk straight. Act reasonably sober. He had told Dr. Wales' assistant that he was okay, that he had to go to his office. He must have gotten there. But how in hell had he gotten on this damn plane?

He knew why he was here. He was going to see Monica. Monica and Jimmy were in Pasadena and a straight line was the shortest distance between two points. A plane flew as a crow flies. He'd been smart to find a plane. You could sleep in a plane. Rocked in the cradle of the deep blue sky. Joe laughed suddenly and the man next to him said, "Well, sir, about time you woke up. We're almost in. Never saw anybody sleep like that. Feel kinda plane sick myself."

He was a loquacious, friendly fellow in a loud checked suit. By the time they had reached the airport they were boon companions. Strangers were what he needed, Joe thought, this guy didn't remind him of Sylvia.

Joe started in the direction of the big blue bus. He'd go to a hotel, get a bath and a shave and some breakfast. Then he'd call Monica.

The man in the checked suit propelled Joe toward a swanky black limousine. "Here, let me give you a lift. I'll drop you anywhere you say. No use riding in that hearse with the rest of the crowd."

It had seemed like a sound idea. And the suggestion of an eye-opener had appealed to Joe too. The motion of the plane was getting him now. He could feel it in his legs when he started to walk. One drink would set him up.

There was absinthe in it. Joe recognized the odd licorice taste. Absinthe was good for a hangover. Good for what ailed him. He could feel himself getting soberer by the minute. Soberer than he had been in weeks. But the drink was having the opposite effect on the man in the checked suit. He disappeared into the bathroom and Joe could hear him retching. He looked around the big expensive suite at the Biltmore and decided to get the hell out. He didn't seem to have a hat or a coat, or any luggage—which made life much simpler. He'd go to a Turkish bath, get fixed up and then call Monica.

On the street his legs seemed to be behaving better. His memory was functioning too. He remembered the way to a Turkish bath from the time he had been in Hollywood after working on that chicle picture with Rick. Los Angeles was as familiar to him as New York or Boston. He recognized corners, shops—wasn't that the bar where . . . ? He turned and walked back. Opened the door. Yup, by God, this was the place he and Guy Spanning had picked up those two dames. Boy, that had been a laugh on him. Guy had acquired a beauteous brunette who worked in a smart lingerie shop in Beverly Hills, but Joe's female had been a faded blonde. She had begged him to drive her to her new job the next day. He had thought it sort of quaint of her. Sort of touching. Why did the pathetic in women always appeal to him? It had been that way with Sylvia. With Monica. He had wanted to protect them. Maybe that was the trouble. Maybe women didn't want pity. It was different now. He was going to Monica now because he needed her. Desperately. Through all the fog and agony of his drinking that need of Monica must have been working in his subconscious. Now it was clear.

He sat at a small table and ordered a whiskey sour. The Turkish bath would steam it out of him. Guy Spanning had taken him there after that night with the two dames and in the morning he'd actually remembered his promise to the sad little blonde. Actually found her address in his pocket and driven around for her. It had been quaint all right. She had directed him through the winding luxury of Beverly Hills to a stupendous place. Over a huge iron gate electric light bulbs spelled out the name of an important producer—one of the men who was considering the chicle script. This was luck after all, Joe had thought, the blonde must be the guy's new secretary—secretaries had a lot of power in the picture business. It was the way Hollywood made you think—of yourself, of any little drag you could get. Joe had turned into the driveway and the blonde had said, "No, take the other entrance." Joe had backed, gone another hundred yards and seen another sign, "Service."

"What's the idea?" Joe had asked.

"They've engaged me as their cook."

"You walk from here, baby," Joe had said, dumping her bags out unceremoniously, hoping no one had recognized him from the house. And been ashamed ever since that the son of Patrick Aloysius and Bridget O'Brien Kelly had been such a God-damned snob.

But it had been funny. Joe gulped a whiskey sour and roared with laughter at the memory. He had never discovered any of the glamorous gals who were supposed to inhabit Hollywood. And the men he had liked had never been important producers or actors, or successful screen writers, but newspapermen, a football coach from U.C.A.A. and a hermit who was peddling octopus oil for arthritis. Octopus oil!

Joe finished his whiskey sour and laughed until the tears streamed down his unshaven cheeks, his wild, unbrushed red hair standing on end. Two patrons looked at him in alarm and disgust and the bartender glanced in his direction as if deciding whether or not he ought to put the guy out.

Joe jumped up from his table, strode belligerently to the bar, banged down his glass and demanded another whiskey sour.

A straight-backed old codger in a dark blue pinstriped suit, which looked as if it had been fitted by a military tailor, gave the bartender a cold blue-eyed look and lifted his glass to Joe.

"Was that you laughing?" he asked.

"Yup," Joe answered truculently.

"I thought so." The old codger beamed. "It was a good laugh. A soldier's laugh, sir. Only a man who has laughed at death," he went on sententiously, "can laugh at life like that."

"Right you are, General." Joe put an arm around the stiff, erect shoulders.

"General Alarm, my men used to call me." A guffaw shook his grizzled jowls and the neat paunch under his belt. "I was always predicting the worst and the worst always turned up on the Western Front."

"It sure did," Joe agreed.

"Only one thing I haven't learned to laugh at yet—this damn business of being retired. Sitting with my feet on a desk. And don't you tell me somebody has to do it," the General barked. "I've heard that one too often. Another thing I can't laugh at is the lousy cognac in this town." The General's cold blue eye was fixed on the bartender again. "Filthy stuff. Have one on me." He nodded to the bartender and marched across the room to Joe's table with the walk of an old cavalryman. "And this port is cherry juice. A good drink, *porto*. Not appreciated in this country."

"Cognac and *porto blanc*. Sounds like the Battle of Paris." Joe laughed.

"You there?"

"Yup. Captain. Artillery." Funny, if you talked about the last war you could forget about this one. And the General talked. He ordered drinks and he talked, but he didn't seem to get tight. He just wanted an audience. Joe listened and drank and suddenly the conversation seemed to have gotten around to this war. The General's son was in it. A paratrooper, of all things. Wouldn't go to West Point. Went to Princeton. Played baseball there. The General seemed proud. It seemed to make up to him for the fact that his son had unaccountably refused to go to the Point.

Joe tugged at his red forelock. "Me too. Not for Princeton. For Harvard. Look, I'll show you, General." There was a billiard room back of the bar. He and Guy Spanning had played a couple of games before they picked up those dames. He got up from the table now and came back with a cue, holding it near the small end. With his right hand he took a pretzel off the table. Dropped it. A peanut might do. Too light. The General had ordered olives and celery. Joe picked an olive pit out of an ashtray, hefted the cue in his left hand like a southpaw coming up to the plate. "Two on, two out, Princeton two runs ahead. Red Kelly up. The pitcher pours in a high hard one. Zowie." Joe tossed the olive pit, slipped his right hand onto the cue below his left and socked the pit into the entrance door with a zing that made the bartender jump. "Harvard three, Princeton two." Joe stood the cue next to the wall, waved to the bartender, "'S all right, Mac," sat down and leaned confidentially toward the General.

"Wanted to knock the hell out of Princeton then. Now I've gotten sorta fond of the place." It was Jim Bradway's college. Monica wanted Jimmy to go there. They had taken him down for a long weekend, seen one of the early games, sat on the bleachers in the warm spring twilight watching the boys practice. Monica was crazy about baseball, knew the batting averages of all the big leaguers. Only woman he had ever known who understood inside baseball. He had taken Sylvia to the Yankee stadium this summer. She hadn't known what it was all about. Mustn't think about Sylvia. Think about Monica and Jimmy. Call them up. But first he wanted to explain to the General how he felt about Princeton.

"You meet the spring at Princeton," he said, his voice taking on its intonation of vastness. "You leave Connecticut, where I live, and it's still grey and wintry-looking and you get off the train and there it is. Yellow forsythia and a green field. Is any place ever as green as a baseball field? Princeton in April. Boy, that's America. That's what your son is fighting for, General. The click of a ball . . . click-click-click through the warm spring twilight. Not real batting practice—just meeting the ball, not socking it . . . click-click-click. And the white balls bouncing over the new green turf to shadowy figures. It's getting pretty dark and you can just see the orange stripes on their stockings. And now those same kids swooping in great silver bombers or dangling from white parachutes, floating—drifting. . . ."

"You're a poet, Captain Red." The General puffed out his white mustache in astonishment. "Like to have seen you play ball. What do you do now? Newspaperman? Pictures?"

"Hell, no. Not pictures. Advertising. Nearly as bad. Tightens you up. Can't write if you're tense any more than you can play ball. You gotta be loose, free-swinging like Ted—that Red Sox outfielder."

"Ted Williams."

"Yeah, Ted Williams. Best natural hitter I ever saw. Never saw Wagner or Donlin or Lajoie, though."

"I did." The General started to reminisce and checked himself. This Red Kelly was wound up now. Needed to throw words around. The General motioned to Mac to fill their glasses.

"Or Tinker to Evers to Chance." Joe sang out the names.

Again the General started to say, "I did," but kept still. He was a bit of a psychologist, the General. You had to be when you'd pulled men through the messes he had at Soissons and Chateau Thierry.

"I saw Tony Lazzeri, though," Joe went on, "the best fielding second baseman I ever watched scoop up a slow one. And Gehrig hitting a three-bagger. Why do I remember that more than Ruth, more than Gehrig hitting a homer?" He was talking to himself now. "Because it was more spectacular. These damn fenced-in parks, fencing for commercialism. Hell, a home run's just a long fly now. But a three-bagger inside the park, that's what I call a hit. That's running. And sliding. There you are, emerging out of a cloud of dust on third, where people have to look at you . . . not just doffing your cap as you disappear into the dugout. A three-bagger is the most dramatic hit in baseball . . . as a long, run-back kickoff is the most dramatic thing in football . . . as a long, dodging, back-tracking reversing, arriving-at-last-in-a-cloud-of-dust sentence is the most dramatic thing, stylistically, in literature. Like Henry Miller coaching a three-base sentence."

"Which Miller is that? Where'd he play?"

"Montmartre. He was traded by the home team to the Left Bank." Joe laughed.

The General laughed too. "Never heard of him. Thought I knew something about American literature for an old Army fellow. My boy used to keep me up to scratch."

"You aren't the only one, General. Not by a long shot. Bet you half the English departments of Harvard, Yale, Princeton—the big three—never heard of Miller. His books are printed in France in English—most of them—but you can get *Cosmological Eye* here." Pell had lent it to him. And *Tropic of Cancer*. He owed Miller Pell. Pell to Kelly to General Alarm. Tinker to Evers to Chance. He picked up his fresh drink, took a deep swallow. "Here's to Henry Miller, the guy with the free-swinging, Ted Williams style. Bet he drinks too. That's what booze does for a writer. Loosens him up. Tedwilliams him. Yup, booze Tedwilliams . . . s."

The red head wavered, went down on the table. Red Kelly of Harvard had passed out.

The General looked at him, the way he had looked at his men being carried back of the lines on stretchers. The General went into action. He ordered the bartender to phone for a taxi—not any taxi—the General had a telephone number, he had a special driver, an old army sergeant. The General liked him. He liked almost any man who had been overseas in the last war. In about fifteen minutes a big guy lumbered in, gave the General a snappy salute, picked Joe up, bundled him into his cab and helped the General take him up to his suite at the Biltmore. He didn't approve of the General's habit of picking up stray drunks, but he would have defended with his life the General's right to do what he damned pleased—not that he had ever heard of Voltaire.

When Joe came to, he was lying on a couch in a room that looked exactly like the one he had been in that morning. He lifted himself cautiously on one elbow—the guy in the checked suit didn't seem to be anywhere in sight. He couldn't still be retching in the bathroom. Then he saw the General. There was a light on a big table and the General was packing a big suitcase, packing neatly and efficiently but as if he were used to having a striker to do chores like this for him.

"Hey," Joe said. "What time is it?"

"Nearly train time," the General said. "I've got a drawing room. And a case of Scotch. And I'd like to hear more about Henry Miller. Better come back to New York with me. Unless you have other plans."

Plans. Other plans. Joe sat up like a red setter that has been lying too long in front of a fire. Plans, Monica. He'd jumped on a plane to see Monica and he hadn't seen her. Hadn't even called her. "Got to telephone my wife in Pasadena." The word Pasadena didn't come out well. The s slurred. It sounded mixed up. Monica wouldn't like it if he talked to her like that. Monica would know that he had been drinking. Monica didn't like him when he drank. He looked at the General. The General didn't act as if he had been drinking.

"Tell you what," he said, "you call my wife for me. Tell her . . . tell her I asked you to call. Tell her I had a business appointment with you and I've just left. Tell her I'll pick her up at seven and take her to dinner." He could get the valet of the hotel to press his suit. He could take a cold shower. Shave. Drink a gallon of coffee. He could make it. He could see Monica. The General had handed him a phone book. Finding her name—Mrs. Joseph A. Kelly, right there in print, among all the other names—had given him confidence.

The General looked at Joe, but he didn't ask any questions. He picked up the receiver and barked a number. Joe waited. Joe listened in an agony of suspense. He couldn't make anything out of the General's harrumphs and ahums.

"That settles it, Captain Red." The General put the receiver back on the hook and turned toward Joe in his commanding manner. "Mrs. Kelly left yesterday for Hope Ranch, near Santa Barbara, and expects to be gone two weeks. Retire to New York and reorganize your forces. That's my advice, Captain."

Hope Ranch. Christ, life could be funny. Joe laughed. He couldn't hang around Los Angeles for two weeks waiting for Monica to come back. He couldn't make tracks for Hope Ranch, either. Monica wouldn't appreciate a husband who barged in on her like that. It wasn't the way he had planned it anyhow—his subconscious had planned it but not like that. The General was right. Retire to New York—or was retreat the word? There was a bottle on the end table beside him. He reached for it, not bothering to look for a glass, took a long pull and bellowed:

"I became a drunkard
So that I could see
Who believed in himself,
Who believed in me."

"Swell." The General snapped the lock on his suitcase. "Is that by your Henry Miller?"

"God, no. That fine quatrain is by Red Kelly of Harvard, Captain Kelly of the A.E.F."

It was the last thing he remembered. He drew a blank again. Wonderful protective mechanism—drawing a blank—shutting your mind away from pain. But pain was there waiting to pounce like a jaguar. The pain of Sylvia. The pain of Monica.

XXIII

SAVING POWERS

Joe's disappearing act was getting Rick down. Joe had returned from his crazy jaunt to the Coast in worse shape than ever, had spent a few days in High Pines and then vanished again into thin air.

Gail kept saying, "Don't worry so, please, Daddy. Gunnar is sure Joe will be all right." Now that her engagement to Gunnar was official, Gail went around in a beatific state, quoting Gunnar's opinion on everything from art to A.A. Once Rick would have been annoyed, but now he was amused and charmed by Gail's devotion. Besides, he found himself repeating Emily's remarks in much the same spirit.

Emily was doing her best to steady him but it was no use. He couldn't rest until he had located Joe. This time no cop pal of Hank Frost's had phoned to say that Joe was at a wop joint in Mianus getting pretty well stewed and someone sure ought to take care of the guy. No hotel bartender had reported to A.A. that there was a drunk he hated to turn over to the police.

Rick had looked everywhere he thought Joe could possibly be. He had kidded himself with the old story of the village idiot who had found the horse by thinking where he would go if he were a horse. He had substituted "drunk" for "horse" but it had been no use.

He sat in the A.A. clubhouse in New York with Bill Griffith, Jane Post, Kidd Whistler and a bunch of A.A.s after the Thursday night closed meeting. They were all hoping Joe might wander in, sick of bingeing, looking for help where he knew it could be found.

Suddenly Rick pulled himself wearily out of his chair. Joe might be at the Monks Club. He hadn't tried that—hadn't wanted to try it. "Has anyone here seen Kelly?" he asked. "What, Kelly of the Emerald Isle?" Someone at the bar took it up and the ridiculous old chorus boomed in his ears. "Have a drink on that one, big boy." A member turned to look at Rick in vague recognition. "Haven't seen you around here in a long time yourself." And you aren't likely to, brother, Rick thought, hurrying into the street. He'd drop in at the Algonquin once more. Joe had always liked the Algonquin bar. But no Joe.

Finally at three a.m. he had checked in at the Harvard Club, absolutely shot. *Clockwise. Counter-clockwise.* He had slept off his own last bender here. And Joe had helped him. Now the tables were turned and he wasn't helping Joe. He pulled off his clothes, intending to take a shower. Turned on the water, saw his face in the mirror over the wash-stand . . . a face in the mirror over a bar—not a drunken face, thank God. . . . Thank God?... "Oh, Thou Power Greater than myself, save Joe Kelly . . . God of Joe Kelly, God of my fathers. Yes, *my* God save him. Help me to find him. Help me to help him. . . ." On and on and on, jumbled words, a jumbled prayer—the first prayer in thirty years—rushed out of him as water poured out of the shower. The smitten rock. The gushing spring. The parted waters of the Red Sea.

Peace came over him. The peace that passeth understanding. He could not understand it. Could not explain why the thought of Cambridge entered his head, but it did. Had his subconscious been tracking Joe down, back-tracking over their whole long friendship, emerging at last with the word, Cambridge, tossing it on the shore of his outer mind like a bottle containing the last message of a shipwrecked mariner?

He showered, slept—the urgency, the tenseness gone, he woke to the same strange certainty. After breakfast he phoned his office, caught a morning train for Boston, still not hurrying, still never doubting that he would find Joe, never questioning that this time his rescue would be successful. He had only to keep his conscious mind quiet so that he could listen to the still small voice his ancestors had called conscience, follow the flight of instinct as even earlier men had followed the flight of birds let loose by the oracle of Delphi.

In Cambridge he let his feet lead him down a shabby, familiar street into a small saloon where he and Joe had gone to celebrate whenever Joe's training was over for the season.

Joe was sitting at a small table in a corner, a bottle of beer in front of him. He looked up with Rick opened the door, waved as if he were not in the least surprised to see Rick—as if they had met by appointment, rushing out between classes for a drink.

Rick said, "Hi, boy," and sat down, not knowing where to begin.

"Which side do you dress?" Joe asked.

"What the hell?"

"I had an uncle who was a tailor," Joe explained with a faraway look in his red setter eyes. "My mother's brother, that was. He used to make over my father's old suits for us kids—for free. Punk little shop he had— not the sort of place you'd ever have put an Abercrombie shoe or a Brooks trouser into, Rick. Uncle Michael was always asking his customers that question. It got on his nerves. Started him thinking. 'Men ought to wear skirts,' he would shout in the middle of Sunday dinner at our house, and we kids would snigger, 'Every nursemaid knows that.' Uncle Michael would glare at us. 'Or kilts like them Scotchmen.' Uncle Michael would pound the table. 'Only good sense them Scots ever showed that makes 'em better than the Irish. Give me Irish whiskey any day, eh what, Patrick, but give me kilts—kilts or togas. Men had ought to stop twisting 'emselves. Crooked trousers—crooked minds!" My father would let out a howl of laughter and wink at my brothers and me, and my mother would get red in the face and flounce out to the kitchen, muttering that she 'never heard such talk in all her born days—and on a Sabbath, too.' But it wasn't funny to my Uncle Michael, God rest his soul, landed him in the State booby Hatch, that's what it did. His customers thought he was crazy—crazy, hell, the guy was sane, or his nephew is going nuts, too."

"You're not nuts, Red." And he wasn't too drunk either, thank God.

"My sister thought the world of Uncle Michael," Joe went on, lost in a world Rick had never shared.

"The one you made the bargain with in your own blood that you'd never touch a drop of liquor so long as you lived?" Rick was glad he had remembered this from Joe's speech at White Plains. It might give Joe pause now. Something had to give Joe pause sometime. Something somebody said had to ring the bell.

But Joe didn't seem to hear. Rick might as well have been in New York for all of Joe. Joe was alone again, talking to himself in his lonely continuity of black despair. "Eileen Martha Kelly—she had curly black hair and Irish blue eyes and a golden heart that was set on her kid brother getting an education at Harvard College. And she, saving every penny she earned at the shoe factory, keeping nothing for herself, not even for the doctor. Not till it was too late, not till the lump on her breast was too big to save her. . . ." Joe drained his glass of beer . . . Eileen's Irish blue eyes, Monica's soft dark hair, Sylvia's pointed face . . . beer wasn't strong enough, beer didn't blind him to this haunting, composite vision. He had been trying to taper off with beer for three days, but beer wasn't any good. The only thing that *was* any good was drawing a blank—going out like a light.

He had crawled to Cambridge because he had been happy there once. Something Dr. Wales had said about roots, about digging out the old troubles, the old injuries, had sent him rushing off to Lowell, Massachusetts. He had been sober, had soberly decided to face the past physically, thinking that it just might help him to face it mentally. And his past began in Lowell, Massachusetts.

Lowell was the same ugly factory town he had hated as a child and escaped from as a young man. Time same but changed. There was a garage and filling station where the Kelly house had stood. You looked for your past and you found a gas station. That was a laugh. Joe had wandered on. There was no member of his family he could look up, his mother had died years before and his brothers had scattered to small towns out west. He hadn't even heard from any of them in a long time. It was places he had been looking for—landmarks—the corner cigar store out of which Patrick Aloysius Kelly had formed the sorry habit of sneaking for a couple of beers, and come rolling home at dawn shouting fit to wake the dead and the neighbors. A shining red Five and Ten brightened the corner. Joe had wandered on again.

The shoe factory where Eileen had worked had spread its hideous grey frame structure over the entire block, engulfing Uncle Michael's tailor shop. Eileen used to race down the street, her black curls flying, her tin lunch box flashing in the sun. She would perch on the cutting table in Uncle Michael's back room, smelling the steam iron, looking at the old-fashioned gas fixtures flaunting naked electric light bulbs, waiting for Uncle Michael to get rid of any customer he happened to have and come beaming in to set the kettle on the little stove and brew her a good strong cup of tea. Sometimes Joe would scoot down from the Loyola Parochial School and join them. The small back room was gone. Uncle Michael was gone. Eileen was gone.

Joe had wandered on. Down to the station. The station was the same—almost. The big round flower beds of red cannas had disappeared and the mound with Lowell spelled out in white pebbles, which he used to admire, was missing, but trains still ran to Boston, and across the Charles was Cambridge. Harvard—his first bright step up, his first shining hope that he, Joseph Augustine Kelly, would not turn into a drunken bum like his old man.

So now, here he was, sitting in a shabby bar in Cambridge. A drunk like his father. What the hell difference did it make whether the bar was located in Lowell or Cambridge, New York or Los Angeles? It was a bar, wasn't it? It was his destiny, wasn't it?

"Character is destiny," Joe muttered.

Rick looked at him with commiseration. He couldn't follow the twisting of Joe's mind through his past, couldn't say to him, "Aren't you letting your sister down—not by going to Harvard, which she wanted, but by the way you're acting now?" Nobody knew that better than Joe himself. "Character *is* destiny. But not predestined, Joe, don't forget that," Rick said. "And part of what a man is depends on what he puts in his stomach." He could at least get Joe to eat something. "What'd you have for breakfast, and when?" he added.

"A double martini," Joe grinned feebly. "No, honestly, Rick, I'm kidding. A cup of coffee, I guess. I don't remember, but I haven't touched anything stronger than beer for a couple of days. Been trying to taper off. You don't think I want to drink like this, do you? You don't think I'm enjoying myself?"

It had been fun once, years ago—breezing into a bar, feeling the world was your friend, clapping strangers on the back, shouting, "Set 'em up, Mike, this round's on me." Fun to have the money to treat all and sundry without counting your pennies, to go to the most expensive restaurant and grab the check, not bothering to add it up, pulling out a wad of bills and saying, "Keep the change, waiter."

When Joe had gotten his first big salary raise, he had thought, this calls for a celebration. And suddenly he knew the place he wanted to celebrate, the place he wanted to throw that dough around. The Touraine Hotel in Boston. It meant something to him, something secure and wealthy—not flashy like the hotels in New York—it meant the Saturdays after football games and the sharp November air and girls with red carnations and girls with big yellow chrysanthemums pinned on fur coats and Red Kelly ducking out, not going along with the crowd because he'd be damned if he'd sponge even on Rick. . . . The Touraine, where everyone used to go after the Club tea dances, hadn't been the same place when Joe Kelly finally got there. It had seemed a bit down at the heel, *passé*, dull, but just being there had given Joe an incomprehensible sense of achievement.

He had never wanted to go to the Touraine again, though. It had never entered his mind to go there when he took the train from Lowell. He had headed straight for this little dump where he and Rick had once been happy, joking, making great plans for the future. Rick was part of that picture . . . but Rick was here now.

"How the hell did you happen to turn up here?" Joe asked, as if realizing for the first time that Rick was not just some projection of his own recollections.

"Believe it or not," Rick said gravely, "I prayed to a Power Greater Than Myself to help me find you and I came straight here."

Joe tugged at his untidy red forelock, blinked, and his voice boomed out with its old intonation of vastness, "It only took you a year. Maybe my binge served a purpose after all. God works in his mysterious ways his wonders to perform. You look the way you looked in college and at Plattsburg, Rick. Young. Confident." Joe slumped down in his chair. "And I look like hell. You needn't tell me. I know. I know I'm letting A.A. down. I know all you guys are worried. I know I ought to stop. Christ, it isn't any fun—I'm telling you it isn't any fun."

"And it isn't the answer either," Rick said steadily.

"Nope, it isn't the answer. Hell, there isn't any answer."

Food wasn't an answer either, but it was a First Things First step. If he could get Joe to eat now, keep him from drinking for awhile, get him on a train and take him home, sober him up enough to go to a meeting, then A.A. would pull him back. Rick was confident A.A. would put Joe on the beam again. Rick beckoned a waiter. "They used to have pigs knuckles and sauerkraut here. That's what I want."

"Me too," Joe nodded indifferently. Then he gave the skinny, pale kid in a big white apron an appraising look. "Working your way through college, eh? Not much fun, is it? Ever play ball? Ever hear of Red Kelly?"

"Yes. I mean no," the waiter stammered. "I'm a student at Harvard," he said it with a flash of pride, "but I'm 4F in the draft and I don't play ball and I never heard of Red Kelly and will it be two pigs knuckles and kraut and two coffees and how about beer?"

"Fame," Joe laughed, "fame."

"No beer," Rick said firmly at the same moment, and Joe didn't contradict him. Didn't argue, for a wonder.

"Look, Red." Rick wondered if it was safe to leave Joe alone for five minutes, decided it was. "I'd like to call Emily, tell her I've found you, tell her we'll be taking an afternoon train, okay?"

"Okay." Joe grinned. "I won't take a powder on you."

Rick located a phone booth near the men's room, behind the bar, dropped change in slots, waited for Emily's voice.

"Emerald called me to say that there was a wire for Mr. Kelly from Pasadena, California," Emily said, "and I persuaded Western Union to give me the message. I practically had to swear I was Mrs. Kelly to get it." Emily's laugh came over the wire and Rick swore, "Like hell you are."

"Don't interrupt, darling, I'm always worried about extra minutes and extra quarters on long distance. Listen, Rick, have you got a pencil? Darling, I was sure you'd call. I was sure you'd find Joe. That's why I lied to Western Union and it's a miracle. The miracle we needed. Ready?"

Rick put an envelope with scribbled words in front of Joe. Joe blinked. "What the hell? I can't read that scrawl."

Rick picked it up, his voice as small as if he had been running up a mountain. "DEAREST JOE. JUST SAW YOUR TRAGIC NEWS IN OLD NEW YORK PAPER. HAVE BEEN VERY STUPID. PLEASE DARLING FORGIVE ME. JIMMY AND I ARE TAKING CHIEF TODAY FOR NEW YORK. ALL MY LOVE, MONICA."

XXIV

SEPTEMBER REMEMBER

Gail and Gunnar were sitting close together on a circular red leather bench in a small Greenwich restaurant. People, hurrying in from the chill September rain, their minds on a drink and dinner, paused to look at the two blonde heads because they were young and in love and Gail was beautiful.

At the back of the room a Negro was playing *As Time Goes By* from *Casablanca,* turning on a revolving stool from the keyboard of a small piano to a still smaller organ, striking a chord here with one hand, there with the other, crooning in a rich, sorrowful voice.

Gail smiled. The nostalgic refrain made her heart run like a child playing in the attic on a rainy day, opening trunks of memories, rushing to her with bright, lovely treasures. "Remember this, remember that," her heart kept saying. . . . Gunnar at the A.A. meeting telling Hank that the Nordstroms had boats and liquor in their blood more than money or women. Her smile deepened. "Remember *Le Matelot?* We didn't know then it was going to be a special memory, did we?"

"I wanted to kiss you, though. You had on that toreador hat," Gunnar laughed, not the booming roar of the quarterdeck but the low, sure laughter of a man in love, "but I never thought I would."

Gail laughed too. "You didn't act as if you wanted to. You acted like Great Uncle Gunnar scolding a half-witted niece. And you had on the most dreadful, Sunday-go-to-meeting suit, darling. Only I didn't care. But this one is wonderful." She put her hand on Gunnar's sleeve, feeling the soft prickly tweed. "I like the funny little brown and yellow speckles in the tan and I'll bet it smells of peat bogs the way Daddy's do."

"It ought to. I guess you pay extra for that smell." Gunnar grinned. "Rick helped me pick it out. I asked him." He had told Rick, "I don't know a damn thing about clothes except uniforms and overalls, but I want Gail to think what I wear is okay. I guess it's important to her and I've been noticing things a bit, myself. I don't like those stiff blue and grey stripes Mac and some of the men wear, but I do like your suits." Rick had been pleased by Gunnar's admiration and his lack of false pride. Gunnar was a good guy.

"I'll bet Daddy picked out that tie too."

"What's wrong with the tie?"

"It's green, darling."

"Sure, it's green. I'm not color blind."

"But Daddy is. He must have thought it was brown. Brown would be nicer. Never mind, I'll be going with you to buy ties and things soon."

"Okay, Mrs. Cézanne."

They were being married the first week in October. Gunnar had finally arranged a transfer back to Hank's boatyard and Hank was giving him two weeks off for a honeymoon. "Not much time, but the most I can spare you," Hank had said. He had never found a satisfactory man to take Gunnar's place, satisfactory men were as scarce as hen's teeth these days. "But more time than a guy in the Marines would get," Gunnar had said grimly. The old resentment that he couldn't be in the middle of the fight was quieting but it still flared up occasionally, and he still drove himself in spite of his leg, still tried to do the work of three men.

"As time goes by." The provocative song wove in and out of their thoughts, in and out of the thoughts of everyone in the small restaurant, bringing regret to some but to Gail a sense of childish impatience.

"Time doesn't go fast enough to suit me," she said, her hand tightening on Gunnar's arm. "Oh, darling, a month is such an endless, endless number of days. Suppose something happened—but something has happened, something marvelous and I've been forgetting to tell you. Daddy has bought the 'shack' and he's giving it to us for a wedding present! He just heard at six o'clock. The real estate man called up. The sculptor is staying in Mexico and the statue has been sold and it's being moved next week and you'll have your studio."

"But how about Rick and Emily?" Gunnar's voice was deep and hesitant. It was damn generous of Rick but he didn't feel happy about it.

Not if it meant putting Rick out of a house that had seemed to fit him.

"Oh, they don't want it. They want to go to South America as soon as the war is over and to Moscow—of all places in winter—and besides, Aunt Emily misses the tide. She told Daddy so. She always liked Joe's house better than the 'shack.' She wants to be where she can smell mud-flats and watch the gulls and the sandpipers and the big white herons, but I like the cedars and the dogwood and our little pond. Please be happy about it, Gunnar, please."

"I am happy, Mrs. Cézanne. I'd be happy in that punk little room in Bridgeport if you were around—but I guess you wouldn't."

"Of course I would." Gail's grey eyes were serious, mature. "But I'm thinking about you—you do love the studio. You know you do. And besides, I'm giving Daddy and Aunt Emily the house in New York for their wedding present. It sort of evens things up."

"I thought Rick hated it. Hated New York. He never ought to live there, Gail." Gunnar frowned. This casual giving of houses like silver tea sets bothered him. Even silver tea sets were something he'd have to get used to.

"They can sell it," Gail explained. "Aunt Emily doesn't like it either, but I figured out that Daddy needed some money. You see, when my mother died he went sort of crazy and put everything she had and all his own money in trust for me. It's all pretty silly, now. I found out that I have more money than he has. You're just a fortune hunter, darling. Didn't you know?"

Gunnar pushed his hand through his thick pale hair. "I guess that's right." He tried to smile, but the whole business still bothered him. "Look, Gail, I'm glad you did that about the house but—couldn't you give him back the rest of the cash?"

"Daddy wouldn't take it. He has a big salary anyway and besides— our children will need money. I won't be able to work at the plant when . . . oh, and there's another thing I've been meaning to tell you. A girl in my department has been drinking a lot. Her boyfriend's overseas and she came in plastered today and they fired her. They had to, really, but I went to the coatroom with her and she was crying and I told her about A.A. She'd read about it somewhere and she went to a meeting in New York about a month ago and she promised me she'd come tonight."

"Good for you, infant."

Gunnar still liked to tease Gail by calling her infant, but she didn't resent it any more. She knew that he depended on her in the way her father depended on Aunt Emily. Her Aunt's serenity no longer seemed like middle-aged acquiescence to Gail, it was a symbol of hard-won adultness.

Gunnar pulled out his watch, clicked open the old-fashioned case.

Gail could see a thin, tired Norseman in the living room of the house in the East Sixties, saying there was a picture he wanted to see, asking her to come along as an afterthought. He was still thin but his face was alive with confidence in life and in her.

"Hurry and finish your ice cream." Gunnar took the last swallow of coffee from his cup and reached for the check. "We don't want to be late. Not with your father leading the meeting and Joe back. It's a great night, Mrs. Cézanne."

"Don't forget Monica. She'll be there too. I'm so happy for Joe." Gail didn't call him Uncle Joe any more and she was finding it pleased and amused her father when she called him Rick. "You'll like Monica."

"Maybe I will," Gunnar said. "I still don't like the way she walked out on Joe."

"I couldn't understand it either. I used to think he was falling for Sylvia and I wouldn't have blamed him a bit, but Aunt Emily always said we didn't know Monica's side of it. And Aunt Emily was right." Gail smiled. "People are always telling her things. Monica told her yesterday that she was sure Joe was in love with Sylvia. That's the main reason she went away. She thought Joe had married *her* because he was sorry for her and she said that just wasn't good enough and she wanted to give him a chance to find out if he cared about Sylvia. And she was waiting and waiting in Pasadena thinking he would ask her to give him a divorce. And she would have, because she didn't think it was fair not to. And the hardest part was Jimmy—he kept talking about Joe and wanting to go home. She really did have a hell of a time. And you know that crazy trip Joe made to California, well, Monica cried when she heard about it. She would have been so darn glad to see him, drunk or sober, and to know most of all that he needed her. So Aunt Emily told Daddy and me about it and Monica doesn't care who knows—she wants all Joe's friends to know how she felt. Daddy's going to tell Hank Frost tonight. Hank was sort of down on her, thought she was a snob, or something. And we've got to be nice to her and make her feel we like her. Not just Joe. You know how everyone always likes his wild, funny ways when he's sober. I mean when he's not drinking—sober isn't the word—and Monica's sort of quiet and reserved and she just likes to sit back and watch him."

"Like me," Gunnar smiled at Gail. "Don't grow up too fast, infant. I like your silly gaiety."

Gail slid into her white raincoat and pulled the hood over her bright hair. The wind was blowing the rain in gusts as they opened the door and hurried down the Avenue. Gunnar headed into it, his heavy shoulders thrust forward, Gail's hand tucked firmly under his arm.

"Rick said he'd pick us up but I told him we liked to walk," Gail shouted.

When they reached the top of the steep hill overlooking the railroad station, the lights of the museum glittered on wet asphalt and every turn of the road was jammed with parked cars.

"Big turnout," Gunnar said, opening the door for Gail. "Ought to be a good meeting."

And it was. Kidd Whistler was the first to congratulate Rick after the concluding prayer. Two carloads had driven over from White Plains, Jane Post and several men had come out by train from New York, Gunnar's bunch from Bridgeport had turned up, every Greenwich and Stamford member, old and new, was there and, best of all, Pell had brought the group that had split off in June—Mrs. Baby, Mr. Junior, the Watsons and some new people they had added to their membership. The hard feelings that had grown out of the local schism seemed to have vanished. Pell had taken Rick aside before the speeches began. "Told 'em I was riding with my old comrade, Light-Horse Harry Lee, saved my life, sir, in the battle of Darien, October 15, 1943. Gratitude, sir. Told my boarders I'd consider it mutiny if they failed to follow me. Watson was with me. Said his wife enjoyed going to people's houses, but he couldn't see any reason why we shouldn't go to both meetings if we felt like it."

"Good idea," Rick had agreed. Everything struck him as good tonight—wasn't Joe back, and Monica, wasn't Gail coming with Gunnar, wasn't Emily sitting in the front row and hadn't he been dry a whole miraculous year?

Kidd Whistler teetered up on his toes like a cheerleader, "Never thought you'd make the grade that night Joe brought you to White Plains. Lost a bet to Joe when you went out to phone. Never thought Joe would slip, either, or that you'd be the one to bring him back to the fold. Well, that's A.A. for you! Where *is* the old buzzard?"

Rick and Kidd elbowed their way through the crowded room with mooseheads and Rocky Mountain goats looking down on this odd assemblage. Joe was surrounded by people who were trying to welcome him back without seeming to rub it in that he had been off the beam. Joe, his red hair smooth, his brown eyes twinkling, was grinning to himself over their obvious predicament. "I feel like one of the monkeys in the cages out there. The prize exhibition of foolishness. There's the big boy you ought to be patting on the back. This is Rick's night."

"Refreshments," Mrs. Hank Frost called.

"Yeah, come and get it," Hank boomed.

Through a door to the left as you faced the speaker's table, they pushed into a long room lined with glass showcases displaying Connecticut in the Pleistocene Epoch.

"It looks nice and peaceful," Rick commented, "What in hell will they call our age? . . . two bloody wars in my generation."

"The age of the alcoholic," Joe laughed. It was good to laugh again. Good to look across a room and see Monica's straight, boyish figure, see the alert, quick turn of her dark head, catch the warm certainty of her smile. She and Emily were busy helping Mrs. Hank, pouring coffee into paper cups, handing out sandwiches. In the center of the table was a large white cake with a single red candle.

Everyone seemed to notice it at once. Everyone looked at Rick and began to sing, "Happy Birthday to you. . . ."

Rick caught Emily's eye and grinned like a kid embarrassed by the applause of his classmates. To an outsider the cake, candle and song might seem a childish celebration, but to him it was finer than the laurel

crown for the conqueror of a great city . . . "he who conquers himself."
. . . A year in A.A. . . . a year of sobriety . . . a year of desperate daily bat-
tles . . . a year of trying to learn the parental patience of a quiet man on
a dock at Falmouth . . . a year with Emily. But back of his happiness,
underneath his thankfulness over Joe's comeback, lay one shadow. No
one had mentioned Sylvia Landon but he knew others were thinking of
her now. Would always think of her. Sylvia in a blue linen dress at the
White Plains meeting a year and two days ago, her words reaching
through the fog of his hangover, making him feel he was no longer alone.

It was what they all felt. What they all must keep. He looked around
the crowded room. These were his friends. These men and women who,
as Joe put it, had been through Belleau Wood together. He could see the
change in every face in a year. Not changes—change. For the look was
the same always. It was in the eyes and around the mouth. Strength. Purpose. Peace. It was in Mac—Mac who had been his yardstick. Mac had
a good job with a law firm in Greenwich. Mac had spoken tonight of
the way his old friends greeted him with a surprised, "You look like a
new man," "You look different," "What have you been doing to yourself?
You look ten years younger." They had all heard similar comments, all
laughed in reply, "I must have looked like hell when you knew me." All
had known that the change was not external, was valid. Change is valor,
but confusion is a stinking swamp. Alcoholism was a stinking swamp.

The singing was petering out into laughter and talk. Rick overheard
Mrs. Baby and Mrs. Watson take up an interrupted argument. There
were two women he could do without, he thought, with a grin at his
uncharitableness.

"Don't you think I'm right? Don't you think it's a mistake to let anyone into a meeting in such a condition," Mrs. Watson was insisting,
"especially a woman? I do think it's shocking. I told Mr. Watson when
that girl came in looking drunk and disorderly and nearly falling off her
chair that I thought someone really ought to ask her to leave, but he's
such a milquetoast . . . I do wish one of the men would speak to her. It
makes such a bad impression. . . ."

"I'll speak to her," Mrs. Bentley-Young drew herself up, her baby-
blue eyes flashing with contempt, "but it won't be what you want. You're

a very unkind, stupid person and you're not a member of A.A. and you evidently haven't learned a damn thing about it. Where is this girl?"

Mrs. Watson's stiff grey hair seemed to grow stiffer with indignation, "I believe she stayed in the other room when we all came in here. I'm sure Mr. Watson will resent your remarks to me. You've been very rude."

"Oh, let me out of here." Mrs. Baby pushed past the spluttering, well-corseted figure and bumped headlong into Rick. "Sorry," she exclaimed, "but I'm so mad I could spit in her eye."

"Good for you." Rick felt a sudden admiration for this small, furious female whom he had always considered completely trivial. He followed her into the next room where Gail and Gunnar were talking to a thin girl in a black and white-checked suit. She had a silly red cap on her head which kept sliding over one eye and she kept twisting a red flowered handkerchief.

"Oh, Rick, I'm glad you came." Gail rushed to meet them at the door. "That's the girl I told you about. She worked in my department and she got fired today and she's been showing Gunnar and me a Navy E she was given for her work—and she's terribly proud of it and terribly unhappy. Please Daddy, help her."

But it was Mrs. Baby who took charge. Mrs. Baby who sat down beside the girl and motioned the rest of them away. Mrs. Baby who listened to the girl's story of how she had promised Gail to come but she had had to take a couple of drinks on the way to get up her courage.

"I know," Mrs. Baby nodded.

The girl looked at her with bleary, incredulous eyes. "You can't know. You couldn't have been such a mess as I am."

"Worse." Mrs. Bentley-Young's voice carried conviction. "I was a mean drunk. I got mad at my husband once and I threw his great grand-mother's soup tureen at him. He was awfully proud of his great grand-mother. He was always bragging about what a gentlewoman she was and how she sipped her sherry."

"Gosh," the girl muttered, "gosh."

"If I can stop drinking you can," Mrs. Bentley-Young said firmly. "You just ask God to help you to stay dry for twenty-four hours. Any dope can lay off it that long and you're not a dope, you've got a Navy E."

The girl kept staring at the pretty, blue-eyed face. Finally belief and a faint ray of hope came into her wavering smile.

Rick, standing across the room with Gunnar and Gail, recognized the expression. He must have looked like that himself a year ago in the Greek joint where he and Joe had stopped for coffee. Now he was on the road this girl was starting. Sylvia in a white dress leaning against the column of Joe's porch, Sylvia saying, "It doesn't matter where you get A.A., or how, so long as you get it. . . ." H. Peculiar Henry, Mrs. Baby had certainly taught him a lesson—a lesson in tolerance. Judge not that ye be not judged or something. "Even if some of them learn slowly, even if some of them fail," Sylvia had said.

Driving home with Joe and Monica in the back seat and Emily and Gail in front, Rick watched the road, his hands on the wheel relaxed and steady. The asphalt was wet, black, slippery but it was *not* a dark, pervasive liquid engulfing both the past and the present. Clockwise. Counterclockwise. The windshield wiper jerked two precisely uniform arcs against the rain.

"Useful gadget," Rick said, "you can see the road ahead."

"It's a good road," Emily smiled, "a road to Moscow—a road to Timbuctoo."

"It's a wonderful, marvelous road," Gail laughed, "and its name is Cognewaugh."

The End